After the Rain

by
Brandy Bruce

Bling!
Romance
Lighthouse Publishing of the Carolinas

AFTER THE RAIN BY BRANDY BRUCE
Published by Bling! Romance
an imprint of Lighthouse Publishing of the Carolinas
2333 Barton Oaks Dr., Raleigh, NC 27614

ISBN: 978-1-946016-73-7
Copyright © 2019 by Brandy Bruce
Cover design by Elaina Lee
Interior design by Karthick Srinivasan

Available in print from your local bookstore, online, or from the publisher at:
ShopLPC.com

For more information on this book and this author visit:
www.authorbrandybruce.com

This is a work of fiction. Names, characters, and incidents are all products of the author's imagination or are used for fictional purposes. Any mentioned brand names, places, and trademarks remain the property of their respective owners, bear no association with the author or the publisher, and are used for fictional purposes only.

All scripture quotations, unless otherwise indicated, are taken from the Holy Bible, New International Version®, NIV®. Copyright ©1973, 1978, 1984, 2011 by Biblica, Inc.™ Used by permission of Zondervan. All rights reserved worldwide. www.zondervan.com. "NIV" and "New International Version" are trademarks registered in the United States Patent and Trademark Office by Biblica, Inc.™

Brought to you by the creative team at Lighthouse Publishing of the Carolinas:
Eddie Jones, Shonda Savage, Jessica Nelson

Library of Congress Cataloging-in-Publication Data
Bruce, Brandy.
After the Rain / Brandy Bruce 1st ed.

Printed in the United States of America

PRAISE FOR *AFTER THE RAIN*

Once I started reading *After the Rain*, pausing for the "real world" felt like a cruel method of torture! Truly, this heartfelt sequel of rallying after life's breathtaking disappointments is everything I could have hoped for and more. Brandy Bruce has weaved together a bittersweet tale that had me laughing and crying within a mere three words. Filled with loss, love, and beautiful life, *After the Rain* will forever be in my heart, sitting on my shelf of favorites.

~V. Joy Palmer
Author of *Love, Lace, and Minor Alterations*

After the Rain is a brave story of heartbreak and hope, of picking up the pieces and starting over. Debra's story of a life sent detouring down roads she never wanted or imagined and finding beauty and healing in the unexpected will stay with you long after you turn the final page.

~Kara Isaac
RITA® Award–winning author of *Then There Was You*

This story will strum its way into your heart like the chords of a great love song. Debra Hart's journey from broken to free is a beautiful testament to the powerful love God sings over us all. *After the Rain* is more than a typical inspirational romance—it offers a glimpse into the hard questions of faith and trust and what it really means to love. For rock stars and wannabes and everyone who appreciates the art of music and falling in love.

~Lindsey Brackett
Award-winning author of *Still Waters*

Brandy Bruce has done it again with this moving romance featuring heart-broken Debra Hart, who is rebuilding her life in Denver after losing everything that mattered to her in Texas. The splashes of humor, vibrant characters, and realistic picture of emotional healing add up to a gripping story that offers laughter, tears, and love.

~Liz Duckworth
Author of *A Perfect Word for Every Occasion* and *Wildflower Living*

After the Rain is Brandy Bruce's highly anticipated sequel to *The Last Summer*. A brilliant standalone novel that will tug on your heartstrings and inspire you to cheer for Debra.

~Narelle Atkins
Author of *Solo Tu*

For Ashtyn and Lincoln and Lillian.
There will never be one moment of your lives
when I am not hopelessly in love with all three of you.

Chapter One

All love can end in a snap.
West Side Story

Deb, I miss you. I think about you. Just wanted to say it again.

I read the text from Lillian—Lily—Spencer as the elevator doors opened. Then I tucked the phone into my small purse. I walked toward the exit of the condominium building I called home now, catching a glimpse of myself in one of the mirrors on the wall.

This woman—with short hair, ringlets barely brushing my shoulders. Dark colors, chocolate-colored eyeliner—nervous about a simple thing like going to a coffee bar. I didn't recognize her.

I stopped mid-hallway and leaned against the wall, my heart hurting.

I'm starting all over.

No.

I closed my eyes. I'd cried all the tears already. None were left. But the pain didn't stop. A reminder of how much I'd loved Luke Anderson. How ready I'd been to link my story to his for forever.

But he'd chosen my friend Sara.

Quiet, ladylike, sophisticated, predictable Sara.

"Debra?"

My eyes opened. Cassidy and Jake, my neighbors, stood in the hallway, looking worried. I must have seemed ill. With one hand, Jake carried a baby car seat. Inside it, their five-month-old daughter, Gilly, slept soundly.

I pushed myself off the wall. "I'm okay," I said without eye contact. I walked straight out of the building to my car and drove downtown.

Here's the thing about 16th Street in downtown Denver—it's crazy. The old me would love it. The post-heartbreak-and-devastation me only half liked it. I parked in the cheapest parking lot I could find, then walked down the busy outdoor mall to reach Percival's Island. I passed a multicolored statue of a bull and a man who was entirely spray-painted in gold. He seemed to be pretending to be a statue. I'm okay with weird, but that was downright creepy.

I'd finally texted my new and only friend, Paige, letting her know I was joining her and her friends at Percival's for an Irish coffee and some live music. Now my phone dinged every second. Paige seemed beyond excited that I'd said yes after two months of refusing to go out on the town with her and her friends. Really, one friend was all I needed, but Paige took persistent to another level. The last text had five smiley-faced emojis and three pink hearts and a message letting me know she'd be waiting outside for me.

Paige liked me and I liked her. But she didn't know me. Not really. Only the shadow me. The post-Texas version of myself.

I walked fast, the Colorado breeze blowing through my hair and tickling my neck.

As promised, Paige stood out front, beaming at the sight of me. With her ruffled shirt, baggy jeans, and glowing skin without much makeup, all Paige needed were some daisies in her hair and she'd look like the perfect flower child. A leather pouch was slung over her head, looped from her shoulder, and rested on her hip. Turquoise earrings dangled to her shoulder. In another life, I would have wanted those earrings.

"Yay!" She hugged me tight, then pulled me inside. The place pulsed, and I began to relax with the beat. The light looked a bit hazy and people filled every table in sight. Paige ordered two Irish coffees and we joined a group of her friends right near the stage. The crowd didn't bother me. Once upon a time I had liked places like this.

We edged in at the corner; two chairs had been saved for us. I had a perfect view of the stage and the band as they were setting up. A guy grabbed the microphone and the crowd started to yell.

I sipped my spiked coffee.

Paige squealed with excitement. The drums started slow, then picked up. People started to clap, pound tables, whistle.

Then he started to sing.

And gosh, that sound. The whistles died down as his voice started low, building. The room quieted under the spellbinding sound of his voice. Low, melodic, hypnotizing, honest.

Music had done nothing for me for months.

I'd loved singing for as long as I could remember and had played the guitar since high school. During my time in Texas, I'd taught music lessons to a few middle schoolers. I'd worked at radio stations since college, being surrounded by music day in and day out. Going to concerts had literally been part of my day job.

After Luke broke up with me, music had lost its sway with me. I couldn't care less about harmony and composition and lyrics. Music didn't comfort me. It didn't spark me to rage. It didn't bring me to tears—God knows I didn't need music for that.

But at that moment, in time with the compelling beat, something small moved in me.

He sang about lost love, about heartbreak, shattered pieces being glued back together. In the haze of the blue lights, it was difficult to really see the singer's face. I'd never heard of the band or the song. None of that mattered. It was the music that reached me.

When the song finally ended, the room burst out in applause. The lead singer thanked the crowd for coming and within moments, they began a second song.

"Deb." Paige touched my shoulder as she stood. "I'm going to get two more coffees." I nodded, but the drums were distracting me. Deep and rhythmic. A perfect match for the rich baritone of the lead guy. The bass player was all kinds of cool, thrumming chords and moving his head to the music, every movement in perfect sync with the guy out front. By the third song, I was hooked and wanted to download everything this group played. After several more songs, the singer pulled over a barstool to perch on and then grabbed his acoustic guitar.

"Feel this one with me, guys," he said, and I held my breath with the rest of the room. The backup singer—unfairly pretty with straight black hair, a slim figure, and black boots that any girl would kill for—started humming first, and I couldn't believe how good she was just at humming! Her hair swished as she moved and started scaling notes.

The singer joined in with her, and he sang about looking for something. Lyrics about searching, for a girl at first, then he realizes that she's not what he's after. And he's searching—thirsty, wanting, seeking. The seeking makes him feel alive.

I loved every note. After that, he seemed a bit emotionally spent, and when the applause died down, he told the crowd the band was taking a short break. The backup singer stepped up and squeezed his shoulder before exiting the stage. One of *those* couples. The ones that fit so well and whom everyone envies.

For the record, I don't like those couples.

Paige scooted her chair even closer to mine, which was barely possible. Now that the music had been replaced by loud, growing chatter, Paige introduced me to everyone at the table. After the hellos, she nudged me. "So?"

"Okay, okay. You're right, they're really good. What's the name of this band again?"

"Twenty-Four Tears."

"They must be local. I'm shocked I haven't heard of them before. Do they have a label?"

"Paige."

Paige twisted around. I did too, responding to that voice. The lead singer had suddenly appeared directly behind us.

"Ben!" She tried to stand, but our chairs were basically hitched, so the guy just leaned down for a hug. A sweaty hug, I might add. He was drenched. I understood, of course. I felt drained and I hadn't even been the one singing.

"This is my friend Debra," Paige said, pointing at me.

The guy looked at me. "Ben Price." He shook my hand.

"Hi." I wanted to tell him how much I loved the music, but I couldn't find the words. Or my voice.

"Can I sit with you guys for a second?" he asked, grabbing an empty chair nearby. The crowd had dissipated, mostly migrating to the bar for refreshments before the music started back up. But still, he was stopped every other second by people talking to him. I liked how gracious he was, taking time to say thank you. Once he sat down, right by me, nearly everyone at the long table greeted him. I realized that he and Paige knew the same people because they all interacted like friends.

I felt a bit odd since I really didn't know anyone except Paige.

"How are we doing so far?" Ben asked, leaning over a bit closer to me.

I looked at Paige, then figured out he was talking only to me. "Um, good. I mean, great."

He just smiled. He smelled like sweat, to be honest. But like concert sweat, which I was cool with. I didn't want to look at him, but he was there, talking to me, so I had to.

He was cute.

I looked away as much as possible. He had rock-star appeal down to a T. Lean but muscular. Permanent stubble on his face. A tattoo snaking its way down his arm. Longish hair. Damp from water or sweat, I didn't want to know. Callused fingers from years of playing the guitar. A smile that sizzled.

What seemed like a lifetime ago, I might have flirted with him. Certainly I would have been chatty, asking him questions and telling him exactly what I liked about every song. But chatty took too much work these days.

Paige had been drawn into conversation with the group at the other end of the table, so it was just me and Ben. That did make me feel sorry for him. It was his night and he was stuck talking to me.

"Paige invited me," I told him, just for something to say.

He nodded. "How'd that last song go? It's our first night playing it." He looked genuinely concerned.

"It was perfect," I assured him. "Your backup singer is a powerhouse."

"Yeah, she's legit. Karis can hit crazy notes. She should be headlining her own band, but she doesn't feel ready yet. Twenty-Four is lucky to have her." His hair was thick all over but longer on top than in the back, and he tucked swooped bangs back behind his ear.

"How long have you guys been together?" I asked, speaking of the band.

"Me and Karis? We're not a thing. Just friends."

I had no doubt my face flushed red at that moment. "I meant, how long have you guys been a band?"

"Oh!" He laughed. "A little over a year. And Bryce, the bass player, and I have been friends since college. I've known Seth for a year. He can play almost anything. We're tight. We're all tight." He sipped his bottle of water. "So the song was perfect, huh?"

I made the mistake of making eye contact with him. "I thought so. You sang it like you've lived it. The crescendo felt like magic."

He blinked. Light brown eyes, dark brown lashes. Tan skin—there was no doubt he spent a lot of time outside. He finished his water bottle, and I spotted another tattoo on the inside of his wrist.

"You know music," he said in a matter-of-fact kind of way.

That was too much. The guy was intuitive to a fault. Good songwriters always are, and I had a feeling he'd written those words he'd sung.

I looked up at the stage, where the others were setting back up. "I used to."

"Ben!" The drummer called his name, but he kept his eyes directed at me. "Debra."

My neck tightened at the sound of my own name. Crazy maybe, but I didn't want to hear a guy say my name. It took me back to that night in my apartment.

Luke, looking stricken and begging me to let him go. *"Debra."* Pain and regret saturating his voice. And I didn't care. I just wanted him to take it all back and stop breaking my heart and ruining my life.

"Debra," Ben said again. I sighed before looking up at him. He was searching my eyes, I could tell. Looking for my story.

I could have told him that it wasn't worth telling. The drummer called for him again, and with a final look, he joined the others onstage.

Late that night, after the last song, Paige and I left Percival's together. Even in June, the Colorado night air could get a bit cool. I didn't mind. We trailed behind a couple of her other friends as we walked down 16th Street, which was in no way ready to go to sleep despite the late hour.

"I'm going to ask because I'm on a roll here. Will you please come to my church Sunday?"

I laughed. "You're on a roll? I finally say yes to one night out, and . . ."

"And that's progress," Paige insisted. "It was fun."

I linked my arm through hers. "Yes, it was great, and I'm glad I came. Church is another story and you know it."

"I know," she agreed. "Just come. Please. One time. It's a great church. I think you'll like it. If you don't, no pressure to ever come back. Let's go Sunday and I'll treat you to brunch after."

Ugh. Relentless.

Still, my only friend.

"Fine."

We came to a crosswalk. Paige had parked in a garage a block to the left, and my car was in an open parking lot just ahead. I felt nervous. Downtown Denver was fun but felt a little scary late at night. Paige asked one of the guys—Milo was his name—if he'd walk me to my car.

"Absolutely," Milo said, hanging back while the others crossed the street.

"Thanks for walking me," I told him.

He nodded. "No problem whatsoever. I'm glad to do it." He was just a couple of inches taller than me, with a nice smile and a really great sense of style. His blond hair reminded me of Luke. But nothing else. Luke was tall, serious. As we walked, Milo joked and teased—not Luke's way at all. Still, I felt a ridiculous rush just walking alone with someone intent on protecting me. Another reminder to me that the level of rejection I'd felt from Luke had been intense, deconstructing who I felt I was.

My loneliness reached deep and wide, but it felt safe. I listened and politely laughed when appropriate. We got to my car and Milo ensured that I was safe inside before waving and running off to join the others.

I drove south, thoughts of the songs rushing through my head. When I got home, I looked up the band online and downloaded all eight songs that were available. Charged from the excitement of the night and not quite ready for sleep, I searched a couple of websites and jotted down notes for my celebrity gossip segment Monday, all while listening to songs by Twenty-Four Tears. Every now and then, images of the song leader invaded my mind. Ben adjusting the mic stand, that tattoo of his twisting down his arm. His eyes closed as his mouth moved over the microphone. His damp hair. The ease with which he strummed his guitar. The energy he carried with him onstage and off. And those light brown eyes, searching for my soul.

When I finally lay down to sleep that night, song lyrics still ran through my mind.

I was restless on my way,
Nothing knew me.
But when I stopped and had my say,
You wouldn't let go.
Holding me like a prisoner,
I can't be me without you anymore.
You've ruined us both.
I dream of you, and you need me,
Don't pretend you don't.
Scars stretch over me, but I don't care.
Love come find me.

I closed my eyes, rest overtaking me. Those lines haunting me. Ben's smooth voice dancing in my head.

I can't be me without you anymore. You've ruined us both.

Saturday morning, I woke early and went downstairs to the gym. Working out had never been my top priority, but after trying out a few of the elliptical machines one evening (all right, after I'd eaten a large supreme pizza completely by myself), I'd been hooked. Moving my body seemed to offer a small release to the pent-up aggression I'd been fighting off.

My condominium building was fairly new, with modern decor (by that I mean a lot of abstract art and random sculptures that resembled either bricks or clownfish, and a wall fountain that made it sound as though it were constantly raining in the hallway). I liked the clean feeling of new carpet and freshly painted walls. Cream colors punctuated with colorful blue and green accents and all that.

The gym was small but filled with top-of-the-line equipment, which didn't matter to me since I had no intention of getting on anything more complicated than a stair-climber. The room, framed mostly by windows and mirrored walls, was empty when I entered. I jumped on the treadmill and concentrated on the feeling of putting one foot in front of the other. Once my pulse was racing and I couldn't go any farther, I slowed down. I could feel each heartbeat.

I sighed at the reminder that it was still there. My heart, I mean. Working for me. I'd thought it had shattered completely, but here I was, breathing, moving. Six months since Luke Anderson had broken up with me, snatching away my hopes and dreams for our happily ever after. Six months since the most dependable man I'd ever known had decided he didn't love me anymore. Now he was dating one of my former friends. I knew he and Sara had been close—we all knew it—but when he'd assured me they were just best friends, I'd believed him.

There was no doubt in my mind that they were headed straight for the altar. Maybe they were already engaged.

That tall blond guy with the steady green eyes, with the chiseled jaw that begged to be kissed . . . that guy with the strong hands that felt both safe and exciting . . . that guy whom I could make laugh even when he was mad . . . *he was supposed to be mine.*

I kept walking despite the burning sensation creeping up my legs. After an hour down in the gym, a shower, and a bowl of cereal, I ran into the issue that was now my life—time alone.

Since Paige was my only friend and I'd seen her the day before and would be seeing her (assuming I didn't back out) the next morning, I didn't feel I could call her. Plus, she usually worked Saturdays.

I was reminded again that a second friend to hang out with might be a good idea.

After placing my cereal bowl in the dishwasher and wiping the kitchen counters, I put on comfortable walking shoes and grabbed my keys.

As much as I'd liked Texas, the summers were brutal. Hot and even more humid than Minnesota. And the mosquitos! But summer in Colorado was near perfection. Hot but dry. The mountains reached across the western expanse, standing regally, meeting the sky. I almost couldn't wait to see them covered in snow. Before the move, I'd been to Colorado once, last summer on a trip with Luke to meet his mom.

Standing by a river way up near the mountains, where his mother lived, I'd told him I loved him for the first time. He'd just stared at me for a moment. Then he told me he loved me too and cupped my face in his hands and kissed me.

The memory came, and I tried to quickly redirect my thoughts, knowing that those kinds of memories tended to stop me dead in my tracks like cement around my feet, making it too hard to move.

On a clear day like this one, the mountain view was so beautiful that I wanted to be outside and just drink it in. I turned the radio up and drove west for about forty-five minutes, stopping at a little town closer to the mountains. I parked on the street and browsed touristy shops, then stopped at a café for a cappuccino. I sat at an old, rickety table for two on the sidewalk outside the café and breathed in the cool, fresh air. My sunglasses shielded my eyes as I watched people passing by, quickly, slowly, some in groups, others toting children, couples holding hands.

Even though I was alone, being there amid people helped somewhat with the loneliness. I wasn't part of *them*—the crowd—but I was close enough. I didn't partake in the sounds of laughter and conversation, but they were all around me.

My mind wandered to forbidden territory. Did Luke ever think about me? Had he asked Sara to marry him? Did she ever think about me? How could the two of them have hurt me so badly and then just *moved on*?

What. About. Me.

I left a tip on the table and started walking down the sidewalk, very slowly, in the direction of my car. The sounds of an acoustic guitar began floating on the air. By a large water fountain, a street performer was playing. People stopped to listen, throwing coins in his open guitar case. I stopped and sat on a bench near the fountain and watched the guy, with long dreadlocks and tattered clothing, playing with abandon. He didn't sing. The music was his song.

I hadn't picked up my guitar since before Christmas.

I closed my eyes and just listened, waiting to see if it would happen again. If the music moved me, even a little.

How long did it take to come back to life once everything stopped? How long until acceptance seemed like the best course of action and a person would willingly choose it? How long would it take for me to be me again?

I enjoyed the music, but my hands didn't itch to touch my own guitar.

Fear swept over me as I sat with my eyes closed. What if this was it for me? What if one devastating moment changed who I was forever? There in the shadow of the Rocky Mountains, the bell-like sounds of a guitar ringing in my ears, I stood up and walked back toward my car. And on a sidewalk in a tiny mountain town where I knew absolutely no one, I could breathe. Far enough away that I was free from friends and family and questions and conversations. I didn't have to answer text messages. I didn't need to listen to voicemails. Emails went unanswered. No one was expecting me anywhere and I could do as I pleased.

I'd thought I was free once. My mind drifted to those moments before I reined them back in. I could hear myself laughing, feel Luke's arms around me, sense the rain weighing down my hair and soaking my shirt. Just a few months ago, there had been times when I'd thought I'd found my soulmate. I was home. Free to be myself and love completely.

That sense of home turned out to be just a state of mind. And I learned that real freedom's a lot less dreamy.

But I planned to have it regardless.

Chapter Two

There are times I almost think I am not sure of what I absolutely know.
The King and I

Sunday morning, I dressed in all black. It was the only thing that felt comfortable to me. Black capris, a loose black top, and black sandals. My unmanageable hair seemed more unmanageable than usual, but it was too short to do anything with, so I just shook it back, put in a little product, and went with it. A few months before, I'd cut my massive mane of curly brown hair after . . . well, after *it* happened. But short curly hair proved to be just as unmanageable. Proof that this was not my year to catch a break in any way, shape, or form.

Truly, I felt sick on the way to Paige's church.

But much like Percival's, I needed to get this over with so she'd stop asking.

A parking team directed me to a spot; just to be contrary, I ignored the person in orange waving his hand and drove closer to the door, where I found another spot. The last thing I needed was someone bossing me around before I even entered the building. I got out, took three breaths and told myself to pull it all together and be a grown-up, and marched in. There were people stationed at every corner, saying hello and smiling bright, even though I knew that in reality they couldn't care less about me and would never see me again—pretend friendship.

I knew the church drill and it wasn't my thing anymore.

Paige and I had agreed to meet directly in front of the sanctuary doors. There she stood, wearing a cute, long orange-and-navy skirt and leather belt, grinning and holding out a Lost Coffee cup. At least I knew *her* smile—her warmth—wasn't fake. I accepted the coffee.

"You're still paying for brunch," I told her, and her head bobbed up and down.

"Of course I am! Let's go in."

"I want to sit in the back."

She pretended not to hear and pulled me forward. "Milo is saving seats for us."

Well, she was going to make sure I absorbed every bit of this service. We walked down to the front. Paige hadn't mentioned that her church was so huge. Milo waved at us from the left side of the *second row*. We got settled in our joined, padded seats, I said hello to Milo, and the worship music started. I turned off the ringer on my phone.

"Sing with me, everybody. Let's do this together."

My eyes darted upward to the stage.

Brown hair, light brown eyes, a white collared cotton shirt, fitted khaki pants, white sneakers, and a tattoo swirling down his arm.

Ben Price. His acoustic guitar strapped on, he raised his hands and clapped to the sound of the beat of the drum. The crowd clapped with him, following his lead. He started singing, calling the people to worship.

I just watched. The congregation sat down after the second song for prayers and announcements and the usual stuff. I sneaked a look up at Ben and nearly choked when I saw him staring right at me.

He's not looking at me. People always think the pastor or whoever is looking at them, speaking directly to them, but they usually can't even see them. No big deal.

After the announcements, when Ben took the microphone again, he pointed at me and waved, really quickly.

What in the world?

Paige leaned close to me. "I think Ben's waving at you," she said, as confused as I was.

"No, it's the people behind me, I think."

Paige swung around to check and I poked her.

I finally just smiled at him, hoping that was enough acknowledgment. It seemed to be, because he segued into the next song and everyone jumped back up.

Church was nothing new to me. I knew the songs. Even the pastor—who, I later admitted to Paige, was a good speaker—read passages from the Bible that I'd read a hundred times, tying those passages to the same topics as usual.

While the songs weren't new, I enjoyed hearing Ben sing them. Like any good worship leader, he primed the audience, getting them ready to receive whatever it was the pastor wanted to teach them. He brought that same energy I'd seen onstage at Percival's and what seemed to be authentic enthusiasm. The people responded to him. How could they not? He was a born performer. Dynamic smile, smooth voice, funny at moments, perfectly at ease in front of hundreds of people. But I knew from experience that performing well wasn't quite the same as leading worship well. Ben managed both. The songs were obviously ones that the congregation enjoyed, judging by the number of voices joining in and hands lifted. Ben's voice stayed steady and true, easy to follow and accompany. Several times he stepped back, allowing the backup singers to shine. He engaged the crowd and the worship team; I even found myself, *nearly*, singing along.

Once the service was over, Paige and I walked out with Milo. The warm Colorado sunshine seemed to invigorate everyone. Lots of people in shorts and flip-flops milled about the lobby and sidewalk beyond.

"I feel like I know you from somewhere, Deb," Milo said, wagging his finger at me. "It's like I know your voice."

"Debra and I are going to brunch. I was thinking The Egg and I," Paige told Milo, tucking her phone in her purse after sending a text. She seemed to have missed what he'd said about thinking he knew me. "Want to join?"

I bit my lip and nodded when Milo looked at me, eyebrows raised, possibly to see if I was okay with that, which I wasn't, but whatever. He was nice enough. We had just reached the sidewalk when someone called my name. I turned around.

Ben jogged up to us. "Hey there!" He smiled at me, shook hands with Milo, and then accepted the side hug Paige gave him.

"We're headed to brunch; can you come?" Paige asked.

"Yeah, absolutely. What did you think of the service, Debra?"

"I liked the music."

His smile reached his eyes. "I'm glad to hear it."

Everything felt familiar. Meeting friends at church, making lunch plans. Like Texas.

I stepped back. "I don't think I can make it, Paige, but thanks. I'll text you for lunch this week."

Paige's face fell. "What?"

I hurriedly pulled my keys out of my purse. Paige stepped close to me and we turned away from the guys.

"Deb, please come," she said, her voice lowered. "It's just brunch. Not a big thing. I want you to be there."

"Paige, I—I don't think I can."

"You can," she said gently. "I know the alternative is you going home alone, and maybe that sounds better, but it's not really. You don't have to talk much. Order some massive plate so you can just concentrate on eating."

I laughed at that, despite myself.

"Look at this weather today. It's too pretty to go home. Come with us. Be my friend. Let me be yours." Paige reached down and squeezed my crossed forearm. "Come. Please."

A breeze blew back my hair; she was right about the weather.

"I shouldn't have invited the guys," she said with regret. I squinted at her, against the sunlight, and I felt a twinge of guilt that now I'd made her feel bad. Behind her, I could see Ben and Milo waiting, watching.

"All right, I guess. I'll meet you there."

She hugged me.

I drove to The Egg and I, trying my best to ignore all the self-doubt that swirled through me. Once I got there, I saw Ben standing out front, waiting for me.

"Thanks for waiting," I told him as I walked up.

He brushed that off. "My pleasure. Milo and Paige are at the table."

I followed him, suddenly hungry. Paige and Milo sat side by side in a booth—not what I would have picked, but I slid in and Ben sat next to me.

I ordered waffles and listened to the three of them talk, contributing a little so I didn't seem aloof and rude. No one pushed me to talk too much. Maybe Paige had warned them. I didn't know or care, but I was thankful not to be pushed. Over Belgian waffles, maple syrup, and sausage, I learned that Ben and Milo and Paige had been friends for two years, ever since Ben had taken over the position of worship leader. Milo helped out with the sound system at church, and he and Ben had been instant friends. Paige volunteered a lot with different church events, and they'd all ended up becoming friends, along with the rest of the gang who'd been at Percival's Friday.

We divvied up checks and paid the bill—I refused when Paige tried to pay for me. She'd been right. Hanging out was better than being alone.

Milo tucked his credit card back in his wallet and then snapped his fingers. "Miss Lonely Heart!"

Inwardly I groaned.

"I knew I recognized your voice." He looked thrilled to have figured out the puzzle that apparently had been in his head. Ben looked at me in surprise.

"Who's Miss Lonely Heart?"

"Debra is," Paige supplied. "The morning show on KGBL."

"You're on the morning show for KGBL?" Ben sounded shocked.

"Yeah." I scrawled my name on the credit card receipt.

"Have you never heard the Miss Lonely Heart segment?" Milo asked.

Ben shook his head. "I don't think so."

"It's not a big deal," I said quickly, pushing the check aside. "I mean, it's a morning show, just the usual morning show stuff. I was lucky to get the job."

Paige stood up and grabbed her purse. "I've got to get going. Lots of errands to run today. Deb, let's walk out together."

Thankful, I slid out of the booth. "Brunch was great. It was nice getting to know you guys a little better."

Paige and I left, slowing down in the parking lot.

"Thanks for that," I said. "I didn't want to explain Miss Lonely Heart to those two."

"I know." She touched my hand. "Thanks for coming."

I wanted to explain but I wasn't sure how. "It's just . . . it was like this in Texas for me. You know, becoming friends with a group of people at church. And it didn't turn out well. I'm not looking for that again."

Paige nodded, her face solemn. "You don't have to come to my church to be my friend, Deb. I hope I wasn't pushing too hard. I'm glad you came today, but the next time you want to visit, it's completely your choice. No prodding from me. And even if you're leery of making church friends, I promise that Milo and Ben are the most regular, down-to-earth guys you'll ever meet. Neither of them requires church membership for friendship." The corners of her mouth tilted up slightly.

I cocked my head to the side. "Do you like Milo or something?"

She flushed. "What? No! Of course not."

"You do." I tapped my temple. "It's all making sense."

"I don't! I mean, I like him as much as I like anyone in the world."

I laughed out loud. "Anyone in the world, huh?"

She glared at me. "You know what I mean. He's my friend."

"It's fine, Paige. It's not like I'm going to tell anyone."

Her shoulders slumped. "He doesn't like me in that way."

My heart squeezed painfully at her tone. I knew that feeling times one thousand. "Paige," I said in a quiet voice, though nothing else came to me. I decided to redirect. "Hey, you didn't tell me Ben was the worship leader too!"

She shrugged. "Didn't I? I guess not." Her gaze fell back down to her phone. "I've got to run. Lunch next week? Our usual spot?"

I nodded my agreement. Ever since we'd met two months before, Paige and I'd started meeting for lunch at Checkered, a diner midway between both our places of employment, in my case, the KGBL radio studio and, in Paige's case, a small clothing boutique off 18th Street in Denver.

After a quick trip to the grocery store, I headed back to my outrageously priced one-bedroom apartment. I walked inside and set the grocery bags on the counter, thinking, not for the first time, that I could own a plantation in Texas for what I paid to live near downtown Denver.

Meh. What does square footage matter when it comes to peace of mind?

Cozy is good.

I kept thinking about Milo and Ben and the Miss Lonely Heart thing.

It was the one segment of the morning show that gave me more anxiety than it should. Near the end of my shift, we took live calls, where people dished on relationship problems. More often than not, women or men called in to either cry over or complain about the person who broke their heart. Something I could, unfortunately, empathize with. The first time we'd taken call-ins, it had just been a random idea for the morning show. But in answering calls, my story—or pseudo-story—came out, bit by bit, garnering the sympathy of the audience, along with a lot of shared bitterness.

Apparently, the segment was a hit. So we kept it up, which in all honesty, I didn't mind at first. Misery loves company and all that—but week after week, well, it got old. Bashing exes and whining about cheaters gets a little tedious after a while.

I'd been lucky to get the job of course. I had desperately needed a new radio gig anywhere outside Houston, and KGBL had needed someone immediately. They liked the slight Southern accent, which was forced, since I was born in Minnesota, not Texas.

They liked the broken heart.

At least it was good for something.

I'd just pulled up Netflix when my phone rang.

Addison Powell.

I didn't want to answer. But something came over me right before I knew the call was bound to go to voicemail, and I clicked the green phone button.

"Addi?"

"Debra, I'm glad you answered this time!"

I didn't respond to that uncomfortable remark.

"How are you? I miss you. How's the weather in Denver right now? It's miserable hot today. I forgot to wear deodorant to work Friday—I know, how could I?—and the air condition at the school seems to be set on the highest setting possible. I mean, I know they want to keep costs down, but it's Texas, people. We need cold air. Remind me not to sign up for summer school next year."

Addison paused and I smiled. I'd missed her chatter.

My turn. "I'm fine."

She didn't say anything for a few seconds, so I felt as if I had to continue. "I like the new job a lot. The mountains out here are gorgeous. There's no humidity, Addison."

She laughed. "I can't even imagine that."

I laughed too. As my laughter faded, I cleared my throat and asked the question I had to ask. "So how is everybody?" *Except Luke and Sara.*

"Good! Lily is a little more than seven months along now, I think. Don't tell her I said this, but she's got the cutest waddle now that she's showing more. She's been craving asparagus all the time. It's crazy. I'd never seen her eat an asparagus before. Sam's business is going well. They contracted with some company downtown to do all their outdoor lawn design and maintenance, so he's staying busy and just hired another guy to help. They're happy and so excited about the baby coming. Glen and I are fine. It's been a wonderful summer. Glen—well—"

"Go on," I prompted.

"Our head pastor has cancer and is stepping down. Glen applied for the position."

"Wow, Addi. That's big. I'm sorry to hear about Pastor Deleon, though. Do you think Glen will get it?"

She was quiet for a second. "I don't know. Maybe. He loves being the youth pastor, but this would be a dream come true for him. He's always hoped to one day be the head pastor of a church. We thought that would probably take us to a smaller, start-up church somewhere, but this opportunity opened, and he's going for it. We'll see."

"How's Jason?"

"He's Jason," she said, and I could feel her smile across the miles. "He got a job as a line cook at a steakhouse downtown, right in the heart of the city. He's loving it. We don't see him that much since his evenings are tied up."

"Dating anybody?"

"I don't think so. He's serious about this cooking stuff, still taking a couple of courses on weekends and then working all the time."

And then quiet. Because I wanted to hear nothing about the last two people in the group I'd been part of.

Just seven friends who went to the same church and somehow became a family. Until we weren't. Luke and I had started dating—a dream come true for me—and I'd been a goner for him from day one. Even now, miles away, starting over, it hurt to think of how beautiful he was to me. How happy I'd been for a while.

After eight months of a picture-perfect relationship, everything had unraveled so fast that it made my head spin, ending with him breaking up with me on Christmas Eve.

Yes.

Worst. Holiday. Ever.

The ring I'd been hoping for never came. The future I'd planned in my head vanished. The circle of friends ... well, I left that circle.

I'd learned fast that moving on takes more than a change of address, and I missed Addi and Lily and Sam and Jason like crazy.

Addison started talking again, updating me on her home renovations and Lily and Sam's inability to agree on a baby name for their first child. When she asked if I'd been to the theater district in Denver yet, I clicked the phone on speaker and started pulling out ingredients for tacos for dinner.

"I've been there. It's not that far from the radio station actually. But I haven't seen any plays or ballets or musicals yet. You know me. I will eventually. I signed up for news alerts so I know what's coming." I'd been obsessed with musicals since childhood. Addi's question sparked a mental note to ask Paige if she liked the theater. A friend to go with would be nice.

"You're planning on staying out there, huh?"

I stopped chopping the tomato on my cutting board and wiped my hands. I picked the phone back up. "Of course I'm staying, Addi. I just got here."

"I know. I just—I'm a little worried about you and I wish you were closer."

Her soft voice reached my heart. "I'm doing better. Honest."

"You're so far from friends and family."

I hopped up on the counter and crossed my feet. "I didn't know anybody when I left Minnesota for Texas, Addison. Remember? I went to Houston for a job and I met people. I'll do the same thing here. It'll be fine."

"The goal is to stay and settle there, then? Do you think you'll try to buy a house eventually?"

"I doubt I could ever afford a house out here. Housing is outrageous. Especially in the city. Maybe I'll find a townhome eventually." I tucked that thought away to think over later. "I'm in this apartment for a year at least. As for staying and settling—" How could I explain that, at the moment, working and functioning took all my energy? I didn't need long-term goals. Addison, who'd never lived outside Texas, couldn't possibly understand my feelings. She'd met Glen, the love of her life, and in short order they'd dated, gotten engaged and had a beautiful wedding, and were now living in married bliss. She'd never picked up and moved on a whim. I knew she couldn't even imagine starting over, alone, in a different state, without knowing one person there.

But I'd done it before. I would do it again.

"I need a fresh start, Addison."

"You've started, then?" she asked, with that uncanny—downright annoying—intuition of hers. I knew she was asking whether I'd truly begun the business of moving on.

"I'm working on it," I answered. After a few moments of awkward silence, I hopped off the counter. "I've changed, Addison," I admitted in a quiet voice. Because if I couldn't tell her, who could I tell?

"That's allowed," she said gently. "We all change, Deb."

I'd been holding my breath unknowingly. At those words, I exhaled.

"Change can be good," Addi continued. "As long as you're being true to who you are."

"I have no idea if I'm being true to myself, Addison," I said with a snap in my voice. "Who am I supposed to be?" We were both quiet for a moment and I regretted the snap. I tried to think of a way to smooth things over, but no words came.

"I know life took a drastic turn for you," Addison finally said. "And when that happens, we tend to reevaluate everything."

Yes, I supposed that was true.

"But, Debra"—her voice dipped low—"you're still *you.*"

I closed my eyes and, with my free hand, rubbed my left temple. "I want to be someone else right now. This is a new beginning for me." I attempted to sound positive there at the end. "That's the good thing about moving somewhere. You can remake your identity. This time around, I'm going for more 'mysterious,' less 'open book.'"

"Are you now?" I could almost see the smile I heard in Addi's tone.

"Just wait and see." I narrowed my gaze. "New town. New place. New job. New me."

"Will that make you happy?"

"Close enough."

She sighed and I did too. I cared less about being happy and more about never being blindsided again. Let the new life commence.

Chapter Three

*The difference between a lady and a flower girl is not how she behaves,
but how she is treated.*
My Fair Lady

I tucked a runaway curl behind my left ear and glanced at the digital clock on the wall and then at Mark, the producer, who was behind the glass, nodding at me. Then I slid the thick headphones over my ears.

And we're on.

"So Andy was telling us that he doesn't believe in love at first sight."

My cohost, Andy Bartlett, leaned into his mic. "Oh come on, you can't tell me you believe in that stuff, Deb."

"You're right. Love is hypothetical at this point."

He laughed. "That's my girl. I mean, I *could* believe in love at first sight. I haven't met J.Lo in person yet. But does 'love at first sight' have to work both ways? What if I fall for J.Lo but Cupid's arrow doesn't hit her?"

Then your life is over and you pine for her forever and you need therapy.

"Well, I think Lana would have a problem with all of that." He grinned at the mention of his wife, who, thankfully, was a great sport at being mentioned constantly on air.

"What does Miss Lonely Heart recommend, though? *That* is the question." Andy winked. Yeah, yeah. Good segue. I could see the lines blinking. Calls pouring in.

"Rather than waste my sage advice on your imaginary love affair with Jennifer Lopez, let's take a call and hear from someone with real problems." I pushed line one. "Miss Lonely Heart speaking. How can I help?"

"Hi, I'm Ruthy. I can't believe you answered. I tried to call yesterday and never made it through."

Andy snapped his fingers. *Get her talking.*

"Tell us your story, Ruthy," I said.

"I'm pretty sure my husband is cheating on me."

My heart sank. "Oh, Ruthy. I'm sorry to hear that."

"What makes you think he's cheating?" Andy asked.

The woman on the phone sniffed. "Well, he's been coming home late. And he's suddenly secretive about his phone. I've noticed that he keeps it on him all the time. He won't put it down, even at home. The other night his phone rang, late. I saw the name that came up. He says she's a work colleague and they're partners on a new project. But he seemed guilty. We've only been married two years! What can I do?"

Andy looked at me expectantly. Ugh.

"Well, if I were you, sweetheart, I'd confront him right away," I told her. "See if he fesses up. If he does and he wants to work it out—only you can know if you're willing to do that. I lean toward the 'once a cheater, always a cheater' line of thinking, but that's just the Southern streak in me. If he doesn't confess, and you're still suspicious, see if you can do that thing where you link your phones so you can see where he is at all times. Doesn't Lana do that to you, Andy?"

His head bobbed. "Oh, yeah. I can't go to the bathroom without that woman knowing where I am. I stopped at The Old Turnkey after shift one afternoon, and she showed up within fifteen minutes. Standing by the door with her hand on her hip, saying, 'Doing some day drinking are we, baby?'" He gave me a thumbs-up.

"Do you have access to his email?" I asked. "His password might be something simple like his birthday. And start showing up at his workplace unannounced. Bring bagels so it doesn't seem weird."

Andy leaned away from the mic and covered his mouth as he laughed.

"Find out the truth. You deserve the truth, Ruthy."

"Right." Her voice steadied. "I deserve that and more."

"That's what I'm saying." I wished her luck, and Mark held up two fingers. Fine. Two more call-ins and that was it.

A few hours later, I yawned as I walked through the parking garage. Every day felt the same. Broken hearts. Tabloid gossip. Commercials for everything from vitamins to laser hair removal. The same songs over and over. Even the laughter had grown stilted for me. Still, it's what I did. I enjoyed being on the radio, and the job was ideal. Andy was funny and not overly demanding for someone who had a lot more name recognition than I had. The last morning show cohost had left unexpectedly to go to a competitor, and I knew it angered him. Not just him—the whole crew. Maybe that was why they were so open toward me, so eager to help me succeed, to replace the radio host who had been disloyal. I knew that a radio crew could grow close like a family. Fortunately for me, they'd needed another member and had welcomed me with open arms.

I climbed in my car and drove the short distance to Checkered, my stomach growling in anticipation for lunch. Within twenty minutes, Paige and I were tucked away in a back corner. I moved slightly to the left in my seat to avoid the torn vinyl on my side of the booth. Even though the decor at Checkered could use some help, the establishment had the recipes for mouth-watering burgers and onion rings and fries down pat. The cheeseburger with jalapeños kept me coming back for more, despite the fact that a person could gain five pounds just from breathing in the smell of bacon frying in the kitchen.

A memory flashed in my head. Me and Luke and our gang, having a cook-out at Addison's house. Everyone smiling and happy. Sara was there, of course.

"Are you listening, Deb?"

I blinked. "Sorry. My mind is all over the place today. What were you saying?" I forced myself to focus on Paige.

She dipped a fried chicken tender in a side of ranch. "I *said*, wasn't Friday night so fun? I need to ask Ben when Twenty-Four Tears is playing again. Actually, Ben and Milo and some others are getting together for dinner tonight—just pasta at my friends Ashley and Kevin's house. Want to come?"

"Thanks for the invite, but I've got a busy night ahead of me."

Paige glowered. "Netflix and pizza is not a busy night."

"Netflix just got a couple of old musicals, and I'm a total sucker for musicals. Not even kidding a little bit. So I have a date with Fred Astaire. By the way, do you like live theater?"

"You're changing the subject."

I swallowed a swig of water in my glass and popped a French fry in my mouth. "I'm tired. I was on the air at five thirty this morning. A night with Netflix sounds good to me."

"Okay."

"But ... if you find out when Twenty-Four Tears is playing again, I would possibly be up for that."

"Excellent." Paige's countenance brightened. She glanced at her phone. Our lunch date was coming to a close. "I better get back to work. I'm hoping to get off a little early tonight. Next week, let's plan to meet at Subway or something. These fries are becoming an addiction for me."

I stayed behind, scrolling through Google, reading a few emails, before gathering my things and heading back to my apartment. I kicked off my shoes and went to the bedroom in search of my phone charger. My room, which was barely large enough to fit my queen-sized bed in, looked like a royal mess. Tidiness had never been one of my shining qualities, but now, living in a matchbox, I'd started to crave a little more organization.

Once my phone was charging on the nightstand, I sat on the edge of my bed, looking over the mess that was my wardrobe. Clothes and shoes flowed out of the closet like a waterfall, but nothing matched me anymore.

Bright sundresses were pushed to the back. My favorite red pants had been crammed at the top of the closet underneath my yellow pants. Striped shirts and sparkly sandals caught my eye. Ripped jeans and rock-band T-shirts and boots cluttered the floor. Bold colors. Flashy outfits with lots of jewelry. Bright purses and pink lipstick.

None of that seemed like me anymore.

Those belonged to a girl who moved with confidence, who liked to be seen, who wanted to be part of the action.

Not me.

Silently I began to fold and stack jeans and T-shirts. Addison's words came back to me: *The goal is to stay and settle?*

Was that the goal? It seemed like a good place to start. I'd come for the job, of course. Setting down roots hadn't exactly been at the forefront of my mind. I'd needed out of Texas, so here I was, and I liked Colorado.

I'd told Addi that I'd started over once and I'd do it again, but the more I thought about it, the circumstances had been so entirely different. I'd left Minnesota, brimming with excitement, eager to make friends and find my place. Here, other than going to work and stumbling into a friendship with Paige at a coffee shop one day downtown, I felt the very opposite of eager or excited.

And yet, this couldn't be it. I finished folding (and was reminded that I hate folding) and then fell back onto the bed and blew my hair out of my face.

I needed to snap out of this melancholy somehow.

How did someone go about putting their heart back together once it split?

No ideas came to me. Not even Miss Lonely Heart knew the answer to that question.

I went to bed early that night, breathing a bit easier in my now-clean room. My phone buzzed right after I'd brushed my teeth. Paige.

Ben asked about you at dinner.

I stared down at the text but couldn't think of a reply. The phone buzzed again.

I told him we would go to 24 Tears's next gig and he seemed really glad.

I waited a few seconds, then typed back.

When's their next gig?

Two weeks, I think. But he's a regular at this church I know.

I sent her an eye-rolling emoji but couldn't help smiling at her humor.

I'd been asleep for at least a half hour when my phone started buzzing again, dancing on the wooden nightstand. I blindly reached over and felt around on the nightstand until I found it.

Are you up? Can we talk?

Addison. I looked at the clock. Ten o'clock. Eleven o'clock in Texas.

I didn't want to talk. We'd just talked a couple of days ago. What could be so important? A second text dinged.

Deb, we need to talk. I'm calling.

I held the phone and waited and felt sick. Something about the text evoked urgency, and my breathing quickened.

I answered as soon as the phone rang. "Hi, Addi."

"Deb, how are you?"

"I'm okay. What's up?"

"I'm sorry to call late. I know it's ten, and I know you work the morning shift." She paused and I felt like I should say something.

"That's all right. How are you and Glen?"

"We're fine. We're still waiting to hear on the pastor position. I miss you, Deb."

"I miss you too." I clutched the comforter, waiting.

"I need to tell you something," she said gently.

"Tell me fast."

"Luke and Sara are engaged."

The sensation that I was freefalling came over me. "I knew it would happen," I managed to say.

"I don't expect that makes it easier." Addison's voice was soft and flowed over me, trying to reach me.

I couldn't be reached. "I hope they're miserable." I said the words, knowing I shouldn't. Addison just sighed. No scolding. After a quiet moment, I braved a question. "Is there a wedding date yet?"

"No," she answered. "But I think they are aiming for six months."

My stomach tightened. "Well, then. I guess when you know, you know."

"Debra." Addison said my name, sympathy saturating her voice, and I had a feeling she was crying. A lump was forming in my throat and I knew I'd be crying too soon.

"I better go. I have to get up early."

"I love you. We haven't forgotten you. You're part of us forever."

But he's marrying her.

I couldn't even gasp. I choked. "Good night, Addi. We'll talk again. When I can." It was all I could say.

"Okay. I love you, Deb. Friends forever."

I hung up the phone and the tears came hard. I rolled to my side and screamed silent screams and thought bad thoughts and hurt all over.

Nearly two weeks had passed since the revelation of the engagement. Eventually the freefalling sensation I'd felt during the phone call had collided with the sensation of my heart slamming into pavement. Other than doling out scathing advice on air as Miss Lonely Heart, I tried to act normal, but after one phone conversation with my mother, she was alarmed enough to say that if I didn't schedule a meeting with a therapist *this very minute*, she'd be on a plane and living with me in my itty-bitty apartment for the foreseeable future.

Gerri Hart doesn't make idle threats.

I looked up a few therapists online, read reviews, picked a random person and made an appointment and went. Now, Thursday afternoon, here I sat for our second appointment, in a cream-colored overstuffed chair, across from a woman with leopard-print glasses and hair that was so shiny and black and long, I thought of Disney's version of Pocahontas every time I looked at her. That first session had been just a retelling of my story—explaining why I suddenly was a very unhappy twenty-eight-year-old woman who now fantasized about showing up at her friends' wedding in all black.

Pocahontas's real name was Dr. Clark. That first day, she'd listened in silence, an unreadable expression on her face. Today her expression was more pinched.

"You are isolating yourself, Debra. In maybe subconscious ways, such as moving to a new place where you didn't know anyone, but that can be explained through a new job and a need for change—and more obvious ways, such as avoiding calls from friends and family, not trying to find any community in the new place where you've settled, changing your appearance to blend in rather than stand out, and sleeping more, as we've discussed."

I licked my lips. The dryness in Colorado left me constantly needing lip balm and lotion.

"Do I need medication for depression?" My mother had insisted I at least ask.

Dr. Clark inhaled and looked down at her desk. "Possibly. If you do, we will certainly go in that direction. But this is only our second session. I want to let you talk through this more and see what we can do about processing the pain, then letting it go."

Process the pain. Let it go.

"Sounds like a plan," I told her.

"I know that it's easier said than done. But it can be done, Debra. One way or another, I believe we can get you back to a place where you want to engage, rather than disengage, with the world around you. It takes time to move on from this kind of betrayal and disappointment."

"My parents are worried about me," I informed her.

She nodded. "That's good. I'm glad you have people who are concerned about you. That means there are people out there who love you." This moved the conversation more toward the topic of family. Dr. Clark wanted to hear about my childhood and my current relationships with my parents and my brother. So I described growing up outside Minneapolis. Fighting with my brother, who was only eighteen months older than me, taking music lessons, fishing with my dad, singing with my mother, spending two weeks every summer at my nana's house on the lake. And always having the dream and desire to spread my wings and experience new places and meet new people. Jumping at the chance to move to Texas. I'd missed my family, but not Minnesota. I loved going back to visit, but my heart wasn't there anymore. I'd thought I'd found home in Texas—with Luke.

The search continues.

"Do you see 'home' as a relationship?" Dr. Clark asked.

I shrugged. "I've always wanted to get married and have a family of my own. Before now, I was never introverted. I wanted people and conversation and activity. I guess I never dreamed about a certain place or a house or anything like that."

"What did you dream of?"

I thought for a moment. "Someone to watch movies with at night. Someone to travel with. Someone there at my side in the hospital when I have my first baby. Dinner parties with lots of people around our table."

She tapped the desk with her pen. "Did you think about those dreams a lot, before you met Luke?"

I tried to remember. "No." I slowly shook my head. "I mean, since college I've hoped I'd meet the right guy and get married. But I wasn't thinking about it constantly. I worked a lot and loved my job. I had an amazing group of friends who I spent all my time with. And even before Luke, I dated guys. But nothing ever came from those relationships. Not until Luke. Then it felt right and wonderful and I wanted to get married as soon as possible and start our life together. Suddenly everything seemed to be right there, within grasp. A wedding. Babies and vacations. Intimacy and security and happiness. It was right there for me. I thought we'd get married and buy a house. Plant roots. Have a family."

My throat tightened. Goosebumps covered my arms.

"Life doesn't always go as planned," Dr. Clark said gently. "But there can be new dreams in place of disappointments. I want you to think about what your dreams for your life are *now*. Apart from Luke."

I didn't answer.

"The difficulty with happiness being tied up in another person is that we have no control over that person. So they have the power to destroy our happiness."

"What do we do when that happens?" I whispered.

"You take back the power." She leaned over her desk and folded her hands. "You discover that happiness doesn't have to come from someone else. It's starts with you. You will be happy again eventually, Debra. It might start slowly, laughing with a friend, experiencing something new, doing something for someone else, tasting something delicious. Happiness comes with positive experiences. But that's not entirely what we're after here. I want you to find peace. With yourself, with your situation, even with Luke and Sara."

I visibly stiffened, but she only smiled. "It's okay. Like I said, this is a process. It will take some time. We can't control whether someone will enter your life who can make you feel the way Luke did—though I have confidence it will happen eventually. What we *can* do is work at getting to a place where you feel secure and at peace with who you are and where you are. At that point, I think you'll be open and ready for whatever direction life takes you." She took off her glasses and started to clean them with a cloth. "What do you think, Debra? Is that a journey you're willing to take with me?"

To be honest, I felt overwhelmed just listening to her. Still, it did seem as though I needed a goal, something to work toward. If the alternative was life with my mother in a one-bedroom apartment or me turning into a crazy woman straight out of a made-for-TV movie, showing up at my ex's wedding, crying and making a scene—well, I wanted a life beyond both of those scenarios. I supposed I had to start somewhere.

"I'll try."

Chapter Four

The number one reason behind all bad hair decisions is love.
Legally Blonde, the Musical

That night I went home, physically spent from my conversation with Dr. Clark. I sent a quick text to my mother, assuring her that I'd gone to my second appointment and intended to continue going. Then I changed into my favorite pajamas. My hair was so unruly that I had to put on a headband to push it back. I stood in front of the pantry, looking for something to eat, but nothing sounded good.

All those things that Dr. Clark had mentioned—laughter, service, experience, even enjoying food—the thought of any of them made me tired.

I closed the pantry and sat on the sofa, cross legged. I stared at the TV, even though it was turned off.

This was not going to be easy.

Paige texted me that Twenty-Four Tears was playing Friday night and she'd told Ben we'd be there. I stretched out on the couch and yawned. A small part of me wanted to go and hear the band again. A larger part wanted to stay on my couch indefinitely.

Dr. Clark had said for me to think about my dreams for the future. New dreams that belonged to me alone. I mulled that thought over. I didn't have Luke, but I did have a job that plenty of people would jump at the chance to get. And I was grateful for it. I considered Addison's question to me about buying a house. Financially there was no way I could swing that at the moment, but eventually—yeah, I'd like to buy a place of my own. I knew from my experience in Texas that setting down roots included building community, which, at the moment, was not on my dreams list. Things like going to church or joining a book club or going out with Paige and her friends—none of that appealed to me.

That left me and my couch.

I thought about Minnesota. My nana had an old house with creaky floors. I remembered it could get drafty at times during the long Minnesota winters, but she had those ancient standing heaters that would warm up spaces. When I was little, I'd run into the house and plant myself in front of one of those heaters until my skin felt nearly scalded. Then Nana would set a mug of hot cocoa with jumbo marshmallows on the round antique table in her kitchen.

Dr. Clark had asked me about home. When I thought of home, I thought of that table at my nana's house.

I closed my eyes and pictured it. How does one find home when they've grown up and moved away? I couldn't spend my life eating jumbo marshmallows at my grandma's table. I opened my eyes and sat up, taking a moment to scan my tiny apartment. Small as it was, I liked having my own space. I needed a place of my own. Maybe a two-bedroom townhome. And I'd buy a rustic, round wooden table to go in the kitchen.

There. I looked at the calendar on my phone. In about nine months, I'd try to buy a townhouse. I set aside the phone and reached for the remote. Therapy was helping already.

Friday, after leaving the studio, I decided to swing by the boutique where Paige worked, maybe finalize plans for seeing Twenty-Four Tears late that night. The nice weather must have brought out shoppers because the small store buzzed with activity. Paige waved from the counter and I browsed while I waited for her to have a minute to talk.

The clothes at the boutique were pricier than I normally would go for, but I looked through the clearance section. A large, cute stark-white purse caught my eye. I picked it up but set it back down. I looked through a couple of racks of tops, but nothing interested me.

"Hi!" Paige rushed over. "I'm so glad you stopped by. It's been busy today. I want to show you something." Paige pulled me to a rack near the tiny dressing rooms. "I thought of you the minute I saw this shirt. What do you think? I think it would look great on you. Oh! They need me up front. I'll be right back. Try it on." Paige wagged her finger at me with insistence before running over to the counter. I hadn't managed to get in one word. I looked at the shirt. Flowy and light, cream and lacy. I just stared at it.

What was wrong with me? So much effort to try on something I would have loved before. Everything took so much effort. I found a medium-sized one and waited until someone came out of the dressing room. Once inside, I slipped off my black T-shirt and tried on the blouse.

I stared at myself. Trying to find me.

Dark wavy hair that barely brushed my shoulders and contrasted nicely with the cream color of the shirt. My cheeks had a little color from the hiking I'd been doing lately. No jewelry. The shirt hung easily on me and felt comfortable.

Beauty starts inside, then comes out and draws people to you, my mother used to tell me. *Be who you are with confidence.*

You light up a room like a seventy-five watt, Debbie. That's my girl, my father used to say with a chuckle.

I turned from side to side, recognizing myself but not. When someone knocked on the door, I quickly pulled off the shirt and donned my old one. I held the shirt in my hand as I walked the perimeter of the boutique, not quite willing to let it go. Paige motioned for me to come up when there was an opening at the counter.

Small steps, Dr. Clark had said, *in any form.*

I bought the shirt.

That night, while waiting for Paige to pick me up so we could ride together all the way to Boulder, where Twenty-Four Tears was playing near the college campus, I examined my outfit for the evening. The light shirt went well with my favorite ripped jeans and my gold sandals. I stuck in some gold stud earrings and twirled my mascara wand over my lashes. When my phone buzzed, I knew Paige had arrived and I rushed down to the parking lot. I blinked in surprise at the sight of Paige standing next to Milo's car.

"He asked if we wanted to ride with him." Paige's eyes were bright, and I didn't want to put a damper on her excitement so I managed a smile.

"Great. That was nice of him." I slipped into the back seat of his Honda, saying hello and buckling up. Paige and Milo chatted on the way and I spoke up when forced. The drive felt long and I spent most of it wishing I'd driven myself. Being with Paige was one thing. I could tell her if I felt uncomfortable and wanted to leave. Riding with Milo made me feel trapped, which was ridiculous.

I shouldn't have even come.

Finally we arrived at the small bar/café near the University of Colorado, Boulder campus. Even after eight in the evening, the sun hadn't quite dipped low enough to disappear. Milo parked, and once out of the car, I looked up at the orange sunset over the gorgeous Boulder mountain landscape. It looked like fire rising from the mountain. Paige stood next to me.

"Now *that* is why I live in Colorado," she said. Milo joined us and we walked over to the Black Horse bar.

"Is anyone else you know coming?" I asked Paige. She shook her head.

"Not that I know of. Boulder's a little far to drive."

Tell me about it.

We went in and the place was about half full. Ben and the band were already setting up on a stage in the corner. Milo suggested we find a table near the band and order something to eat. I hadn't eaten dinner, so food sounded like a great idea. We ordered drinks and appetizers to split; then Ben and the others came over to say hi. Ben sat down next to me and snagged a coconut-crusted shrimp.

"Hey." Ben's gaze lingered. "You look really great."

Well.

I sipped my lemonade. "Thanks."

He looked great too, though I didn't say anything. His dark hair looked subtly styled to perfection. I liked his striped shirt and dark jeans. One worn, scratched silver ring graced the left finger on his right hand. Milo reached over and slapped Ben on the back, and they started talking, along with the bass player. Paige scooted closer as the waiter brought a second order of jalapeño poppers. The bar kept filling up with people as time ticked by. I knew the guys were supposed to start singing around nine.

"Nervous?" I asked, when the chatter at our table died down.

Ben shrugged. "Just enough to make me work for it."

The space was getting warm. My palms suddenly felt sweaty, so I rubbed my hands on my jeans.

"I'm really glad you came," he said in a low voice. I grabbed a napkin to wipe away the condensation from my glass.

"Me too." Sort of.

"How've you been?" Ben asked, still talking quiet enough so that only I heard him.

I glanced over and the serious look in his eyes caught me off guard. The table was small, and we were all crowded around it, so Ben was close enough for our shoulders to brush every time either of us reached toward the platters of food.

"I've ... had some stuff going on."

He raised an eyebrow. I wasn't about to say anything about my new extra-curricular activity that involved seeing a shrink to process my ex's engagement.

"I've been listening to your show every morning," Ben said. I had a feeling that would happen. "Sounded like a couple of rough call-ins last week." His eyes winced with empathy. My shoulders fell a bit without warning at the reminder of the Miss Lonely Heart calls I'd fielded lately. So many broken hearts and so much anger.

"Yeah."

Karis motioned for Ben to come up to the stage.

"I've got to get up there." He stood, then stepped back and leaned over, one hand on the table. "And, really, I mean it, Debra. You look great tonight." He dipped his head. I watched him jog over to the stage and hop up on it. The drummer started to play, and Karis moved side to side, holding her microphone.

"So this is not a question," Paige said, her voice in my ear. "Ben is into you."

I shrugged her away and grabbed the last stuffed jalapeño. But the realization that he'd been tuning into the morning show every day struck me.

I wasn't quite sure how I felt about that. Hearing me crack jokes with Andy and talk about celebrity gossip was one thing; Miss Lonely Heart was another.

The beat of the drums went through the bar and I could see heads bobbing and people clapping. Then Ben stepped up to the microphone, adjusting his guitar strap. He bit a red pick between his teeth as he tuned the guitar for a moment. Then that smooth voice emanated. He stomped his right foot, keeping in time, and started to play his guitar, fast but perfectly methodical. I moved with the music. I just couldn't help it. Karis's voice merged with his, and the sound filled the room, lighting up the crowd.

He stopped playing for a moment and cupped his hands around the microphone as he sang.

They sang "Ruin" for the third song, and I sat there, captured by the song and by the way Ben brought it to life.

"Deb?" Paige placed her hand on my shoulder. "Deb, here." She pressed a napkin to my hand.

"What?" I jolted, blinking as I looked over at her. Then I realized I'd been crying. My face felt wet. I took the napkin, embarrassed.

"I'll be right back." I jumped up and found the restroom. Inside the tiny bathroom, I wiped my face and freshened up what little makeup I was wearing. Then I stared at myself in the mirror.

Get it together. Your boyfriend dumped you. So what? It's happened to a million girls and will happen to a million more. So he's marrying one of your former best friends. He's forgotten all about you. You thought he loved you. He didn't. Move on and stop being a loser.

The mirror wasn't helping. I went back to the table. Paige and Milo both glanced at me with worry.

I felt ridiculous and embarrassed and wished I could leave.

Instead of sitting down, I glanced back over at the stage. Ben had the crowd on their feet in a moment, clapping in rhythm with the drums. Rather than face Paige and Milo, I started clapping too and fixed my attention on the band. Milo and Paige jumped up to join me. The small bar practically shook with sound, and somehow, in that moment when I felt so frustrated with myself, the music made me feel just a little bit better.

I ignored everything around me, kept my gaze on the stage, and listened to Ben sing.

The final song started right around eleven forty-five, and by that time, I was trying to keep from yawning. The song ended, and I grabbed my purse, ready to leave with Milo and Paige. We were just outside the bar when I heard Ben call out Milo's name. The three of us turned around and Ben squeezed through the crowded door.

"Hey!" He panted. "Debra, would you ride back with me?"

Paige turned to look at me, her eyes like saucers. Milo grinned.

What. In. The. World.

"Um…"

"I have to help the guys finish loading the van, but I brought my jeep, so if you don't mind waiting…" The three of them stood there, waiting for my answer. I was so tired that standing around while the band loaded up equipment sounded like the opposite of what I should be doing. I shot a glance in Paige's direction and caught the glimmer of excitement in her eyes. The long ride back—just her and Milo.

"Okay," I answered.

"Cool." He gave Milo a chin-up. "See you later, man. Thanks so much for coming."

Paige gave me a short, energetic hug that again told me she was way too excited for the fact that I was not riding with her and Milo, and I followed Ben back into the bar.

"Can I help?" I asked.

Ben shook his head. "We've got it. Just have a seat right by the stage and we'll be ready soon."

Okie dokie. I sat down, stifling another yawn. After a few minutes, Karis came and sat with me.

"We haven't officially met. I'm Karis." She pulled up a chair next to me and handed me a Styrofoam cup of coffee. I took it gratefully.

"I'm Debra. How on earth did you get coffee?"

She grinned. "I told James, the bartender, that the band would definitely need caffeine for the drive back. He hooked us up." She blew the steam wafting up from her cup. "What did you think of the show?"

"You guys were great. Every song was flawless." I cupped my hands around the coffee cup, enjoying the warmth seeping through.

She smiled. "Ben brings the magic. But we all do our part."

"How do you guys know each other?"

"We met through Bryce, who I met through Bryce's ex-girlfriend."

"Ben says you should have your own band eventually."

Karis smiled. "He's sweet like that. Maybe one day. This is really good experience for me right now, and it's about all I can manage."

"Oh?" I didn't want to pry but I also didn't want her to think I wasn't interested in what she had going on.

Karis took another sip. "My mother has breast cancer. It's been a rough year. I moved back home to help out."

"I'm so sorry," I whispered.

After a brief moment, she shrugged helplessly. "Thanks. I know it's kind of a downer to bring up in conversation, but it's what's real for me."

I appreciated how she said it—just truth.

"Hey, Karis, you about ready?" One of the guys called over. Ben came up in the next minute, pushing his hair back and sliding on a ballcap. Those cappuccino-colored eyes of his met mine.

"Thanks for waiting, Debra. We can go now."

Karis looked at both of us and smiled. "Nice talking to you. I'll see you again, I'm sure."

"It was nice talking to you too. Thanks for the coffee."

Ben and I fell into step across the sidewalk and to the parking lot beyond. The moon lit up the night like a spotlight. We reached his jeep and I climbed into the passenger side. I told him where I lived and he plugged it into his GPS. Once we were well on our way back toward Denver and had chitchatted about how the gig had gone, Ben switched gears on topics. He asked about my job and where I'd gone to college. We traded history on where we were from. He was a native Coloradan but had been ice fishing in Minnesota once. Conversation stayed safe and light for most of the drive.

I looked over at him, his face forward. So handsome even in the darkness. We were quiet for a moment. An uncomfortable quiet, at least for me.

"Ben, why did you ask me to ride with you?" I had to ask.

"It's a long drive back, you know, to make alone. I'm worn out, honestly. Company is good."

Well, that sounded reasonable enough.

"I love your song 'Ruin.' What's it about?" I asked.

"It's about a lot of things, I guess. I think it's Karis's voice that makes the song seem so haunted. When I sing it without her, it's not as effective."

I shook my head. "It's the lyrics, Ben. Not Karis. I mean, she helps. But the lyrics are haunting on their own. And when you drop into the lower register, it's beautiful," I told him. "When did you write it?"

"A long time ago. The words came to me completely, before the music, which is a little unusual for my style. I didn't do anything with them for a while, but eventually I decided to put them to music. I had a few ideas on melody, but I was struggling. I gave the lyrics to Bryce and shared my ideas with him, and he helped me find the music."

"Helped you find it?"

"It was in me. It needed to be drawn out." Ben gave me a sideways glance. "Can I tell you something?"

"Of course."

"I sense the music in you. I think you need help finding it."

I don't know why that touched me. He was wrong. I knew he was wrong, but for someone to care enough to dig for anything in me—well, I wasn't too proud to appreciate that. "It's gone, Ben," I told him truthfully. "I don't even want to find it."

"Can you tell me why?"

"No. Don't ask. I'm just—like I said, going through something right now. It's private."

"Okay."

I looked out the side window until my eyes closed. The next thing I knew, Ben was poking my shoulder.

I jerked upward. He smiled. "We're at your condo, Debra."

"What?" I rushed to rub my mouth and smooth my hair.

"You fell asleep."

I realized we were in the parking lot of my condo building and I unbuckled my seatbelt. "I get up really early, Ben. I'm usually wiped by nine o'clock."

"I'm not complaining. You stayed up to hear Twenty-Four Tears. I'm honored."

"I'm a fan, what can I say?" I hoped I wasn't a fan with completely frizzy hair at that moment. I reached for the handle.

"Wait," Ben said and I paused and looked at him. In that moment, part of me realized that most single girls would be totally up for being alone in a jeep with a guy who looked like a rock star and could sing like an angel. His side-swept dark hair and the angles of his face and the rough eleven o'clock shadow on his jaw, long brown lashes and perfectly formed lips—sadly, lost on me.

Rather than hoping for romance, I fell asleep. Despite his good looks and his overall sex appeal (that I was fairly certain a worship pastor shouldn't have), I wanted nothing from him. Nothing from anyone.

"Are you doing anything Sunday afternoon?" Ben asked. "I'm going hiking. Want to go with me?"

"Sunday? I don't think so. Thanks for the invite, though."

I got out of the car and blinked in surprise when Ben got out as well.

"I'll feel better if I walk you to the lobby at least," he said, walking forward, letting me know it wasn't up for negotiation. We walked inside together and stopped by the water fountain.

"I've been thinking about 'Ruin.' I told you that song came to me fast," Ben said, shifting his weight from one foot to the other and shaking his keys. "You know how I told you it's about a lot of things?" I nodded. "Well, it's about something that I … I don't like to talk about."

"You don't have to tell me," I said quickly, hoping he wouldn't.

He didn't respond for a moment, then looked at me, straight in my eyes, and gosh, there was so much depth. He was a guy with layers upon layers.

"I want to. I ….. had an older sister named Sadie. She was three years older than I was and she died her first year of college. A car accident, she and some friends were out, and she wasn't wearing her seatbelt, and a drunk driver hit them. I can't really explain how that wrecked me. Sadie was everything. Losing her was the catalyst to a lot of bad choices on my part. I went to college and just—tried to be someone else for a while."

"I'm so sorry." I could barely hear my own voice. The rushing water behind us sounded louder, or maybe it was just me, hypersensitive since the conversation had taken such a turn.

"There are a lot of ways to read those lyrics. But the truth is, I wrote it for Sadie. The fact that it reaches you—that you connect to it—I just—" He stared into my eyes, searching for the right words. "I saw you crying tonight when I sang the song. That matters to me. Of course, any writer is glad when people connect with their message. But that song especially …" We were alone in the lobby, with only that sound of running water and a faint smell of citrus air freshener around us, and suddenly I felt very nervous.

Was Paige right? Did Ben like me? What was going on here? Nothing felt romantic. Even at that moment, I felt too numb for romance. I didn't want it. Couldn't want it. Not when Luke still haunted my dreams. I hoped Ben didn't like me; I'd hate for him to start down a road of inevitable disappointment. With all his friends, with how likable he was—I didn't doubt he could find a more suitable girl, someone sure of herself, a woman of faith, someone ready and eager to be the partner he needed. Why in the world did he want to hang out with me? Was I a charity case to him? Why would he confide in me?

"Would you—reconsider about hiking Sunday? I'm leading worship that morning, but after, I could pick you up whenever you wanted." His voice was small and hopeful.

I didn't see how I could say no after he'd shared something so personal with me. That seemed almost cruel.

I said yes.

Chapter Five

Now life has killed the dream I dreamed.
Les Misérables

Saturday morning was my nana's birthday. A reminder on my phone popped up, telling me to call her. I pulled up her contact info and clicked on her name before even getting out of bed. I sang her "Happy Birthday" as soon as she answered.

"Debbie!" She giggled with delight at the sound of my voice. "How's my girl?"

At the sound of her giggle, I couldn't help but grin. "I'm fine, Nana. What fun plans do you have for your birthday?"

"Well, let's see. Mary and I are going to get our hair done in about an hour. Then we're going out for lunch. Then I'm going to your parents' house for dinner tonight. I expect there will be a cake."

Nana and Mary had met as young moms and had stayed friends through thick and thin. For a few years, Mary had moved to Kansas for her husband's job. I remember how thrilled Nana had been when work brought them back to Minnesota.

"Nana, how long has Mary been your best friend?"

"Good grief. Four decades or more. Over the years, friends have come and gone, of course. She and I hold to each other. I've never needed lots of friends. Just one good one is enough."

"I suppose that's true."

"Now you, little Miss Social Butterfly, growing up, you always had a pack of friends. When you were small, and then when you got older. I remember all those sleepovers you used to have. You were the life of the party."

She was right. I'd thrived on friends and activities and a busy schedule—and I'd cried whenever I felt left out of anything.

"Other than social media online, I don't really keep in touch with hardly anyone from high school, much less farther back than that. I can't think of one special friend I've held on to for that many years. I'm glad you have Mary." I snuggled down deeper under my comforter, my hair splaying out behind my head on my pillow.

"Well, it seems to me that when you moved to Texas, you had a good group out there. You must miss those people."

My breath caught in my throat, and I stared up at the ceiling. "I do miss them, but I've made new friends."

"I don't doubt it one bit. People are drawn to you, Debbie. Always have been. Tell me about your new friends." I proceeded to tell her all about Paige and Ben. I added in Milo for an extra person because two seemed a little embarrassing after she'd just said people were drawn to me. I made sure to tell her about the gorgeous scenery and the excitement of working downtown every day.

"Colorado sounds wonderful, Debbie Ann. I might have to come visit you out there."

"You're welcome anytime, Nana."

"I'm glad to hear you're doing well. We've been ... worried, honey."

Don't cry.

Twenty-eight years old and my chin was quivering. I closed my eyes and held the phone away for a second. "I'm much better." Except for the tremble in my voice.

"Are you lonely, Debra?"

It was getting harder to breathe. "Sometimes."

"Listen to me. I learned a long time ago that we're all lonely sometimes."

Even Sara and Luke? I wondered.

"You can be in a crowded room and feel lonely. There were days when I was stuck at home all day with three small children, and I'd never felt lonelier. Your grandpa and I would go to church and sing hymns, standing in a full congregation, but at times I still felt alone. It's not so much about who you're with as how those people make you feel. I drink my coffee alone on the back porch every morning during summer, and I just listen to the birds, and I feel perfectly at ease. Just me and God. There's something about being at peace with yourself. It helps with being lonely."

I tried to swallow the huge lump that had formed in my throat. "I'm working toward that, Nana."

"You'll get there. Sometimes there's too much noise around us to even think, and we need to be alone, if only to hear that whisper in our heart, telling us who we are."

All the emotion had made my nose start to run. I sat up straight.

The truth was that I'd had a revolving door of friends while growing up, but never felt truly close with anyone. It didn't seem to matter. I loved being around lots of people and working and saying yes to any and every activity. I'd joined the group in Texas, thinking it would be the same. People to hang around, girlfriends to shop with—what I'd found was a circle of friends that wanted to do life with me, whether that meant crying together or laughing over pizza. I'd felt close to Addison and Lily and Sara and Luke and Jason and Sam in a way that felt deep and real. Finding that again felt impossible. And risky.

"What if I'm not quite the same girl I was, growing up in Minnesota?"

There was quiet for a moment; then her warm voice drifted in my ears. "Take it from a woman who turned seventy just this morning, honey. Knowing who we are takes years. Twists and turns and mistakes and growth. You're a woman. We're complicated creatures. There will be moments when you lose yourself in passion, and times when you find yourself in love. Days you want to freeze time, and nights when you'll cry until you can't breathe. None of them are wasted." Nana inhaled and I could almost see tears in her eyes as she spoke to me. If I needed to hold her, I knew she needed to hold me too. "You become the woman *you* want to be, Debbie. I'll love that girl, no matter who she is." States away, she gave me what she could. Her words held me.

After we said goodbye, I went down to the gym for an hour, then came upstairs and put in a load of laundry. Still thinking of Nana, I found my DVD copy of *My Fair Lady*, curled up on the sofa, and hummed along to every number.

Around one thirty Sunday afternoon, I was sitting in the passenger side of Ben's jeep. Luckily he had the top off and it was far too windy for conversation. Mixed emotions of both regret for agreeing to go and pleasure for being out on such a clear, gorgeous day kept swirling around inside me. I ended up just inwardly yelling at myself to get a grip and enjoy the hike. Ben seemed easygoing enough that I figured if I asked him to take me home, he'd just do it.

We drove about thirty minutes out of town to a popular hiking spot. I climbed down from the jeep and shook back my windblown hair, trying not to picture what it must look like. I shaded my eyes and looked up at the climb before us.

"You ready?" Ben asked.

"I'm ready."

We hiked in silence for a few minutes, but we weren't alone. People walked ahead of us and behind us. The sounds of conversation and laughter surrounded us. Once we hit our stride, Ben started telling me all his favorite hiking spots in Colorado, then his fishing spots, and then conversation shifted to his job at the church.

"You're the worship leader at a church and the lead singer of a band," I said, trying not to huff. While working out had been pretty much my only pastime for the last few months, the Colorado altitude was no joke. "Is it hard to be both?"

Ben shook his head. "Not exactly. I'm not expecting the band to hit it big and start touring."

"You don't want that?" I asked.

He lifted one shoulder and dropped it. "I'm not saying that. Music is a huge part of my life. And yeah, it would be a dream come true to get signed and hear my stuff on the radio and all that. But my life direction changed course a while back. I stopped making decisions that were solely based on what I wanted to do, and I started searching for a purpose that felt more real. Leading worship is fulfilling for me. I feel like this is where I'm supposed to be."

"Do you love it? Like you love being in a band?"

"Yeah, I do. It's about more than me. When the band plays, the spotlight is on us—when I lead worship, it's not about me."

When the band plays, you are the spotlight. I kept those thoughts to myself.

"Did you have a church you went to back in Texas?" he asked. To be fair, he couldn't know he'd just endangered his life by bringing that up.

"Yeah," I answered, trying to think of a subject change. Thoughts of Luke and Sara's engagement started to swirl through me and I got quiet. Here I was, thousands of miles away, trying to piece together a new life for myself, while they enjoyed their happily ever after. I supposed I'd made it easy on them. I left. Addi and Lily and Sam and Jason were probably brimming over with congratulations and happiness for Luke and Sara.

I tried—really, I did—to slow down my rage and pivot to other thoughts. "You said you've been leading worship for two years. What did you do before that?"

Ben stopped, opened his water bottle, and took a drink before answering my question. "A few different things."

Sara would be trying on wedding dresses and the girls would be twirling in bridesmaids' dresses—all while pretending I didn't exist. They'd all moved on like I was nothing to them.

Something inside me snapped.

"Why are you here with me?" I rested my hands on my hips. "You're the worship pastor. The worship pastor is always part of the popular crowd at church. You should have lots of people clamoring for your time, right? You're one of the cool kids. Probably always have been." My words rushed out, bitter and angry, and to my embarrassment, I couldn't stop them. "I'm nobody. You shouldn't waste time on me. I'm sure you've got lots of friends and people—girls to hang out with. I can tell you now, I'm not that interesting. You should be with all those perfect people, who go to church and act like their lives are perfect. And only hang out with people just like them. People who all speak the same churchy language. I used to speak that language and now I hate it. I hate it!"

Tears were pooling in my eyes and I couldn't breathe.

Oh God. I think I'm going crazy. Maybe my mom was right, maybe I'm seriously depressed.

Ben tightened the cap back on his water bottle. He looked at me, no words.

"I'm okay," I said brusquely, trying to actually *be* okay.

Breathe. Breathe. Breathe.

He tapped the water bottle against the side of his leg. "What I'm hearing from you is that you used to believe and you don't anymore." His tone was curious, nonthreatening. I folded my arms.

"No. Yes. I don't know." I inhaled through my nose, then looked back upward toward the top of the trail. I wiped my eyes. "I still believe in God. I've tried not to, but I do. But we're not on speaking terms." Then I looked back at Ben, daring him to say something cliché. He just nodded. He pointed up the trail.

"There's a bench at the top, waiting for us. I'd like to sit on that bench and talk. Want to keep going with me?"

My heart rate slowed just a little. "What if someone else is sitting on the bench?" I asked.

He smiled. "We'll make do, I guess."

We started slow, walking side by side. "I'm sorry," I whispered finally. He didn't say anything. "I know," I continued, my voice raspy. "I seem crazy." And then I wanted to talk. I desperately needed to talk to anyone who cared enough to listen. A tear dropped from my eye and I brushed it away.

"You don't. Not to me." His voice was tender and quiet, like we were alone, not on a busy hiking trail.

"My boyfriend broke up with me. That sounds trivial, but I loved him. I still love him. I think I'll always love him. He's ruined me." I gasped for breath, my heart rate accelerating again. "I thought we would get married. Every day we were together, I knew my future was supposed to be with him."

We reached the bench, which was empty, and sat down. Ben rested his arm on the back of the bench, behind me.

"Tell me," he said simply.

I cried—after months of my tears having dried up—they were pouring out of me again as I told him the story, sparked by my anger at the engagement. I told him all about the group of seven friends who meant everything to me. Who I missed so badly that my heart couldn't heal. Me and Luke coming together, falling in love, then falling apart. Him choosing Sara over me. All my dreams shattering. Running away to Colorado to escape the people I'd loved. Now, living so far from family and friends, sometimes the loneliness made it difficult to move at all. I even told him about Miss Lonely Heart, about how at first it felt therapeutic but now some days it felt toxic. It kept the pain always present. I shared how my parents thought I was depressed and called me, worried, every week.

When it was all out, laid bare between us, when the tears subsided, Ben leaned forward, resting his elbows on his knees. He was quiet for a couple of minutes. Then leaned back.

"Before I took the job at the church, I worked at a youth camp. I was the music director. I'd been working there for about three years. Before that, I worked at this place up in the mountains. I ran rafting tours during the summer and taught skiing during the winter. Before that, I lived with Jane."

I blinked. Hadn't seen that coming.

He took a deep breath. "I grew up in a good family. My parents are great. They still live up north of Denver. My dad is retired now. I have a good relationship with both of them. But when I hit college, I just ... wanted to try everything. I wanted to play music and party. So that's what I did. Then I met Jane. We were inseparable from the first night we met. And we partied a lot. I have no idea how I even passed my classes. I loved her. I did. But it wasn't a healthy kind of love. Not selfless. More like destructive. Then one day she told me she'd been pregnant, and she'd had an abortion the day before. It made sense to her; she wasn't ready. Neither was I, she pointed out. We weren't ready."

He looked at me, and the pain in his eyes was enough for me to reach over and squeeze his arm.

"I grew up the day she told me that. We had a fight and basically ripped each other's hearts to shreds. The next morning, I moved out. She didn't try to stop me. We couldn't keep going as we were." He sighed. "I went to a friend's house—his name is Cooper. We've been friends since elementary school. He's a pastor of a church now, but back then he was in seminary. I slept on his couch for a month. And he helped me process and get some clarity on my life. Then one of my dad's friends got me a job at a river rafting place up in Breckenridge. I rented a basement apartment and worked as much as I could. But I missed music. Music has been it for me since high school. I needed to play again. I went to a little church up there and worship music started to fill the emptiness in me.

"Coop helped me get the job at the camp. And that was perfect. I was singing worship music, helping kids focus and hopefully avoid some of the mistakes I made. Then the worship pastor thing came open, and again, Cooper called me. He's friends with Eric, the pastor at Rock Community. I didn't really want it, but I'd started to feel like I couldn't spend my whole life at camp. This seemed like an opportunity to move forward. And it's been amazing. Then I reconnected with Bryce and we started talking and decided to pull together a band. We started playing in Bryce's garage, and it felt good. We formed Twenty-Four Tears."

"Where did the name come from?" I asked him.

"I don't know. It just came to me. When I left Jane, I drove straight to Cooper's. I cried for what felt like a whole day straight. Then I breathed again. That was seven years ago. I was just twenty-three years old. Right out of college. Listen, Debra." He looked me straight in the eyes and leaned a little closer in. "If there's a popular crowd at church, I could not care less about being part of that. Don't get me wrong. I've got great friends at Rock. And the staff there is real—they want to help people. But, yeah, you're right. There are cliques everywhere. At church. On staff. Sitting in the pews. There are people judging people. People who only want to be with people who are exactly like them. That's not my scene.

"As for being perfect, I'm about as far from perfect as you'll meet. Honestly, I'm just as comfortable up on stage in a smoky bar, singing and playing my guitar, as I am onstage at church, asking God to meet us where we are. I'm more comfortable in the bar, actually. Why am I here with you?" He turned to face me on the bench, placing his arm on the back again. "When I met you at Percival's, it seemed like you were hurting. I only recognize that because I've been in that kind of dark place. Then you show up at church, and it's like God put you in front of me again—"

I opened my mouth to protest but he held up his hand. "I know—you're not on speaking terms. Totally fine. I am, though." His tone was unpretentious and he left the words there. I relaxed. "I didn't want to miss my chance to tell you that I want to be your friend."

My friend.

My eyes filled back up with tears.

"You sure you have room for me? Even if I'm not on speaking terms with God? Even if I don't want to go to church?" I asked. His face softened, and he stared at me in that way again, like he was searching for my soul.

"Yes and yes and yes."

I wiped the runaway tears from my face. "I don't think I'm very good friend material these days, Ben. You seem like a good guy. Less hypocritical than a lot of church people I've known. Maybe you're trying to save me. That won't work. This is the best I can do right now."

"Debra," he said, his voice soft and smooth, almost like a song, and I bit the inside of my mouth at the sound. We both heard a dog barking somewhere on the trail. "I can see you've been hurt. I get that." He stood up abruptly for a moment, stared out at the view, then sat back down. That dog was still barking somewhere in the distance. "I used to dream sometimes that I had a kid." Ben's voice cracked and he stared off at the mountains. "A boy actually. He looked different every time. Sometimes he looked just like Jane." He drew in a sharp breath and then looked at me. "I've never told anyone that. Except Cooper."

I felt the urge to reach over and take his hand but I didn't.

"So trust me—I know something about profound hurt."

And he didn't belittle mine.

"I've got room for you, Debra."

Chapter Six

There are bridges you cross you didn't know you crossed until you've crossed them.
Wicked

The following Wednesday morning, I leaned into my microphone after a traffic update and Hollywood gossip segment. Andy pointed at me to take the lead.

"To all our KGBL fans, we're going to be out at the music festival in Denver September sixth. The lineup of artists is amazing; there will be fantastic food—it's going to be a great time. We want all of you to stop by our booth and say hi."

"This is your chance to meet Miss Lonely Heart in person," Andy cut in. "Come party with us, you guys. We'll have T-shirts, water bottles—"

"We welcome cookies, by the way," I added.

Andy nodded. "Absolutely, we accept gourmet cookies. Stop by, bring cookies if you're so inclined, and meet us in person."

"But keep your expectations low," I instructed. "You know what they say—people go into radio for a reason."

Andy guffawed. "So true. People always meet me and say, 'You can't be Andy!' And I'm like, 'Why not?' And they say, 'Andy has hair. I know he does.'"

I giggled.

"Too bad I can't borrow some of Debra's hair." Andy smiled. "You guys, Miss Lonely Heart has crazy hair."

I fingered the ends of my curls. "It used to be long. I cut it after the breakup."

"Typical," Andy said with a snort. "What is it with dumped girls chopping off their hair? Like it's liberating or something. You're back on the market! Think about what you're doing. When Lana and I got back from our honeymoon, I came home from work maybe two days later, and she's got this pixie cut. I'm like, 'WHAT?' She just shrugs and says, 'It's too much work to fix it.' She gets the marriage license; off goes the hair." Andy snapped his fingers.

"Go, Lana!" I cheered. "Will she be at the festival?"

Andy adjusted his headphones. "Yeah, Lana and Timmy, the child who stays in his terrible twos even though he's four. They'll be around."

I laughed out loud. We talked a lot about Timmy, Andy's adorable son who also tended toward being a terror. Cute, though. And regardless of his joking, every time Lana and Timmy stopped by the studio, Andy was like a magnet for Timmy. The kid beelined to Andy's arms.

He gave a few more details regarding the music festival coming up; then it was time for my Miss Lonely Heart shtick. I ignored the knots in my stomach and watched the lines light up. I pushed line three.

"Tell me your story, Richard," I said after introductions.

"Well, I've been in a relationship with this girl for a few months. Now, don't hate me, but I've started having feelings for her best friend."

The knots could no longer be ignored. I started to clench and unclench my fists.

"Something happened between us the other night, and now I know that Ju—I mean, her best friend, has feelings for me too. How can I go about this without hurting my current girlfriend? I want a clean break. This other girl and I—I mean, we've got to give this a try. I never thought a girl like her would like someone like me. What do I do?"

"How long have you and your girlfriend been together?" Andy asked.

"About three months. But it's not going anywhere. I mean, I don't see myself with her long-term."

"Of course you don't," I snapped. "You're too busy looking at her best friend."

Andy's eyebrows shot up like a spiked radar going off. He coughed.

"It's not like that," Richard insisted. "I didn't go looking for a connection with her best friend. It just happened."

"Ugh. I hate that excuse so much. 'It just happened.' Like grown adults have no control over what they do." I shook back my hair and tried to keep my voice from shaking.

"Okay," Andy intervened, obviously attempting to calm things down. "What if you break up with the girlfriend, wait a little while, then start dating the best friend? Maybe give her time to move on too."

"I don't know. Things are heating up with me and the best friend, and I feel like this is our moment."

"I guess the question is, do you want to be a cruel, narcissistic jerk? Or do you want to be a human being?" I said, my chair swiveling with my anger. "Your girlfriend has no idea that you—and her best friend—are about to ruin her life because you're so selfish. You seriously can't slow things down? Why not? Are you sixteen years old and have zero control over your hormones?"

"Ouch," Richard said, and I could hear the building irritation in his voice as well. "Someone's angry."

I couldn't speak. Andy held his hand out to me, indicating for me to sit back and stop.

"Dude, that's probably just a touch of the anger you're about to get from your girlfriend. If you ever cared about her, which I'm thinking you did, since you're worried about her reaction, then maybe you should just be up front with her. Let her go before things get more serious and she ends up really hurt."

Oh, she's going to be hurt either way.

"Yeah," Richard mumbled. Andy's easygoing tone seemed to defuse Richard's defensiveness.

It didn't work that way for me.

The call ended and I stood up. Andy went to break and pushed away his microphone.

"You okay?"

I crossed my arms. "I don't want to do this stupid segment anymore."

Someone tapped on the glass. Andy waved them off.

"You know how popular it is, Deb. We get flooded with calls every day. No one's going to be on board with cutting something that's hot right now."

He was right and I knew it. I'd gotten myself into a mess.

"The lines are blowing up. Have you got this or what?"

"Yeah, yeah. Let's get it over with. One more call." I sat down with a huff, blowing my hair out of my face. I grabbed my headphones and pushed the button for line one with a vengeance.

"Miss Lonely Heart here. Tell me your problems and we'll see what kind of revenge we can dish out today."

When the segment finally ended, I took off my headphones, my hands trembling. Andy took us to break and then he did the same.

"Hey." He rolled his chair closer to mine. "You've got to get a hold of whatever's going on here."

I couldn't answer. I just gave a brief nod.

"Deb." His voice was calm. I managed eye contact. He continued. "I know this isn't easy for you. You need to take it for what it is at this point. You're playing a role on the show. And however you feel, you're great at it."

"Thanks," I said in a small voice.

He nodded, his eyes still serious. "Keep in mind that this segment is doing things for your career. You're building an audience. Our listeners like you. I worried when Ellie left that we'd struggle to find someone who connected with our base. You stepped in and it's been so easy. I know you worked at a smaller station before, but this place will open doors for you. How far you want to take it is up to you. Whatever happened with that jerk who dumped you—shake that off."

My heart twinged without warning. *He wasn't a jerk. He was everything. That's why this hurts so much.*

Andy's quiet voice spoke to me, low enough that I knew he wanted to keep this conversation between us. "You've got a great career here if you want it. And the longer you're here, the more valuable you are to the network. You'll be able to negotiate for a larger salary eventually. You could buy a house, travel, whatever you want. We'll be at festivals in Nashville next year, doing some great interviews. If everything goes as it should, you'll be with me at the iHeartRadio awards next year too. You're going to make so many contacts."

He pushed his chair back to his microphone as time wound down on the break. I slid my headphones back on and shot Andy a grateful look. He gave me a thumbs-up and moved us into an advertising stint. I couldn't verbalize how much it meant to me to have someone rooting for me, but I think he knew. This job was about all I had left going for me. I needed to make it work.

My phone buzzed, and once I reached the stoplight near my apartment, I checked it.

Want to do coffee?

Ben. He'd insisted we trade numbers after our tell-all on the mountain Sunday afternoon. I still didn't know how I felt about the confession session (as I'd grown to call it in my head). But the truth was, I'd never been a secretive person. I didn't want to rehash my sob story every moment, but I didn't want to pretend it never happened.

Well, most days I wished I *could* pretend, but it was so encompassing that pretending wasn't possible, not when just functioning took so much effort.

He'd shared his story with me too, after all.

He was easy to talk to.

I drove home without answering, realizing that therein lay the problem.

I didn't want to hang out with cute singers who were easy to talk to. I couldn't chance any feelings forming and more disappointment in my life. Oh, I hoped I'd move on eventually. I certainly didn't want to find myself all alone and joining a knitting club for companionship. (Not that I had anything against knitters, since I'd known how to do a garter stitch since the age of nine, courtesy of my nana.) But the new me imagined herself settling down later, with someone older maybe (well-off financially isn't a sin either). We could have a few children and I'd talk politely with the wives of his friends while our kids did water polo or something.

The point was, good-looking musicians were dangerous at the best of times. I was not even close to the best of times.

I looked at the clock. It was already eleven.

My phone buzzed again.

Or how about lunch? I'm hungry.

My stomach growled. I looked down at what I was wearing. Some mornings I was so bleary-eyed that I showed up to the station wearing no makeup and a ballcap on my head. As I looked at my cuffed-up jean capris, white Converse shoes, and one of my old favorites, a loose black Johnny Cash T-shirt—I figured I looked presentable enough. I could reapply eyeliner. I grabbed my phone.

Okay. Where should we meet?

Fifteen minutes later, I was sitting at Tokyo Joe's, sipping a soda. I watched Ben jog through the parking lot. With Nike shoes and long, loose shorts, he looked like he'd been either at the gym or on a basketball court. The top half of his hair was pulled back in a topknot, which somehow looked perfect on him.

"Hey." He stopped in front of me, catching his breath.

"Where did you come from?" I grabbed my purse and stood up, then we walked together to the counter to order.

"Basketball at the rec. I play every week."

We both ordered bowls of steaming teriyaki chicken and then went back to our table. I kept looking at that tattoo on his arm.

"Tell me about your tattoos." I took another sip of my drink.

He looked down at his arm and ran his hand over the ink.

"This one is old, from way back in college. Honestly, I don't know what I was thinking or why I ever thought it was cool. No special meaning or anything. I liked it because it made me think of skiing or surfing. At least, I think that's why I liked it. I do still really like the movement of it. I added this later." Along the side of the curved stripe read *Isaiah 43:19*. I made a mental note to look that up later. Ben flipped his left wrist and held it out to me. "This one was a few years after college." I leaned closer. One word.

Healed.

I tried to swallow but my mouth felt parched-dry.

"It's a reminder to me that no matter how broken I feel or what I do, God healed what matters." He flipped over his right wrist and my heart twinged at the sight of one name. *Sadie.* Above his wrist, on the inside of his forearm, there were these words: *When the brokenhearted people living in the world agree, there will be an answer, Let It Be.* "I got this one in college as well. It seems to be the time for bad decisions."

"The Beatles," I said and he nodded. "I like it," I told him. Without thinking, I reached out and touched the tattoo. I looked up to find him staring at me, so I quickly withdrew my hand and cleared my throat.

"Any other ones you want to tell me about?" I finally asked.

He grinned a wicked grin—and this from a worship pastor! "Not yet."

I rolled my eyes. He chuckled as he devoured the teriyaki bowl in front of him. I refilled my soda and sat back down. "I was wondering who influenced you musically. I love the definite edge of rock in all your music, but you're not afraid to infuse some pop to lighten it up."

"Just a tad," Ben said, holding up his thumb and forefinger to indicate an inch or less. I smiled.

"I'm eclectic in my taste," he told me. "I'll give anything a try, and I think there's value in all kinds of music. I grew up on gospel and I still love it. My dad always liked Johnny Cash; there's no doubt Cash made an impression on me. So … that shirt you're wearing? Yeah, I like it." He winked at me. I looked down at The Man in Black on my T-shirt and then glanced back up. I couldn't help thinking Ben should be careful with those winks. A girl could get carried away. Ben continued, "The Beatles are probably my favorite band ever. They changed everything. Bob Dylan. Steven Tyler. Pearl Jam. U2. Skillet. Radiohead, of course. Nirvana. Even Coldplay reaches me. Now, I follow lots of indie bands. There's so much music out there, it's hard to tap into everything. Twenty-Four definitely leans into rock, but I like so many genres, I'm always open to mixing things up."

"I get that." I nodded. "I listen to everything from showtunes to hip hop, depending on my mood. First concert you ever went to?"

He cracked his knuckles and folded his hands. "Red Hot Chili Peppers."

I grinned at that. "Mine was Shania Twain. My mother loved her—she still does—and took me to hear her."

Ben laughed. "Awesome."

"I enjoyed it a lot." I shrugged. "But the first time I was blown away was when my mother took me to see *Les Misérables.* I was ten, I think. I cried."

"You love theater, then?"

"Passionately."

"But you went into radio?"

"I'm terrible onstage. I tried in high school. I always get so wrapped up in the story that I forget my lines or want to sing along with someone else's song. I get way more out of it by buying a ticket. And truly, I enjoy radio so much. For the most part. All the advertising can get annoying."

"I listened to your show this morning," he told me. "You're really good on-air, Deb. You and that guy have good chemistry."

"Thanks. Andy's really nice. He's been doing this for longer than I have and he's made a name for himself around here."

"You did this in Texas too?"

I nodded, wiping my mouth after finishing the last bite of my lunch. "Yeah, I worked for a Christian radio station for a few years. It was a good experience. One of the women who worked there had a contact here at KGBL. She helped get me the job. Patty is her name. She knew I needed a change."

"What made you get into this line of work?"

I leaned over and rested my chin on the palm of my hand. "I majored in communications and minored in music. I love both and I had a goal of working in radio from early on. So I worked at the radio station on campus at the college I went to. Then I did an unpaid internship with a more well-known radio station. Money was tight, I lived at home, but the experience was worth it, and I made good contacts. That ended up helping me get the job in Texas. I was totally ready to go—ready for an adventure. I moved without knowing anybody. Now I'm here."

"What do you play? Or do you sing?"

Neither at the moment.

"I taught guitar lessons for extra money in Texas. I used to sing sometimes at church. But music—well, I'm concentrating on work right now."

He nodded.

"Tell me about Twenty-Four Tears. I think I've already memorized all your songs."

His eyes lit up like fireworks. "Really? Well, Bryce and I have written most of the songs. A couple I wrote, he wrote a few, and we collaborate on everything. Karis has been with us about seven months. Xander is our drummer. Seth plays keys. Sometimes Milo comes around to help us with sound."

"Have you tried to get signed?"

He sighed. "Not exactly. We paid for studio time and have about half an album available online or burned on CDs. We do a lot of cover songs too. We've been playing fairly consistently in Denver and the nearby cities. We all have jobs outside of the band, of course, so it can be hard to work around schedules. Xander and his wife have a new baby. But we love performing together. So we keep at it."

I ran my finger over one of the grooves on the table. He studied me closer. "I'd love to hear you sing sometime."

Never. Going. To. Happen.

I dropped my crumpled-up napkin in the plastic bowl, preparing to throw away trash. "I don't have an extraordinary voice or anything. I've just always been drawn to music. I think I'm pretty good at recognizing talent, though. That's helpful in radio." I walked to the nearby trash can. When I got back to the table, Ben was cleaning up as well. The line of customers had reached the door and nearly every table was claimed.

"What do you have going on for the rest of the day?" he asked me once we were walking back toward our cars.

"Not much. Sometimes I sleep after my shift, since I work so early in the mornings."

"Well, my schedule is all over the place. I work full-time as the music minister at Rock Community, but that carries over into doing whatever Eric needs. I try to help out where I can. Wednesday nights the band practices. Saturday morning the worship team practices. Sometimes I help Drake and Shauna—they run our teen ministry." He chuckled. "I think since I don't have a wife or kids, everyone on staff sees me as the go-to guy for anything."

"Do you mind?" I wondered aloud. He shook his head.

"Nah. I say no when I need to. I like being around people. And really, I like being busy. The only time I want everyone to give me space is when I'm working on a song. Sometimes I have to hole up when I need to write. Have you ever written a song?"

"I'm not a songwriter. Do songs about turtles count? I think I wrote three songs about my turtle, Zach, when I was in the fifth grade."

Ben laughed, and I liked the way his eyes crinkled at the corners. "You had a turtle? Not a dog or a cat or a hamster?"

"Nope. Zach the turtle," I stated, and he laughed again, a warm and happy sound.

"You've been here two months, right? That's what Paige was saying."

I nodded.

"Have you seen much of Denver yet? Or Colorado for that matter?"

I leaned against my car. "No. I flew out ahead of time and found my condo. Then I drove out with a U-Haul over a weekend, started working on Monday, and basically hit the ground running. I work all week. I met Paige, but she usually works Saturdays, so we haven't hung out much other than lunch dates and dinner a few times. I've been to a few malls—I like the outlets at Castle Rock, and 16th Street is cool. But no, I haven't explored the area much yet."

"Excellent. Colorado is awesome, especially during summer, and I volunteer to help show it to you. Starting with our turtles." Ben rocked back and forth on the balls of his feet.

"Turtles?"

"I'm free today. You're free. Let's go to the zoo. When was the last time you went to a really good zoo?"

"Well, in Texas, you could die from heatstroke during the summer, so I never went to the zoo. I went to one in Minneapolis when I was a kid."

"The zoo in Denver is great. The one in Colorado Springs is even better. But the one in Denver is closer. Want to go?"

This guy. Boundless energy.

"You want to spend your afternoon at the zoo, with me?" I shook my head in disbelief.

"All right, I admit it. I love the zoo and no one else ever wants to go with me. I'm hoping I found a new friend who likes the tigers as much as I do. Also, I'd like a reason to avoid setting up for the women's Bible study held at the church tomorrow morning."

I laughed at the sincerity in his voice. "You and me and the turtles and tigers. Let's go."

Chapter Seven

You could get lonesome being that free.
Funny Girl

I patted the sweat from my forehead with a napkin and slid my shades up like a headband. Ben came running back over with two lemoncellos.

I reached for mine. "Fabulous. I'm thinking Denver could rival Texas on heat today."

He shook his head. "It's a dry heat, Debra."

I dug my spoon into the icy lemon treat. "So you keep telling me."

We found a shaded bench and looked over the zoo map. The truth was that I had only vague memories of going to the zoo as a child, and I found that, hot as it was, I loved the Denver Zoo.

"We still have to see the gorillas. I saw a sign saying they have a baby gorilla, which I need to see," I informed him.

He was halfway through his lemoncello but he nodded his agreement. "I want to see the penguins."

I paused and looked at him, hot and sweaty, damp hair curled up at the neck, bright blue Nike running shoes. He'd taken down the topknot and replaced it with a backward ball cap.

"Penguins?" I echoed, a smile hiding as I watched him study the map.

"Yeah." He was too busy inspecting the trails on the map to catch my amusement. After our treat, we walked slowly together through the park. Families were everywhere, kids crying, kids screeching, parents talking. I didn't mind. But I appreciated simplicity of Ben and I just walking together, stopping when we wanted to. We looked at the gorillas, then the penguins, and yes, we saw a turtle—several adorable ones actually—then stopped again for fries and corn dogs. We sat on two iron chairs at a round table under a red umbrella. A gorgeous peacock wandered too close to my personal space, snagging bits of bread from the ground.

"What were you like before?" Ben asked.

"Before?" I repeated, stalling.

"Before the breakup with Luke." He dipped his corn dog in mustard.

I stabbed my soda straw down into the cup, past the ice, trying to get the last bit to drink. "I was more like you, probably. But this is me now." I ate another fry, thinking they were pretty stellar for being zoo food.

Next to where we were eating, an outdoor amphitheater of sorts was filling up for the upcoming elephant show. Ben glanced over as a large family passed by us, looking for seats.

"Thanks for coming today. I was being honest when I said I really like the zoo. My parents used to take me and Sadie to the zoo all the time when we were kids. I've always loved it."

I was glad he'd looked away and that he didn't see me wince when he mentioned Sadie. I wanted him to feel safe enough with me to mention her, but the story still broke my heart. "Guess what? I like it too. And I need to see more of Colorado, Ben. So thanks for asking me."

His eyes looked over my crazy hair, to my eyes, to Johnny Cash on my shirt, and a smile filled his face. "Want a cotton candy and then we can watch the elephants swim?" he asked.

I nodded. "I absolutely want a cotton candy and to see the elephants swim. Good plan."

We left the zoo after four, both sweaty and tired and yet in great spirits. Ben took me back to Whitestone. On the drive back, we hit traffic and I rested my head on the back of the passenger seat.

"I need a shower, something to eat, and sleep. Five in the morning comes early." My eyes couldn't stay open.

"But you had fun, right?" Ben asked.

I turned my head and my eyes slanted open. "I had so much fun."

He grinned. "Me too.

The next thing I knew, someone was calling my name. I opened my eyes and jolted up. Ben's lips were pressed together, his eyes bright with amusement.

"We're here."

"What?"

"We're here. That's the second time you've fallen asleep with me, Debra Hart."

I wiped my mouth quickly, hoping I hadn't drooled. "Sorry. It was a long day."

"It was," he agreed. "But it was a really good day. Thanks for that, Debra. I hope we hang out again soon."

I grabbed my purse. "You're one of my only two friends. I'm the one who'll be hoping we can hang out again." I opened the door and looked back at Ben and there was a moment that scared me to death. Him, looking tired and beautiful and smiling.

And me, suddenly panicked that even being friends could lead to me being hurt.

I'd been avoiding any kind of social networking for months. Back in Texas, whenever our group would hang together, Addison would post tons of pictures in online albums. She was a picture taker, so every get-together was well documented. "Weekend at the Lake" or "Jason's Birthday" or "Girls' Night Out." Albums for everything. Even before I'd left for Colorado, I'd "unfriended" both Luke and Sara on our mutual networking site and had decided to take a long-term hiatus from any social sites where I might run into photos of the gang. To my surprise, staying away from it felt freeing. I'd gotten to the point where I didn't even want to check social media anymore.

But this text came to me from Addison Thursday morning:

We had Lily's baby shower this past weekend. The pictures are online now if you want to see.

I didn't respond.

Of course, I wanted to see the pictures of Lily, cute and pregnant and glowing. The problem was Lily's closest friend, also known as Sara Witherspoon (soon to be Sara Anderson), and most likely the hostess of the shower. I couldn't see Sara. She would probably be beaming and happy and there might be a glimpse of that diamond on her finger. Finally, Friday after my shift, I texted back.

Could you just text me one picture of Lily?

Sweet Addison complied, texting me three pictures of the shower, none of which included Sara. I couldn't stop the smile that came over me as I studied Lily, that very round belly of hers and the pinkness of her cheeks. Her blonde hair cut short again. A very small part of me wished I could have been there to celebrate her, to touch the belly, and to buy something adorable for baby boy Spencer. Addison and Lily were together in one of the pictures. Addi's auburn hair was longer than when I'd last seen it. She looked tan—summer in Texas, of course. She had one arm around Lily's shoulders and one hand on Lily's tummy, and there were smiles all around.

I reminded myself to buy a baby gift and mail it soon. I wanted there to be something from me there, some mark that I existed in Lily's life. I was sitting on my sofa, scrutinizing the photos of Lily, when my phone rang. For some reason, hearing the phone ring now made my stomach clench. I hated talking on the phone. A name flashed on the screen.

Paige.

I texted her.

CAN'T TALK RIGHT NOW.

Two seconds later, she texted back.

I'M BORED AND LONELY. CAN I PICK UP A PIZZA AND COME OVER?

I blinked and I looked at my apartment. Clean. But still.

Ugh. I shut my eyes tight.

Pizza sounded good, though.

ONLY IF YOU WATCH A MUSICAL WITH ME.

She sent a string of laughing emojis, along with dancing emojis, and I had to smile.

DEAL.

Forty minutes later, Paige sat next to me on my comfy gray sofa, also cross legged. An open pizza box sat on the round white coffee table. The smell of pepperoni and mushroom and bell pepper and pineapple filled the room. I held a pizza slice in my hand and took a big bite.

"Explain to me again why you love musicals. What's the draw?" Paige asked, her brows pinched in confusion as she watched the first song-and-dance sequence in *Newsies*.

"Well, this is one of my all-time favorites. I fell in love with *Newsies* as a kid. I've seen it onstage and it's life changing."

"Hm." Paige stared at the screen, unconvinced.

I reached for my water bottle. "My love for musicals started with my nana, I suppose. When I'd stay with her during summer vacation, we'd watch *West Side Story* and *The Sound of Music* and *Singin' in the Rain*. I've seen probably every movie ever made with Fred Astaire. I think *The Royal Wedding* is my favorite. Also, we sang a lot at my house when I was growing up. My mother has a beautiful voice. We'd go to Minneapolis and go to the symphony or to the theater. It's been part of my life forever. I was in the drama club in high school. I just love it. When I'm really happy, I want to be one of those people, dancing around my apartment and bursting into song."

More accurately, I used to want to be one of those people.

"Can you dance?" she wondered.

I shrugged. "I took tap and ballet as a child. My dad taught me to swing dance when I was in high school. And I used to go out dancing all the time back in college. I would *love* to ballroom dance. Maybe, if I ever get engaged, I'll take professional lessons before the wedding."

"Why wait for that? There are dance studios everywhere. Take a dance class now."

Good point. However, I was now paying for therapy to avoid turning into a character from a Lifetime movie. "I don't think I can afford it right now. Maybe next year."

Paige nodded, munching on a bite of pizza.

"Tell me about Milo." I nudged her knee with mine.

She sighed. "It's not a big thing. He's nice, and you can see how cute and friendly he is. But he's like that with everyone. He was dating another girl at church last year, which was fine. The thing is, I do think he kind of likes me. He asks me to help him with projects and we run errands together and stuff. We work well together as a team. But when we're in groups, he doesn't single me out for special attention or anything. And when we're alone, he can be a little flirty with me. But when we're with other people, he's not like that."

"Mixed signals," I murmured.

"Yeah. But what can I do about that? I'm not ready to put myself out there and tell him that I'd like us to start dating. Because what if he doesn't want to? What if I'm reading the signals wrong?"

I remembered when I started dating Luke. I'd been crushing on him for what seemed like forever, and at the first sign of interest, I pushed him for more. I told him how much I liked him and that if he was interested, we should start dating. He agreed. Would he ever have pursued me on his own? I had no way of knowing. But his personality was different from mine—more introverted and cautious. I had a feeling I would have been waiting a very long time.

"That's tricky" was the only response I could think of. I was in no place to offer advice.

"What would Miss Lonely Heart say?" Paige teased.

"She'd probably tell you not to let it reach a point where you feel used. Where he leads you on in private but keeps his options open in public."

Paige sobered up and I felt bad. I touched her hand. "But I also don't advise giving much thought to Miss Lonely Heart."

"No, you're right. And I think it's good advice." Paige reached for another pizza slice. "I want you to know how glad I am that you moved here, Deb.

Honestly, I've had several girlfriends at church, and I like the women at the boutique, but I haven't had a *really* close friend in a long time. Someone to talk to about serious things or to meet up with for lunch—the two of us. With my friends from church, everything turns into a group thing. Which is fun, but it's hard to share personal stuff in that setting."

"Well." I cleared my throat. "Obviously, I'm thankful we met. Since, without you, I would have minus zero friends."

"Ben seems to like you *a lot*," she said, her voice overly innocent.

"I only know him because of you," I reminded her. "Also, he seems to like everyone."

She frowned for a moment. "Yes, I mean, Ben is nice to everyone and he's very well liked. He's got lots of charisma, as you know. And he's easy on the eyes. I can tell you now, most girls I know would jump at the chance to go out with him. But honestly, I haven't seen him single anyone out the way he has with you."

I waved that off. "The reason is obvious. He's probably hoping to help me see the light, get me back in church, something like that. Being friends with poor, lonely Debra is the right thing to do—I bet he's thinking about it in that way."

She snorted. "He's not like that. I think because he's on staff, he's overly careful not to give anyone the wrong impression. But he seems very interested in you." She looked at me, a thoughtful expression on her face. "What do you think about him?"

"Well, like you said, he's nice and good looking. We went to the zoo together."

Her mouth fell open. "You went on a date with Ben Price and didn't tell me? When was this?"

I shook my head. "It was in no way a date. We went on Wednesday. Randomly he asked me to meet him for lunch, then after lunch, he asked if we could go to the zoo."

"Two dates in one day!" she squawked.

I narrowed my eyes. "Neither was a date. I told you we went hiking that one day. Well, I guess we just sort of established a friendship. He told me he wanted to be *friends*. That's what we are. We have stuff in common, like music, I guess."

She nodded. "That's true. So ... you're not attracted to him or anything?"

I shifted uncomfortably. "Just like any girl, I'm aware of how cute he is. But I'm not looking for love at the moment, Paige. You know this. I'm not looking for anything. If I thought that's what he wanted, I'd run in the opposite direction. Because he'd probably change his mind in the end."

"Would you get back together with Luke if he wanted to?"

I sucked in a sharp breath and looked at the TV. "He's engaged to Sara now. We're never getting back together."

"Oh, Debra." I could hear the ache in her voice for me, and Paige reached over and took my hand in hers. I hadn't realized how desperate I was for physical touch. Without warning, I squeezed her hand back.

"It's going to be okay," she whispered. I swallowed but couldn't manage to talk. Paige didn't care. She scooted closer to me, grabbed the DVD remote, stopping and restarting the movie. "I think we need more dancing and singing about Santa Fe," she said. A small laugh erupted from me and I blinked away the heavy moisture in my eyes.

Saturday, I drove to Castle Rock, about thirty minutes outside the city, and went back to the hiking spot that Ben had taken me to. I hiked up to the top of "the rock" alone, saw the bench, which was occupied, so I found a flat rock to sit on, and I looked out over the town. The sky was so crystal clear that I could see mountains stretched out for miles and miles, blue and beautiful.

Despite the other hikers, including families with young kids, something about the setting calmed me. As I drank in the postcard view and the crisp, fresh air, I stuck in my earbuds and turned on the playlist on my iPhone, starting with Twenty-Four Tears.

An awareness came over me, a feeling of fragility. I didn't like it.

My body was strong enough to hike this rock. I could run miles in the gym at the condo. I could lift weights. On the radio, I could work and talk and make people laugh. I could pay my bills and take care of myself.

And yet, I felt frail. I could run and hike and be strong, but that wouldn't mend anything that felt broken. I drew my knees up to my chest, my scuffed-up tennis shoes flat on the rock. Dr. Clark had spoken of new dreams to replace disappointment. She said it would take time.

For some reason, I thought of the verse on Ben's arm. On my phone, I plugged Isaiah 43:19 into a search engine and waited to see what came up.

For I am about to do something new. See, I have already begun! Do you not see it? I will make a pathway through the wilderness. I will create rivers in the dry wasteland.

That tattoo, snaking its way down his arm like a river, reminding him of who he was. I read the verse three times; then I pulled up my text messages on my phone and scrolled down to Ben's name. I typed out a text. He was, after all, my second friend.

I HIKED THE CASTLE ROCK AGAIN TODAY. THX FOR SHARING THIS SPOT WITH ME.

Then I stood up and started making my way back down the trail. I felt my phone buzz on the way but kept my stride and waited till I reached the parking lot to check his response.

IT'S A GOOD ONE. ANY CHANCE YOU'RE UP FOR MORE EXPLORING SOON? WANNA ZIP LINE WITH ME NEXT SATURDAY?

Did I? I got in my car and turned on the air-conditioning.

SOUNDS A LITTLE LIFE-THREATENING.

WE CAN BRAVE IT. I'VE GOT WORSHIP PRACTICE THAT A.M. COULD YOU MEET ME AT THE CHURCH AFTER?

The thought of a good adrenaline rush *did* sound kind of fun to me.

I said yes to him.

Again.

Chapter Eight

Seize the day.
Newsies

When I pulled into the church parking lot the next weekend, I sat in my car, watching the minutes on the clock pass before finally deciding to just go inside and listen in on the last few minutes of practice. I could hear Ben before I entered the sanctuary. I stood at the back and watched him, foot stomping in time, playing his guitar like it was easy, his voice filling the empty auditorium. Words about God being the breath in our lungs. I sank down in the last row, watching him. Even in practice, he seemed to give it all he had.

I couldn't help thinking of my church in Texas, my place on the worship team. Every Sunday, standing to the far left of Michael, the worship leader. My hands outstretched, breathing deep and singing out all those same words now coming from Ben. Believing those words and singing until my breath was lost.

The words seemed fake now to me. All of it felt like make-believe. A show for the people.

Then I looked at Ben. There were no people. Just me, and I barely counted.

And he poured himself out like he meant every word.

The song finally ended and Ben stepped away from the mic and was talking to the worship team.

"Hi, are you waiting for someone?"

I looked to the right and saw a woman with red hair and cute freckles, probably my age, standing at the edge of the pew. It seemed like practice had ended, so I stood up and grabbed my purse. "I was waiting for Ben."

"He should be finished any minute. The team prays after practice."

"Okay, I'll wait in the lobby."

She fell into step next to me. "I'm Mikayla, by the way. Do you go to church here?"

"No, I'm just friends with Ben." And I realized I meant it.

"Hmm," she said, and her tone struck me as weird.

I took a moment to study her. "Do you work here?" I asked.

Her head bobbed. "I'm the children's ministry pastor. We're prepping for tomorrow."

At that moment, Ben walked up. "Debra, ready for our life-threatening zip-lining adventure?" He was smiling and teasing, but I watched as Mikayla's face fell.

Oh dear.

Someone who appreciated Ben's charms in a more romantic kind of way.

I wanted to assure her that he was just being nice, that I was a wayward soul he hoped to bring back to the fold, and that my heart wasn't available regardless. But none of that would be appropriate. So I just smiled and we both said goodbye to Mikayla; then Ben and I went outside to his parked jeep.

"I think Mikayla may be interested in you," I told him once we were on our way to the zip-lining place. Since guys tend to be clueless about girls, I figured I could help her out on that point, at least.

Ben turned up the radio like I'd brought up a nonissue. "Nah. I think she's dating someone else."

Doubtful.

We drove to the zip-lining place and I shielded my eyes from the sun as I looked up at the structure. "I think I just want to watch you do it," I said.

He shook his head. "No way. We do this together. Come on. It's a very Colorado-type thing to do."

"I'm not a real Coloradan."

"That's okay—most people here are transplants. We'll make a real Coloradan of you."

"I don't know that I'm staying," I said, my eyes still upward.

"Really?" Ben asked. I glanced at him. Why had I said that?

"I mean, of course I'm staying." But my heart fluttered. Did I want to leave? And go where? Minnesota? Never Texas. Never again. I needed to stay. Plug in. Buy a place. Advance my career. Hold on to what I had. Ben didn't say anything, but I wanted to get past this moment. I looked back up at the lines so high above us.

"Let's go to the top. If you still don't want to do it at that point, I'll go alone. But if not, we'll do it together," Ben said.

"Fine." We signed forms and Ben insisted on paying since it was his idea. I told him he was trying to make me feel guilty if I didn't go through with it and he just laughed. We got to the top and Ben told the people who worked the lines that we needed a minute to decide whether I wanted to do this. I liked how he said it, simply, again, just keeping things real. For a rock-star kind of guy, he was very undramatic.

I stood at the edge. Ben stepped back, and I looked out at the line, going all the way to the next structure on rock formations that looked, to me, too far away. A sharp, warm breeze whipped past me.

What was I afraid of?

Not this. Being hurt again, yes. Being alone forever, yes. Losing myself, yes. Not this, though.

I looked at Ben. "I'm ready."

He stepped forward like he'd known all along. "Cool. Let's do it." We were strapped in—despite my sudden bout of courage, I was very relieved that we were doing this tied together. And in a moment, we were flying. Brave or not, I screamed.

"Ben!" We'd just made it back down from zip-lining and were halfway to the parking lot when someone called Ben's name and we both turned.

"Drake, hey, man, how's it going? I didn't know you were coming out here today," Ben said as the guy stepped close and patted him on the back. I vaguely remembered Ben mentioning the name Drake.

"Are you here with Venture?" Ben asked.

"Just a couple of the guys. It's not an official youth group outing."

Right. The youth group.

Ben introduced me, and Drake reached out to shake my hand. "Debra, it's nice to finally meet you."

I felt the smile freeze on my face. I half expected him to tell me he'd been praying for me. At that moment, the teens Drake had been talking about surfaced, all obviously excited for zip-lining or whatever else they were doing, surrounding Ben and talking over each other. I moved to the side. Ben glanced in my direction.

"All right, we've got to go. I'll see you guys later." Ben extracted himself from the group and we walked together.

"What's wrong?" he asked, once we reached the jeep.

"What have you told Drake about me? He acted as though he'd already heard about me from you."

Ben faced me. "Yeah, I saw him later in the evening, that day we went to the zoo. So I told him about you."

"I see." I looked down at the pavement.

"Hey," he said in a slow, easy voice. "Why? Is this a secret?"

"What? Us hanging out together? No, of course not. We're just friends. It's not a big deal." I pursed my lips, went to the passenger door, and climbed inside. Ben got in the driver's side and turned the ignition.

"I just …. I don't want to be on anyone's prayer list. And I don't want anyone talking about me behind my back."

I snuck a fast glance over at him and saw his jaw tighten and his brow furrow.

Not happy.

"First, you're not on any prayer lists. Except mine. And I can pray for you if I want, so don't argue that one. Two, I'm not talking about you behind your back. Everything we talk about is between us."

I didn't say anything as we drove back to the church, but I couldn't help feeling slightly chastened. I knew he wasn't talking about me like that—why was I so defensive?

Because my life has taken a painful detour and I don't trust anyone. And if that's not obvious to him … then he's less intuitive than I thought.

The rest of the drive was entirely silent, and I kept thinking I should apologize, but it felt too hard. I just wanted to go home, curl up in bed, and avoid people for the rest of my life.

Ben swung the jeep into the parking spot next to my SUV and I got out without a word. He jumped out.

"Debra."

I turned halfway to look at him. "I'm sorry."

"I'm sorry."

We said the words in sync and I couldn't stop the teeny smile that crept up on my face. He moved to stand right in front of me.

"You don't trust me," he stated.

I leaned against the car. "Ben, we've known each other just a few weeks. And I don't trust easy anymore. But …" Again I wondered why he wanted to spend time with me, with so many options. What was he looking for? I decided I'd just ask. "Ben, are you ever lonely?"

He pressed his lips together in a straight line for a moment. "Everyone's lonely at times, Debra."

Nana had said the same thing. Maybe it was true. I looked at him, trying to ignore how attractive he looked in that moment, casual in every way, except for those eyes, staring at me so seriously. I crossed my arms, just for something to do with my hands. "Ben Price, you are my second friend. If I lose you, I'm down to one. Which is kind of sad."

Lines crinkled by his eyes as he smiled. "Well, it's nice to be needed."

Tuesday morning after my shift ended, Andy informed me that Producer Mark needed to talk with me in his office. I made my way down the long hallway from our studio to Mark's office, then took a seat in a bowler chair across from his cluttered desk.

"We've been amazed by how popular the Miss Lonely Heart segment is, Debra." My stomach tightened at the producer's words. "But over the past two weeks, to be honest, you seem a bit lackluster when it comes to taking calls and giving advice."

I held my hands tight together in my lap and tried to act indifferent. "The thing is, I'm not a professional counselor. You know this, right? I'm not an unending well of advice." I chuckled uneasily, hoping to keep the conversation civil. Mark gave me a tight smile that didn't feel very friendly.

"Our numbers spike during that hour. People love listening to the show and they love calling in and talking about their problems. I'm not asking you to be anyone's therapist, Debra. You're there to be entertaining. And you are. We feel very fortunate to have you on our team here at KGBL. You have a very bright future with us here. Andy likes you. And you came up with this segment—"

"Not exactly," I reminded him. "I talked about my ex, and I said, 'You can just call me Miss Lonely Heart.' That's it."

"Well, it stuck. And it's a hit. I'd like to see you perk up a bit more during the calls."

"What do you mean?"

"The call yesterday—"

I knew we'd get to this eventually. The reason I'd been called in to see Mark, without Andy. "I was fairly perky yesterday."

Mark's gaze narrowed. "The caller was highly offended."

"So was I. She chose to call in, and she's a moron, and I called her on that."

"Calling our listeners morons isn't what I'm looking for in a morning show cohost."

My mouth went dry. Was he going to fire me? I could suddenly see my future in Minnesota, having failed at life at the age of twenty-eight, back at my parents' house, sleeping on the sofa since my mother had turned my old room into an office for my dad that doubled as a place to store boxes of her collection of ceramic cows.

Knots tightened in my stomach. "Mark, did you listen to the call-in? Her boyfriend has cheated on her like five times, and she's weeping about how much she loves him and needs him to stay. Are you kidding me? I told her to get a life and move on."

"Yes, I know. You told her she's pathetic and that he never loved her and he never would and she needed to get a grip on reality."

"All of that is true."

His lips pressed together and his fingers strummed his desk. "You're right. It's true. But did it help her? Did it make anyone laugh? You were the one who ended up sounding cruel and angry. Part of the draw of Miss Lonely Heart is that you empathize with these people."

"And part of the draw is that I'm honest with them. Life sucks sometimes and we move on."

Mark just studied me. "I want you to go on the air and apologize. You don't have to call her personally or anything, but during the next segment, we need you to acknowledge that you were a little heartless yesterday and that's not your intention. Can you do that?"

I felt like screaming. Instead, I just swallowed and thought of all my mom's ceramic cows.

"Okay, fine. Sure, I can do that."

His brow smoothed and relief filled his eyes. "Excellent."

"And I understand that Miss Lonely Heart is popular for the radio station, but I can't do this forever. I'm running low on funny ideas for revenge."

"Well, our afternoon show has been running the Five O'Clock Phone Calls, where Tim and John let people call in and talk about how much they hate their jobs, for six years. When something works, we keep going until it doesn't."

How encouraging.

Mark turned his attention to his buzzing phone and spoke without looking up, effectively dismissing me. "I'm glad we're on the same page, Debra. I look forward to hearing the segment tomorrow."

Wednesday, after the traffic and weather update, Andy pointed at me, a sympathetic look on his face.

Yeah, yeah. The apology. I wasn't going to shirk my duty and chance an immediate future in Minnesota.

"So . . . things got a bit tense yesterday," Andy began.

I sighed, loud enough to be heard on air. "That's true. And, you know, I think I came across as kind of mean. Not my intention at all. Some girls have unending patience with shmucks. I'm not in that camp. But to each her own."

Andy ran one pointer finger over the other. *Shame on me.* Apparently, the apology wasn't good enough.

Grr.

"So I'm a little bitter. It's to be expected. I was oblivious to the fact that I was in a dead-end relationship. I hate to see other women in dead-end relationships too. We need more than that."

Andy nodded, adjusting his headset. "Fair enough."

A lump formed in my throat. "And, Carol from yesterday, if you're listening … you could have more than a dead-end relationship. You could shut the door on someone who hasn't valued you as he should and be brave enough to see if there's more out there for you."

Andy watched me, seemingly unsure as to how to respond to that. I was busy trying to breathe around the lump and keep my emotions in check. "Let's take a call," I suggested, the blinking lines in my peripheral. I punched a button. "Miss Lonely Heart here. Who've we got?"

A sniffle. "I'm Rebecca. Thank you so much for what you just said. I've been needing to close a door on a dead-end relationship. I've just been holding on because I hate to be alone."

"Well, Rebecca, we get that. Right, Andy? No one wants to be alone."

"Technically, I'm looking for more alone time in my life. Timmy has started climbing into our bed at night and we still sleep on a double."

"Okay, everyone but Andy, then. Don't listen to him, Rebecca. Tell me about your relationship."

"I'm unhappy. My boyfriend was great in the beginning—lots of fun dates and conversation. But we've been together two years now and we fight constantly. The thing is, I'm about to turn thirty-one … and it sounds stupid maybe, but I want kids … and marriage. What if …"

My heart pinched. "Rebecca, you are definitely not alone in feeling that way. Lots of us understand that. But if you're already unhappy now—that's not a good sign for later. Maybe he's unhappy too. Maybe it's time to grab hold of a different dream and go after it. Do you like your job?"

"Not really."

"Maybe this is your year for a job change. Change is good."

"I know. And I know I should break up with him. I just need to do it. I think I'll be lonely, though."

A face came into my mind. Dark hair and café-au-lait-colored eyes. "I was talking with a friend of mine recently and he told me that we're all lonely sometimes, Rebecca. I think he's right. Be brave anyway."

"Thank you for listening."

I ended the call, and after one more call-in, we shifted to a music block and

I took off my headphones.

Andy did the same. "Nailed it. Officially out of the woods. Not as much drama as I like, but all those female listeners will appreciate the heart."

I sat back in my swivel chair, breathing hard. I hadn't realized that my hands were sweating. Or how fast my heart was racing. I jumped up, telling Andy I needed a water bottle before the break ended, and went to the staff kitchen as fast as I could.

At lunch, I went to a nearby deli to meet Paige. I spotted her at an outdoor table. Her long hair was twisted high in a loose bun, a long, beaded necklace around her neck, and she wore black sunglasses. Her attention was on her phone, but I paused at the table to ask whether she'd ordered already, then darted inside to order a club sandwich before joining her at the table. Over baked chips and a delicious club, I told her about the meeting with Mark and the subsequent apology via radio. She ate every crouton from her Caesar salad as she listened.

When I finished my story, Paige kept digging through her lettuce, looking for croutons. "I listened to the show this morning. I'm kind of addicted, Deb. I have to hear your morning show every day now. I almost called in yesterday to talk about Milo."

I laughed, then choked on a chip and had to drink half my water bottle. "If you ever do that, you better change the names. Milo listens in too, remember."

"Oh, right. I'll keep that in mind." She looked perplexed.

I picked up my last fourth of club sandwich and leaned over. "So what's new with you and Milo?" I asked before taking a bite.

She twisted her mouth and shrugged. "Same. Basically nothing. Well, sort of nothing. He asked me to help move one of the church interns into a new place—she's staying in the basement of one of our church families. But it's not working out—the dogs are making her crazy—so we're moving her to bunk with another single gal who needed a roommate anyway. I helped out with that last night, which I was happy to do. Then we stopped for burgers after on the way home ..."

I looked up. "And?"

"Okay, this sounds dumb, but he didn't offer to pay for me. And I'd just helped move all those crates for that girl! It's not that I was hoping it was a date, exactly, but—"

"That would have annoyed me too," I assured her.

"I mean, I helped because he asked me. Not that I minded. But I didn't really know her."

I nodded my understanding. "I get it."

She propped her elbows up on the table and folded her hands beneath her chin. "So someone else asked me out."

My eyes widened. "Really? Who?"

"My boss's son. Which sounds weird, I know."

"It only sounds weird if he's ten years old."

Paige laughed. "No, my boss, Trisha, is my mother's age. She's the manager at the boutique. Her son and I are the same age. He's military, stationed in Monterey, and he's in town this weekend, and his mom is trying to set us up. She gave me his email and we've been writing back and forth for a week. I've checked him out on Facebook. He seems normal."

"Normal is good."

"He asked me if I'd like to go out to dinner on Saturday." She paused to look for more croutons.

"Well, are you going to go?"

"Maybe." She tore her baguette in half. "I don't like the yo-yo thing I've got going on with Milo."

"If you don't end up liking Military Guy, will it be awkward with his mom?" I had to ask.

Paige inhaled and gritted her teeth. "Oh gosh. I hadn't even thought of that."

"It'll be fine, don't worry," I said quickly, thinking I should listen more and talk less.

"Military Guy's name is Deacon."

"I like that name," I said, hoping to bring more positivity to the conversation.

"Me too. But—I think maybe I'm going to hold off," Paige decided suddenly.

"Okay."

"He's only in town for the weekend, and I think—well, I'm just looking for someone more available. Plus, his emails have been really formal. I need someone casual and fun loving."

Like Milo, I thought, but this time kept my mouth shut. I had a feeling Milo wasn't *the one*, but no doubt Paige would find that out eventually.

"Have you seen Ben lately?" Paige asked. She seemed to have given up on croutons and stabbed a piece of chicken.

"We went zip-lining the other day."

She put down her fork. "What? More dating with you two?"

I bit off the end of a dill pickle and dropped the rest in my lunch basket. "I told you, we're not dating. Repeat after me: Debra is not dating Ben. We're just friends, Paige. I'm not the kind of person Ben is looking for."

She looked amused. Those freckles across her face scrunched up with her grin. "What kind is that?"

I finished the pickle wedge and wiped my hands on a paper napkin. "The church kind. You know what I mean. He's in full-time ministry. I would imagine he'd need to date girls who go to church and talk to God. Like that Mikayla girl."

Paige pursed her lips. "Mikayla? The children's pastor? Do you know her? How did you know she likes Ben?"

I shook my bag of chips, looking for crumbs. "I met her at the church before our zip-lining thing. And I could tell she likes him because, *come on.*" I gave her a look.

Paige nodded as though she knew this already. "Well, regardless, Ben seems to want to spend time with you. You should give him a chance. What's not to like about him? I mean, the guy can rock a man bun. He's the embodiment of cool. Is he … is he anything like Luke?" she asked, her voice quieting at that last part.

I didn't want to talk about Luke, but—it was sort of a relief to have a friend who wasn't afraid to bring him up. Paige wanted to know me. I looked at her sadly eating chicken because her croutons were gone. She wanted to be real friends. Beyond surface level.

I wanted that too.

I thought of my nana saying she only really needed one good friend. Maybe that was all I needed too. There was no doubt that Denver felt more like home, knowing I had a friend in Paige.

"No, he's not like Luke. For one thing, Luke has short blond hair. No man bun. Also, Luke is serious. He's organized and logical and disciplined. Not that he's rigid—he'll do anything for anyone. But his personality is quieter. He'd never be comfortable being on stage, like Ben. Ben is laid-back and constantly easy-going, and he's fine being in the spotlight. He can engage with a roomful of people. He's very spontaneous. That's not Luke. Luke—he's good one on one. When you have his full attention, you just feel—" My voice trailed off and my throat tightened at the thought of those moments when I'd had Luke's sole attention. "They're different," I surmised and pushed away the last bite of my sandwich.

"Well, I still think you should give Ben a chance. He's fun, and his voice …" This time, she was the one giving me the knowing look, and I nodded.

"Oh yeah, that voice." I could hear my phone ringing and pulled it from my purse and just stared at the Texas number.

Jason.

Jason never called me. Not like Lily and Addi did. He'd text now and then, but calling wasn't his style.

"I need to take this, Paige."

She waved me off as a waitress stopped to refill water glasses.

I jumped up and walked a few paces away. "Jason?"

"Deb!"

The sound of his voice brought an immediate smile to my face. "Hi, is everything okay?"

"Yeah. I'm wondering if I can crash on your couch for a few days next week, into the weekend?"

My jaw dropped. "What?"

"I'm coming out to Denver for this cooking seminar. The guy is a well-known chef and he's teaching and doing a workshop on restaurant ownership. It's like two days of classes—Thursday and Friday. Then I was hoping we could hang out over the weekend. What do you say?"

I shook my head, still trying to wrap my head around the fact that Jason had called, was coming to Denver, and was apparently crashing at my apartment. "Of course you can stay with me."

"Thanks."

"Do you need me to pick you up from the airport?"

"I better rent a car so I can get to my classes."

"I work downtown, Jason. I'm sure I can take you or you can borrow my car and I can take the train."

"Really? That would be awesome! My flight gets in Wednesday night at like ten. Too late?"

"I can manage. Next Wednesday?"

"Yeah." He paused. "I can't wait to see you, Deb. We've all really missed you."

A pang touched my heart. "I can't wait to see you either. It will be fun to catch up."

I went back to the table and relayed the conversation to Paige. She took off her sunglasses and her mouth rounded into an O.

"That is so fun! You have to make plans for where to take him next weekend."

I licked my lips, starting to feel a thrill of excitement at spending time with Jason. "I wonder if Twenty-Four Tears is playing anywhere. I'll have to ask Ben."

"Totally. If they are, let's all go. I want to meet your friend."

I texted Ben later that evening and didn't hear back; then I remembered him saying the band practiced on Wednesday nights. By nine thirty I was in pajamas, worn out from my long day that had included the apology on air. I was just about to fall asleep when I heard a *ding*. The light from my phone illuminated the nightstand. I reached for it.

Ben.

Sorry. Practice. Want to meet up sometime tomorrow?

I laid back, my head on the pillow, and held my phone up, scowling at the light while texting my response.

Yes. I'm free any time after work.

I waited a few seconds for another *ding*.

You need to experience Denver taco trucks. pick you up around four thirty. Ok?

I smiled. Full of surprises, that one.

You and me and the taco trucks. See you then.

Chapter Nine

Life is out there waiting, so go get it.
Mary Poppins

"What do you recommend?" I asked, peering up at the menu on the side of a red food truck.

"I swear everything is good. I really like the chorizo tacos, but the green chili and shredded chicken are awesome as well. And that migas one—it's like eggs and tortillas and—"

"I know what migas are," I interrupted.

He held up both hands and grinned. "Order away."

We both ended up getting chorizo tacos, which were more like burritos, in my opinion. There were picnic benches nearby and Ben and I found an empty one. He'd brought two bottles of water for us, and we sat across from each other. I took one bite, closed my eyes without warning, and uttered a long *Mmmm*.

He laughed, then wiped his mouth. "Told you. As good as Texas?"

I opened one eye. "All right. Yes."

He finished two tacos in a matter of minutes, then threw back that water bottle. "Twenty-Four Tears isn't playing next weekend, but I have something to ask you."

I nodded, still eating my second taco.

"Want to go to the mountains with me? I'm going up to Breck. The place where I used to work as a river guide needs a hand. They're booked solid and need another guide around because one of their guys is out with an injury. It's fun for me and the extra money is good. I'm driving up Friday afternoon, and I'll help out with the tours all day Saturday. Hiking and rafting and fishing and camping overnight. We could come back late Sunday or stay till Monday."

"And you want me to go with you?" I echoed in surprise. He nodded.

"Yeah. It'll be a lot of fun. There are a couple of groups and guides, and so far, my raft has extra room. Will you ... I mean, I'd really like you to come, if you want." His eyes and voice were hopeful and I couldn't keep the regret from my tone.

"I wish I could, Ben. The reason I was asking about next weekend is because my friend from Texas, Jason—I told you about him; he was part of the gang—is coming into town. He's coming out for a cooking seminar and he's staying with me. I just thought if Twenty-Four Tears was playing, I would take him to hear you guys."

A slight frown shadowed his face. "Your friend Jason is coming to Denver? He's staying with you?"

I nodded patiently. "Yes. He was one of my best friends in Texas. Jase asked if he could crash on my couch for a few days. He'll be here through the weekend. Too bad you'll be gone. I wish you could meet him."

Ben stared past me at the parking lot for a moment, then crumpled the taco wrappings on the table into a ball. "Well, do you want to bring him along? Does he like white water rafting? I could get him a discounted rate. You guys could drive up Saturday morning instead of coming with me Friday night."

I opened my mouth to protest, then stopped. Jason would probably *love* rafting and hiking and fishing and whatever else. "I could ask him," I said. "It does sound like a lot of fun." I suddenly thought of Paige. "Oh, wait. Paige was looking forward to meeting him. Maybe I should hold off on plans till I talk to her. I don't want her to feel left out."

Ben sighed. "Bring her along too, then. I can get her the discounted rate as well."

I brightened. "Seriously? Is there room for all of us to go rafting?"

"I might have to ask one of the other guides to squeeze Paige into their boat, but we'll make it work. She can definitely hike and camp overnight with us. Do you have camping stuff?"

I bit my bottom lip and shook my head. He sighed again. "Okay. I'm sure I can scramble up extra stuff for you and Jason. I might have to borrow some equipment from some friends."

"Are you sure? That's such an inconvenience for you ..."

"It's fine, Deb. I want you to come."

His eyes met mine and I felt my face flush. "Thanks, Ben."

The frown slowly vanished from his face and a very small smile emerged. "I listened to your show yesterday."

"Oh yeah? I had to apologize to a listener for being harsh."

"I thought you did a great job. Good advice, Miss Lonely Heart."

Then I remembered. I'd quoted him. The bit about everyone being lonely sometimes. A small smile emerged on my face as well. "It came from this worship pastor I know. He's kind of a rock star, actually."

Then Ben flushed and looked down at the table.

My breathing stopped for a second.

I'm flirting. I'm flirting with Ben. What am I thinking?

"Jason is very easygoing." I redirected the conversation quickly. "You're going to like him. I'm so excited! It's like family is coming to visit!"

Less than a week later, I pulled up to the curb at Denver International Airport, threw my SUV in park, and hopped out at the sight of Jason standing below a United sign, wearing a red backpack, an Astros ball cap, sports pants, and a gray T-shirt. Black hair, black eyes, and a constant tan that stemmed with his Hispanic heritage, he was adorable in every way.

His face lit up when he saw me. I'd told myself sternly that there was no crying allowed, but it didn't work. Tears filled my eyes as a living, breathing reminder of my life in Texas scooped me up in a bear hug. We talked fast, over and around each other, laughing as we tried to slow down. He seemed quite shocked by my short hair and kept exclaiming that he'd never seen me with short hair before. I exited the airport, and Jason scrolled through his phone, answering a slew of texts.

My phone started dinging as well, Addison and Lily asking if Jason had arrived and letting me know they were thoroughly jealous that he and I were having a solo reunion.

I listened as Jason brought me up to date on Addison and Glen and Sam and Lily, specifically Lily's pregnancy. He didn't bring up Sara and Luke—but I knew he would. This was Jason. He'd been there at my lowest moment—when I'd shown up at Sara's apartment and bawled her out. He, more than anyone, had been a front-row witness to my meltdown. He'd also drawn the unlucky straw in driving me to the airport at the crack of dawn on Christmas morning, the day after Luke had shattered my heart. I'd sobbed the whole way.

No, there was no doubt he'd go there eventually.

We got to my apartment around eleven, and Jason dumped his duffle bag and backpack on the floor.

"I like your place," he said, eyes darting around.

"It's like living in a big closet," I said, and he laughed.

"Not even. You've got a separate bedroom and that kitchen island is amazing. And these blank white walls are great." He looked at me and raised an eyebrow. "What's with the boxes over there? How long have you lived here again?"

My gaze followed his, and I flushed at the stack of boxes in the corner of the breakfast area, and yes, the walls, which were picture free. "Yeah, so I haven't finished moving in yet. Blank walls make it feel bigger, I think." I knew what he was thinking. My apartment in Houston had been small but much homier. Framed, signed posters from lots of musicians had lined the walls. Along with vintage movie posters of my favorite musicals. I'd hung up my dad's old acoustic guitar he'd given me. One year on my birthday, the girls had surprised me with a night out to one of those art studios where everyone drinks wine and paints pictures. The pictures were musically themed, and Addi, Lily, and Sara had all given me their pictures when the night was through. I'd proudly displayed our artwork over the sofa in my apartment.

Sara's picture had not made the trip to Colorado, but the others were in a box somewhere.

Jason stretched out on the sofa. "Well, no judgment from me on not hanging stuff up. But not unpacking? Are you staying or what?"

I plopped down next to him. "I'm staying. I want to buy a place of my own when this lease is up. If I can afford it."

He nodded. "The appliances look new. And the lighting is great in here."

"These are newer condominiums. That part is definitely nice."

"Yeah. Last month I moved into a different rental. I think it was built in the seventies." He kicked off his sneakers. "Go to bed, Deb. I know you need sleep to function tomorrow. What's our plan for getting around?"

"You're taking my car. The keys are hanging by the door. My cohost is picking me up in the morning and giving me a ride to the studio; then I'll take the light rail back to my condo. No problem at all. Will you be finished in time for us to have dinner together?"

He nodded. "Definitely. There are a couple of cool chefs I'm excited to learn from at the seminar, but the main guy is Leonardo Romano. He owns two restaurants in Denver. You and I are going to one tomorrow night."

I smiled. "Can't wait. And you're right. I need sleep. Make yourself at home, okay? Seriously, *mi casa es tu casa.*"

Jason grinned, then yawned. "*Buenas noches*, Deb."

Four-thirty a.m. came in a blink and felt brutal. I stumbled out the door of the lobby to where Andy sat waiting for me. Bless him, he had a grande Starbucks cup waiting on me, which I accepted gratefully. We got to work and the caffeine boost helped as we jumped into the morning show. Anything new in our lives was considered fodder for the show, so I talked all about Jason being in town. His arrival helped with the Miss Lonely Heart segment as I shared, in the most humorous way I could, his being there for me at my worst moments. I had one call-in where a girl told us how her fiancé had heartbreakingly left her standing alone at the altar, deciding at the last minute that she couldn't make him happy. My blood pressure had risen as I listened to her story, at which point I recommended she create flyers with his face on them and their story and distribute them as far and wide as possible.

By noon, I was running on adrenaline. I walked to Union Station to catch the train back to Whitestone, still fuming about all the liars and cheats in this world. When I got back to my apartment, I collapsed onto my bed, fumbled for the comforter, which I pulled up to my chin, and slept hard for a few hours.

I woke up with a headache, glancing at the clock. Three thirty. I took a hot shower, which helped with the headache, then got ready for dinner out with Jason. He walked through the door at five thirty and we left almost immediately for the restaurant. I'd seen one of the Romano restaurants downtown, but Jason wanted to try the branch on Franklin Street, so we used GPS to get us there. After a short wait, we were seated at a table in the large, family-style restaurant, complete with a huge water fountain in the waiting area.

I ordered chicken Parmesan and a glass of merlot and listened to Jason gush over how much he'd enjoyed the seminar. Over the past year, he'd decided to change careers from computer programming to cooking. One of his first catering gigs had been to take charge of the food for Addison's wedding, at which point we all realized how gifted Jason was in the kitchen. As far as I'd known, he'd been working as a line cook at a steakhouse in Houston, but he told me he'd recently applied for the sous chef position and was waiting to find out whether he got it.

"This seminar was sort of a 'continuing education.' My boss was the one who recommended it to me. I'm so glad it worked out." Jason dipped a piece of bread into the crab dip appetizer we'd decided to split.

"Who was that last girl you were dating? Mia? Are you guys still together?"

He shook his head. "That lasted like fifteen minutes. Addison set me up with someone from her church." He rolled his eyes. "After I told her not to. That was awkward and didn't go anywhere. I've been working a lot. And I work nights, so it's not like there's a lot of time to socialize." He shrugged. "I'm good. I like where I'm at. Lily is ready to pop. She could have that kid like any minute. Are you going to fly to Texas when he's born?"

Eek. I hadn't even thought of that. "I don't know. Maybe, I guess."

He raised an eyebrow at me, and I reached for the last piece of bread.

"She misses you. We all do. I miss seeing you up on the stage on Sunday mornings. Are you singing out here?"

I sipped my wine. "Um, no. I'm not going to church anywhere."

His eyebrows rose. "Why?"

"Because I needed a break. Because I'm reinventing myself, Jason. Because a lot has changed for me."

He nodded, undeterred by my rising voice. One of Jason's best qualities—he wasn't easily ruffled.

"What did you think of that chicken parm?" he asked.

I glanced at my empty plate. "Really good."

He nodded. "The chicken marsala was excellent. I'm going to have another glass of wine. Want one?"

I shook my head. "I think I'll order a cappuccino. Let's split a dessert. Your choice."

The restaurant had filled with groups and families and couples, but we were seated at a small square table for two, tucked away in a corner. Ideal for private conversation and lingering at the table. Over a piece of cheesecake, one more glass of Pinot Noir for Jason and a steaming cappuccino for me, Jason brought up the subject that had been hovering.

"So ... how are you doing with all of it?"

I looked at the fancy white leaf someone had artistically made on my cappuccino cream. "I'm doing better. I'm seeing a therapist, and I think that's been helpful. How are they? Wedding planning and all that?"

I saw the pain and sympathy that filled those black eyes. His fork sliced off a piece of cheesecake. "Yeah. The wedding is in December, like Addi's was. They're fine. The same, I guess. Sara's still working at the museum. Luke's still at the architecture firm. Sara's mom had a fall and ended up with a slight bone fracture in her hip last month."

I winced. "Poor Suzanne."

Jason nodded. "It's not the same without you, if you've wondered. Which I would. But things have changed, you know. Glen and Addi are crazy busy. I feel like I never see them, even though Addi is good about intentionally keeping in touch. And with the pregnancy, Lily has been tired and sick a lot. Sam's been working overtime, trying to make extra money. I still hang out with Sam and Luke. We try to do lunch once or twice a month. We still play basketball the first Saturday morning of every month."

He was quiet for a moment, and I took a bite of cheesecake, thinking of what was unsaid.

Life goes on.

"I miss all of you too," I finally said, my voice small. "But my job is good here. I've got a couple of friends, who are both excited to meet you, and I've started exploring a bit. Ben took me to the zoo and zip-lining."

"Ben?" Jason's brow furrowed.

"Yeah. He's cool. I think you're going to like him. Oh, that reminds me! Do you want to go up to the mountains this weekend? Ben invited us to go rafting and fishing and camping overnight. What better way to see Colorado than in the mountains, on a river, right?" My tone spiked with excitement.

"Camping? Deb, I've got nothing with me for camping."

I waved that off. "He's borrowing stuff for both of us. Please, Jason? I think it will be awesome. If you say yes, we'll drive up to Breckenridge Saturday morning early, then meet up with Ben. We'll go white-water rafting and hiking and then we'll camp in tents that night. Oh, I forgot to mention that Paige is coming with us."

"Who is Paige? Your other friend?"

"Yeah. Paige and Ben."

"Are you into Ben or what? Are you dating him?"

"No. We're just friends."

He gave me a look. "Just friends, but he invites you up to the mountains for the weekend?"

I glared at him. "It's not like that. And if it were, so what? You think no guy will ever like me again since Luke doesn't?" I snapped, unable to hold back.

His jaw tightened immediately. "Of course I don't think that. *I'm* here, aren't I? Wanting to see you? I like you."

The tension in my neck pulled at me.

"Hey," he said, his voice easier. "You don't have to be defensive with me, Deb. I was there. I know how it was. Luke breaking things off was about him. You're amazing. You always have been. Maybe I'm just being protective. Remember, you were my friend before you were theirs."

That right there.

Jason, his open hand reaching across the table to me, melted my guardedness.

I breathed out. "Sorry." My hand slid into his, and he squeezed it, then released. I took a sip of my cappuccino. "Ben and Paige go to the same church. Ben is the worship pastor. I went once. C'mon, Jase. I've worked so much since I moved here that I've never gotten to go up to the mountains, and getting to go up with you will be double fun. Please?"

He held up both hands. "Okay, okay. If you want to go, I'm up for it."

Chapter Ten

Even the darkest night will end, and the sun will rise.
Les Misérables

Debra, you realize we'll be camping *one* night, right? And we'll be sleeping in tents?" Ben stood at the door of my apartment, mouth open. His eyes took in my luggage.

"Well, yes. But it's been a while since I've been camping. I don't want to forget anything I might need."

"How could you possibly need this much stuff?"

"You can come inside, you know." I crossed my arms. "You don't have to stand in the doorway. My luggage doesn't bite."

"It will as we're hiking." Ben took three steps inside. "You have to condense. You need maybe one change of clothes." He held up one finger to emphasize. "Is that a pillow?" He pointed to my obvious pink pillow-cased pillow.

"It's my favorite!"

He didn't respond. I huffed out a sigh as I looked at my bags that included toiletries, a book or two, my camera case, and more.

Ben maneuvered his way around my bags and sat on the sofa. "I'll tell you what you need while you unpack. I'm limiting you to one backpack." He held up that one finger again.

"Grr. Fine."

An hour later, we were barely speaking. Well, I was barely speaking. Ben was fine.

"This is not going to be enough." I motioned to the backpack and shoulder bag I'd packed.

"Trust me—it will be enough. The hike to the campsite isn't far, but after rafting, everyone will be exhausted. It's not a strenuous hike. Do you think Jason will be able to handle it?"

I nodded. "Probably better than I will. Assuming the altitude doesn't bother him." I snapped my fingers. "I should pack some aspirin."

"Make sure he drinks plenty of water. Staying hydrated will help avoid the symptoms of altitude sickness. I'm going to text you the address where we'll be. It'll take you guys about two and a half hours to get from your apartment to Breckenridge, so try to leave by nine at the latest. Actually, aim for eight thirty. I'm doing a half-day raft that morning with a group. When you guys get there, we'll suit up and raft for a few hours. You should eat lunch beforehand. At the spot down the river where we stop for the night, we'll unload. The company will have brought down all our luggage and gear already. We'll load up and hike—it's not very far—to our camping spot. Don't go crazy, but you and Jason and Paige should stop and pick up some small snacks." He gave me a pointed look. "Like granola bars or something, not a bag of groceries. I'll have water filters. We'll cook dinner. The guides will have planned out the meals for dinner that night and breakfast the next morning.

"There will probably be two other groups staying with us at the campsite. Sunday we'll hike back to the outpost, where vans will pick us up and take us back to the main building. I was thinking we'd hang out in Breck for a while. I have some friends I'd like to see. Then we can all head back to Denver at some point. Have Jason try those on." He pointed to a pair of hiking boots. Jason had told me his size and I'd passed the word on to Ben. "We're the same size, so I think he'll be okay. He needs really thick socks."

I nodded. "We'll run to the store tonight for whatever we need."

Ben stood up and I followed suit. "Okay, then. I'm going to go. I need to get on the road. I'm staying with some buddies tonight in Breck. Text me any questions. I should have decent cell service once I'm there, but it could be spotty on the way up."

I followed him to the front door. "Ben," I said. He faced me. "Thanks. Truly. For inviting me, then inviting Jason, then inviting Paige. I'm really excited to do this."

A half smile inched its way to his face. We stood a bit awkwardly. Unlike my Texas friends, Ben wasn't a hugger. Or he wasn't with me anyway.

"I'm glad you're coming. When I said I wanted to introduce you to Colorado—well, this is the best way to see it." He stuck his hands in his pockets and moved into the outside hallway. I leaned against the doorframe.

"I'll see you tomorrow and I'll text you before then."

"You and me and the mountains," he said with a wink, borrowing my tagline. I grinned.

When Jason came home that evening, we made homemade pizza together and then ran to three different stores for snacks and socks and everything else Ben said we should get. Excitement was building in both of us. Paige too. She texted me every three minutes and had agreed to be at my apartment the next morning at eight fifteen. After making sure we were packed and ready, I said good night to Jason and went to bed, leaving him to watch TV until he was tired enough to go to sleep.

Paige knocked on the door at eight fifteen on the dot. Her hair was in her signature side braid and she wore long shorts and a hoodie and her usual Birks. With a yawn, Jason shook her hand and said hello; then he loaded up my SUV with all our stuff and we headed out. Jason insisted Paige sit in the front, and he climbed in the back, pulled his ball cap down over his eyes, and fell back asleep. Paige and I were jittery with excitement. After about a half hour, Jason perked up, and we pulled into a drive-thru for breakfast sandwiches. Jason wanted to drive, so Paige moved to the back. She peppered both of us with questions the whole way, wanting to know about Jason's life in Texas, how our group had been formed—she was smart enough to avoid any mention of Luke and Sara and just stuck to general questions about our friendships and Texas and so on.

The farther we got up in the mountains, hardly any of the radio stations were getting a good signal. Paige tucked into the corner of the car and closed her eyes to rest, and I tried to read for a while. Reading and winding roads didn't seem to mix for me, and I stopped when I felt a hint of motion sickness. We stopped for gas and a bathroom break a little more than three quarters of the way into the drive. Jason bought an energy drink. Paige was acting bubbly at that point, chatting and bright-eyed, and I was feeling sleepy, so we switched spots, and I fell asleep. I woke to the sound of Paige and Jason talking in quiet voices about the scenery. I sat up and tucked back my hair, looking out the window. We were basically on the side of a mountain, with netting hanging to keep any falling rocks from hitting vehicles. On the other side of the road, beyond oncoming traffic, was a river, snaking its way around rocks and fallen logs. And beyond that, wide open space led upward to more mountains, covered in Evergreens.

Having lived in Minnesota and Texas, mountains were new to me. They stood so majestic and powerful, I felt small just looking out the window. Paige glanced back at me.

"You're awake. We're almost there. Should we pick up something for lunch before we go to River Run?" she asked.

I stretched and nodded. "Ben said we'll definitely want to have a good lunch before we leave for rafting. I didn't even think to ask, but have either of you rafted before?"

Paige nodded. "Oh, sure. Every summer since I was a kid. It's tons of fun."

"Does tubing the Guadalupe count?" Jason asked, and I chuckled.

"I hope. That's as close as I've come too. And I flipped my tube and fell into the river, remember?"

"Oh, right. I thought that was Addi. Well, fingers crossed none of us falls into the river this time."

"Don't worry," Paige assured us. "We'll all be fine. Even if someone went for an unintentional swim, the guides will give instructions beforehand so you know what to do. Last time I went rafting, one of the girls in our group fell out of the boat. It was scary, of course—for one thing, the water was high, we're at the end of the season here, and it was a fairly dry spring, so I have a feeling the rivers won't be bursting at the seams. But she was okay. A little scraped up and shaky, but she lived to tell the tale."

Jason and I were quiet. "Um, that wasn't a very reassuring story, Paige," I finally said, and Jason laughed.

"That's what I was thinking."

Paige looked sheepish. "Sorry. But honestly, the guides know what they're doing. Ben did this for years. We'll be fine. You're going to love it!"

We stopped in Breckenridge for lunch, and Jason and I kept gushing over what a fun town it was. Touristy shops everywhere and restaurants lined the streets of the mountain town, home to ski resorts. We ate cheeseburgers while sitting at an outdoor table at a local burger joint, with a mountain backdrop to our lunch. Then I took over at the wheel, and we made our way to River Run Rafters, about ten miles outside the town.

The gravel parking lot was packed. I finally found a spot at the very back of the lot and we left our bags in the SUV while we went to find Ben. He stood waiting on the front porch of the building, which looked very much like a large, rectangle log cabin. I waved at him as we got close. He held the remnants of a sub sandwich wrapping in his hands, so I figured he'd just had lunch.

"Hey!" Paige jumped forward and gave Ben a hug, then I introduced him to Jason. The two guys shook hands but both seemed guarded. I glanced back and forth at them, a bit surprised, since I knew them both to be two of the friendliest guys I'd ever known. This aloofness seemed weird.

"We'll get you guys wet suits and all that. There are forms to sign. I've told Lee, the girl at the front desk, that we're all together, so you'll get a discounted rate. Before you change, you should bring out all your gear. They'll load a van full of our stuff. There are two other couples riding with us. Paige"—Ben looked at her—"are you okay with going with the second raft? They had an open spot."

She nodded immediately. "Absolutely. But I'm camping with you guys, right?"

"Yes. We'll all meet up at the outpost and hike to the site together and make camp."

Even from the log-cabin base, we could see the river, calm at the outset. Jason and Paige and I retrieved our luggage and piled it on the front porch. My stomach tightened, a mixture of nerves and excitement, as we filled out the forms and got our wet suits and splash jackets and water shoes. Paige and Jason both paid and then browsed the small section that sold T-shirts and souvenirs while they waited for me. I stepped up to the counter and gave Lee my information. She shook her head.

"Ben already paid for you, Debra. You're covered."

My eyes widened. Even with the discount, the cost of rafting and overnight camping was just over a hundred dollars. "That can't be right. Am I supposed to pay him?"

She looked at the paperwork. "You could ask him, I suppose. But he made the reservation for all of you, then paid your balance." She then asked my size and handed me a wetsuit, pointing to where the restrooms were. I took the wetsuit, and Paige and I made our way to the restrooms to change. Jason had already disappeared into the men's bathroom. From one stall over, Paige talked to me.

"You didn't mention that your friend is basically a hot tamale."

I burst out laughing at her description of Jason. "I guess Jase is pretty cute. And I know for a fact that he can make a very decent tamale. He's a talented cook. Did I tell you he catered my friend Addison's wedding?" I zipped up the already damp wetsuit, then wrinkled my nose. "This feels disgusting. I'm trying not to think about the person who already sweated in this."

Paige stepped out of the stall, a pained look on her face. "I feel like a seal, slippery and cold. And I look ridiculous."

"Ben says the wetsuits will keep us from freezing when that white water hits us. He better be right."

We waddled out of the bathroom, giggling at each other. Jason seemed unaffected by the cold ickiness of the suit. He clapped his hands. "Let's get this show on the road. I'm ready to hit the river."

Lee waved us over and told us to make our way around the side of the building to find Ben. The three of us slathered on sunscreen and then walked down closer to the river, all of us feeling a bit ridiculous in our wetsuits. I sighed with relief when I saw Ben in swim shorts, a neoprene shirt, and waterproof shoes, down by the river, talking to four other people. A stack of huge rafts stood piled on the riverbank. Ben motioned for us to join him.

"Hey, guys, this is Chloe and Kyle, and Greg and Rita. They'll be joining us on the raft and camping tonight." We all introduced ourselves. They all looked about our age or older. I assumed they were in their very early thirties. I didn't see wedding rings, but both sets of people were obviously couples by the hand holding. They all seemed nice enough. As we grouped together and listened to Ben's instructions, warnings, and advice, Jason casually threw his arm across my shoulders. Having known Jason for years, this was completely natural for me. But midspeech, I saw Ben do a double take.

The fact that Ben had paid for my excursion niggled at my mind. I appreciated the gesture very much—but it made me a little nervous. Again, there didn't seem to be anything romantic between us, but he kept doing these nice things. Always including me. Paying for me. At this point, I obviously had to consider the reality that he liked me in a romantic way. For that matter, I knew I was trying not to like him in a romantic way—a task that was starting to take more effort.

Of course, there was that whole "he's in ministry" aspect. I could explain away some of his behavior just by acknowledging his expression of Christianity—reaching out, being kind to the new girl, offering friendship to someone struggling with faith.

Still ... did that extend to noticing when Jason put his arm around me?

I didn't like the confusion, but if the alternative was awkwardness or resulted in hurt feelings, I decided I'd choose ignorance.

With a gulp, I realized I'd spent most of Ben's lecture dissecting our friendship, rather than listening to the rules of the river. Not to mention his distracting habit of being attractive. The man bun was back, and Ben wore dark sunglasses and kept flashing that white smile. And he somehow made a splash jacket, board shorts, and swim booties look cool.

A second group joined us, along with another guide. Ben introduced the other guide—Emmie was her name—and explained that we'd be tag teaming this trip, including camping near each other. Paige joined the second group.

Jason leaned closer to me. "Doesn't sound so bad."

"I feel like I was daydreaming and didn't hear a word he said," I whispered furiously. Jason scowled at me.

"What the heck? You need to sit in the middle, then. That's the safest spot. If I fall out, tell my parents I loved them." I poked Jason hard at that scary comment.

We started strapping on life jackets. As it wound up, I did sit in the middle in the very front of the raft, between Jason and Kyle, and Chloe and Rita and Greg were in the very back. Ben was in the middle, steering with double oars. Once our raft was in the water, I felt a quick tug on the back of my suit. I turned around. Ben smiled at me.

"Ready for some fun?"

I grinned back at him. "Definitely."

We drifted downstream, Ben talking and pointing out certain rocks and flowers and talking about the upcoming rapids. I drank in the scenery. This, *this* was Colorado. Unpredictable rivers and white clouds over gray-and-green mountains, fresh air. Evergreen trees and wildflowers.

I'd wanted more of it ever since I came to visit with Luke. Here I was, so many months later, without him.

But still experiencing adventure.

The thought startled me.

"This is incredible," Jason murmured next to me, his shaded eyes scanning the river and mountains beyond. "I'm glad you talked me into it."

I nudged him. "I'm happy you're here."

"All right, people," Ben called out. "We've got white water ahead. Remember my instructions. When I say 'Right,' paddle hard right. When I say 'Left,' paddle hard left. When I say 'Back two,' paddle back two times. It gets crazy when we're in it, but listen for my voice."

Rita and I, both sandwiched in the middle of the rows, didn't have paddles, but I held on to the rope in front of me as though my life depended on it. As the water grew choppier, my stomach dropped. Then we were smack-dab in the rapids—Ben yelling to paddle left and right. Jason dug into the water with his paddle. Water splashed over us and I screeched. I heard other shouts and laughs and Ben's voice—a distant sound amid the roar of the torrents—yell, "Be ready. We haven't seen anything yet!"

The rapids were relentless. Stark white water crashed over rocks and over us. Suddenly our raft tilted to the left and lodged in rocks. Ben used his oars to push us back into the water. We turned and dipped and then the entire front of our raft, including those three people named Jason, Debra, and Kyle, were submerged in ice water.

The moment I breathed air, I screamed, drenched to the bone. My hands lost the rope and I scrambled to grab it. Jason started to slide off the edge of the raft and with my left hand I grabbed him and held on tight. Ben was yelling but I couldn't hear a word he was saying. My face stung from the cold, and I heaved deep breaths, and finally, the river calmed.

Jason and I looked at each other, water dripping from our noses. He still had a white-knuckle grip on the paddle he was holding. Wide grins spread across both our faces, in tandem. Whoops and breathless laughs erupted among our group. I turned back to see Ben. His gaze was right on me, and he winked.

"More to come. Hold on," he told me.

I laughed, shaking back my hair, water droplets flying. The sun shone high overhead, quickly warming my face, and the river rolled out in front of us for as far as I could see. My racing pulse slowed a bit as our raft glided easily downstream. But Ben assured us that a few miles forward, around the bend, stronger rapids were waiting. I breathed deep, loving the breeze in my hair and the sun on my cheeks, the exhilarating dips and turns and rushes of the river.

It wasn't long before we heard the roar of the water again. My hand tightened around the rope and I braced myself.

"Ready, guys?" Ben called out.

I gritted my teeth and squinted with the glare of the sun.

Bring it.

About three and half hours later, we hit our last group of rapids, flying fast, maneuvering around and over rock formations in the water. I'd been drenched multiple times by this point—funny how Ben didn't mention that being in the front was a *guarantee* I'd be doused regularly. Ben shouted instructions and encouragement, deftly steering us down one course and then another. I heard him yell, "Hard left! Hard left!" then I heard screams from the back. I couldn't twist to see, not with the jerking back and forth. Suddenly our raft was going up on the left. Up, up, up . . . I'd fallen over on Jason completely and he was half in the water. I felt Kyle grab the back of my suit and try to pull me back.

"Hold on!" Ben shouted.

From the corner of my eye I saw Ben working his oars, standing, then sitting—and then our raft landed flat again, Jason falling on me this time.

"Almost there, guys. I need three paddles forward!"

Jason inhaled, grabbing his paddle and going back to work. And in moments, we were back in calm waters. I looked back and saw a very soaked Chloe in the back row, and I had a feeling she'd gotten up close and personal with the river back there. The river carried us farther down, and Ben slowed us even further. We came to a standstill right next to a huge flat rock.

"We call this rock 'the jump,'" Ben explained. "We're less than half a mile from where we'll disembark. The river is deep here, deep and safe enough to jump in. I don't have to tell you—the water is *cold*. But anyone who wants to jump from the rock can." With that, Ben secured the oars, reached over, and held the rock as he climbed on. I watched, my eyes huge. No hesitation, he dove into the water like a fish, coming up just moments after. Paige's raft was just ahead of ours, and everyone in both rafts applauded for Ben. He swam back to the raft, and Jason helped pull him in. Ben wiped the water from his face and got back into his spot.

"Who's next?" he asked. I twisted back around, and Ben stared at me, both eyebrows raised in question.

I didn't have the ease of decision Ben had. My heart pounded in my ears as I looked at the rock.

But then I was up. I climbed over Jason, reached for the rock, and scrambled up on it. The groups were cheering, but I didn't listen.

The water will be freezing! You're crazy.

My hands clenched and unclenched at my sides. I looked over at Jason and he nodded encouragingly. His eyes told me he knew me; he knew I could do this. Then I glanced at Ben. And his gaze stared almost into my soul.

He knows you can do it. He wants to see if you will.

I looked at the water—constant movement, slow as it was. Calling me. Stirring me.

I dove in.

Intense cold shocked my body. My legs kicked, and my arms reached above me, parting the water and pushing myself to the surface. Then I was out, gasping for breath, hearing the muffled cheers through my water-clogged ears. My wet hair hung around my face. I side-stroked to the raft, and Jason pulled me in, his face beaming. He hugged me despite the fact that we were now even ickier in our saturated wet suits. Immediately after, he climbed onto the rock and cannonball jumped into the river with a whoop.

Ben leaned forward once I was settled back in my spot. "How do you feel?" he asked me. Soaked and freezing and shaking, I looked back at him. And I smiled.

"Alive."

Chapter Eleven

Still, you're not alone. No one is alone.
Into the Woods

At the outpost, there was a makeshift tent up for us to change out of our wetsuits, and portable toilets, which Ben highly recommended we use before we left the outpost. (I was very concerned with the bathroom arrangements going forward, which included something like a box and no doors. And Ben explained that *everything* came back down with us. I didn't ask for further explanation.) The River Run van was there with all our backpacks and equipment, along with a case of water bottles. I grabbed one and downed the whole thing; then I pulled out my change of clothes, and Paige and I went into the tent together to change quickly, laughing and shivering the whole time.

After we changed, Paige and I sat next to each other on a log while we waited for everyone else to get ready.

"I cannot believe you jumped. That water is ice cold!" she squealed.

"Believe me, I know. I don't know what came over me." I tilted my head back to feel the sun's rays on my face. The warmth was quickly drying my hair. I tried not to think about the inevitable frizz that would follow.

"It's the river, I think. And nature in general. It brings us to life."

I nodded in agreement. "I did feel so alive. Every pore on my body prickling, the cold hitting me like a wave." Jason joined us then.

Paige shaded her eyes and glanced up at him as he moved to sit next to me. "Can you believe Deb jumped?" she asked. He shrugged, his shoulder now right next to mine.

"Of course. This is Debra. I once saw her bungee jump in Galveston when no one else in our group would, making me look like a chicken."

Paige was quiet and I knew what she was thinking.

Not the same Debra.

Maybe that was it, partly. Jason being here. I couldn't help but feel like myself again. What Jason didn't remember about that particular moment, and I did, was that I'd been trying to impress Luke with my adventurous spirit. And

I'd been terrified.

But afterward ... I'd loved it. And in the end, I wasn't thinking about Luke. The whole experience had made me feel euphoric and even brave.

Like jumping in the river.

Maybe the old me wasn't completely gone. Ben called us over to the van and we loaded up with huge backpacks. Paige stayed with our group. Guide Emmie stood about twenty feet away, talking to her group. The campsite was not too far but up a rather steep incline. We hiked the trail. I fell into step next to Ben up front. Jason seemed a bit more worn out—from all that paddling, no doubt. And he stayed behind. Paige had paddled on her boat as well and seemed a little more winded. They brought up the caboose of our team.

"So what did you think?" Ben wondered. I tore open a granola bar.

"Oh, it was perfect. Every minute of it. I think I missed my calling. I should have been a rafting guide."

He chuckled. "Yeah, I loved it when I worked out here. Very physical work, but the payoff is experiencing nature. Getting your hands dirty. There's nothing like it. Kathy and Rob started River Run a decade ago. It's a mom-and-pop business. They built it from the ground up. When I worked here, their preteen daughter worked the cash register and cleaned bathrooms and that sort of thing. Their son was in college then; he'd come home and work during every break. They're a great family. They want their customers to have memorable excursions, and they treat all the guides with respect. I'm always glad to come back here and see everybody. Some of the guides are lifers—they'll be out in these mountains forever. Some are just college kids, here for a season."

"What's our plan for when we reach the campsite?" I asked.

"When we get to the clearing, we'll get the tents up and make a fire and I'll work on dinner. Emmie and I will tag team. Don't worry—the meal will be good. During training, they teach all of us to grill and cook meals. Satisfying meals are supposed to be a selling point. Before I became a guide, I could make macaroni and cheese and microwave Hot Pockets. I learned to cook over a fire."

"You should get Jason to help. He's practically a professional chef. He'd probably really enjoy doing whatever you need him to."

Ben put one foot in front of the other. "Yeah, I might. So ... what's the story with you guys?"

I looked at him, bemused. "What do you mean? I already told you. He was part of my group of friends back in Texas. We're close."

"Is that it, though? Him coming out here ..."

"He's out here for a seminar, Ben. And even if he wasn't, if he came here just for me, that would be fine. Jason and I—well, he was there for me at more than one of my worst moments in life. We have a bond. I love him like a brother." I accidentally kicked a rock and stumbled. Ben stopped and grabbed my arm, steadying me. We kept moving once I had my bearings. "In fact, having him here—I don't know how to explain it. I feel more at home, just having him around."

Ben didn't answer. I was starting to huff with exhaustion.

"Nearly there," he assured me. Trees had lined most of our path, but then they dissipated and we reached the clearing. I could hear sighs of relief from behind us. We were all worn out. Ben clapped his hands and rallied our troop. He showed us the places to set up tents, scattered around where we'd have a campfire. I drank another bottle of water, and then Paige and I set to work getting our tent up.

The second group reached the clearing and went past us to the other side to set up more tents. Paige and I struggled with our tent but finally got it and rolled out our sleeping bags inside. I thought wistfully of my pink pillow that hadn't made the cut. Ben and Jason's tent was up and ready, and Jason was helping sort the cooking utensils while Ben got the fire going.

There were several camping chairs—I hadn't carried one myself, but Ben had a couple of extras. Easy to unfold and set out around the fire. Emmie came over to our site, and she and Ben started powwowing over dinner. Jason seemed to be part of their cooking crew of three, and I appreciated Ben's graciousness in including him. Paige and I chatted with our other two couples and we got our backpacks and personal things squared away and settled before nightfall. Not far from us, I could see Emmie's group doing the same thing.

The enticing smell of grilled chicken wafted through the air and my stomach grumbled. I could smell peppers and see foil-wrapped potatoes. Paige and I decided to hike around the clearing, checking out the wildflowers. Ben asked us to stay within sight, and I promised him we would.

"Do you miss your friends in Texas?" Paige asked. "I know you've talked about them—it's just, when we met, you seemed so hurt. In my mind, I assumed you were all fractured beyond repair. Now I see you with Jason, and it's like—I don't know—I have this inkling of what it was like, how you all were a family. That makes it worse, I imagine." She gave me a look of sympathy. "But it also makes me wonder how much of yourself you left back there. Being with Jason—does that make you wish you could go back?"

I plucked a flower and ran the stem between my fingers and thumb. "No ... I don't think I could ever go back. As much as I love Jason and Addison and Lily and Sam. And I don't just mean go back to Texas. I don't think we'll ever be the same. So much has changed for all of us. I think my leaving helped—no one had to take sides. I just took myself out of the equation. They can all get together and be happy and not have to feel guilty that I'm not there." A twinge of bitterness laced my voice. "But I can't be there, and they know it. I could never be around all of them again. Me alone, while Luke and Sara are standing on the other side of the room, married and in love? No way."

We stopped and looked out at the view, flowers here and there, trees surrounding the clearing.

"The distance helps," I acknowledged. "I have a new life here. New friends." I looked at her gratefully. She smiled. Fresh-faced, pink cheeks, her hair now in two golden braids, Paige stood there wearing cutoff jean shorts and a loose, tangerine-colored sleeveless top, in a patch of wildflowers. She certainly belonged in Colorado.

Did I?

I shielded my eyes from the sun and squinted up at the mountain peaks in the far distance. "I've been thinking I should buy a place. What do you think? My lease isn't up until May but I might start looking at neighborhoods and pricing out places. I feel like I need to own something."

She nodded. "Well, as you've probably realized, housing prices out here are a little different from Texas."

I frowned. "Yes. I'm not sure what I'll be able to afford. I can renegotiate my contract and salary after a year. I do have savings, though."

"They're building new paired homes right near where I live. We could go look at them together. Prices are more affordable not so close to downtown. And the commute wouldn't be bad at all if you took the light rail."

"That's true. Let's go look next week. I just want to start moving in that direction. You know, get to know the housing market and know what area I'm interested in."

"Putting down roots, huh?" Paige said with a smile. I shrugged.

I glanced at the campsite and saw Jason waving for us to come back.

Paige cleared her throat. "Did you ever ... I mean, did you ever think of Jason like that?"

A V formed between my eyebrows. "Jason? Think of him like what? Like Luke?"

"Like *romantic*."

I laughed. "No. In a point of total irony, Jason first dated Sara. He was crazy about her. They dated for about a year, I think. It was so long ago. Then she broke things off with him. I knew it wouldn't last between them. She never looked at him the way she looked at Luke." I picked another flower as we slowly walked back toward camp. "He's dated on and off, but no one serious since Sara.

Come to think of it, that might be why we have such a strong bond. He had this unrequited love for Sara, and I had it for Luke, and we both know what it feels like to *not be the one*."

"I'm surprised you never crushed on Jason. Or that Sara would give him up—he seems so fun. And he's so good-looking."

I blinked at Paige's pensive tone and her gaze off toward the campsite.

She cleared her throat a second time. "What if his feelings for you changed? I mean, look how he is with you. Affectionate and teasing and he jumps on board with whatever you want to do."

I smiled. "That's who he is, Paige. He's been that way since the very first moment I met Jason. We're not romantic. His joking and teasing could drive Lily crazy sometimes. But we all were that way with each other—affectionate and real. I could call anyone in that group, at any hour of the day, and they'd drop whatever to help. That—*that* is what I miss. But ..." My voice caught and my next words came out several notches lower. "I'm glad I had it for a while."

"If I could have that with just one person..." Paige stopped and looked down at the purple flowers. "I think it would be enough. Safety and security and trust. I've been thinking a lot about Milo today. When we get back, I think it's time for us to talk. He's either interested or he's not."

"And if he is?" I asked.

She shrugged. "I don't know. But I'd like to know where he stands." We started walking again, picking up our pace. Our group was milling around Jason and Ben. The aroma of cooked chicken inundated my senses and suddenly I was starving.

Jason had a huge smile on his face. "Ready to eat?"

"More than."

Ben waved us all closer. "Jason's going to help with the assembly line, guys. We've got grilled chicken with peppers, baked potatoes, and baked beans. And we've got lemonade as well." I grabbed a plate and got in line behind Paige. Ben dished out the chicken and peppers, and Jason divvied out the baked potatoes and beans. There were butter and sour cream packets for the potatoes. After hours on the river and the short hike up to the clearing, nothing had ever tasted so good as that grilled chicken. We sat in a circle around the bonfire, eating—fast at first and then slowing down as our bellies filled. I savored the red peppers and juicy chicken, then ate every scrap of my baked potato. The lemonade was tart and sweet and I gulped it down.

Jason sat next to me, devouring his plate of food. Even around six o'clock, the sun shone bright but a bit lower. I was so tired that I looked forward to nightfall. After dinner, Ben passed out gourmet cookies and told us they were made locally at a bakery in Breckenridge. Someone asked Ben about wild animals and my ears perked up.

"Of course, we're in the mountains, so there are animals around. But we make a lot of noise out here and we're a large group. We're intimidating to them, just like they are to us. The closer you are to the campsite, the safer you'll be. And we'll package everything up—food wise—tight and sealed, to avoid tempting any bears."

I didn't like the sound of bears. Or any type of wild animal. I glanced over at our tent, which looked small and flimsy against, say, a mountain lion.

Paige swallowed a bite of her oatmeal cookie. "We'll be fine, Debra," she said, brushing off my rising concern. After dessert, we helped Ben clean up and get everything put away.

"You know what this reminds me of?" Jason asked, once we were sitting back around the fire. He didn't wait for my answer. "Summers at the lake house."

"Hmm." That was the only response I could think of. I didn't want reminders of Addison's parents' lake house, the place where our group had gathered year after year. Skiing and fishing, s'mores by the fire pit, playing games and eating dinner on the deck. I wondered whether everyone had gone back without me, but I didn't ask. If the answer was yes, which I was sure it would be, it would hurt too much. My attention diverted to Kyle and Chloe and Rita and Greg. They'd brought out a bunch of mini bottles of liquor.

"Do you think Ben's okay with them drinking?" I asked Jason in a low voice. He nodded.

"Yeah, he told me alcohol is allowed as long as no one brings glass bottles. He also told me he doesn't like it when the guests get sloshed and he has to babysit."

I bit my lip. "I'm sure it won't get to that."

Jason glanced at our extended crew. "Stranger things have happened. I'm not worried, though." Paige joined us then. She'd donned a sweatshirt and pants, and I was thinking of doing the same. August or not, as the sun began to set, the temperature lowered significantly at our high elevation. I left Jason and Paige and climbed into our tent, digging through my backpack and finding my warm hoodie and yoga pants and extra socks. Once I changed, I went back out to the fire. The sun hung low, disappearing behind the mountains and casting a yellow glow to the coming darkness. The fire glowed orange, sparking and popping. Ben came out of his tent at the same time, having changed as well. I walked over to join him.

"Hey." His eyes brightened. "Are you having a good time?"

"Of course," I said, waving at the sight of our gorgeous sunset, the blazing bonfire, and the overall splendor of being under a Colorado evening sky. "This is perfect, Ben. I want to do it all again."

He smiled, his shoulders dropping a bit as he tugged on his hoodie and shoved his hands in his pockets. "Yeah, the summer season won't last too much longer. That's part of the reason I really wanted you to come. River Run doesn't usually do rafting past early September."

A burst of loud laughter came from Chloe and Rita, and Ben's eyes darted to where they'd congregated on the other side of the bonfire.

When his gaze turned back to me, I raised one eyebrow.

"It's cool," he told me. "I've just had a couple of bad experiences where the guests drank way too much. I like to have a good time as much as anyone, but it's not so fun when people start puking or fighting or getting obnoxious." He scuffed his shoe into the dirt. "C'mon, let's go sit by the fire. I've got instant cider or cocoa. Either sound good?"

"Cider sounds perfect," I told him. I went with him to the stash of supplies and we filled mugs with powder; then Ben set a pot of water over the fire to boil. I sat back down next to Jason and scooted closer to him as a brisk breeze whipped through my hair. Ben asked Kyle and Chloe and the others whether they'd like to roast marshmallows. Who wouldn't want to roast marshmallows? We all wanted to. We settled in around the fire. I could hear singing coming from across the clearing over at Emmie's group.

"Should we sing 'Kumbaya'?" Greg asked with a snort.

Ben smiled good-naturedly. "We don't have to, but—" He reached behind his chair and pulled out a small bongo drum. He thrummed his hands across, the beat carrying with the breeze. The sun had disappeared, but I could see Ben in the glow of the fire, sitting next to Paige. His dark hair was loose, tucked behind his ears. He wore a navy hoodie and black pants. There was at least two days' growth of hair on his chin and cheeks and he looked ruggedly handsome in the firelight.

"Any requests?" he asked, continuing to stir the silence with sound.

"'I Can't Help Falling in Love,'" Rita called out with a giggle, snuggling up to Greg. Ben nodded. I waited in anticipation. I noticed Chloe hold out a mug and Kyle empty another mini bottle of alcohol into it.

"You should sing with him," Jason whispered. I grimaced and barely shook my head, flustered by the very idea. Then Ben started to sing, and we all went still, captured by that irresistible voice singing the song made famous by Elvis Presley.

When Ben finished, we all clapped. Then Chloe fell over in her chair and the foursome fell into high-pitched laughter. Kyle stood up and pulled Chloe up with him. "I think this one needs some sleep. We're going to retire to our tent," he said with a chuckle. Ben nodded. I thought I sensed relief flash across his eyes. The two of them made their way to their tent, stumbling every now and then.

"Another song!" Rita said, and I was very inclined to agree. Ben and I made eye contact and I could see a blinking question in his eyes.

Good grief, he wanted me to sing. I shook my head slightly, and he just nodded and looked back down at the bongo.

I exhaled, relieved—and something else. I couldn't quite pinpoint it.

Something about the way he respected my feelings without further ado.

Something about the way we'd just had a conversation with our eyes.

And something about the way I wished I could download Ben singing "I Can't Help Falling in Love" ... something about all those things made me anxious and uncomfortable.

I drank the rest of my cider, fidgeting in my chair, wanting to move, go to my tent—something. I didn't want to be near Ben Price. I didn't want to feel anything for him.

Then he started to sing again, his version of a current pop song. Jason leaned in close to my ear.

"He's *good*, Deb."

Yeah, yeah. I know.

"Can you get him on the radio?" Jason whispered. The million-dollar question. Of course Jason would be audacious enough to ask it. I elbowed him and he shrank back just a bit.

"I think he likes you," he whispered again. I looked at him, my eyes narrowed. Jason didn't shrink back at that.

"I'm just saying."

I faced forward again, then felt Jason lean close again.

"It's okay to move on, Deb. To be open." His voice was low, right in my ear.

My eyes, staring at the fire, began to burn.

Move on? Be open?

I wanted to cry.

Jason's arm went around me, his hand squeezing my shoulder.

The music stopped and I looked up. Ben's eyes were on me, his face taut in a frown. Jason moved over quickly.

"Ben, seriously, you have a good voice," Rita exclaimed. "You should do something with that. Not that you're not a good guide ..."

Ben laughed. "Thanks, Rita. Well, actually, I'm only a guide this weekend. I'm a worship pastor."

"What's that?" Greg asked.

"I lead music at a church," Ben said simply.

"Oh, you're religious," Greg said, obvious disdain in his voice. Ben, as usual, seemed unaffected, cool, composed.

"I am, yeah."

"He's amazing at what he does," I heard myself speak up defensively.

Ben's gaze came back to me, soft surprise covering his face.

"Thanks, Deb." He blinked and set the bongo aside. "I'm going to make sure all our supplies are secure. If anyone wants anything, let me know." He jumped up.

Paige and Jason both turned their attention to me.

"What?" I said, exasperation spilling over at both of their amused expressions.

"Go talk to him," Paige said in a fast whisper. I looked at Jason.

He studied me. "You know I'm here. And I'll be here. If you feel something for Ben, go talk to him. What can it hurt?"

I'd been taking shallow breaths and I exhaled sharply at that comment. "It could hurt *me*. I don't want that again. You have to know that, Jase." My tone changed from pleading to anger. Without warning, moisture filled my eyes. "How can you want me to be hurt again?"

Jason frowned. "I don't want that. You know I don't. I want you to be happy. And that will take risk, eventually."

I pushed myself out of my chair and marched to my tent, then crawled inside and sat cross-legged, my breath ragged. After a few moments, I lay flat on top of my sleeping bag, trying to take measured breaths.

Do I like Ben that way?

I reminded myself that of all the nice things Ben had done for me, never had the line crossed into romantic.

Did I want it to?

Eight months ago I was hoping Luke Anderson would propose to me. I wanted nothing more than to spend my life with him.

No, I don't want anything from anyone.

I crossed my arms over my face. The flap to our tent opened. Paige unzipped it all the way and crawled in.

"Deb," she whispered. I didn't answer.

"Don't even act like you're asleep," she said, her voice normal and blunt.

"Fine." I opened my eyes and moved my arms.

"Jason's worried about you," she said.

I blew my hair out of my face. "He's probably been worried about me since last Christmas, with good reason."

Paige sat next to me. We were quiet for several moments; then she finally spoke. "I think Jason is so incredibly cute. And nice. And thoughtful."

Huh.

I sat up immediately. Knees to knees, we looked at each other. My eyes had adjusted to the darkness. "He is," I replied.

"And Ben—gosh, Deb. He's splendid. Can't you see that?"

I threw my head back. "I *know*. But there's no real reason to think he likes me—"

A small burst of mirthless laughter came from Paige. "No reason? You've got to be kidding. Except that ever since that day at The Egg and I, he's been singling you out. Asking you to do stuff. Making time to be alone with you. At least give him a chance, Debra."

I leaned over and placed my elbows on my knees and pressed my hands to my cheeks. "He asked me to let him be my friend. That's what I'm doing. I'm here. We're friends. I can't do more, and he hasn't asked. I can barely be me. I can't think about being me in another relationship. I can't think about another relationship ending. I can't think about who I would be then. I somehow lost everything I wanted; I have to figure out where that leaves me." My voice rose, and Paige didn't respond.

After several tense moments of silence, Paige's shoulders slumped. "Maybe I'm trying to project where I am on where you are." She reached over and squeezed my forearm. "I'm sorry for that. I'm ready for a relationship. I'm ready to dive into something new and see what happens. But ... that's me. You've got these guys in your life—like Jason and Ben—who want to be around you and care about you. I can't even get Milo to ask me on a real date. You've been in love and come close to happily ever after and it fell apart. I don't know what that feels like. But I'm very sorry you went through it. It's totally fair to think you're not ready for another relationship. Whatever happens with you and Ben is between you guys."

My defensiveness eased.

"But, Debra," Paige added, "I've known Ben awhile now. Long enough to know that he's not running a charity based on helping brokenhearted single girls."

I almost smiled at that.

"He's got his reasons for reaching out to you, sure. But he's different with you. That's all I'm saying. And I doubt he's ever brought another girl up here camping. Do what you want with that—but his heart matters too."

My neck stiffened.

Ben's heart matters too.

After a moment, I just nodded. "You're right."

"Let's go roast more marshmallows. Chloe and Kyle started making out— um, hello, we're all sitting right there—and Jason quipped that they should get a tent, and then they did." Even in the dark of the tent, I could see the whites of Paige's very large eyes in an *Eek! That's awkward!* look. I chuckled.

"I'm up for more marshmallows." I followed Paige back to our now low-burning fire. Jason glanced up at me, worry all over his face. I shook my head and sat next to him.

"Are you okay?" he asked me in a whisper.

"Yes. No. Sometimes." It was the best I could manage. Jason pulled me into a side hug.

"Where's Ben?" Paige asked.

"He went over to touch base with Emmie about tomorrow. He should be back soon."

Paige nodded, digging through the bag of marshmallows. She dragged her chair a bit closer to the embers. Once she was settled, a toasty, bubbly marshmallow sticking to her fingers, she looked back at me and Jase. "What do you think of Colorado, Jason?"

"Toss me that bag of marshmallows," he told her. Paige grinned and threw the bag at him. He popped a regular one into his mouth. "I think it's incredible. I went to California once for a cousin's wedding and saw the Sierra mountain range. But I've never been out here before. These Rocky Mountains and rivers are awesome. I can see why my girl Debra loves it so much."

I smiled. "You could give up the humidity and move out here," I teased. He looked shocked.

"The humidity is one thing—the food is another."

I nodded in not-quite-mock sadness. "True. I'll take Colorado's lack of humidity and the lack of bugs, but I *do* miss the food in Texas."

In the corner of my eye, I could see a shadowy figure coming closer through the clearing, a flashlight beaming this way and that. Ben clicked off the flashlight as he joined us at the fire. He grabbed a chair and pulled it next to Paige.

"Food is Jason's life. Music is Ben's." Paige twisted her mouth for a moment. "What's mine?"

"Hippie clothes?" Ben guessed, and I laughed, then choked, trying to stop quickly. Paige scowled at us but ended up smiling.

"*No,*" she responded. "I mean, I like clothes. But they're not my life."

"What was your major in college?" Jason asked. Paige crossed her arms as the night air got even chillier.

"English literature."

No one said anything.

"Hey, I like literature," Paige protested.

"What did you want to do with it? Did you hope to be a teacher?" Jason asked.

She shook her head. "Not really. I just liked learning about all that stuff."

"I get that," Jason said, stretching out in his tiny chair. "I majored in computer science and worked as a programmer for a while. And then I got sick of it. I felt like I wasn't living, just boring myself to death. I'd always loved food. My grandmother owned a big Mexican restaurant down by the border for years. I could live off her enchiladas. Not kidding. And my *tía* Marina—my aunt, I mean—has a small café where she sells breakfast tacos and tamales and that sort of thing. So I started cooking, experimenting. I signed up for a night cooking class. And it all clicked. I wanted to work with food."

"Do you want to be a chef?" Ben asked.

Jase shrugged. "Maybe. I'm also interested in having my own food truck. Drive around Houston at lunchtime and feed hungry people, you know?"

I smiled, completely able to picture Jason Garcia in a food truck. "My life is radio, I guess," I offered, thinking I should contribute to the conversation.

"What about Miss Lonely Heart?" Paige asked. "Are they going to make you keep doing that?"

Jason wasn't up to speed on Miss Lonely Heart, so I filled him in. His brow furrowed as I talked, but he didn't say much more, thankfully. I wasn't up for disapproval.

"But it's not all negative, Debra," Ben spoke up. I looked over at him. "It's not," he insisted. "When I've listened—which is pretty regularly—it seems to me that you give people a place to talk about what they're going through or have already gone through. People want to be heard. You empathize more often than not—" He grinned. "Except when you get angry."

I snorted and Jason laughed.

"But you let people know their feelings are valid and you listen. The revenge part ... well, who knew there was such a thing as a 'revenge body'? I'm learning a lot from Miss Lonely Heart," he joked with a chuckle.

"It's not my favorite part of the job, but it is what it is. What about you, Ben?" I asked. "If you had the opportunity to go on tour or sign with a label, would you? Or do you feel like you'll be a worship pastor long-term?"

Ben grabbed a stick and poked at the fire, trying to stir up more flames. "I don't know. I'll do this until God shows me I should do something else."

"Yeah, well, sometimes life changes directions, with or without God's help."

So that came out sounding more bitter than I meant for it to.

"Sometimes *we* change directions," Jason broke in, his voice easy and calm. "Like with my job. I don't think God cares too much if I'm a cook or a programmer. I think—I hope—who I am is more than either of those things."

"But maybe that's different from a calling," Paige piped up. "Like being a pastor or a missionary. Do you believe God calls people for certain purposes?"

Jason tilted his head, thoughtful. "Yeah, sure. But whether you're a missionary or a dishwasher, I think God wants the same things from us, right? Love people. Love each other. Have faith."

Paige nodded. And by the way she was looking at Jason, I started to worry that her admiration of him might be inching up quickly. Too quickly when it came to someone who'd be on a plane home in two days.

"I feel the same," Ben agreed. He leaned back and looked at the stars. "But living out faith in a church looks different from living out faith on a tour bus. For me, I'm okay where I'm planted right now."

I was quiet.

"Deb?" Ben said my name, bringing me back to the discussion.

"Living out faith just isn't on my radar right now."

"Tell me why," Jason said, leaning over and looking straight at me.

Ugh. The boldness of close friends.

"Deb, talk to me. Whatever the reason, I want to hear. Is it Luke? Do you think God made Luke break up with you?"

"No. I blame Luke. And Sara. You know I blame her."

Jason sighed and shook his head, looking down at the dirt. "Okay, where does faith factor in?"

I felt anger slowly rising in me. "It doesn't. That's the problem. I went through the worst moment of my life—and I was alone. I didn't feel any God or spirit holding me. Those are clichés, Jason, and you know it. 'Hold me, Jesus,' and all those things we pray and say. It still amounts to us being on our own. There was no comfort, not to mention justice, since they're off happy as can be while I'm left to glue myself back together."

"Deb—" Jason started but I kept going.

"So, yeah, I'm not sure if any of it is real anymore. I sang up there with the worship team at Christ Community for years. Hands raised, crying, all kinds of feelings. But that's what it was—*feelings*. Everything shattered for me, and I'm trying to put my life back together. And it's *me* working every day, paying my bills. It's *me* taking care of myself. That's just truth." Tears sprang to my eyes. "I'm alone in my apartment. There's no great Spirit talking to me, holding me, going before me and making everything work out." I tightened my fist at the harsh reality. The cold fact that I'd never felt so alone in my life as I had over the past eight months.

"It's fine that God didn't stop Luke from breaking my heart. I know Luke gets to make his choices like I get to make mine. But the fact that amid all of it—I never sensed God. Nothing happened to show me he was there or that he's real. Nothing. I don't know, Jase. I can't look at the beauty of nature and the complexity of humans and think it's all an accident. But as for the whole 'relationship with God,' 'he loves us so much' lingo—I just don't think he's all that involved. If he's involved, explain poverty. Explain abuse. Explain starvation. Explain genocide." I crossed my arms firmly.

There.

I'd said it out loud. They could argue my points, but I'd been honest. I'd said the words I'd been thinking for months. I'd given voice to the doubts that had invaded my heart and mind and that I couldn't brush off. I felt different about God now, and there was no going back, as far as I could tell.

"It's hard, I know," Ben suddenly said, his tone as soft as snow falling. "When he doesn't seem to show up. When nothing changes. It's hard to believe the same way. When Sadie died—I kept thinking, *Surely God could have kept it from happening.* Made them leave a few minutes earlier or later or kept her home sick—anything to keep that car from hitting them."

"Who is Sadie?" Jason asked, his voice hushed.

"My sister," Ben said. He looked down at his hands. "She died in a car crash."

"Oh, Ben," Paige whispered, and I realized that she hadn't known.

But he'd told me.

"How ... how did you reconcile that?" I asked, needing to know. "Those questions about God with the faith you still have?"

Ben rested his elbows on his knees and loosely laced his fingers together. "For me—and this is part of why I feel so strongly that each person's journey with God is their own and looks different at certain seasons of life—I was in this conundrum. Sadie and I were close, so the thought of never seeing her again, the thought that nothing of her existed anymore—that couldn't be true. I couldn't even go there. My anger and frustration at God manifested itself in some self-destructive ways. I spiraled for a few years. But always, I had to hold on to the belief that there's more, that Sadie wasn't lost forever. I couldn't seem to let go of my faith. I needed it too much. From someone on the outside looking at me during those years, they might have thought that I'd abandoned my faith. But they would have been wrong. I was holding on the best that I could."

Ben straightened and tucked his hair back. "But that's *my* story. People react to things differently. People struggle with different levels of doubt or unbelief. It's *okay*." And then Ben was staring straight at me, reaching down in my soul for music and faith and happiness. Like someone digging in a purse or a suitcase, feeling around for what they're looking for, pushing aside what doesn't matter.

How he could do that with just his eyes was beyond me, but I felt spent just making eye contact with so much intensity.

"Maybe your faith journey will look different from here on out, Deb. Maybe you'll know God in a different way. Maybe one day something will happen. Maybe he'll show up in a huge, unmistakable way, and you'll dissolve and every piece of you will cry out with faith. Maybe you'll just barely scratch the surface of faith, but it'll be enough to get you there. I can tell you this—the day Sadie died, my mother changed forever. She was never the same woman again. It kills me to think about it, how part of her died that day too and has never come back to life. She takes faith in small doses. Enough to keep her going but not so much to consume her. I think she's afraid of the rage. And I understand."

Next to him, Paige wiped tears from her cheeks.

"Even in those small doses, I think Jesus walks with her day in and day out."

And Ben's eyes were wet now, burning red like the embers. "The hard questions never get answered in this life. Not really. Anyone who says differently is probably in denial, or maybe just grasping for something to make sense. But the worst of what you mentioned—families starving to death, children raped and abused, people praying for rescue who never will be, old people unloved and abandoned, senseless accidents—I don't think there's an easy way to reconcile those things with a loving God.

"Sometimes it just comes down to choice. Choosing that there's more to this than we understand. Believing that he's a complete balance of mercy and justice and he'll make it right in the end. Accepting that his plan isn't ours, but that doesn't erase who he is. Faith can be a difficult choice. The people in the Bible—their stories are messy, Debra. It's always been a hard choice." Ben rubbed his hands together. We were all cold at this point, with our fire nearly snuffed out. "Whatever your faith looks like going forward or if you lose it entirely, you're not alone in the struggle." Ben's words drifted over to me, like snippets of heat from the fire, reaching my heart.

Jason's arm was around me again, the warmth and closeness of real friendship. The dying embers suddenly popped and I jerked at the sound. Ben stood up. "I should get some sleep. I'm the cook on duty for breakfast, after all."

Jason stood up, and I joined him. "I'll help, man. Whatever you need." Paige hopped up as well, and she and I started to walk, arm in arm, back to our tent. Then I stopped and turned around.

"Ben," I called out. He paused, near his tent. Without thinking, I ran over to him and threw my arms around him. I hugged him tight under an endless blanket of stars.

"Thank you," I whispered.

Chapter Twelve

When you know the notes to sing, you can sing most anything.
The Sound of Music

"Do I smell bacon?"

I buried myself farther in my sleeping bag, ignoring the question from Paige. But my nose perked up, sniffing. Yep. A faint waft of bacon.

I groaned. Sleeping on the ground was not my favorite. My body yelled silently in protest. Paige sat up, groaning as well. "Brrr. It's cold!"

"Then get back in your sleeping bag," I said, snuggling down farther.

"But there's bacon," Paige argued. "And probably coffee. Who knows what else. I'm hungry."

At the mention of coffee, my limbs moved without permission. I sat up, then patted my hair. "I'm terrified of how I must look. And I need a shower so bad."

"Oh, me too," Paige said. But she looked fine. In five seconds, she'd twisted that hair of hers into a messy-but-cute bun on top of her head. There was no doubt my hair had the messy part down, minus cuteness. I shook it back and tried to finger-comb my curls.

"Actually"—Paige cocked her head and studied my face—"you look pretty. You got quite a bit of sun yesterday and your cheeks are pink. Your eyeliner is still smudged from yesterday, but it kind of looks smoky and accents your eyes. Your hair …" Her voice trailed off and I laughed. "I recommend a little lip gloss for shine, and you're ready to face the boys."

I poked her. "Find me some lip gloss, then."

She handed me a white tube. "Sorry, ChapStick will have to do."

We both giggled. Once I was ChapStick-presentable, we climbed out of our tent. Everyone else was up, and Ben had reignited the bonfire. Paige and I shuffled close to it, trying to warm up. I could see people meandering about over at Emmie's side of the clearing too.

"Breakfast!" Ben called out. The smell of bacon was stronger now and my stomach growled impatiently. I got in line behind Chloe, and Jason divvied out hot scrambled eggs, crispy bacon, and pancakes. Ben poured coffee and even had individual coffee creamers for us.

I sat back in my chair and ate everything on my plate, hardly taking a breath between bites. Maybe it was just being out in the fresh mountain air, but everything tasted extra delicious. Over second cups of coffee, our group wandered around the campsite, enjoying a cool, cloudless morning.

Ben was busy, first cooking enough for everyone and then cleaning up and packaging everything as tightly and compactly as possibly. Jason helped him every step of the way. The two seemed to work well together. Paige and I packed up our tent and backpacks, then hiked around the clearing, keeping our conversation light. After the heaviness of the previous night's discussion, I needed time to process how I was feeling.

Ben had shared his heart beautifully. And I couldn't help feeling closer to him for it.

But still ... there was that question about how he felt about me. How I felt about him. When I'd hugged him the night before, he'd been shocked but tightened his arms around me too. It had occurred to me later—while lying awake in my sleeping bag—that was the first time we had hugged. Of all the times we'd hung out together, a hug goodbye or good night had never happened.

Until last night.

Trees lined our path back down to the river and outpost. We were all loaded with backpacks and extra gear. (Greg got the unfortunate job of having to carry down the garbage bag with who knows what inside it.) Jason and I walked the trail together.

"I don't want you to leave," I admitted.

He gave me a half grin. "You know I'll miss you too. And I'll miss Colorado." He motioned to the general surroundings. "I could get used to this—camping, rafting, hiking. The dry air, the views—I love it. Ben told me next time I'm in town, he'll teach me to fly-fish."

"Planning to come back, are you?" I asked with a smile.

"If I'm invited," he teased.

"Standing invitation," I assured him.

Jason nodded. We stopped for a moment, both needing a water break. "You can come back and visit us too, you know," he said, before taking a long sip. "You don't have to see Luke and Sara."

I tightened the cap on my water bottle. "Maybe."

The group was getting a little ahead of us, so I pushed off the tree I'd leaned on, and we started back on the trail. "Come back this winter and go skiing with me," I suggested.

Jason brightened. "That would be great! If I can get the time off, I'd love to."

"I think Paige would like to see you again too," I mentioned.

"She's nice," Jason acknowledged. "I've enjoyed my time with both of you. But I've got to get back to Houston and hopefully get the sous chef position. I need to concentrate on work. I spent a lot of time as a programmer and I feel like I'm starting late with my passion."

"Better late than never," I reminded him.

"Yeah. Did Ben tell you he wants us to hang out in Breck for a while after we get back to base?"

My head bobbed as we walked faster downhill. "Yeah. But I feel gross after being out here all night, not to mention yesterday's dunk in the river. I need a shower in the worst way."

"Ben told me we could stop by his buddy's house and clean up before going to dinner in town."

"Really? I'm on board with that."

We reached the outpost and I immediately took advantage of the portable restrooms again. Then we loaded into one of the River Run vans and drove the sixteen miles back up to the base building. After unloading all the equipment, the staff handed out sub sandwiches and chips for a picnic lunch. Paige and Ben and Jason and I sat at a picnic table together; Chloe, Kyle, Greg, and Rita sat at another one near us, and we enjoyed lunch right next to the river. I loved the constant sound of the water flowing.

After lunch, we said our goodbyes to Greg, Rita, Chloe, and Kyle. They thanked Ben for being such a good guide, and then Jason decided to buy a T-shirt in the gift shop. I hadn't realized it, but midway through the rafting excursions, someone was positioned to take a professional photo of each group that passed. I about fell over laughing when I saw ours. All you could see was the top of my mess of curls; the rest of my body was submerged in the river. Jason's arm and paddle were visible, the rest of him was underwater with me. We got a good laugh over the photos. But there was a second one that made my heart skip. A photo at 'the jump' of me diving into the river.

I didn't want to spend money on a photo of just me, but I kept looking at it onscreen as we stood there, waiting for Jason to buy his T-shirt. The river, the rock, and me—choosing to jump. I loved it.

Ben texted me his friend Mike's address and then said he had to finish a few things at River Run and would meet us at Mike's. All of us were eager for showers, so we drove straight over to Mike's small apartment, where he kindly let us in and gave us full use of his bathroom and anything else we needed. Now knowing we'd be having dinner in Breckenridge, I was thankful I'd brought an extra pair of clean clothes for the ride back and left them in my SUV. After showering and towel-drying my hair, I put on some makeup. Paige had been right that I'd gotten quite a bit of sun, and I didn't mind the pinkness in my cheeks at all. At the bottom of my purse, I found a tube of pink lipstick. I held the tube in my hand for a moment. I hadn't reached for it in months, hadn't wanted to wear it.

I could almost see Dr. Clark's pinched smile. The voice in my head sounded like hers.

If you can dive into a freezing cold river, you can certainly wear pink lipstick.

"Are we sure this is it?" Paige asked, head tilted back, studying the hanging sign over what looked like a rather old café. The tattered sign read, *The Drunken Frog.*

Jason laughed and steered her forward. "Sometimes these little local dives can have the most amazing food. Sometimes not. We'll see." On the ground next to the doorway, a chalkboard had been propped up. I read the scrawled writing: *Sunday Night Karaoke. Throwback to the '90s!*

I scanned the sidewalk for Ben but didn't see him, so I followed Jason and Paige into the small building, made of a mix of brick and chipped-painted wood. A very worn wooden bar lined three quarters of the left wall. Round, scuffed-up, and scratched tables filled a crowded dining area. And a stage occupied the far side of the bar, complete with barstools and microphones. The bartender waved as we walked in, and a waitress passed by us.

"Take a seat anywhere," she called over her shoulder.

"Let's get a seat near the stage," Jason said, leading the way through the maze of tables. Before I could remind him that it was *karaoke night*, not exactly an established band, and that things could get loud and crazy and *did we need to be right up front?* he'd chosen a table and Paige was sitting down.

Only a few other tables were taken, but a steady stream of customers were coming in. We looked at menus and ordered drinks while waiting for Ben. The chatter in the room grew as minutes ticked by. I saw Paige sit straight and wave toward the door, and I turned, knowing it had to be Ben.

Sure enough. He looked showered and as animated as ever. That dark hair was styled back in waves. He had on loose jeans and a red T-shirt; I didn't recognize the band on the front. The stubble on his face was reaching the level of a beard, and somehow it just made him more attractive. Ben waved back at Paige, then stopped at the bar, slapping hands with the bartender, who must have been a friend of his. Paige looked back down at her menu and Jason pointed something out to her. I sneaked another look at Ben at the bar. One of the waitresses stopped and hugged him, saying something that made him laugh.

All the questions that had been jumbled in my mind at the campsite came back.

If I were in a different space of mind—not a girl who'd been wildly in love with someone else eight months ago—what would my reaction to Ben look like?

He bumped fists with the bartender and headed in our direction, pausing as he caught me staring at him. Flustered, I dropped my menu, then picked it up and pretended to study it scrupulously.

What's wrong with you? You're nervous. You've been around Ben a bunch of times … and now you're nervous? No. Get over it.

Ben sat down next to me. "Hey, everybody. Sorry it took so long to get here. They needed more help over at River Run, so I had to stay longer."

"Totally fine," Paige said.

"What are you drinking?" Ben asked me with a smile, taking the menu from my hands. I looked at my drink.

"Um, something fruity with a little kick. Paige ordered our drinks."

"Mind if I taste?" he asked, reaching over.

I managed a nod and watched Ben Price take a sip of my peach fusion. He pushed the drink back my way, an amused look in his eyes.

"What do you think?"

"I like it," he told me.

But do you like me? Do I like you? What's happening between us?

"What's good here?" Jason asked Ben.

"Steak tenders and onion rings—the batter is from scratch and it's stellar. The crab cakes are excellent. The only thing I don't recommend is the clam chowder. Too salty."

The waitress appeared at our table and we all ordered.

"Did you used to come here a lot?" Paige handed Jason her phone and jumped up to squeeze next to me. "Take a picture of me and Debra, please." Jason obliged, and Paige and I leaned in together and smiled; then she insisted on taking one of me and Jason.

Before anyone could suggest a picture of me and Ben, he started talking. "Yeah, I came here all the time when I lived in Breck. It's a popular hangout for locals."

Jason wanted to relive our rafting adventure, so we started talking about the water, and the raft flipping on its side, and the jump, and how much fun we'd all had. Our meal arrived and Ben was right—the crab cakes were delectable and I kept stealing onion rings from Jason until he ordered another basketful. We were all laughing over Paige's hilarious version of going down the river with Emmie's team (which included Paige being pitched from the back row to the front, with her bottom in the air, at one point during a vicious set of rapids) when a guy jumped up on stage and grabbed the microphone.

"Hello! Welcome to The Drunken Frog. It's karaoke night if you didn't know." He paused and the whole café burst into applause. "I hope you're ready to flashback to the nineties"—more cheering—"and on top of the rad night we're about to have, we've got a local boy back home tonight." The guy pointed to Ben. "Ben Price, get up here. You're going to get this party started!"

"Oh, man," Ben muttered. Paige whistled and I started to clap.

"You've got to do it," Jason said with a chuckle.

Ben looked at me and I winked. "Bring down the house."

He just stared at me for a moment, then took a sip of water and stood up to the raucous applause of the crowd. Ben grabbed the microphone and waited for the music, his eyes on the screen where the lyrics were about to appear. An old Counting Crows song came on and everyone in the building, myself included, knew the words by heart. I could see Ben coming alive, reacting to the energy of the people.

And he killed it.

Slam dunk.

I watched him on stage—no band, no guitar, no Karis for backup—just Ben up there, singing karaoke. His hands on the mic, his voice filling the room. I watched his every rhythmic move. Again he stomped his foot in time to the beat. He hit every note and made the song his own.

"The guy's a rock star." Jason drew close so I could hear him. I took a drink from my water glass; my peach fusion had been finished long ago.

"He could be," I answered, my voice low, but Jason heard. He put his arm on the back of my chair.

"You told me his original music is really good. Maybe you should try to get him on the radio." He broached the topic again.

"It's not that easy," I pushed back. "But ... you're right. He belongs on the radio."

The song ended and the crowd cheered as Ben came off stage. Someone else jumped up to sing. Ben took his seat on the other side of me. Paige and Jason praised him. Then he looked at me, eyebrows up.

"Not bad," I said with a barely suppressed smile.

He dipped his chin. "Thanks."

Knowing we had a long drive back, I ordered a coffee, and after two songs—one that was painfully off key—Jason nudged my shoulder before taking a bite of an onion ring.

"Go on, Deb. You love karaoke."

I shot daggers at him through my eyes but he shrugged.

"Correction: I used to love karaoke."

"C'mon, Deb!" Paige added to the ridiculousness of this moment.

I glanced at my phone. "Don't you think we should get going soon? It's such a long drive back."

"You don't have to sing if you don't want to, Debra." Ben touched the table in front of me. I set down my phone. "But if you *do* want to, I'll sing with you."

The sound of someone destroying a high note squeaked through the mic at that moment and I winced. Ben grinned and leaned closer. He whispered in my ear, "What's your favorite nineties song?"

"It's kind of cheesy," I said. "You probably don't know it." I whispered the title to him.

Are you seriously thinking of doing this? You haven't sung in months. You haven't warmed up. This could be one of the most embarrassing moments of your life.

But I was right next to Ben, looking at those light brown eyes, and suddenly feeling so close to something. I wasn't sure what.

Who cares if you're embarrassed? You don't know anyone here. Why not?

That used to be my motto.

Why not tell Luke how I felt? Who knows what might happen? Take a chance and see. You'll never know until you try.

And look where that had gotten me.

What are you afraid of, Miss Lonely Heart?

Ben sat back, waiting. Jason touched my shoulder.

"I know you can do this, Debra. I've heard you sing karaoke a million times."

That small reminder that he knew me. I felt a little bit braver.

Jason placed his finger under my chin and gently lifted my face to look at him. "I want to be here when you get your voice back," he said. I looked at him and another moment flashed in my memory. Me and Jason at the airport the morning after the breakup. His hands cupping my face, promising I would be okay. That there would be more for me than Luke. Standing on the curb in front of Bush Intercontinental Airport, I'd been crying too hard to listen.

Ben stood up and I saw him walk over to the deejay. And then he moved to the stage, and the crowd started to clap. He perched on a barstool and just watched me. I knew he'd sing it for me if I couldn't do it.

On wobbly legs, I stood up and walked to the stage. His eyes followed me; then he reached down for my hand and pulled me up. He gave me his barstool and pulled up a second one, grabbing another microphone from the floor. And the music started. The crowd quieted.

The music began to play. Alison Krauss's nineties version of "When You Say Nothing at All." I closed my eyes; my quaking hands held the mic; I opened my mouth and sang. About halfway through, my voice faltered. But there was Ben, picking up the slack and keeping us going.

And when the last, shaky note was drawn from me, I gulped for breath. The room broke out into applause. Jason stood up, clapping, his eyes shining. I looked sideways at Ben.

The astonished look in his eyes sent a shudder through me. I pushed away the microphone and raised myself up. Ben set down the mic he'd held, stood up, reached for my hand ...

And then he kissed me in front of every person at The Drunken Frog.

Chapter Thirteen

Life and love go on, let the music play.
Johnny Cash

D o you want to tell me what you're feeling right now?" Jason asked calmly.
"No," I told him.

We were an hour outside Breckenridge. With Jason at the wheel, I'd curled up as tightly as I could in the passenger seat, nearly plastering myself to the door, my head resting on the window. Paige was in the backseat, either asleep or pretending to be asleep. I couldn't know for sure.

"I'll talk, then. So ... I *think* Ben likes you," Jason said in a light voice. I covered my ears. "I just want to know if you like him."

I sighed loudly, trying to communicate extreme exasperation.

"*I* like him," Jason continued, and a glimmer of a smile worked its way to my lips. I rested my head back on the seat. "But that's just me," Jason went on. "He seems like a cool guy. I think Addi and Lily and Sam would like him too."

I faced the window again and touched the cold pane. I couldn't see the mountains this time. Just the darkness. "Of course I like him, Jase. He's sweet and fun and I could listen to him sing all day long. But I'm not interested in dating right now. I don't know when I'll be ready for that. There's no way I'm ready to chance another heartache. Plus ..." My heart hurt. The cold from the window seeped into my hand. "Plus, Luke is still in me. I wake up thinking about him sometimes. Not as much as I used to. But when I found out they were engaged—" My throat tightened as I thought of that night.

Jason didn't respond for a while and the curving road began to make me sleepy. The last thing I heard him say was "Luke is your past, Debra. I think your future just might rock your whole world."

I cried when Jason left. I'd gone into work the next morning after just a couple hours' sleep, feeling like a zombie. Then I'd driven Jason to the airport right after lunch. I'd hugged him, bawling, and he'd tried to console me, promising he'd come back again. I drove back home, crawled into my bed, and slept until nightfall. I woke up to the feeling of my stomach rumbling, then shuffled to the kitchen for something fast and easy. When I opened the fridge, I blinked in surprise at a ready-made casserole.

Jason.

He must have made it for me while I was at work that morning. Thankful, I reached for it, dished out at least two portions, and heated my meal in the microwave. With a steaming plate of chicken-and-rice casserole, I sat on the sofa and turned on the TV. *The Sound of Music* was on The Movie Channel, and thrilled, I settled in to watch Maria fall in love with Captain von Trapp. From the coffee table, my phone dinged and I reached for it. Jason's name popped up.

MADE IT HOME. BEST WEEKEND EVER.

I smiled and typed my reply.

MOVE HERE.

He sent me a string of laughing emojis.

AND THANK YOU FOR DINNER. DELICIOUS.

A second later, another text came through.

YOU'RE WELCOME. AND IF YOU DIDN'T SEE, I LEFT SOMETHING ON YOUR NIGHTSTAND. BEN ASKED ME TO GIVE IT TO YOU.

A second surprise. I set my empty plate on the coffee table and ran to my bedroom (all of about six steps away). A large envelope sat on the nightstand. I slid my hand inside and pulled out the contents.

The photo from our rafting day, of me diving into the river. I looked at the dark color of the water, the bright turquoise blue of the sky, the large gray flat rock—and me, in flight.

Thoughts of the trip inevitably turned to Ben, to what happened after.

I'd stood, frozen as a log in winter, after he'd kissed me. He'd looked a bit startled himself. Every corner of the small café had erupted in an ovation at that kiss. I'd blinked, stunned, too numb to feel anything at first. Then I'd blinked again and Ben came into focus. The room was too loud to hear much, but he'd leaned close to my ear and said, "I meant it." Then he'd taken my hand, maybe knowing I was basically catatonic, and led me off the stage. Paige was clapping, eyes as round as dinner plates, and Jason had looked too shocked to react.

Then someone else was up on stage singing "Losin' My Religion," and Ben led me through the café, out onto the front sidewalk. A few paces away, a couple of people were smoking cigarettes on a bench. In the evening light, I could see a red glow after every few moments.

Then I found my voice all right. "What was that?" I snapped, a swirl of mixed feelings rushing through me.

Ben folded his arms. "It was just automatic. It's not like I planned it."

"Yeah, yeah. 'You feel something and you go with it.' I remember. That's not okay when it comes to kissing me in front of a room full of people."

He'd pressed his lips into a thin line, then exhaled. "Maybe the timing wasn't right. But I'm okay with people knowing how I feel about you."

"I—you—what—" I just kept sputtering, trying to find something coherent to say. "How you feel about me? You could've just said something. You know that, right? We hang out all the time. You could have told me how you feel. Then maybe I wouldn't be caught off guard when you kiss me in front of one of my closest friends. Two of them, come to think of it."

He'd frowned at that. "What does it matter that I kissed you in front of Jason and Paige? I knew it." He stepped back and ran his fingers through his hair. "I knew you liked Jason."

"No." At that point, I was losing steam and needing us to get back to the heart of the argument. "Jason and I are just friends. It's—you should have said something before."

"How could you not have known?" He'd raised his hands, palms up. "I ask you to do stuff with me all the time."

"Yeah, but ... I thought you were just being nice. You're—you're nice to everyone, Ben. You're a worship pastor, for goodness' sake. I'm a girl who feels uncomfortable sitting in church."

He'd crossed his arms again, head down.

"You said you wanted to be my friend," I had reminded him, trying not to sound accusatory, but it didn't work.

"I did say that," he agreed. "And I do. If that's all you want, we can just be friends."

Not likely. Not when he'd just kissed me after drawing the music back out of me.

"I can't—I mean, it's too soon. I'm not ready to even think about, you know, dating or anything."

"Too soon?" His brow furrowed and his voice rose a notch.

I felt prickles on my neck, my guard jumping up. "It's not just about Luke. My whole life has changed. *I* changed. I started over when I moved out here. You didn't know me before; you don't know how different things are for me. My hair is short! I still barely recognize myself in the mirror." Emotion started rising in my throat. "I was this other person—happy and outgoing and ready to start my life with Luke. Busy all the time, hardly ever alone. I'd stand on the platform and sing at church on Sundays, not struggling with doubt. Now ... I don't know anything. My faith felt good back then. Singing to peppy songs, surrounded by fog and lights, swaying to the sound of the drums. But you know what? That peppy religion was like the smoke and colored lights ... ridiculous. It didn't really mean anything."

"You say you're different. That's okay. You struggle with faith now. A lot of us do. You're trying to find yourself—but I already see you."

All that emotion started to choke me.

"No one sees me." I could only whisper the words.

Ben's face smoothed and he stepped closer. He put both of his hands on my shoulders. "I do."

"But Luke—"

Ben stepped back and gritted his teeth. "I wish I could get that guy out of your head!"

My breath stopped for a moment.

I wish that too.

To see calm and easygoing Ben lose his cool—my heart started pounding, this time from desire, not so much anger. To see passion evoked in him, because of *me* ... Without warning, I took a step closer to him.

"Ben."

He looked up at me, still annoyed but a hint of hope in his eyes, handsome and kind and more than a little frustrated at that moment. I touched his face, and all the fight in me drained away. Then I kissed him back.

This time, I absorbed the moment, feeling his lips—warm and soft—against mine. Not since Luke had I connected with someone like this, and with Luke, I'd been all in from the first kiss. I wasn't that girl anymore. But even with my hesitation, I let myself tap into this experience of linking part of myself with Ben. I could feel the scruffiness of his beard beneath my fingers, taste the remnants of whatever it was he'd been drinking, sense the pounding of his heart closing in closer to mine. Ben was frozen in surprise for all of two seconds, then his arms wrapped around me and he kissed me—gentle but with enough urgency to jump-start my heart rate. I relaxed in his arms.

Then I heard and felt his deep sigh of relief.

And I knew, instinctively, that he was all in.

"And how do you feel about that?" Dr. Clark asked after I'd recounted the story to her at our next session. I didn't answer. "Debra, remember, this is a safe place to say anything."

I bit my lower lip and pulled my legs up under me on the couch, shifting uncomfortably. Then I stood up. "I don't know. He's—Ben, I mean—he's so abrupt with things. After the gig in Boulder, he comes running out and asks me to ride with him—alone—in front of Paige and Milo, like it's not a big deal! Then he asks me to go hiking when we barely know each other. And he tells me his life story. He's wide open. And I *think* he's that way with everyone; then I'm shocked on the camping trip when Paige had no idea that he had a sister who died. So maybe he's not that way with everyone. And now this ... in front of a packed bar, he kisses me. We've never even been on a date."

Dr. Clark took off her glasses and, as usual, began to clean them. "I think the argument could be made that you've been on lots of dates. You just didn't categorize them that way."

"Fine, fine!" I agreed with annoyance. "Luke wasn't like this. If I hadn't suggested we start dating, he would have taken forever to ask me out. He thinks through every scenario of life before making a move."

Dr. Clark nodded. "Some people are like that. Ben seems a bit more impulsive."

"You think?" My voice came out high pitched and maddened.

"Ben is more like you."

I didn't say anything for a moment. "It didn't matter that Luke was different from me. I loved him anyway. In fact, maybe I liked how intentional and thoughtful he was."

Dr. Clark slid those glasses back on and I sat back down. "Do you wish Ben was more like that?"

I shook my head. "That's not who Ben is. Well, he *is* intentional and thoughtful. He's just—I don't know. He's not very guarded."

"Why did you kiss him a second time?"

Why on earth did I do that?

"I don't know. He seemed sad. I felt pulled to him. When he kissed me on the stage, it was rushed and unexpected, and I was so shocked that I barely registered that it was happening. I suppose I was curious as to what it would be like to kiss Ben without all those factors."

"And what *was* it like?"

"Different from Luke."

Dr. Clark leaned over her desk. "That's okay. Let's take Luke out of this for a moment."

I nodded, nibbling on my bottom lip again. After a quiet minute, I spoke up. "Ben is every kind of cool, without even trying. He's beautiful and nice and people are drawn to him. When he sings, he leaves nothing behind. It's all out there. And when he kissed me—or, actually, when I kissed him—that's how it was. He doesn't hold back."

Dr. Clark blew out softly, almost a whistle, and I blushed, slightly embarrassed by my own description.

"I *do* like him," I confessed. "But there's no way we wouldn't run into roadblocks. I mean—him and his job and the church, and me and where I am right now."

"I think Ben understands that where you are right now may not be where you are six months from now. Where you are at this moment is completely different to where you were a year ago. Things change. Circumstances change. People change. We grow. You're in transition, Debra. In a lot of ways. Faith included. I want you to give yourself space to figure out where you want to end up. Ben sounds willing to do that as well."

"Maybe," I whispered.

"Do you feel ready to move on from Luke? We know that he has moved on, but this is about *you* and your feelings and what you want."

I sank farther into the couch cushion and mindlessly ran my fingers over one of the pillows. I thought about going to the zoo with Ben, eating tacos in a parking lot, riding the rapids, and roasting marshmallows under a starry sky. Finding my voice in a karaoke bar, singing one of my favorite songs. Kissing Ben while standing on a cracked sidewalk, in a haze of nearby cigarette smoke, navy-blue mountains in the distance and a stark-white moon.

This is dangerous. I think I just might be willing to risk my heart again.

Without speaking, I looked back at Dr. Clark, who sat peering at me, a quizzical look on her face.

"Maybe kiss him again and see how it goes," she suggested, and I laughed.

Chapter Fourteen

Sometimes the dreams you came in with aren't always the dreams you leave with, but they still rock.
Rock of Ages

Midmorning Tuesday, during a twelve-in-a-row song session, I pulled up my personal playlist.

"I want you to hear this guy. He's local. I've heard him in a couple of venues and I'm obsessed."

Andy rolled his eyes. "C'mon, please tell me you haven't found a diamond in the rough for us to discover."

I glared at him. "I know *good* when I hear it. So do you. So stop being grouchy and just listen. I wouldn't ask you if I didn't think this guy has incredible talent. I've downloaded every song his band plays, and he's written most of them."

Andy acted like I was asking him to climb Pike's Peak, but he stuck my earbuds into his ears anyway. "He better not be good-looking," Andy said before pushing play, and I had to fight to keep a straight face. I left him in the studio while I went to grab a bottle of juice from the staff room. After about five minutes, I returned. Andy was still listening but scrolling through text messages on his iPhone.

He took out the earbuds and dropped them on the table. I sat in my swivel chair and rocked back.

"Well?"

He shrugged. "Meh. He's not bad."

At least I tried. I reached for my phone.

"I mean, he's okay," Andy said, emphasis on *okay*, and acting like he was suddenly the most important judge on a reality talent show or something.

"All right, thanks for listening." I pulled up Twitter, then glanced at the clock. "We're on in two."

"What's his history? Failed label? Newbie?"

"His band, Twenty-Four Tears, has been together a little over a year. He also leads music at a church."

Andy frowned. "Super religious."

I gave him a look. "He's actually really cool. You should hear him live."

Andy rubbed his chin. "Not a bad idea. Let me know the next time he's playing, and we'll go see him. We'll take Lana too. She's very good at sniffing out new talent. Also, she's desperate for time away from Timmy."

I grabbed my headphones and put them on as the producer began counting down on his fingers.

Andy did the same. "And like I said, he better not be good looking."

To my utter frustration, after texting Ben, I learned that Twenty-Four Tears didn't have anything lined up until late September. Somehow, a miracle truly, I talked Andy into visiting Ben's church with me the next Sunday morning to hear him sing. I enticed Lana with the fact that they provided free childcare for an hour and a half.

At the last second, I started to worry about Ben seeing me in the congregation. Remembering how he'd waved to me from the stage that one time, I pursed my lips, then found a pair of glasses I used sometimes for reading. I also grabbed a floppy hat. I figured his church was so casual, no one would care about a girl wearing a floppy hat.

I glanced in the mirror at myself incognito.

In the masses of people, I had no doubt he wouldn't notice me, especially like this. I sent Lana a quick text, telling her to meet me right outside the building, then dashed out to my car, running a tad late, and sped to the church. I was furious at myself for being late, since being late meant possibly missing the music. I ignored the parking lot attendants again, finding a spot as close as possible to the front. Lana had texted that they were going to go in and figure out where to leave Timmy. I ran in just as they were walking, hand in hand, out of the kids' section.

"Do we really have to go to church?" Andy asked, checking his watch. "Timmy's set for more than an hour. This is freedom. Let's go have coffee."

Lana cocked her head to the side. "Are you in disguise or something?"

"Or something." I grabbed Andy's arm and pulled him to the sanctuary, where the service had already begun. We found seats in the back. It wasn't the best lineup of songs to showcase Ben's voice, but it wasn't bad. Andy and Lana didn't sing along with the music. I kept stealing glances at Andy, wondering what he was thinking.

One thing I *knew* he'd recognize was how good Ben was with a crowd. How he engaged with the audience and how they responded to him.

After the music ended, we sat back down, and Andy passed me a note written on the church bulletin.

Lucky he's not good looking or anything.

I swallowed a giggle and elbowed him. Once the worship team was off stage, I took off my glasses, which were giving me a headache. I rubbed my eyes.

"So, as most of you know, Eric's father passed away last night. He'd been battling cancer for a long time, and the family knew this was coming. He was surrounded by his wife and children as he met Jesus. But because of that, I'm speaking today. Let's pray for Eric." I blinked in surprise at seeing Ben onstage again. He perched on a stool.

Ben is speaking? My pulse raced with nerves; I wasn't sure why.

"Is he a preacher too?" Lana leaned across Andy and whispered to me. I shook my head.

"No, he's just helping out today. I had no idea."

After the prayer, Ben took a breath. Even though we were in the back, I shrank against the seat, hoping he wouldn't see me.

"Eric asked me to speak to you about loss. I can't do that without telling you about Sadie."

Then I sat straight up. And I listened, heart pounding, as Ben shared the story of the sister he loved so much. At one point, I saw, out of the corner of my eye, Lana wiping away tears. Ben talked about hope amid hurt. And being real with people and with God. And being brave enough to love with what we have left.

I could hardly breathe as he said the words again slowly.

Love with what you have left.

I was crying too by the end of it.

At the end, Ben sang. Just Ben. He sang "Amazing Grace" a capella, and before he could finish, nearly every person in the church was standing, hands raised, singing in unison.

Afterward, Andy and Lana and I walked into the lobby. And by the way Lana was still wiping tears from her eyes and Andy's jovial manner now seemed pensive, I had a feeling that rather than me introducing them to Ben, Ben had just introduced them to God.

Milo had caught me in the lobby and said hello while Lana and Andy picked up Timmy. Once we were out on the sidewalk, I squinted at Andy. "What did you think?"

"It wasn't what I expected," Andy said, sliding on his sunglasses.

"I feel worn out," Lana told me. "That was such an emotional experience.

You're right, Deb. He's got an incredible voice. But there's more to him than that."

Oh, I knew it.

Lana slid her purse strap over her shoulder. "Come to lunch with us, Debra. Let's talk about it more."

I didn't feel like being alone, but I looked over my shoulder a bit regretfully. Now that I was here, so close to where Ben was, I half-hoped to see him. But I didn't see Ben in the sea of faces, so I turned back around and agreed to meet Lana and Andy at a nearby Mexican restaurant.

Fifteen minutes after sitting down in a booth with Andy's family (Timmy was stationed by me), I understood the reason Andy and Lana were desperate for a break from sweet Timmy. I was sitting on a booth covered in tortilla chip particles, Lana's water glass had been knocked over, and now Timmy was screeching, begging to play on the iPad, which Lana was frantically digging through her purse to find. When she realized she didn't have it, she and Andy exchanged a look of horror. The sheet of paper and three crayons the waitress had provided were very insufficient for our situation. Andy quickly downloaded a free game on his phone and passed it over to Timmy, and the three of us heaved a collective sigh of temporary reprieve.

"Kids are delightful," Lana assured me, "just not at restaurants. Every time we take Timmy out, we swear we'll never do it again; then we forget. Then we're reminded."

I nodded with fake understanding. *How* could you forget?

Our meal couldn't arrive fast enough; then we ate like a pack of wolves. And my seat was covered in rice, along with the chips.

"Andy, can you guys get him on the radio, or what?" Lana asked, taking a breath once she'd finished her plate of enchiladas.

Andy wiped his mouth, eyeing Timmy, who was back on his phone. "Maybe. I should run it by Mark, but I can most likely talk him into it. We could do one of those things where we play a song and let people call in and say 'Yea' or 'Nay.'"

"What's the story with you two?" Lana asked, suspicion lighting her eyes. "He's really cute . . . for a preacher."

Andy glared at me again. I laughed.

"He's *not* a preacher. He just leads the music. And he has a band on the side. Ben and I are just friends." I coughed and sipped my water, thinking of the kiss outside The Drunken Frog. "I met him through a mutual friend. The next time Twenty-Four Tears plays, we should go. He's a great performer, and the band treats each other like family."

Lana pulled out her phone and started searching for songs to download.

"Just friends?" Andy raised both eyebrows.

I flushed and looked down at our very messy table. "I mean, we've gone out a couple of times. He's a nice guy. But he doesn't even know I invited you today. I don't want to get his hopes up or anything. Ben is content where he is, but I think he's got what it takes to take Twenty-Four Tears to the next level."

Andy nodded seriously. "You're probably right. I can see that too. Let's see what Mark says. If I can get the green light, we'll highlight one of his songs next week. You choose."

"That would be so fantastic, Andy!" I tried not to get too excited. "I'd probably choose 'Ruin.' It's my favorite."

"Got it," Lana said, downloading the song onto her phone. Her eyes widened as Timmy abandoned Andy's phone and stuck his whole fist into the bowl of salsa. Within seconds, she'd grabbed that little fist with an iron grip and was wiping it clean while Timmy howled. Thankfully, our check came. Andy paid for my meal, ignoring my protest. Then we escaped the restaurant.

In the parking lot, Andy threw Timmy over his shoulder. Lana and I slowed our step as we walked together.

"I'm glad to hear you're dating again," she said in a soft voice. A regular listener, of course she knew my whole Miss Lonely Heart story.

"We're not really dating. I mean, we've just hung out a few times. But I do like him," I admitted. "I'm just a little worried because I'm not sure I can take another bad breakup."

Lana stopped and held me back. "Debra, you know, don't you, how strong you are? I listen to you guys on the radio and hear you holding your own with Andy—not always easy. I see this talented woman who picked herself up and started over in a brand-new state without knowing anyone. You are completely self-sufficient and capable. You're hilarious on the radio. You're beautiful and thoughtful. Andy says the studio got lucky the day you showed up."

I felt my heart squeeze at that. "Really?"

Lana nodded and smiled. "He's right. Whatever you've got going with that cute preacher, singer, whatever he is, run with it."

The last thing I'd said to Ben that night in Breckenridge was that I needed time to think. Other than texting him about when Twenty-Four Tears played again, we hadn't been in contact. But I was ready to talk. I had no idea what I wanted to say, but I wanted to talk to Ben Price.

After lunch Sunday, I put a load of laundry on and then sat on the sofa and texted him.

NICE SERVICE AT CHURCH TODAY.

A minute later, he replied.

MILO TOLD ME HE SAW YOU. I'M HEADED OVER TO ERIC'S HOUSE, TO BE WITH HIS FAMILY. CAN WE TALK SOON?

I waited just a second before typing back. MAYBE LUNCH THIS WEEK?

YES.

If possible, I wanted to talk to him in person about playing "Ruin" on the radio, once Andy was sure we could. It was a gamble, if we did what Andy suggested and let callers decide whether we'd keep playing the song or not. But it was one I was willing to bet on. I had a feeling listeners would connect with the song. And I'd make a plug for it on my Miss Lonely Heart segment. But by Tuesday, Ben was running ragged and I doubted I'd see him before the following week. Eric needed time off for the funeral and time to grieve, so Ben and the other staff were picking up the slack, handling all the things Eric normally took care of.

Thursday, Andy met me in the hallway at five fifteen in the morning. We were getting ready to go on the air. He gave me a thumbs-up.

"Mark said yes. We can play your boy's song. We'll do the call-in thing, so fingers crossed people like it. I'd like to do it as soon as possible. Go tell Jake to download the song so we're ready. And get your guys on the phone so we can get them to sign permissions and stuff."

My stomach dropped.

Oh gosh. I need to tell him. I hope Ben is cool with it.

I shot Ben a quick text to call me, then ran to the studio room to tell Jake, our music guy, and then was just able to slide into my chair and put my headphones on as we went live.

I didn't hear back right away, so I texted Paige too, asking her to give me Bryce's number. Then I had to set my phone aside because we were back and Andy was talking about our lunch date Sunday, specifically Timmy's role at the restaurant. We segued into celebrity gossip, which I was pathetically low on, and then went back to music. I grabbed my phone and called Bryce, glad Paige was responding even if Ben wasn't.

Bryce was more than thrilled. He assured me he'd get everything signed and back to our business department ASAP. He thanked me profusely for such a great opportunity and told me he'd be in touch. I felt a sense of strange relief that he'd be the one talking over everything with Ben. Surely Ben would be thrilled. Surely.

All I got from Ben was a quick text that night, letting me know that Bryce had called a meeting with the band and they were reading all the documents and signing everything.

You would have thought I was the singer for "Ruin." I was so edgy when ten o'clock rolled around the next day. I'd already mentioned it during my Miss Lonely Heart spiel. Andy led in, telling people to call right after and let us know whether they wanted us to keep it or trash it.

And then it was playing and I couldn't even breathe.

Paige was texting me, beyond excited, letting me know she'd told every person at the church and everyone would be listening in. I texted her back that she and Milo and every friend they had better call in to vouch for the song. The lines were lighting up and Andy had me answering them—apparently, he wasn't aware of the near out-of-body experience that was happening to me. Out of dozens of calls, I sighed with relief that only a handful of people said it wasn't for them.

When our shift ended, Andy gave me a high five. "Diamond in the rough, it is! We'll keep playing it. Good call, Hart. I've got a gut instinct that things are going to happen for preacher boy."

My gut was twisting, still nervous to talk to Ben. He had to be happy about the response. He had to.

"I cannot *believe* you got Twenty-Four Tears on the radio!" Paige squealed so loud that I flinched. I'd driven to her place right after my shift and we'd agreed to ride together to the new builds near her neighborhood. She parked out front of the model home and we walked up the sidewalk together.

Paige opened the door and we walked into a small office. A woman sat at a large mahogany desk. She gave us a folder of information with prices on the styles of paired homes that were being built and then told us to take our time walking through the model home.

"Wow," Paige breathed as we opened the nine-foot black front door and stepped onto gleaming dark hardwood floors.

"*Wow* is right," I muttered, flipping through the folder of prices. "Keep in mind that everything we see is an upgrade. I'd be downgrading to basic on everything."

Paige didn't respond. She was running her hand over the granite countertops and oohing and ahhing over the extended-length cabinets. Downgrade or not, I liked the idea of getting to pick out my own colors and styles throughout the house. The two-bedroom paired home was the ideal size for me. High ceilings made the rooms feel large, and I loved the big walk-in closet in the master bedroom. The kitchen reminded me of the one in my condo with good lighting and a nice island. The backyard was miniscule but still large enough for a small patio. I could buy an outdoor table-and-chairs set and spend gorgeous Colorado evenings outside. Maybe I would plant a small garden. I could create a home to my exact taste.

All by myself.

Well, maybe. There was the whole paying-for-it part that could get discouraging.

I took all the information and the saleswoman's number and promised to come in soon for a consultation. I wanted to come without Paige for that. Discussing finances seemed personal enough that it should be done alone. Plus, I figured I'd continue to price neighborhoods closer to downtown in the meantime. Still, having walked through the model house, being able to imagine having a place that was all mine—I was hooked on the idea. A home of my own would put an end to that question of *Was I staying?*

We drove back to Paige's house and Ben invaded my thoughts again. "How did Ben sound when you called him?" I asked. "I feel like he's being weird and not excited."

Paige frowned. "Huh. Well, he seemed shocked, but of course he would be. I'm sure he's thrilled, Deb. Anyone would be!"

In a perfect world, yes. I needed to talk to him.

Chapter Fifteen

Here's to the hearts that break.
La La Land

B en"—I leaned against the island in my kitchen on Saturday morning, my phone gripped in my hand—"are you mad or something? I'm sorry I didn't tell you before. I really meant to. I just wanted to tell you in person; then you were so busy at the church that week—and when we got a 'yes' from our producer to do it, we had to. I couldn't let that opportunity slip by. There was no guarantee it would come back around. That's why I called Bryce."

"I get it. I'm not mad."

I closed my eyes and rubbed my temples with my left hand. "What are you, then? Something seems off."

He sighed. "It's cool. The band is really thrilled. And we're getting crazy numbers of downloads everywhere—iTunes, Google Play, Pandora, you name it. I guess it was just a shock. That's not a bad thing, though—and I know you did it because you believe in us. That means a lot."

"I believe in *you*," I said, my tone dropping a notch.

"Thank you," he said, and I knew he meant it. For the first time in about twenty-four hours, I breathed a little easier.

"We should celebrate. Your song got on the radio!" I told him, eagerness finally creeping back into my voice.

"Yeah, definitely. This week was brutal, though. And I've got worship tomorrow. Can we do lunch Monday?"

"Sure," I agreed easily.

At the last minute, I went to church on Sunday. I figured I wasn't the first girl to go to church with ulterior motives of seeing a guy. I told myself I didn't have to stay for the message—I'd just go for the music. I'd just go to hear Ben. But then the pastor got up, after having lost his dad the week before, and I felt too guilty to skip out at that point. I was on the very back row, far left-hand side. The lights dimmed a bit as the pastor stood up to speak, and then Ben was squeezing in next to me.

"How did you know I was here?" I whispered, astounded that he found me. He leaned close to whisper back.

"I guess I was looking for you, Miss Lonely Heart."

I smiled. About ten minutes into the message, I felt even more guilty that I was too distracted by the fact that Ben and I were basically hip to hip in the crowded row to concentrate. I was having random thoughts about what it would be like to hold hands (or more) with Ben. The fact that he'd been singing praise songs just a few minutes before made me feel even more mortified. As the pastor began to wind up his message, Ben had to leave to go back onstage with the team.

At the first hint of a benediction, I was out the door, almost colliding with Paige, whose eyes were tinged red.

"Paige!" I exclaimed. She wiped her face.

"Hi. I'm surprised to see you."

"What's wrong?" I asked immediately. She pulled me outside with her and we sat on a bench.

"So I just heard that Milo asked this girl, Angie, out while we were in the mountains. A date! He finally mustered the strength to make a move, but it wasn't with me." Her nose was bright pink as tears filled her eyes again. "I heard about that last night from another friend. Then this morning, I run into him before church, and he's super nice and wondering if I could help him set up the stage and asking if I've got lunch plans."

"What did you tell him?"

"That I was busy and will be busy for a long time."

I nodded. "That was a good response."

"You think? I keep wondering if I should have just helped ... Who refuses to help set up for church? And as for lunch, maybe he was just being nice or maybe it's a group thing—"

"Hey," I interrupted. "Remember how you told me Ben's feelings matter too? Well, *your* feelings matter, Paige. It's okay to give yourself space from him."

Paige nodded, looking down at her hands. A warm gust of wind blew past us, and she had to push back her hair from her face. "I need to tell you something else too."

I felt a spike of trepidation. "Okay. Tell me."

"Jason friended me on social media."

I waited, but she didn't elaborate. "And?"

"That's all. He friended me and I tagged him in the pictures from the weekend in Breck. And he messaged me that he was glad he met me and maybe he'll see me this winter."

I pressed my lips together to avoid laughing at Paige. "Are you worried about how I'll feel about you being in contact with Jase?"

She nodded, sneaking a glance at me.

"Well, worry no more. I love Jason like a brother, but that's where it ends. I think it's great if you guys chat online."

"Are you sure?" she asked timidly.

I hugged her. "Thanks for considering my feelings, but yes, I'm sure. They don't come any better than Jason, Paige."

Monday, I was early to meet Ben for lunch at Tokyo Joe's again. We hadn't talked about the kiss. We hadn't talked about us. We'd barely talked about the radio thing. I sat near the window, watching him in the parking lot. He looked tired, even from a distance. The usual bounce in his step seemed subdued. A backward ball cap held down that hair of his. He ordered and then sat down across from me.

"So," he said.

"So," I responded. "It feels like there's a lot to talk about."

He nodded, taking off his hat, smoothing back his hair, then putting the hat back on. "Twenty-Four Tears got a spot at the Denver Music Festival. One of the bands had to pull out, and Bryce got a call."

My jaw dropped. "That's amazing!"

Both of our meals arrived and Ben started eating.

Why in the world didn't he seem more excited?

"Ben, do you want Twenty-Four Tears to get more exposure?"

He shrugged. "Yeah, sure."

Okay. Next subject. "We haven't talked about the kiss."

He grinned. "Which one?"

"Either."

He took another bite, then wiped his mouth and sucked down half his soda. "I would like for us to start dating. In my mind, we've *been* dating. But obviously, I've been living in a dreamland that's completely one-sided."

I laughed out loud. And he smiled that wicked smile that could induce a whole audience of women to fall in love with him.

"You're a worship pastor," I reminded him. He nodded.

"It's true. I'd forgotten, so it's good you keep reminding me. Can you look past that to my hidden qualities?"

It was hard not to just lean over the table and kiss that cute mouth again, but I restrained myself and managed a fake frown. "What are these hidden qualities?"

"We have to start dating for you to find out." Ben pushed aside his empty bowl, propped his elbows up on the table, and folded his hands.

"Hmm." I shook my cup of ice, needing a refill but not wanting to disrupt our discussion.

He reached over and laid his hand on the table, palm up, waiting for me to take it. That one gesture made my stomach tighten.

I'm not ready. He might change his mind.

I just stared at his hand, wanting to hold it but not quite able to.

He pulled his hand back. "Debra," he said, shaking his head as though frustrated. "Does it bother you that much that I'm on staff at a church?"

I shook my head. "No. It just makes me nervous that this might not work out. That we're not going in the same direction."

"That I would choose God over you?" He looked right in my eyes.

Ouch. My breath caught for a moment.

I let that sink in and tried to hold off the immediate indignation running through me that I would be passed over. That again I'd come in second best. It took effort, but I gave his comment at least *a little* of the attention it required. I had a feeling it would be haunting me for much longer.

I closed my eyes for a moment. Tokyo Joe's seemed like a ridiculous place to have such a serious conversation. When I opened my eyes, Ben was there, waiting on me.

"I don't think I'd ever ask you to choose God over me, Ben," I finally answered, not completely sure, but the words felt right. "The truth is, one of the things I like about you is how real your faith is. How it's all over you, like an old, broken-in, Tom-Petty-and-the-Heartbreakers T-shirt. But the reality is—there might be times you'd want me to go to church with you, and I'm not feeling it. There might be events you'd like me to help at, and for me it wouldn't be real, so I'd end up feeling fake. I might be showing up to that stuff for you, not God. I think that would start to wear at me. You'd want faith to be something that bonds us together. But for me, I needed God to show up and he didn't."

I could see him take every word to heart, his eyes never leaving me, his mouth tightening as I spoke. He inhaled, long and deep, and mixed feelings spiked and fell inside me, like beats on an old stereo. I wanted to hear his response, and then again, I wanted to hold his hand and maybe kiss him until I couldn't breathe. Dive in and let an uncertain future unfold.

"Well . . . we could keep being friends. I'd like us to try something more, but I can wait." He took off his hat and rustled his hands through his hair. "I just wonder if this is about me or about Luke. Is it that you don't want to go out with me, or is it that you still love Luke?"

Fair question, but the hairs on the back of my neck bristled. "Neither. It's not that I don't want us to date. I'm sitting here, right now, wanting to kiss you again."

I was angry, but Ben's eyes lit and his eyebrows jumped. "Really?"

I flushed.

"'Cause we can make that happen," he added, the adorably wicked grin back. But this wasn't fun and games for me.

"I'm *saying*, yes, I like you. But I can't chance getting in too deep again and ending up with a broken heart. I know I'll have to take that chance again one day, but eight months ago, I wanted to marry Luke. I was absolutely ready to have a wedding or elope or run to the justice of the peace—whatever he wanted—if it meant I could be married to him."

Ben sat back abruptly, crossed his arms, and looked away from me. His jaw tightened.

"Ben"—my voice eased up a bit—"I don't know if I still love him. I think—I hope—that I'm letting go of that. How do you just *stop* loving someone you gave your heart to? Keep in mind what this is for me—the love of my life broke up with me on Christmas Eve. Within a year, he's engaged to someone who used to be one of my best friends." I took a sharp, painful breath. "Is it all that surprising that I offer revenge advice as Miss Lonely Heart?"

He didn't answer for a moment. I wished we were alone, maybe on my sofa, where deeper questions could be asked. How did he stop loving Jane? Had he ever really loved her? What was it about me that made him think we should give *us* a try?

"Don't you think—I mean, it seems like you should be dating someone like . . . Mikayla."

He squeezed the bridge of his nose. "Mikayla again?"

"You know what I mean. Someone who wants to go to church with you. Someone who has more in common with you. C'mon, you're on staff. You don't think people might be confused as to why the worship pastor wants to date a girl who doesn't want to go to church?"

"I think you're the one who feels confused about that." He finally made eye contact with me.

"Yes, I am confused about it!" I said with exasperation.

"We need to talk more about this. But not here," Ben said, and I agreed. "We've got the Denver festival next week. Twenty-Four Tears will be one of the start-up bands. You'll be working."

"I'll be at KGBL's booth for hours with Andy. You should stop by and say hello. I'd love to introduce you to Andy."

Ben nodded. We walked out of the restaurant toward the parking lot, and my pulse started to jump, wanting things to be different.

Luke and Sara ... that was unforgivable for me. But the fact that here I was, wanting to hold hands with someone new, eight months after Luke broke up with me—the feeling made me angry at myself.

If I moved on, if I found even a measure of happiness—what if Luke and Sara used that to ease their guilt?

Maybe it was wrong, but I didn't want to help them feel better about hurting me.

Ben stopped in front of my car.

"Thank you for the picture. I loved how I felt in that moment and I don't want to forget it," I told him.

The corners of his mouth just barely tilted up. "You were fearless."

"No. I was nervous. I just did it anyway."

He stepped closer to me and I tried to take measured breaths. I sneaked a look up at him.

Dr. Clark's advice seemed extremely relevant.

Ben touched one of my wayward curls. "I can see the faith thing stresses you out, Deb. It doesn't stress me. God loves you. He holds us when we don't have faith to hold him. Remember Peter, trying to walk on water? He failed. God didn't let him drown. He just pulled him back up. If all it takes is faith as small as a mustard seed to move mountains—" He leaned his head down closer to me and whispered, "You can move mountains, Deb. *I* believe in you. You keep thinking I'm looking for perfect. You keep thinking I'm looking for someone who fits a stereotype." He shook his head.

"You don't realize—I *wasn't* looking. At all. I haven't for a really long time. So when you show up—messy in all kinds of ways—and I feel *something* ... Well, we all want to feel something, right?" His fingers lightly strummed their way down my arm, all the way to my wrist, and he took my hand in his, and I was shaking all over at that touch. "Faith is an unpredictable journey. I'll walk on it with you, if you want me to. Even as your friend. And wherever you land with it, I'm here."

He kissed my forehead, then stepped back, his warm fingers still intertwined with mine. "I'll text you this week, and we'll see each other at the festival next

Saturday. The next couple of weeks are going to be busy for me. Eric's decided to take a little more time off. He needs to. Now I've got studies to lead and visits to make and lots of meetings to go to."

Then he left. I just stood there, thinking, *So that's what it's like, holding hands with Ben Price.*

I'm in trouble.

"Does Twenty-Four Tears have a manager?" Andy asked me. We'd played "Ruin" again on Wednesday and had great response from listeners, both calling in and emailing, asking for more information about the band. "A friend of mine asked about them. And what's that next venue they'll be at?"

I sipped my second cup of coffee and plugged Twenty-Four Tears in the search engine on my laptop. "They actually got a spot at the music festival in Denver. You'll hear them live. And then they're playing at Percival's Island again at the end of September." I searched web results. "I'm not even seeing a website. Hmm. Ben told me that Bryce was the one who got the call about the opening at Denver Fest. Maybe he's working as pseudomanager, lining stuff up for them." I scrolled down. "They do have a Facebook page. It needs a little work—a few more pictures, more info."

"You better help this guy out, Deb. People are taking notice right now. I wonder how many downloads of 'Ruin' they've had."

"I don't know. Ben only said it was crazy how many they were getting."

I friended Karis online and sent her a quick message, asking who set up gigs for them and whether they'd had any professional photos taken or considered creating a website. Then we were back on the air and wasting way too much time talking about the latest A-list celebrity couple to split.

"I watched E! last night and they did this whole spiel about how amicable the split is and how they'll be best friends forever and blah blah blah." I swiveled in my chair. "Why are they always supposedly amicable? Why are they always going to be friends after?"

"Well," Andy countered, "they're not *always* amicable. Especially when it comes to younger celebrities, don't you think? I mean, there are all these songs written about exes. And then there are compromising photos leaked by someone who had access."

"Yeah, yeah." I waved him off. "But for the most part, they say the same things again and again. 'We're focusing on our careers' or 'With tons of love and respect, we've decided we can no longer stand to be in the same ten-thousand-square-foot house.'"

Andy nearly spit out the mouthful of Mountain Dew he'd just thrown back. He choked, then howled with laughter. "Okay, you're right. Celebrity breakups do sound like that most of the time. I've known a lot of people who've broken up, and yeah, for the most, it's not amicable. They usually make the best of it, but it can take years to get to a point where it's all good and easy. Not for everyone, of course." Andy leaned into his mic. "Don't flood us with calls about how you and your ex give each other new relationship advice. We're talking celebrity breakup statements."

"I think regular people should be able to send out statements as well. Oh gosh, that first holiday after my breakup, I wished I could just wear a sign around my neck that read, 'He dumped me. Don't ask.'"

Andy chuckled. "Bad?"

"Like I said, don't ask."

"Well, whenever I broke up with someone—this was back in my younger days, before the leaking of private photos, thank goodness." Andy tapped his phone on the table. "The textbook line was that I hoped we could still be friends." I snorted my disapproval at Andy. "Come on, Deb. You're saying when your boyfriend broke up with you, he didn't say that he hoped you guys could still be friends?"

I didn't even want to remember that horrible night. But I knew without a doubt, Luke had *not* said that. "He knew that was never going to happen. And he wasn't the kind of guy to say things just for the sake of saying them." My breath stopped short. No, Luke didn't like to waste words.

"Maybe tomorrow we should take a few call-ins, hear about what people have said during breakups. To stay friends or not to stay friends—that is the question," Andy said, grinning at his own cleverness. "What do you say, Miss Lonely Heart?"

Ugh. Talk about wasting words. When would I learn to keep my mouth shut?

Chapter Sixteen

Why didn't you tell me I was in love with you?
Easter Parade

I wasn't sure what to expect when it came to September in Colorado. To be honest, after several years in Texas, I was looking forward to enjoying a fall season with cool breezes and colored leaves. But we were halfway into September and it still felt like summer, just with cooler nights. I'd put on sunscreen for the Denver Music Festival as well as brought a hoodie. It seemed like in Colorado, the weather changed by the hour. I'd decided to take the light rail that afternoon, rather than drive to 16th Street, where the festival was taking place. By the time I found our booth, everything was set up and Andy was waiting for me. The crowd was starting slow and building.

Karis had messaged me back about the fact that Bryce usually did their booking for them and, no, they didn't have a website or professional band photos. She seemed more talkative than Ben when it came to the band, so we exchanged numbers. She'd told me Twenty-Four Tears was going to be one of the first bands playing at the music festival, sometime around three o'clock. I'd texted Paige to see whether she wanted to come, and she assured me that their group of friends from church was coming to see Twenty-Four Tears. She also said she'd ask Milo (despite the fact that she was avoiding him) whether he could bring his good camera to the festival and take a few shots of the band.

All good things.

Andy and I weren't near the stage, which saddened me, but I'd hear the bands just fine from our booth. I wanted desperately to see Twenty-Four Tears, but I had to man the table at that time. I made a plug for them on the radio, of course. Paige and Milo and their friends stopped by the booth to say hello. Paige had brought me churros from a nearby vendor, and I decided our friendship was now settled for all time.

I'd been shocked by how many people stopped by to "meet" Miss Lonely Heart. Andy had built up the fact that she—I mean, I—would be at the booth, and a steady stream of people came over to talk to me. I was tweeting out about the bands and the booth and the food every few minutes.

I felt jittery with excitement as three o'clock rolled around. Karis had told me this festival was the largest venue Twenty-Four Tears had ever played at, thanks to Bryce, who'd been the one to submit their band for consideration and had gotten them on the wait list. And once they started to play, I had to force myself to sit in the booth, rather than run out and bounce up and down with the crowd.

Andy and I were on the air until five, at which time our popular afternoon duo was taking over. Around four forty-five, Ben showed up at the booth, looking like the rock star I knew him to be. Black skinny pants, loose white shirt, half of his hair up in a topknot. I introduced him to Andy, hoping Andy would not attempt to embarrass me.

"So Debra is your number one fan," Andy teased.

Out of luck on the no-embarrassment thing.

"She bribed my wife and me with free childcare to come see you at your church," Andy continued. Where was Lana when I needed her?

Ben blinked in surprise. He stood under the awning of our booth, sweating, an empty water bottle in his hand. "You did?" He looked at me. I was already red faced from the heat of the afternoon, and I hoped my face didn't flush more. I just waved off the whole thing.

"Not a big deal. I wanted him to hear you, and at the time, you guys didn't have anything until the end of September. So we went to church."

"My wife actually really enjoyed hearing you speak. I did too," Andy said, a tad more serious.

"You guys did so good up there today," I said, trying to redirect the conversation. "We could hear you from here. And really, home run, Ben."

"Thanks." He talked shop with Andy a little more, and then Lana and Timmy showed up.

"Ben!" Lana exclaimed. Ben turned to her. "I mean, you don't know me. But Deb's got me hooked on your stuff. I feel like I know you." She flashed him a smile, while Timmy hung on her leg and whined for more ice cream.

"It's great to meet both of you," Ben said, shaking her hand.

"The four of us should get together sometime," Lana said brightly.

"What about our well-behaved son?" Andy asked as we all watched Timmy, now writhing around Andy's leg and moaning loudly that he wanted to leave.

"We can get a sitter or something," Lana hissed at Andy.

Ben and I exchanged a glance. They were talking to us as though we were a couple.

"That would be so fun," I answered.

"I've got a friend who'd be interested in hearing from you if Twenty-Four Tears starts seeking representation," Andy offered. I bit my lower lip. For Andy to offer, that was just nicer than I could have expected. Anxiety bubbled up in me that Ben might not react positively, like the lukewarm way he'd been responding to me about the band lately. But Ben nodded, his face serious.

"Thanks so much, Andy. I really appreciate that. Let me talk to the band. And, Lana, I would love for the four of us—or the five of us—to hang out." He winked at Timmy.

I breathed a sigh of relief. Ben looked over at me. "Do you want to stay and join up with Paige and the others?"

"Sure, let me get my bag. Are you hungry?"

"Starving. I couldn't eat this morning."

"Nerves?" Andy asked with a grin.

Ben nodded. "Yeah. We were all a little shaky."

"You did great," I assured him, then paused. Now I felt like we *were* a couple.

I ignored the uneasy feeling that swirled through my stomach and instead grabbed my bag. We said goodbye to Andy and Lana and Timmy, then made our way to the food vendors because Ben had passed a barbecue sandwich station that, he told me, smelled like heaven and he had to have a sandwich. We both ended up getting smoked sliced-beef sandwiches. Ben got a text from Milo and we found them in the crowd as another band took the stage.

We stayed for hours. Dancing with the crowd as the sun set and the more high-profile bands started to play. Before it got too dark, Paige and I decided to go for a quick bathroom break. I was glad I'd brought a hoodie and pulled it on as the night air dropped several degrees.

"Are you okay being around Milo?" I asked her on our way back.

"Yeah. It's fine. But all day he's been overly nice to me. I haven't heard any more about him and Angie, so maybe the date didn't go so great. I'm keeping my distance, though. I'm upping the bar."

"Oh yeah?" I said with a hint of a smile.

She nodded. "I want someone who looks at me like Ben looks at you," she said. My smile vanished.

"Paige—" I started, but she shook her head.

"No arguments. How you feel about him is one thing. How he feels about you is another." Paige picked up her pace. "Come on. It'll be harder to find everybody once it gets darker." She was right, so we quickly made our way through the crowd. Ben waved at me as we got closer. I slid in next to him.

"I think I might have to leave soon," he said, speaking into my ear so I could hear above the music. "I'm singing at church tomorrow too," he said, almost regretfully. He didn't want to leave.

"Did you drive?" I asked him. He shook his head. "No, I came with Bryce in the van, with all our equipment. Karis has to get back, so maybe I'll catch a ride with her."

"I'm taking the light rail back. Want to go together?" I asked.

"Yes."

We let the gang know we were leaving, then tried to maneuver our way through the crazy crowd back to Union Station. Ben took my hand—I think mainly so we wouldn't lose each other. But that "couple" feeling returned as he led me through downtown. He didn't let go, even as we stood in line to hop on the train.

I didn't let go either.

Once we were on the train, my phone started buzzing. I pulled it out of my bag. Texts were rolling in from Texas.

Lily had her baby! Logan Fox Spencer. Eight pounds 13 ounces. –Addi

The bun is out of the oven. Heading to the hospital now. –Jason

Meet the fox. Lily and Logan are doing great.—Sam

Sam's text included a picture of a sleeping baby with a tuft of blond hair on the top of his head.

I was laughing and smiling and showing Ben. And then I was crying. Because I wasn't there. I wouldn't be there.

Ben's arm was around me, my head on his shoulder, while I cried the whole way home.

It rained Sunday morning. I slept late and stayed in my pajamas most of the day, receiving text messages periodically from Addi, along with a slew of pictures of little Logan Fox Spencer, the cutest baby I'd ever seen, swaddled in forest-themed blankets, a teeny brown beanie on his head. I got online and ordered flowers to have sent to Lily's house in a few days. Then I heated up leftover Chinese food and lounged on the couch. Needing the comfort of something familiar, I turned on one of my favorite musicals ever, *The King and I*, and made popcorn. As Deborah Kerr and Yul Brynner twirled to "Shall We Dance?," I munched on buttery, salty popcorn and tried not to think about Addison and Glen, and Sara and Luke, and Jason, and Sam, all hovering around Lily in a hospital room, taking turns holding that little bundle of joy.

I tried not to think about the ride home the night before. How Ben had held me as we sat on the train. And as tears soaked my face, he'd leaned in and whispered, "It's okay, baby. I'm here." Like I was his. Then he walked me to my car and kissed me, and I came back alone to my apartment.

In short, I tried not to think about how lonely I felt. Late afternoon, Ben texted me that he was thinking about me, which I appreciated. But I didn't feel like responding. My mother called, but I didn't want her to hear the inevitable sadness in my voice and worry her further, so I let the call go to voice mail. The woman from the model home left a message about scheduling a time for our consult. I didn't feel like talking to anyone. Instead, I watched another movie and cleaned my apartment. Finally I ate cereal for dinner and went to bed early.

I worked all week, texting Ben now and then, enjoying a week of afternoon rain showers that mirrored my mood. I spent the next couple of weeks working a lot and staying home a lot. Saturday, September 30, Paige asked me to go with her to Percival's Island to hear Twenty-Four Tears, but I woke up that morning with a bad headache and an overall antisocial attitude. I promised her we'd go together to the next gig, but I stayed hunkered down in my apartment. Late that night, I got a text from Ben.

Missed seeing our number one fan.

I missed hearing you guys. Hope you rocked it. I'll be there next time.

Monday after work, I got a text from Karis.

We took band photos yesterday afternoon! Keep an eye on our new website this week and you'll see them. Thanks for a great idea. We're booked pretty solid through December. The radio play has helped so much. Thanks, Deb.

I was glad to hear that. Though I wondered how Ben was feeling. We'd both been busy and I hadn't heard from him as much. I finally texted him and asked him if he'd like to come over for dinner Friday. Casual. Just spaghetti and salad. My cooking skills didn't go much further than that.

He was set to arrive around six o'clock and I started getting nervous around noon. Wondering why I'd asked him. Wondering what we'd talk about. Wondering if he might kiss me again. Wondering if I was okay with that.

By 5:50 I was a nervous wreck. I'd changed clothes twice. Ending up in just jeans and one of my favorite T-shirts, the one my brother had given me for my birthday the year before—with John Travolta and Olivia Newton-John's faces on it in a *Grease* embrace.

He was five minutes late.

I opened the door, and there stood Ben. Jeans, sneakers, and a green T-shirt. His hair styled to perfection. A simple rope chain bracelet on his wrist.

"I was going to bring flowers—" he started to say.

"This is not a date," I said quickly.

He frowned. "But I brought this instead." He handed me a rolled-up T-shirt. I took the shirt, unrolled it, and held it up.

"A Twenty-Four Tears T-shirt!" I squealed. He was still grimacing from my pointed comment about the nondate. "Thank you." I hugged him, hoping to move past the awkward moment. He held me loosely and barely patted my back before stepping away.

"Bryce thinks we need to make T-shirts. This was trial number one." Plain black tee, the words *Twenty-Four Tears* in stark white, along with a white guitar.

"I like it," I told him. We sat down across from each other at my small high-top table and ate plates of spaghetti and salad. "Karis texted me and said you guys have been getting more gigs, that you're booked through December."

"Yeah." Ben twirled a forkful of spaghetti. "This is good, Deb."

I brushed off the compliment. Spaghetti noodles and meat sauce. Nothing special. "And you took band photos, and you're making T-shirts, and you said you were getting downloads like crazy. Ben, are you thinking about this? Do you want to talk to Andy's friend who's a manager? What did Bryce and the others say?"

"Cautiously optimistic. Bryce has always booked everything for us, but he's open to talking to a manager eventually. But—I don't know—Karis's mom, and Xander and Emily and the new baby, and work for me has been constant. I'm not sure how to fit in more."

He put down his fork and sighed. And I realized how overwhelmed he was.

"So, two days after the festival, Bryce got a call. One of the bands—Chasing Summer, have you heard of the them?—asked if we'd be interested in opening for them during their spring tour. Their manager was scouting for new acts, and they liked Twenty-Four Tears."

My mouth fell open. "Karis did not even tell me. And *have I heard of Chasing Summer*? Um, I work for a radio station. They've had one hit after another. Yes, I've heard of them. Oh, Ben, that is incredible!"

"I don't see how we can, Deb. We all have jobs. We can't just not work."

I sobered. "But it would be such an incredible opportunity. And it could turn into something huge for you guys. This could be your shot."

"Maybe," he agreed, but he seemed hesitant. "We're talking about it. They gave us a couple of weeks to look over schedules and see if we can make it work."

He tapped his fingers on the table. "Karis started saying that I had to do it, even if she couldn't. And Xander said the same thing. I can't do that, Deb. I'm just as locked down here as they are."

We could hear thunder rumble outside, and I could hear the conflict in Ben's voice. The band was like family. And I knew all about having friends who were like family. I stood up and pushed back the floor-length curtain covering the back door. A heavy gray sky let loose a spattering of raindrops, with the promise of more to come.

"Want coffee?" I asked Ben. "I made lemon-cake bars. My mother's recipe."

His smile returned. "Both sound great." I turned on my favorite online playlist while he cleared the table; then I dished out dessert. "Tell me more about your family," he said, leaning over the island as I set a cup of coffee in front of him. Outside, the rain came down harder. The sound of rain falling in sheets reminded me of the rush of the river on our camping trip. The water sounded like life—movement and beauty and intensity. Washing away and replenishing all at once.

I sat on the barstool next to him and we ate lemon-cake bars and sipped coffee, and I told him about my family in Minnesota. Then we moved to the sofa and watched the auditions for one of those reality singing shows, critiquing everybody and cheering for who we thought should make it. And we drank more coffee and shared stories from high school and college. It was after ten when someone pounded on my door, and my heart jumped into my throat. I got up, and Ben did too, walking with me to the door. I checked the peephole and saw my neighbor. I opened the door quickly. There stood Jake.

"Jake, hi. Is everything okay?" I asked him.

He shook his head. "Cassidy is burning up with fever, and I think I need to find a twenty-four-hour Urgent Care. Is there any way you could watch Gilly for us? She's asleep right now, but she'll be up in an hour probably, needing a bottle. Cassidy is so miserable; we need antibiotics or something to help with the fever. She can't help with Gilly, and I—"

"It's not a problem," I said immediately. "This is Ben. Ben, Jake." I made the introduction fast. Jake shook his hand.

"Like I said, Gilly's asleep. If you both want to come over, that's fine. I'm sorry to ask." Jake glanced back nervously at his door, two feet from mine. I grabbed my keys and Ben turned off the TV. We followed Jake into his condo, which was a wreck.

"Sorry for the mess. Cass has been sick a couple of days, and with Gilly—" He shrugged.

"Don't even think about it," I told him. Cassidy came limping out of the bedroom and I gasped. Pale and shaking, circles under her eyes. "Any instructions?" I asked, knowing Gilly was maybe eight months old and I wasn't an expert on babies. Jake and I exchanged cell numbers.

"She's not sleeping through the night yet," Cassidy rasped. Jake put his arm around her waist.

"She'll probably wake up and want a bottle. They're ready-made in the fridge. Just pop it in the bottle warmer on the counter. There are diapers and wipes in her room. And thanks, Debra."

"You guys go." I motioned to the door. Cassidy looked ready to fall to the floor. "If you don't find an Urgent Care open, take her to the ER," I told Jake and he nodded. They left and I locked the door, then turned to look at Ben. His head was downward.

"Ben?" I asked.

He glanced up. "Just praying," he said. Then he looked around the apartment. "Where do we start?" he asked.

I shook back my hair and rubbed my forehead, looking at the condo. "You don't have to stay. I can handle this."

"I'm here, Deb. I want to help you. I can tackle the dishes."

"But we don't want to wake the baby."

"Well, I'm pretty sure they said she'll wake up one way or the other, and I think it would help more if they came home to a cleaner condo."

"True. Okay. You start on the dishes. I'll pick up the living room and see what else I can do."

After throwing away trash and tidying the living area, I peeked into their laundry room, which was overflowing with clothes. It was also missing a washer and dryer. I walked back into the kitchen. "They have a ton of laundry and no washer or dryer."

"Really?" Ben asked, loading the dishwasher. "Do you have one?"

I nodded. "Yeah. I found a used, compact, stacked washer-and-dryer set online. I think I'll take over a load of baby clothes and wash them at my place. Maybe I can do a load of towels too. Be right back."

I carried one of the overflowing hampers to my apartment and loaded the washer, then went back to Jake and Cassidy's. Ben had finished the dishes and was wiping down the counter. Once he finished, I asked him to take the trash bags outside to the dumpster. When he came back, I ran over to my apartment to put the clothes in the dryer. Then he and I sat on the sofa, silent and tired.

"Thanks for staying," I said with a yawn, curling into him. I'd just closed my eyes for a moment when we heard Gilly crying through the monitor. Ben and I traded wide-eyed looks. I jumped up and tiptoed to the room.

"She's already awake, Deb. I don't think you need to tiptoe."

"Right. You stay out here; she might be overwhelmed by two strangers."

Ben nodded. I went into the baby's room and reached for Gilly, who started howling louder when she saw that I was neither of her parents. She was reaching new levels of loudness when Ben peeked into the room.

"How about I hold her and you warm up the bottle? I can't figure out the warmer," he said. I handed her over and dashed to the kitchen. I saw the conundrum about the warmer; it needed water poured in for steam. I ended up guessing on the amount and pushing the button. When it seemed fairly warm, I grabbed the bottle and ran back to the room. There in the dark, Gilly had quieted. Ben stood by the crib, holding her, swaying from side to side, and singing softly. I was frozen by the door, unable to look away. The light from the hallway spilled into the room and I could see Ben as he rubbed Gilly's back gently.

"Deb? The bottle?" he whispered again.

"Here!" I almost tripped going into the room. He handed Gilly over to me. Her eyes were drooping. I sat down in the rocker in the corner of the room and put the bottle to her lips. She went after it like a milkshake. Ben stepped back toward the doorway, then turned and watched us for a second. I wondered if he felt all the things I'd just felt while watching him. With a final glance, he left the room. I rocked Gilly, enjoying the weight of her in my arms. My thoughts went to Lily, what she must be feeling as she rocked Logan. I'd wished I could be there, take my turn holding Lily and Sam's little one.

But here I was, Gilly's sweaty little head against me, her lips smacking as she devoured that bottle. They hadn't said anything about burping her, but she sucked down the bottle so fast that I decided to try. I lifted her to my shoulder, rubbing that tiny back and feeling Gilly sniffle and whimper in my ear. Once she was completely silent, I stood up, my body tense as I tried not to jostle her whatsoever, and I laid her back in the bed, then crept backward out of the room. I tiptoed back into the living room. Ben had turned off the bright lights, leaving on the pendant lamps over the island. He'd brought the hamper of clean baby clothes back. The TV was on, muted. Ben sat on the couch, flipping through channels. I glanced at the clock on the wall. Eleven forty-five. With a huge yawn, I sat down and pulled over the hamper to fold.

"I put the towels in the dryer," Ben told me, resting his arm behind me on the back of the sofa.

"Thank you. For everything. You don't have to stay. I know it's late," I told him. I looked at him, pink onesie in my hand, Ben's head resting on the back of the couch.

He gave me a tired smile. "I'm good."

I tried not to think ridiculous thoughts ... of Ben holding Gilly. Of what it would be like one day for me to live with someone, to warm up bottles for my own baby, to look at someone on the sofa—namely Ben—exchanging weary smiles while our baby slept in the next room.

I folded half the hamper, then leaned back on the sofa next to Ben.

The next thing I knew, someone was saying my name. I opened my eyes.

"Hey, your phone just buzzed. Better check if it's Jake and Cassidy," he said. I rubbed my eyes and sat up, reaching for my phone on the end table.

"They're on their way back," I told him. "Looks like they ended up going to the ER. She's got a really bad case of strep. But they got her on antibiotics and got some fluids in her." I groaned. "I should get the towels."

"Already done. I didn't fold them, but they've got clean towels."

"Oh, good. Thanks."

I rested my head back for a moment.

"That's three, Deb," Ben said.

I gave him a side glance. "Huh?"

"The third time you've fallen asleep when we're together."

I laughed as quietly as possible. "I'm always tired."

His hand found mine, and we both sat there, heads laid back, breathing steadily as the minutes passed midnight and beyond.

"Are we dating or what?" Ben finally spoke.

"I don't know," I whispered. "Do you think you're going on tour?"

"I don't know." He sighed. I sat up, pushing my hair back. He sat up as well, then leaned over and rested his elbows on his knees.

"Hey," I said. He glanced up at me, his eyes glazed with a mixture of weariness and desire; then he leaned over to kiss me. But I was so tired. So unsure. I placed a hand on his chest and gently pushed him back.

"No, Luke. We have to think about this."

I froze. Ben's eyes steeled. "My name is Ben."

We heard the door unlock at that moment, and Jake and Cassidy came in. Ben jumped up and my heart split.

It was an accident.

I'm sorry.

I wanted to pull him back, rewind the moment.

But there was no undoing what had been done. There was no undoing the hurt I felt and the hurt I caused. No going back. Didn't I know that on so many levels? Wasn't that the heavy regret I woke up with and went to sleep with?

Cassidy went straight to bed, dead on her feet from the exertion of being weak and up so late. Jake just kept saying thank you. Ben and I assured him that we were happy to help. Then we moved into the hallway. Their door closed, and Ben immediately turned and walked down the hallway.

"Ben!" I called out.

He kept walking.

Chapter Seventeen

There are moments that the words don't reach.
There is a grace too powerful to name.
Hamilton

Debra," Dr. Clark said calmly. "It's okay. It was a slip of the tongue. He knows that. He'll get over it."

I shook my head as I sat, wrapped in a fleece blanket on the sofa in her office. My curls whipped past my face as my head turned from side to side. "I feel like I should go to Texas. Confront Luke. Scream in his face or something."

Dr. Clark's eyebrows raised and her chin dipped. "Hmm. Well, that can go on our list of options." I tightened the blanket around me. "Do you blame Luke for last night?" Dr. Clark pressed.

"I blame him for everything!" I snapped. Then I squeezed my eyes closed, knowing how that sounded. "No," I corrected. "He wasn't there last night. Or maybe he was. And that's the problem. He's everywhere and I haven't let go yet."

"I think you have," Dr. Clark said after a moment. "I think it was an honest mistake. This happens. People accidentally say the wrong name. It's unfortunate, especially for Ben, of course, but it's not the end of the world. What are you afraid of right now?"

"That Ben won't forgive me. I mean, I know he will. That's who he is. But he might not want to pursue me anymore. I texted him last night, as soon as he left. And I told him I was sorry. He never responded." I hit my forehead with the palm of my hand. "Ben is amazing. Why should he keep trying with a crazy person who can't get over her last breakup?"

"Well, it was a difficult breakup in many ways. The timing alone ..." Dr. Clark got up and came and sat next to me on the sofa. "But I hear you saying that you want Ben to keep pursuing you. That tells me you've moved on more than you'll acknowledge."

I replayed her words in my mind, trying to absorb them.

"What should I do?" I asked.

Dr. Clark crossed her ankles and folded her hands in her lap. "Well, you could do nothing. But that would leave Ben feeling like he doesn't matter and the two of you would never get past this. You could fly to Texas and scream at Luke, but you would end up feeling worse and lose the ground you've gained. Or you could tell Ben that you're sorry—find a way to make him hear you—and let him decide on his next step. Give him the space he needs. One thing you need to do is decide, in your heart, what it is you want from Ben. You've told me before that you've worried Luke was just stringing you along, that he knew deep down that he couldn't marry you.

"Be sure you don't do that to Ben."

I didn't blink. My eyes started to burn. I would never want to hurt anyone the way Luke had hurt me. I'd never want to break a person's heart the way Luke had broken mine.

"Take some time to really evaluate your feelings for Ben. I'm not saying you need to be ready to jump into a long-term commitment with him, Debra. But to be fair, you need to know your own heart." Dr. Clark patted my hand and stood up. "You know what you need to do." She went back to her desk chair and sat down.

I removed the blanket from my shoulders and set it next to me. "I'm thinking I should buy a house. A townhouse actually."

Dr. Clark peered at me over her glasses. "Really? That's a big decision, Debra. What's brought this on?"

I bit my lip for a moment before answering. "I was thinking I need to have something of my own. I told you I thought Luke and I would buy a house and start a family. Well, I can buy my own house without him."

She didn't answer, just studied me for several uncomfortable seconds.

"I mean, maybe I can buy one. Housing is so expensive and I haven't been working out here that long. But I went and looked at some new paired homes. And I called a realtor last week and talked to her about the market right now. I just ... I want something that's mine."

She nodded and then inhaled. "And then you'll know you're staying."

"Right," I agreed, then frowned. "Well, I am staying, of course. Where else would I go? I love it out here. The climate is perfect. My job is ideal."

She gave me a small smile. "I'm not arguing with you, Debra. Buying a home can be a positive thing. It's also a huge life choice, which, since you have a lease until May, you have plenty of time to think about. I like that you want to build a life here. I'm just wondering ..."

"What?" I asked with a tinge of annoyance.

"From what you've described, Luke was your anchor not too long ago. You were tethered to him, and you wanted to be. Without him, maybe you're looking for a new anchor. And maybe that looks like a house right now."

I stopped breathing for a second, then exhaled slowly, letting her words settle. "Is that a bad thing?" I finally asked. She tapped her pen on the table.

"No, not necessarily. Let's keep talking about it as you find out your options. This might be really good for you."

I agreed, relieved she hadn't tried to talk me out of it.

I left her office that Monday afternoon and went home. There were people in the hallway, rolling a dolly out of Jake and Cassidy's apartment. I ran over. Jake was shaking hands with some guy.

"Hi, what's going on?"

Jake looked at me, a look of disbelief on his face. "Debra, some people from Ben's church gave us a washer and dryer. They're used but in great shape. Can you believe that?"

My heart tugged.

Yes, I can believe that.

"That's great, Jake. How's Cassidy doing?"

"She's doing better. It will be a couple of days before she's herself again. She's just tired and weak. I need to run to the grocery store." He scratched his head, and I wondered if he knew there was baby spit-up on his shirt.

"Want to leave Gilly with me so Cassidy can sleep?"

"Are you sure? Would you mind?" Jake looked uncertain. "I can be back in an hour."

"I don't mind, Jake," I told him.

Relief smoothed the lines on his face. "You and Ben have helped us so much. I don't even know how to thank you."

"Hey, we're neighbors. Now go get me that cute baby."

Jake darted back into his apartment. I unlocked my door and left it open. A couple of minutes later, Jake came in, carrying Gilly and her diaper bag. After a few quick instructions, he left for the grocery store, and Gilly and I settled on the living room floor with a few of her baby toys. While Gilly gurgled and gnawed on a plastic giraffe, I grabbed my phone and texted Ben.

Jake and Cass just got the washer and dryer. Thanks for making that happen.

I waited several minutes. No response. I set the phone aside and played with Gilly. When Jake got home, Gilly was on my hip as we surveyed the refrigerator contents. I packed up her things and handed him the diaper bag. "So Gilly and

I are BFFs now. You can ask me to watch her anytime."

Jake smiled and took Gilly, kissing the top of her head. "Thanks so much. It means a lot to me that we have a friend we can count on to help. We moved out here last year for my job, so we don't have any family nearby. Cassidy's made a few friends at a moms' club in the area but no one she's really close to yet. Maybe we'll try Ben's church when Cass is feeling well. It would be nice to know more people."

After Jake left, I made a bowl of soup for dinner and watched TV, thinking about what Dr. Clark had said. We seemed to be in a season of evening rain showers. Thunder rolled overhead again. It reminded me of Texas, where I'd experienced multiple thunderstorms. I hadn't realized I'd missed the rain while here in dry Colorado, but as the thunder boomed, my soul seemed to respond, wanting the water to come down.

My thoughts ran in a million different directions. When the rain finally started to fall, I opened my back door wide, not caring that water splashed indoors. I left the door open so I could hear the splatters on the ground. I sat on a chair and just watched the rain, thinking of Texas, thinking of Luke and our friends, thinking of how my life had looked so different a year before. We'd danced in the rain once, Luke and I. We'd gone out to dinner and he'd brought me back to my apartment. We'd dashed through the parking lot, rain soaking my hair. Then I'd stopped, taken his hand, and pulled him to me, and we'd danced, right there in the parking lot.

I wondered if he ever danced in the rain with Sara.

The rain grew louder and began to change. I got up and moved closer, watching as little icy balls started to hit the ground, clattering as they fell. Harsher than before, hail came down. I closed the back door but kept watching. I used to hate being alone. Not so much anymore.

But I'd hurt Ben. After all he'd done to help, I'd blurted out Luke's name. Was Luke still so much in my head? I reran last night like a movie reel.

It was Ben washing dishes.

Ben praying.

Ben singing to Gilly.

Ben putting towels in the dryer.

Ben waking me up when I fell asleep.

Ben with that look in his light brown eyes that unnerved me—desire and challenge and excitement and intimacy. Ben with his dark hair twisted in a topknot. Ben with stubble on his face and that dark tattoo snaking down his arm as he played the guitar. With Nike sneakers and rock-band T-shirts and a voice that reached me when nothing else could.

Ben ... in my head.

The hail rattled louder, hitting the window, pouring over the roof. I reached for my phone and sent another text.

You're more than my second friend.

The rest of the week passed without a word from Ben. Paige invited me to her place Friday night. She shared a paired home with two roommates in Centennial, a little farther south from where I lived. But one of her roommates was out of town, and the other was a nurse who worked the night shift at Sky Ridge Hospital. She had the place to herself and wanted to cook dinner for me. I showed up at seven with a bottle of Moscato wine. Paige opened the door with a squeal and a big hug.

"I'm so excited that you're here!"

I considered the way I normally greeted Paige when she came to my house—rarely with squeals and hugs. I'd have to work on that. I handed her the wine and followed her into the kitchen.

"Something smells good. What are we having?" I asked, setting my purse on the counter.

"We're having chicken divan. It's Daneal's recipe—she's the nurse. She gave me the recipe and told me to make it whenever I wanted to impress someone. So this is me impressing you. I hope you like broccoli. And curry."

"I'm easy," I assured her. "I like everything when it comes to food."

"Oh, good. Pour us a couple of glasses of that wine. We can dish out plates here and eat at the coffee table. And in honor of you, I got a movie for us to watch. I've never seen it, but it seems right up your alley."

"What is it?" I asked, grabbing a wine glass and filling it halfway with Moscato.

"*La La Land.* Heard of it?"

"Of course. You'll love it."

"Hmm," Paige responded as she filled two plates with large portions of chicken divan.

We sat on the sofa, our plates on our laps, a basket of French bread on the coffee table, along with our wine glasses. The casserole—chunks of chicken in a curry sauce, spread over steamed broccoli stalks and served over white rice—was delicious, and I ended up wiping my plate clean with that French bread, trying to get every bit of the curry sauce.

"I want the recipe," I told her.

She took a bite of bread and chewed while nodding. "You can make it for Ben."

"I doubt that," I muttered.

"What happened?" Paige asked immediately. I figured I might as well tell her—I was desperate to talk about Ben with someone other than Dr. Clark. I told her the whole story of Sunday night. She covered her mouth in horror when I told her I called Ben, Luke.

"Oh no," she whispered.

I lifted and dropped a shoulder. "There's nothing I can do now. He won't respond to my texts."

Paige tore another piece of bread in her hands, her mind obviously turning. "Do you want to fight for Ben, Deb? Do you like him that much? I know you don't want faith to be a big part of your life, the way it is with Ben. I'm asking this as a friend—whichever direction you go in, I'm here to support you—but if faith is the foundation of who Ben is but you can't share that with him, do you think that would eventually come between you two?"

I sighed. I wasn't angry she asked, and I knew that Paige meant it when she said she'd support me. "Faith is this ongoing discussion in my head. I'm trying to work it out. Trying to find a balance I'm comfortable with. God just doesn't feel very real to me anymore. I keep waiting for him to do something to prove to me he's here, prove to me he loves me like the Bible says he does." I set my plate on the counter. "Ben says maybe my faith journey will look different from here on out. That people go through things that change them. That makes me wonder—if I can't go back to how I was before, at church all the time and super involved and reading my little daily dose of Scripture—is there still a place for me? Can I still be a person of faith if it looks different?"

Paige scratched the top of her nose and reached for her glass of wine. "Of course you can. If you find yourself wanting to talk to God, say whatever you're thinking. Yell, cry, share your deepest doubts and fears. Don't hold back. You don't want to go to church? Fine. Go hiking. If you get the urge to go to church, *go*. Don't worry what anyone else thinks. Do what you need to. Just be you."

"That's sounds like a good start actually." I tilted my head to the side.

"What's happening with the house idea?" Paige asked.

"It's still there. I was thinking of going and looking at places with a realtor, but it seems too soon. Maybe after the new year. I'm definitely going to sit down with the lady at the model home nearby for a consult."

"You could always buy a place and then let a roommate rent the second bedroom to help with cost."

I poured another glass of wine for a second. "That's true. But I feel like I want a place to myself if possible. I want to decorate it and make it mine." I pushed away thoughts of the still-packed boxes in my apartment.

Paige smiled. "That sounds really fun actually." She clapped her hands. "Okay, ready for our movie? And maybe some brownies?"

"Yes. On both accounts."

We watched the movie, which Paige ended up loving, but my mind kept wandering to Ben. At the end of *La La Land*, the main two characters end up going in different directions. The ending always made me a bit sad, to be honest. That had already been my story once. I needed a new song and dance.

Chapter Eighteen

Close your eyes and let the music set you free.
Phantom of the Opera

Saturday morning, I woke up to the sound of my phone dinging. I reached to the nightstand and held up the phone. When I saw Ben's name, I sat up straight in bed. I hadn't heard a word from him since that terrible Sunday night.

CAN YOU GO TO A CONCERT AT RED ROCKS WITH ME TONIGHT?

My brow wrinkled. A concert? I scrolled up through our text messages to see whether I'd missed something. Some important text where he acknowledged my apology and told me everything was okay.

No such text.

I leaned back against the headboard. *Who's even playing at Red Rocks tonight?* I did a quick search on my phone and found that a well-known rock band was in town for one night, playing at the infamous Red Rocks amphitheater. I knew their music and had desperately wanted to go to a concert at Red Rocks ever since moving to Colorado—but like this? Were we just pretending nothing had happened?

On the other hand, did I want to go even twenty-four more hours without seeing Ben?

I texted back. YES. AND WE NEED TO TALK.

He told me he'd pick me up at seven thirty. And this—a concert at Red Rocks—I decided I'd treat it like a date. With all the rain and hail we'd had lately, cool weather had slowly replaced our summer warmth. Red Rocks was up near the mountains; the rock formations were legendary, and I couldn't wait to experience a rock concert at such a cool venue, but I had a feeling, especially after dark, that it would be cold. I showered and took extra time with my makeup. It was a rock concert, after all. Dramatic eyeliner and mascara, smoky eye shadow, and pink lipstick. I put a little product in my hair to tame my crazy curls, then went to my closet to find something warm to wear but still worthy of a Red Rocks date.

I found my ripped black jeans and then dug out my favorite cowgirl boots—

the ones that had cost me a fortune back in Texas. I pulled my boots on over my skinny jeans. The boots fit perfectly, and as I looked down at them, the thought crossed my mind that I'd brought a teeny bit of Texas with me after all. I found a long, fitted gray sweater that I'd bought at the Galleria in Houston. Then I spun around in front of my floor-length mirror.

One thing was missing.

I went to my jewelry box and found my sterling silver leaf-shaped earrings. They dangled almost to my shoulders. And as I put them on and stared back in the mirror, I looked and felt like me again. A little changed, sure. This version of me didn't mind some quiet. She didn't mind being on her own. This version hiked and rafted and climbed mountains. She asked hard questions.

She still liked karaoke. Music still echoed through the chambers of her heart. It still called to her.

She still liked dangly earrings.

When I got the text that Ben was waiting outside, I grabbed my old, worn brown leather jacket and my purse. I paused at the door, straightened my shoulders, and enjoyed the few butterflies swirling in my stomach at the thought of seeing Ben. Then I rushed downstairs, ready.

We weren't even out of the parking lot before I turned to Ben.

"I was shocked by your text, inviting me to go tonight. You realize that, don't you? We leave things in an awful way Sunday night, I text you and apologize and try to reach out, and you don't respond for a *week*—then you text me randomly and ask me to go to a concert with you."

"Almost a week," Ben said as we exited the parking lot and headed toward the interstate.

I rolled my eyes. "Okay, fine. What are you thinking? Do you not believe me when I say I'm sorry?"

He exhaled, his gaze fixed on the road. "I believe you."

"But you're still annoyed, right?" I tried to clarify.

"It's like I said in Breck. I wish I could get that guy out of your head. I'm tired of fighting against someone who's not even here. And if you really want *him*, I can't help thinking that I'm wasting my time."

I sort of wished I hadn't pushed for clarification. "So why did you ask me tonight?"

"There's a reason, but I don't want to talk about it yet. And if I haven't said it yet, you look beautiful, Deb."

I smiled, warmth filling me at the compliment.

"I want you to tell me what *you're* thinking," Ben continued. "Why did you say yes tonight?"

"Because I like you. I'm sorry I said Luke's name. I wish I could take it back, but I can't. Even more scary, I can't swear it will never happen again."

Ben worked his jaw and his gaze narrowed a bit.

"I like going to the zoo with you, Ben," I said. "I like hearing you sing. I like camping with you. I like seeing you in my apartment. I liked"—my heart sped up, but I never was one for holding back—"seeing you hold Gilly. I like waking up when you say my name."

Then Ben glanced over at me, his eyes filled with pleasant surprise.

After a few silent moments, he finally spoke.

"I like all of those things too."

As we got closer to Red Rocks, we slowed to a crawl in a long line of cars entering the park for the concert. At eight o'clock, the sun had dipped behind the mountains, but you could still see a glow of orange and yellow shining behind the rocks. That sunset, along with the sight of the huge rock formations flanking the amphitheater, stole my breath. I wanted to soak in the beauty, to somehow take the magic of it with me.

It took forever to park; then we had to go to will-call for our tickets. My eyes rounded as Ben accepted two backstage passes from the clerk.

"What? How did we get those? How long have you had these tickets?" I shrieked as we left the booth. We stopped for drinks before finding our seats.

"I knew Branham Street was coming, but I hadn't planned on trying to get tickets. Then this week I was thinking that I'd like to take you—so I called their manager and left a message for Scotty Van Horn."

I stopped in my tracks. "You left a message for Scotty Van Horn. Like you know him?"

Ben nodded, moving us back in the direction of our seats. "Yeah. I do. Scotty and I went to college together and were friends back then. His manager called back and said he'd be leaving two tickets and backstage passes for me and that myself and a guest were invited to the post-show after-party." He raised one eyebrow at me. "You up for that?"

I almost bounced up and down. "Of course I am! This is going to be so fun!"

Ben, again, seemed to lack the gusto I'd seen in him so many times. But I was excited enough for both of us. We found our seats, midcenter, and the glow of the sunset disappeared, replaced by the chill of night and the bright lights on stage and the beat of a drum.

The crowd was wild and we shared in the energy. Jumping and clapping and singing along, first with the opening act, then later as Branham Street took the stage. Scotty Van Horn, lead singer, grabbed the microphone and started to sing, and the crowd took wild to a new level. And finally, when the encore had finished, Ben and I made the trek to the bottom of the stage. Ben showed security our passes and they let us through. We saw the Red Rocks tunnel, signed by hundreds of singers as they went onstage. I tried to temper my eagerness as we were led to a room with a buffet of food and drinks and people milling about. We were told to help ourselves to whatever we wanted, that it would be a little while before the band arrived, so we got drinks and food and waited.

Finally the band came in, greeted by applause from all of us. They made the rounds around the room, shaking hands with everyone, taking a few pictures. When Scotty Van Horn saw Ben, his bloodshot eyes grew large. He came over and pulled Ben into a sweaty hug. I stepped back, watching as Scotty held Ben tight, patting him hard on the back.

"Dude, I didn't think you'd come. I couldn't believe it when Dennis said you'd called."

Ben nodded, putting a hand on Scotty's shoulder. "It's good to see you, man." Scotty's red eyes moved to me.

"You must be Ben's girl. I'm Scotty." He held out his hand, and I shook it, noticing the jerk in his hand and the way his eyes darted every which way.

Ben's girl.

"I'm Debra Hart. It's really nice to meet you, Scotty." The sickly sweet smell of marijuana and who knows what else drifted around the room and off Scotty. Someone put a drink in his hand and he downed it.

"Let's find some chairs. I want to catch up," Scotty said to Ben. "Jack is over there." Scotty pointed to another corner of the room where a guy was chatting up a group of girls.

"I should say hello," Ben murmured.

Scotty put an arm around me. I tried not to breathe in—the body odor, the weed, the whiskey. "Debra and I will find a place to sit."

Ben looked at me, his eyes blinking question marks. I waved him off. It certainly wasn't the first time I'd been backstage at a concert, though normally I would be taking quotes and interviewing. Scotty steered me to a couple of chairs and we sat down.

"So how long have you and Ben been together?"

"Um. It's new." I didn't know what else to say.

He nodded. "We go way back."

"He told me you guys went to college together."

"Yeah. We were tight. Lived in this cheap apartment with a couple of other guys. At least until Jane and Ben got their own place. We partied hard. Those were good times."

"I can imagine," I said, lightly taken aback at his reference to Jane. I glanced over at Ben, who was being hugged by someone named Jack.

"But you know Benji," Scotty said, his tone now sarcastic. "Always too preoccupied with the afterlife and all that."

I held back a smile.

Well, that's one way to call someone a believer.

"Yeah, there is that."

"He was the best out of all of us. It should be him up on that stage."

"Branham Street wouldn't be on top if you weren't good at what you do," I reminded him. His head bobbed, but his gaze stayed on Ben.

"Thanks." He shook his empty glass.

Ben came back, the other guy with him, and we stood as he introduced me to Jack. They'd all been friends since college. "Did he tell you we lived together on Branham Street?" Ben asked.

"That's where it all started. Do you still sing at all?" Jack asked. I saw the subtle change in Ben. His neck stiffened; he crossed his arms.

"Yeah, I've got a band out here."

Someone handed Scotty a fresh drink, and he sucked it down, looking more on edge.

"Man, you're singing again? Why didn't you let me know? I could hook you up with people."

"Nah, we're just a small band. We play local bars and that sort of thing."

"You writing your own music?" Jack pushed.

"Yeah, mostly," Ben answered, moving to stand by me. I didn't know quite what was going on, but the vibe seemed to have shifted. I took Ben's hand in mine.

"I need a smoke. I'll be back," Scotty said, taking off toward the door.

"You ever see Jane anymore?" Jack asked, and there was trepidation in his voice but not malice.

Ben's grip on my hand got a little more intense. "I haven't seen her in years."

Jack nodded. "It's good to see you, Ben. You were one of us—then you weren't."

"That wasn't anyone's fault but my own. I needed to change some things in my life. And I'm happy for you guys."

"Scotty would help you, if you wanted connections or anything. We all would. We owe you." Jack looked at me. "You know he wrote 'Starfall,' right?"

"Huh?" I racked my brain, trying to think of where I'd heard of that.

"Our first hit. The one that put us on the map. That one's Ben's."

Ben sucked in a shallow breath. "Long time ago. Scotty does it justice."

Then Scotty was back, laughing too loud at something on his way back to us. I winced as he crashed into Ben, putting an arm around his shoulders. Ben didn't even flinch. He just steadied Scotty.

"You should fly back out to L.A. with us, Ben. Bring your girl. We'll get you signed. I can pull strings if I have to. What's the name of your band?"

"Twenty-Four Tears. But I work full-time for a church too. So that trip will have to be put on hold. I appreciate it, though, Scotty. Really. And I'll do better at staying in touch this time."

Scotty shook his head and suddenly there was this weight of emotion between the three guys. In a room crowded with people, filled with laughter, lots of alcohol, and the smell of weed getting stronger—there were these three guys with a history so deep that I could feel it. And I looked at Ben, wondering what was going through his mind, what he was feeling. He was watching Scotty; then he stepped closer to him. And Jack closed in closer as well.

"Your new album is killer, Scotty," Ben said finally. Those red eyes jerked up and met Ben's.

"You checked it out, huh?"

"Every song. It's gold."

The look on Scotty's face was a mix of gratitude and heavy emotion. Jack nodded at Ben, emotion in his eyes as well. "Thanks, man. I think it's our best."

About an hour later, Ben and I made our way back out to his jeep, walking slowly, holding hands under a clear, cold Colorado sky. I shivered, tightening my jacket and staying close to Ben.

"You wrote 'Starfall'?" I echoed.

He sighed. "Yeah. Another life." We reached the jeep and stopped.

It dawned on me then. "You're not afraid of failure or rejection or disappointment." I squinted at him, trying to read his reaction. "It's the opposite, right? You're afraid of success."

"I would argue that my definition of success might be different from what you're thinking."

The image of Scotty was stark in my mind. "Okay. I'll give you that." We were both quiet for a moment. I had to know more. "But, Ben, is that fair to Karis and the others?"

"Is what fair? We've cut songs; we play every month. I'm not trying to sabotage Twenty-Four Tears, Debra."

True enough, but still. "You know you have to want it bad to make it in the music industry. And you don't."

He sighed. "It's not that…well, maybe partly. But I'm content. I don't want to hold anyone back, and I'm not trying to. Karis's got her mom, and Xander's tied to his job—they need insurance for the new baby. He can't pick up and leave. And me … am I leery of success? You saw Scotty. That's not a road I want to go down. And I'm not immune to temptation. I was just like them, Deb. Those guys were my best friends. I still care about them. I always will, but that's not the life I'm looking for."

I understood. We stood there in the stadium parking lot, which was more like just gravel, the moon high over us. Ben opened the jeep door for me and held it. I stepped up and then turned to face him. We were so close, I could see his breathing turn shallow and his eyes zero in on me.

"You could be great, Ben. You've got so much talent, and you're grounded enough that I think you would stay true to who you are, whatever came your way."

I could tell, from that longing in his eyes and the way his gaze kept lowering to my mouth, that kisses had overtaken music in Ben's mind.

My breathing shallowed as well. The sounds of tires on gravel filled my ears. The looming rock formations were the backdrop to our moment.

I'd met so many musicians over the years, so many people with ability and a dream. Ninety-five percent of them didn't make it big. But I knew, instinctively, that Ben was more than talent. He was energy and appeal and authenticity. Combined with the talent I knew he had—he was a rock star already. In the way he would drop everything to help a friend. In the way he could lead a crowd to worship. In the way he was the same, down-to-earth guy singing in a bar to thirty people or hanging out backstage with someone perched precariously at the top of the music charts. He was just Ben, standing there, silently asking me to stop talking and kiss him.

"Maybe it's your turn to be brave," I whispered. He sighed, then moved one hand to my back and pulled me close to him. And both my arms wrapped around his waist. I felt an incredible sense of relief, as though I hadn't realized how much I needed to touch him and how much he needed to touch me.

"You think I'm not?"

"I don't know. I'm afraid. Maybe you are too."

He frowned. "Are you afraid of me, Deb?"

"Not exactly. I'm afraid I'll try and then everything will fall apart. Or you'll change your mind. There's no guarantee you wouldn't, Ben. No matter what you might say, you could change your mind." I suddenly shook all over at the reminder.

"You could change yours," he countered. "That's not a reason not to try." He leaned down. "Please, Deb," he whispered. And the break in his voice was like twinkle lights during summer or aged red wine or the perfect melody—it drew me in and made me want to stay right where I was, wrapped up in Ben.

"What if you're just a rebound fling for me, Ben Price?" I said, forcing those thoughts out loud, needing to be honest.

He just chuckled, unaffected, and leaned in for a kiss I couldn't—wouldn't—fight. "I'll take that chance. And if it's true, I'll probably end up writing a song about you."

Sunday morning, I felt guilty—guilty that even after our late night, Ben was up and leading worship at the crack of dawn. So I dragged myself to church, snuck in late, and found a seat in the back. Ben was already singing. The song segued from a modern worship song to an old hymn, and I watched as Ben closed his eyes, raised both hands, and sang out like there weren't hundreds of us watching.

And the music moved me.

I thought of Paige, telling me to be open, to go with whatever I felt, no matter what anyone thought. Not Ben. Not the people sitting near me. Not the people I'd left behind in Texas. Not my family.

I sat in the pew for a moment, my eyes shut, letting the song seep into me.

As the music rose up inside me, I stood on shaky legs and let myself sing—my heart crying out the words before they ever left my lips.

Chapter Nineteen

The best things happen while you're dancing.
White Christmas

I'm in love with October in Colorado," I told Lily via Facetime on my iPhone almost a week later. "Cornflower-blue snow-capped mountains, bright yellow aspen leaves, cool breezes, and cider at Starbucks."

"That sounds like a movie. Delicious and beautiful. Well, I'm in love with this little guy. He's the spitting image of his daddy," Lily said. She held up Logan for me to see. To me, he looked very small and not at all like Sam, but I kept those thoughts to myself. He did have the cutest yawn ever, and I giggled when I saw it.

"How are you?" I asked. "How was delivery?"

"Absolutely terrifying. I can't believe I'm alive. Thank God Almighty for the epidural. I needed it immediately, but that doctor made me wait. We're doing fine. Exhausted but fine. Have you seen snow yet?" Lily asked, as usual going a mile a minute.

"Not yet. But I've heard it's not unusual to get the first snowfall of the season around Halloween. So maybe soon. I can't wait. The aspen leaves are gorgeous and I love the brisk air. I've been buying way too many sweaters and scarves."

"Don't make me jealous. We probably won't get a cold front until January." Lily paused to lay Logan back down in his bouncer. "Jason told me you're dating someone. Tell me about him."

I decided not to go into the fact that Ben and I hadn't been technically dating when Jason was in town. "He's a musician. He's a lot of things. He works as the worship pastor for a big church around here. And he's the lead singer of a band. And he wears his hair in a topknot. *And* he's got interesting tattoos." I threw those last tidbits in, knowing Lily liked details. Lily chuckled.

"Yes, *please.*"

"He's really a great guy, Lil. Kind and thoughtful and crazy talented."

Lily dropped the phone and picked it back up. "He sounds wonderful. I've already stalked him online, so I've seen pictures. He's gorgeous."

I laughed, not shocked at all.

"You seem happy," she said softly.

"I'm doing all right," I confirmed. "I miss you."

"I miss you too. Come visit. Come meet Logan," she pleaded.

I swallowed. "Um, maybe. I'm new at work, so I don't have a lot of vacation time." From where I stood at the kitchen island, I checked the clock on my microwave. "I've got to go, Lily."

"Wait. I wanted to tell you that Glen finally got the head pastor position for their church. The process took forever, but it's final now. He and Addi are thrilled. And thank you for the adorable stuffed moose! Logan's room is decked out like a forest, trees painted on the walls and everything. Sara helped—" Lily stopped midsentence, her eyes rounding with horror at her mistake. "I'm sorry. I haven't slept. I didn't mean to ..."

To bring up Sara.

"It's okay. But I do have to go. I'm glad you liked the moose. I'll call again."

"All right. I love you, Deb."

My heart tugged. "I love you too."

I ended the call, wishing I could be there with Lily and, at the same time, relieved to be miles away from Luke and Sara. I reached for my sneakers and decided to go for a run. I *had* fallen in love with autumn in Denver. I ran the trails behind my condominium, gulping in the cool air and enjoying the leaves blowing in the wind. I couldn't get enough of the sight of the Rocky Mountains spread across the Front Range. Snowy white peaks reaching the sky even on sunshine-filled days.

A playful cool breeze whipped through my hair, and leaves danced across the trail in front of me. And I didn't feel alone.

That was something.

Saturday evening over bowls of chili at his apartment, I told Ben about finally singing along at church the week before. Ben crushed a handful of tortilla chips over his bowl, then sprinkled cheese on top of the chips, then stirred the whole thing together.

"There's something cool about finding our rhythm with God. To me, that's what it feels like. Like he and I have a rhythm between us. Sort of like you and me," Ben said with a twinkle in his eyes.

"I don't know if I'll get to that place."

"Deb," Ben said, pushing the bag of tortilla chips toward me. "Here's the thing, if you can try—just try—to accept God exactly as he is, mysterious and still and quiet and complicated and layered. If you can accept him as he is— which I know takes faith—maybe you'll start to realize that is exactly how he accepts *you*. Just as you are. And maybe you'll start to find your rhythm."

"Maybe," I said, hoping I didn't sound as doubtful as I felt. I asked him whether Twenty-Four Tears had come to a decision about opening for Chasing Summer.

"The tour is four months, almost five. End of January through May. I don't know how to even ask off for that much time. I might end up losing my job. Also," Ben filled his spoon with a heaping bite of chili. "Bryce called that manager Andy told us about, just to talk. His name is Carlisle Miller. Bryce said it was a really good conversation. I think we're all kind of wary of signing over some control over the band to someone new. We're so used to doing things on our own."

"But a manager could help steer you in the right direction too. He can advocate for you, make sure you get the best deal."

"Yeah. I know. It could be a worthwhile tradeoff." Ben finished another bite and sipped his soda. "Bryce said the guy told him he's pretty confident he could get us signed with a label."

Knowing how nervous all this made Ben, I squashed the giddiness I felt at hearing that. "What about Xander and Karis?"

"Xander says he can't do it. He can't leave Emily and the baby right now. Karis isn't sure. I know she wants so bad to jump at this opportunity. Bryce wants to say yes. Seth too."

"You could call Scotty, see if he knows a drummer who needs a job." I made the suggestion lightly while crunching tortilla chips over my own bowl.

"No, I don't want to do that. I know a guy I could ask, up in Breck. He's young. But he's not like Xander."

Not family.

"If you go with this Carlisle guy, he might be able to get you a drummer."

"Maybe," Ben agreed. "And Seth could move over to drums if we needed him to. He can play almost anything. But he's great on keys. He can sing back-up vocals too. We'd take the hit with Karis, though. You know she's awesome."

"What do you think—I mean, do you have a certain sense of what God wants you to do?"

Ben sighed and leaned back in his chair. "I've prayed about it, of course. But I don't feel strongly either way. I just know—I know God will go with me. But I'm good here. I'm happy with my job and my community. If I were to do this and if my life gets screwed up, it'll be my fault. That worries me, because I know I'm capable of screwing things up."

"Ben," I admonished softly. "You're not going to mess anything up. And if you do, is that a reason not to try?" I asked with a small smile, echoing his words.

But his shoulders just slumped. "It is when people are counting on me." He pushed his hair back out of his face. "You're counting on me," he said.

I reached over and took his hand. "You, Ben Price, are already a rock star to me. I'm with you whatever you choose to do. Do I think you'd kill it on tour? Yes. Does that scare me a little bit? Yes."

"Why?" He sat up, lacing our fingers together. "Why does that scare you, Deb?"

"Because you'll go off and be famous and have girls throwing themselves at you. I can't compete with that." I couldn't even compete with *one* girl, who was supposed to be my friend. I tried to fight off the image in my head of adoring fans, tipsy and willing and obsessed with Ben. My stomach started to tighten into knots.

He scraped the last bite of chili from his bowl. "You wouldn't have to compete with anyone."

I knew different. He knew the business well enough to know different as well. "What if you lost your job? Could you make it?"

He picked up our empty bowls and carried them to the sink. "Yeah." He didn't look at me. "I mean, I still make money off 'Starfall.' It's ridiculous. The song wasn't even that good, and yet I make more money than I should from it."

My mouth fell into an O, but I quickly recovered. For some reason, it hadn't occurred to me, when Jack told me that Ben had written "Starfall," that he still received royalties from it.

"How did that happen?" I asked him.

"I started writing it forever ago, back when the boys and I lived on Branham Street. Then Jane and I moved in together, but Scotty and I were still tight. He always gave me feedback on what I was working on. He knows what happened with me and Jane, but I don't think he ever quite forgave me for moving up to the mountains and leaving those guys. After they got signed, he called me, asked me to send him 'Starfall.' I'd finished it but hadn't done anything with it. I sent it to him, and they ended up using the song, giving me credit and royalties."

I started munching on tortilla chips. Ben came back and sat next to me at the table, putting an arm around my shoulders.

"I can't believe you finally decided to try dating a worship pastor." He winked.

I laughed and snuggled in closer to him. "Me either. Lucky for you, you're very multifaceted."

He kissed the side of my head. "Lucky for you, I'm persistent." He played with my curls as we sat there. "The church is doing a fall festival for families on

Halloween. Want to come?"

"Will you be working a dunking booth or anything?"

He chuckled. "Thankfully, no. I'm helping set up and creating booths and a million things beforehand, so I think I'm off the hook having to run stuff. Who knows, though. If I'm there, they'll probably get me to do something. But we can make candy apples and they have this huge popcorn machine that makes great popcorn."

"Why do you try to entice me with snacks?"

A burst of laughter escaped Ben; then he just smiled. "You just, you know, seem to like snacks. Nothing wrong with that. I like snacks too."

"Hmm."

"Halloween night, we've got a gig downtown. You'll come, right?"

"Of course," I promised him.

"Do you think we should go on tour, Debra? I want your opinion," he asked in a still voice, turning the conversation back and making me realize it was still forefront in his mind.

"It's up to you and the band, of course, Ben. But I've been around a lot of people—ever since college—who would give anything just for a chance to go on tour with a group like Chasing Summer. What if it doesn't go beyond that? It would still be a chance of a lifetime to experience playing before sold-out crowds. I think you know it *would* go beyond that—and that's the real question. If you want that. You guys have that magic. There's no doubt about that. And really, even Karis told me this—*you* bring the magic, Ben. I think you're a born performer. But money and fame don't equal happiness, and you'll be miserable on the road if you do this for any reason other than it's in you to do it."

He folded his arms on the table and put his head down for a moment. I let him think and went to the sink to load the dishwasher. After a few moments, he pushed his chair back.

"We've just started dating. I mean, you don't mind that I might be gone for months?"

I dried my hands on a towel. "You'll need to be able to focus on the tour, without the distraction of me."

"So that's it, then?" I could hear the frustration in his tone.

"Four months is doable, Ben. And you can—I mean, you could date other people, I guess."

He stood up, his eyes narrowed. "Do you want to date other people, Debra?"

I threw the towel down as hard as I could. "Right. Because it was so easy for me to start dating you. If it's hard for me to move on with the most gorgeous, gifted, sweet, and amazing man I've ever met, I doubt I'm going to join a dating website and start going out with someone new every weekend."

He was in front of me in a second, kissing me, pulling me close. My arms went around his neck and I kissed him back. For a moment, the tension in my neck eased, and the warmth of his mouth on mine was like whiskey on ice, melting me. Ben's kiss started slow and then deepened, and I followed his rhythm, matching his need with my own. My lower back pressed into the edge of the counter, but I ignored the discomfort, wanting the sensation of letting go to last a little longer. When I finally pushed him away, needing to breathe, Ben searched my eyes.

"Is that really how you see me?" he asked.

I sighed. "That's how everyone sees you."

"We've just started dating. I don't want to lose you," he whispered. He cupped my face in his hands and stared at me.

"I'll be here. You can tune in to hear Miss Lonely Heart every day online," I said, trying to joke. The truth that he'd be leaving—I had no doubt that four months would turn into longer—and I was the one pushing him to go began to sink in.

Ben, of all people, deserved this chance. He would shine like the stars; I knew he would.

But what about me?

That was always the question.

My eyes darted to the window over the sink and I blinked twice.

"It's snowing! Look, Ben. It's snowing!" I grabbed his hand and pulled him to the back door with me. He laughed as we went outside in the freezing cold, no jackets. On the small back patio of Ben's apartment, I raised my hands and twirled in the lightly falling snow. Ben caught me in his arms, took my hand in his, and slid his other hand around my waist. We danced on the patio, to the music that lived inside both of us.

He danced with me in the snow.

Snowflakes fell, melting on my eyelashes, scattering on Ben's dark hair.

"If this is even a tiny dream in you, I want you to chase it," I told him.

He kissed my cold nose, then closed his eyes. "I'll tell the band we're going."

By the third week in November, I wasn't sure how Ben was juggling his life. The fall schedule at the church seemed packed, and another radio station in Denver had started playing Twenty-Four Tears on the radio, so the band was getting more exposure, especially now that they were set to open for Chasing

Summer. He hardly had time to sleep. Karis had decided to go on tour. She said her mother told her she refused to watch her daughter give up this opportunity. Ben had asked for my help in secretly planning to fly Karis's mom out to San Diego for their first show. He wanted me to go too, but I wasn't sure I could get the time off.

November sixteenth, I dropped a pile of mail on the island counter but didn't go through it until that Saturday morning, the eighteenth. I sipped coffee and tore up credit card offers and threw away grocery advertisements. And then I froze, my hand midair, at the sight of a wedding invitation. I withdrew my hand and just stared at the name Witherspoon in the top left corner of the envelope. I jumped up, went to the sink, and poured out the rest of my coffee.

Sara and Luke's wedding invitation.

I swallowed three times.

How could they send me an invitation?

My breathing started to shallow, and my chin quivered. I walked back to the island, reached for the thick envelope, and made my way to the sofa. I slid my finger under the flap and opened it. My eyes were burning as I pulled out a second envelope.

Dr. and Mrs. Witherspoon formally request the honor of your presence at the marriage of their daughter, Sara Ashley Witherspoon, to Luke Matthew Anderson

My eyes scanned the rest of the details. Lily of the Valley Chapel, December twentieth, four p.m., dinner and dancing to follow.

A handwritten letter dropped to my lap and my breath stopped completely.

Dear Debra,

I wasn't sure whether I should send this—part of me worried that it might hurt you too much. Another part of me felt like I had to send it. And that part won out. I tried to know what to say, but I couldn't find the right words and finally just decided that there are no right words. I wrote this letter anyway. Please know that I don't want to hurt you. I don't want to remind you of things that maybe you're trying to forget. But I can't forget. I can't forget the years we've spent as friends. I can't not invite you to come to my wedding, Deb. I just can't. I don't expect you to come. I know how hard that would be. Maybe I'm the only person who has some understanding of what that might feel like.

Do you remember that conversation we had at the lake house the weekend you told us that you and Luke were dating? You sat me down in the blue room and talked to me. I'll be honest—I didn't want that conversation. It hurt. Now I know why you had to do that. Why you had to acknowledge how I might have been feeling. Why you had to tell me that you cared and understood. You wanted me to know that you still saw me. I knew you were ecstatic to be dating Luke, but you took that moment to tell me I mattered to you too.

That is why I'm writing this letter. You matter to me too.

I know how much you loved Luke. I also know how much he loved you. If you ever doubt that he did, if you start to wonder if it was real, I know that it was and I know that he loved you. We both know that while some relationships do not last, that doesn't mean the feelings weren't real.

I never wanted to take something that was yours. I hope one day you can forgive me for marrying Luke. For loving him too.

I will forever miss the perfect circle that all of us were before last summer. But even if we can't go back, I need you to know that I pray God will bring you love and happiness and peace and all those wonderful things that you deserve. I will always want those things for you.

And you will always matter to me.

Sara

My hands were shaking so badly that the letter dropped. Hot tears welled up from deep inside me, searing my heart. I drew my legs to my chin and wrapped my arms around my knees. Tears spilled down my face, and the only sounds that broke the silence were the sniffs and gasps of a girl letting go of everything.

I remembered the conversation Sara had referenced. And she was right—I'd been giddy with excitement that I was dating Luke, but also, I'd wondered for the longest time if Sara had a crush on Luke, just as I had. They were best friends. In the end, they were meant to be more than best friends.

I didn't know how much time passed before the tears subsided, but eventually my legs straightened, cramping from the tension. I reached for the cream-colored throw blanket on the other end of the couch and pulled it around my shoulders. The gas fireplace in the corner of the room was lit, but I still felt chilled. For a moment, I felt an urge to read the letter a second time, but I didn't. I slid it back into the envelope and pushed it away from me, to the far corner of the coffee table. Then I leaned back into the sofa, and the softness of the blanket warmed me and comforted me. I breathed in and out and considered what I'd just read.

I thought opening that invitation would break me, but something else happened after I'd read Sara's words. I sensed—I knew—that the tears, the ache, now stemmed from more than losing Luke. It was the shattering of that circle. My heart had moved on from Luke. As Sara had said, the love had been real, but I knew it was over now. The pain lingered. I wouldn't go to the wedding—of course I wouldn't go. As for forgiving her, that wasn't currently on my radar, but I could see how I might get there one day.

I didn't hate her anymore. I didn't hate him.

This time, when the tears stopped, I felt free.

I did take the letter with me during my next visit with Dr. Clark. She read it out loud and I was brave enough to listen to it a second time. Then she set it down on her desk and seemed to silently read it again. Then she looked up at me.

"First tell me about that conversation between the two of you."

I did. As best I could remember, in slow detail.

"All right. Now tell me how you felt when you read the letter or how you felt just now, as I read it."

I tucked my feet into the cushion on the couch and relaxed a bit, taking my time with my thoughts. "I think ... I think I needed to hear her say she was sorry, and she finally did. I probably couldn't have heard her before now."

Dr. Clark nodded her agreement. "Do you need to hear Luke say he's sorry?"

I exhaled and asked myself the question again, silently. Then shook my head. "He already did. That night he broke up with me. He apologized over and over. We spoke once after that, and he apologized over and over then too. But I knew he was only sorry for hurting me. Not necessarily sorry for the breakup. I think I know why. His parents' divorce—his perspective and fear when it came to commitment. He wasn't sure about us. And Luke was sure about everything. So for him *not* to be sure about us ... I should have known that it couldn't work."

"What are *you* sure of, Debra?" Dr. Clark asked.

"I'm just trying to be sure of myself," I answered in a small voice. I cleared my throat. "And when—if—I fall in love again, I want someone who is sure of me, sure of us."

"Are you glad she sent the letter and invitation?" Dr. Clark questioned.

Was I?

I hadn't expected to be invited, yet ... now having been invited, I realized that I'd needed to be. If only to be included. If only to know I wasn't forgotten.

I needed to know I mattered. And Sara, perceptive Sara, had known and understood.

"Yes," I answered. "I'm glad. I thought I needed resolution from Luke—but I was wrong. I needed it from Sara."

"Do you think you can forgive her? Forgive them?"

I blew out my breath and tucked my hair back behind my ears. "Yes. One day. Not today, but someday."

Dr. Clark nodded. "You seem lighter, Debra. Do you feel lighter?"

"I feel like maybe I've let go of the anger. So even if there's still some hurt, especially over the broken friendships, I don't know … I feel ready to move on."

"Does Ben factor into this?" Dr. Clark asked. I pictured Ben. I didn't want to be rescued. I didn't need some prince to save me. I'd given up on fairy tales after Luke. Even the best of guys could make mistakes and change their minds.

But Ben, in a small but significant way, had brought me back to life. Stirred desire and hope—things I thought I'd lost forever. Ben, with his frustration and honesty. Ben, his voice like a river, flowing in and around me, breaking over rocks and trickling over pebbles, smooth and straight, then fierce and powerful, like white water crashing, then slowing, easy and calm. Ben, reaching me like a song I wanted to hear on repeat.

"I think this is me, ready to move instead of standing still. Ben might be part of what I'm moving toward. Even if he isn't"—my voice strengthened, that freedom spreading through my body like truth—"I want to keep moving."

Dr. Clark smiled and slid those leopard glasses onto her face. She tucked Sara's letter into the envelope.

"Excellent news, Debra."

Chapter Twenty

All you need is love.
The Beatles

As Thanksgiving closed in and Paige went up to the mountains with her parents and siblings for vacation, I decided to finally go in for the consult about the paired home. After work the Tuesday before the holiday, I went in for a meeting. The woman I'd first spoken with, Denise Shumaker, met me at the door, with a broad smile and firm handshake. She handed me a bottle of water, and I took a seat across from her, a mahogany desk between us.

We talked money and financing—all discouraging topics—then we walked through the model together. Denise pointed out everything that was an upgrade and explained what the more basic house plan was. A few nice upgrades—like granite countertops and hardwood floors in the kitchen—were standard regardless, which made me very happy. Even without a lot of the extras from the model, I liked the floor plan.

Most importantly, if I were able to buy a place, it would be mine. I'd pick the cabinets and countertops and floors and paint shades. I would choose the exterior stone and color. Every piece of the house would be a reflection of my own taste.

When we sat back down at her desk, she pulled out a large map of the new neighborhood plans, showing me which lots were available.

"These"—Denise pointed to a row at the back of the left side of the neighborhood—"will be ready in about six months. End of May."

I swallowed and nodded. End of May. When my lease was up.

"I'll be perfectly honest with you. These spots won't last long. New housing is booming in Denver. And this location is close to the Tech Center and not far from the light rail for people who work downtown. Now, more spots will open up. We're building all the way through here." She waved her hand over the map, indicating the whole region of the new neighborhood. "But if you're looking to have a place ready in May, these would work for you. Because of location, resale will be no problem. A lot of people are investing in these homes for rental purposes later as well. You have some time to think it over, but keep in mind that they'll go fast."

I promised to think about it and get back to her. I walked through the model once more alone before leaving, and it was impossible not to get excited. The bedrooms were, of course, larger than the teeny space of my apartment, and I could envision hanging my vintage musical posters in the bedroom; maybe making the second room an office or music room. I would *want* to unpack in a space like this.

I left and swung by Starbucks to grab a latte on my way home. I'd been preapproved for a loan, but that didn't ease my mind regarding the monthly payments. To me, we were talking about huge numbers I would be attaching myself to. I hadn't mentioned to Paige or Denise the fact that my savings had basically been a gift from my grandfather. He'd passed away two years before and, in his will, had left both me and my brother each a sum of money. If I bought the paired home, I'd be using that sum as a small down payment. The money was mine, of course, and investing it in a home of my own seemed like a good plan. But Dr. Clark had been right—it was a big decision and I felt the weight of it.

Later that evening I sat cross-legged on my bed, my laptop in front of me as I searched homes online. Every house I looked at only made the newness of the paired home more appealing. Ben called and I shoved the laptop aside and stretched out.

"You're invited to Thanksgiving at my parents' house," he told me.

The sound of wind pounding on my windows distracted me. "Ben, Thanksgiving is the day after tomorrow."

"I know. Can you come with me to Fort Collins?"

"Why are you just now asking me?"

"You told me you couldn't go to Minnesota. I just assumed you would come home with me."

I shook my head but smiled. "Next time, let me know more than two days in advance. I'd love to spend Thanksgiving at your parents' house, but I have to work. I'm the newbie at the radio station and there's no way I'm getting a holiday off."

"We can leave right after your shift. Be ready. We can be there in less than two hours. In time for dinner with my parents."

"But you probably want to stay the night. I'll have to work Friday as well."

"Then we'll drive back late Thursday night, and no doubt you'll sleep all the way back."

I bit back a chuckle. "Are you sure?"

"I'm sure. My parents want to meet you."

My first Thanksgiving in Colorado was spent driving to Fort Collins on a crisp, clear, but freezing-cold afternoon. We made it to Ben's parents' home by three o'clock, walking into a one-story house that smelled deliciously of turkey and cornbread. I wondered if holidays usually consisted of just the three of them, because there were no other relatives coming over, and Ben's parents, Connie and Jonathon, seemed thrilled to have me join them. When we walked in, I handed her a homemade chocolate Bundt cake that I'd made and she thanked me over and over.

Connie had set a beautiful table, complete with candles and a fall bouquet of flowers. Ben's dad prayed over the meal and then we ate. I had second helpings of everything. After the meal, Ben and his dad went out to the garage to see some project his dad had been working on, and I helped clear the table.

"Everything was delicious, Connie," I said honestly. She set a pot of coffee to brew and turned to smile at me.

"It's just so nice to have you here. Ben's told us quite a bit about you. And it's been so long since he's wanted to bring anyone home."

Well, that made me both sad and relieved.

"We used to have more family in Colorado, but my sister and her family moved to Iowa a few years ago. Now holidays can be kind of quiet, unless we travel. Since he's a worship pastor, Ben usually needs to stay close to home for holidays. And I don't like to spend holidays away from Ben. He's—he's our only, you know?" she said, her voice wobbling a bit, which broke my heart.

"Yes. He told me about Sadie," I said gently, hoping it wasn't rude to bring her up. Connie sighed. She moved to stand in front of me.

"Can I touch your hair?" she asked, a little embarrassed.

I laughed. "Sure."

"It's so curly!" she exclaimed with delight. "Did Ben tell you that Sadie had curly hair?"

I shook my head. She touched my hair. "Her curls were blonde. Your dark hair is beautiful, just beautiful, Debra."

I hugged her impulsively, and she hugged me back. When I pulled away, there were tears pooled in her eyes. She laughed a bit self-consciously and wiped away any stray tears.

"Would you like coffee?" she asked.

"I'd love some. Can I slice the cake?"

She nodded and pointed me in the direction of dessert plates.

"We don't have to wait for the men," she told me, motioning for us to sit at the table. We sat down and had coffee together. Connie wanted to know about my job and my family. I wondered whether Ben had told her the reason I'd moved from Texas.

I stirred cream into my coffee and looked out the kitchen windows to the backyard. One or two runaway snowflakes drifted on the wind.

"You know my son is in love with you, right?" Connie asked, her tone serious. I blinked fast and stared at my coffee.

"Oh, I don't know."

"I know Ben," Connie said, "and I have to tell you, you'll never find a more wonderful man. I may be biased, but he's perfect."

I smiled at that. "He's definitely wonderful. He—he has really strong faith. My faith doesn't match his." I wasn't sure why I told her—maybe just the need for transparency since she was being so open with me.

Her brow furrowed. "What do you mean?"

I sighed. "This year has been one with a lot of change for me. And in all that change, I sort of lost myself. I realized my faith wasn't as strong as I thought it was."

Connie looked outside. "I have a little experience in realizing your faith isn't as strong as you expected." She looked down at her hands, running her fingers over her wedding ring. "To me, faith is the promise that I'll see Sadie again. It's the peace that eventually came when I didn't think it was possible. It's the ability to forgive that I couldn't have mustered on my own. None of those things were the miracle I wanted—the one I needed. But it's what I got." Connie covered my hand with hers. "You may have lost yourself; you may have lost other things too—you may have lost your faith. But God didn't lose you, Debra. He's hard to see sometimes. He's hard to understand. But he's all we have."

A tear fell down my face.

"There came a point in my life when I had to decide if I would accept God for who he says he is. It was my choice to make. I'll be honest, it took years for me to make the decision, but I did. God is more patient than people, Debra. Hold on and see what happens. Take your time. You came here to Colorado, brave girl, and God brought you to Ben, and now Ben is going after a dream I thought he'd left behind. Who knows what else might happen?" She sniffed and reached for a napkin.

"Will you be sad?" I wondered. "When Ben goes on the road? Do you want him to stay at the church?"

Connie waved her hand. "Ben has a gift. In whatever way he uses it, I just want him to be happy. That's why I'm so pleased he brought you here. We needed another girl in this house."

I had never felt so welcome in my life. In that warm kitchen, over pieces of chocolate cake and cups of strong coffee, I relaxed at Connie's table. And my deep sigh of respite felt like a prayer of gratitude.

The Saturday after Thanksgiving, Paige and I went shopping together all day, stopping only for lunch at the Park Meadows food court. There were so many good sales that we ended up buying presents for ourselves and convincing each other that it would be worse to let the sales pass us by.

"How can you leave me for Christmas?" I pointed my slice of pizza at her. We sat near a huge fireplace, front and center at the food court. She slurped down her lemonade.

"I have to. This year we're all going to my grandma's house in Kansas. You can come too."

"I only have the weekend off, and if I went anywhere, it would have to be Minnesota. My mother is freaking out that I'm not coming home. She's probably having flashbacks of last Christmas—which was the worst holiday of my life."

Paige cocked her head to the side. "But this Christmas will be wonderful. You and Ben are dating!"

"Yes, but then he leaves for the spring tour. And then he'll turn into a legit rock star, and he'll have groupies following him and girls throwing their bras onstage."

Paige put her hands on either side of her face. "Do women still do that?"

I shrugged. "Probably."

We continued eating in silence.

"You've come a long way, Debra, from last Christmas."

"I'm not even the same person."

She smiled. "You're still the same person. At least, I think you are. Jason says you are. You've changed, yes, but change is good. Have you made a decision about the house?"

I took a long sip of my soda. "I'm going to at least tell my parents about it. I know it's my decision, but I have a feeling they'll freak out if I buy a house without telling them. Plus, I want their opinion before I sign anything."

"The thought of building a brand-new house is so exciting. I hope you do it. I can see lots of fun summer evenings on your back porch." Her eyes shone.

"This is going to be a great holiday for you. I know what Ben's getting you for Christmas." She clapped her hands. "It's going to be fabulous."

"Really? What's he getting me?"

Paige immediately sobered and gave me a stern look. "Don't ask. If I accidentally tell you, I'll never forgive myself."

I rolled my eyes. "What should I get him?"

She looked stumped. "I have no idea. He's the kind of guy who will like anything, but you want to get him something he'll *love*."

"Thank you for all that help."

"Anytime."

Paige and I cleaned up our table and continued shopping. We walked together past the Santa station, then stopped at one of the baby stores so I could get Gilly a gift. Finally, worn out from shopping, we made our way to the exit.

"It really is shocking to me that it's been almost a year since Luke broke up with me," I said.

Paige looped her arm through mine. "I'm so glad you moved here."

"Me too," I told her.

When we got back to her car, Paige pulled something out from the trunk while I waited for her in the passenger seat. She hopped into the driver's side and handed me a bag.

"I have a Christmas present for you, and I know it's early, but I want to give it to you now."

"What? We're not doing gifts yet!"

She pushed the bag into my arms. "I can't wait any longer. I made this for you."

"You made it?" I reached my hand into the bag while Paige nodded with excitement. I pulled out a wooden plank, smooth and natural. Stamped onto it in black were the words: *There's no growth without rain. Embrace it. Be the storm.*

"I read something like it online somewhere, and it made me think of you. How much you've gone through and how you don't always realize it, but I think you're fierce and strong—like a tempest."

My hand ran over the words. "I love it, Paige." I turned over the plank, and at the bottom, in tiny letters, it read, *From Friend No. 1.*

I chuckled as Paige turned the ignition and said, "My vital place in your life, etched in wood forever."

Ben was so busy through all of December that other than a few quick lunch dates, it seemed like I hardly ever saw him. I tried not to be overly aware of the calendar dates ticking down to the twentieth, to Sara and Luke's wedding day. A few days before, Ben and I managed to have coffee after worship practice on Saturday morning. I sipped a peppermint mocha latte as Ben slid two tickets across the table at Starbucks.

"What's this?" I asked.

"Your Christmas present," he said, smiling over the top of his spiced chai.

I picked up the tickets. "*White Christmas* is coming to the theater district? You bought me two tickets?" I squealed.

"Technically, one is for me. It will hurt my feelings if you want to go with someone else."

I laughed, leaning over the table and kissing him. Then I looked back down at the tickets. December twentieth.

I swallowed the lump in my throat and looked back up at Ben's beaming face. "Thank you so much."

The Christmas before, I'd left Texas around five in the morning to get to Minnesota. I cried during the whole flight, blubbering my story to a military guy sitting next to me, who never got a word in. When I'd arrived, I'd spent the next week in bed, emerging only for meals. My mother slept next to me that first night back home, smoothing my hair as I whimpered and whispering to me that everything would be okay, that my life wasn't over. She promised me that I was a resilient woman and that I wasn't alone.

This Christmas season, Paige came over and we decorated a tree in the corner of my tiny apartment. I babysat Gilly so Jake and Cassidy could have a night out. I lost all battles of temptation against specialty coffee drinks, drinking way too many pumpkin spice cappuccinos and gingerbread lattes. I baked Christmas cookies and took them to KGBL. I hung a wreath on my door and listened to holiday music.

And on the twentieth of December, I went to the theater with Ben.

We took the train downtown. I'd worn my new knee-length gray coat (my favorite Christmas gift to myself) and white gloves, since it was approximately nineteen degrees outside. Even if we hadn't been going to a musical, the lights and buzz of downtown and the magic of the theater district would have been enough. Ben was adorable, in trim black pants and a gray sweater over a white collared shirt (no, we didn't coordinate ahead of time). He held my hand tight as we walked the short distance from the train station to the auditorium. We stopped at a little bistro before the musical started and had champagne.

Then we went to see *White Christmas*. He didn't know that it had been my favorite Christmas movie of all time since I was eleven years old. He couldn't know that nearly every December of my childhood, I'd spend at least one night at my nana's and we'd watch *White Christmas* together and dance to the "Sister, Sister" number. And he had no idea that while being in the heart of Denver on a cold December night, the smell of snow looming in the air, the hint of Christmas around the corner, I was trying not to think about the fact that somewhere in Texas, Luke and Sara were taking their first dance and cutting cake and, *at this very moment*, were now married. I had no doubt that Sara would have looked beautiful, probably wearing an elegant designer dress, dancing with her own Prince Charming, who at one small point in time had been mine.

I finished my champagne, and then Ben and I went to find our seats in the auditorium. And I cried and applauded with everyone else, because *White Christmas* is perfection. But sometime after the first intermission, I could feel the weight of emotion getting to me. Memories of my childhood, being with Nana, those special moments when I was a little girl, twirling and dancing. Moments that were forever in my heart but now over. The emotion of growing up and moving away from home. The heavy reminder that I was miles away from my family this Christmas. And of course, the pressure on my heart, knowing Sara and Luke were married, maybe making their way to a gorgeous hotel room at that very minute, starting their life together.

Even surrounded by the wonder and magic of my evening with Ben, the emotional weight was like a too-thick blanket, suffocating me.

After the musical, we bundled up and walked back toward the train station. Snow started falling. Through the light surrounding the lampposts, we could see it swirling down.

"Are you going to tell me what's on your mind?" Ben asked, discerning as ever.

"No, I don't want to ruin this perfect night."

Ben stopped walking. "Now you have to tell me. Deb, I need to know what you're thinking."

I cried and told him—all of it. Missing my grandmother. Missing my mom. Thinking of Luke and Sara celebrating with all the people who were my closest friends. Everyone there but me. Because I couldn't be there. I didn't belong there. Ben pulled me into a hug, and we stood there on a snowy street corner.

"Are you upset that everything has changed, or are you hurting because Luke just married Sara?"

I sniffed and dug through my purse for a tissue, then wiped my nose. "I don't know. I'm just sad."

Ben's mouth twisted and he shoved his hands in his pockets as he stared down at me. "I get that it's a lot. And it would make anyone sad ... but are you missing Luke right now?"

"I'm missing everyone, and I'm sort of mad at everyone." It was getting colder; we started walking again, toward the train station. Once we got there, we had to wait awhile for the next train. I wasn't sure how Ben was feeling at that moment, but I was freezing so I tucked my arm through his and stood as close to him as possible. Finally the train came, and we got on, but it was packed, so Ben stood the whole way back. When we were in Ben's jeep, the heater on high, Ben drove me home.

I felt awful and wished I'd been able to keep it all inside. "I'm sorry, Ben. You planned this perfect date, and I ruined it."

He sighed. "You didn't ruin anything. If you can't tell me what you're thinking and feeling, we're not a real couple."

We didn't talk for a few tense moments. My apartment was close to the train hub. Ben swung the jeep into my parking lot.

"Want to come up?" I asked him, my voice more timid than usual. He parked the jeep and we walked upstairs together. Once we were in my apartment, the lights glowing from the tree, the gas fireplace burning, our jackets strewn over the high-top chairs, Ben seemed to relax somewhat. I made coffee; then we sat together on the sofa. If it hadn't been for the incredible awkwardness I'd created, the glow of the twinkle lights and the fire would have been wonderfully romantic.

"Are you happy here, Deb?" Ben asked, restraint tempering his voice.

"For the most part. Is anyone entirely happy?" I asked with a nervous chuckle.

"I am. When I'm with you, I'm happy. When I'm leading worship, I feel joy. When I'm singing with Twenty-Four Tears, I feel a rush of adrenaline." His eyes were cast downward. "Are you ever going to be over Luke?" he asked evenly, and I bristled.

"You think I'm not?"

He gave me a condescending look. "We're still talking about him, aren't we?"

I stood up. "Well, I thought I would marry him, and tonight he married someone else. What do you expect?" I yelled, hands trembling.

Ben stood up too. "I know. But do you know how that makes me feel?" Ben's voice jumped several notches and his eyes narrowed. "Do you know how sick it makes me that you came so close to marrying someone else?" He ran his fingers angrily through his hair. "You might have married him and never moved here and never gone to hear Twenty-Four Tears play. And you'd be his, when—don't you realize?—you were always meant to be mine." Ben's voice fell, he was rigid with tension, and I couldn't make myself breathe. "It's him or me, Deb. Or neither of us, I guess. But he's gone and I'm right here. You have to decide what you want. I need you to be all in if we're going to do this."

Oh, God. I found it again.

Did that count as a prayer?

Yes.

I blinked, frozen, sure that the answer had come from my heart, and recognizing it as a voice I hadn't heard from in a long time. And that one moment—that whisper—drew tears to my eyes. No miracle. Nothing special. Just a nudge that perhaps I wasn't as alone as I thought. Then I remembered that's how it is sometimes.

Just a subtle voice.

Subtle wasn't my favorite.

I blew out a breath, trying to let go of some of the anger.

I could want it to be different, or I could accept how it was.

Ben took hold of my shoulders. "Debra, I haven't loved anyone since Jane, and I didn't love her in the right way. Part of me has held off on anything resembling a serious relationship since then, because I knew the next time I loved someone, I wanted it to feel healthy and real." Ben took a shaky breath, but his eyes stayed on mine. "The next time I make a baby with someone, I want that to mean everything to both of us."

I touched his face, my heart aching. He wanted all that with me. "Ben." His trembling hands squeezed my shoulders slightly.

"I've made mistakes, and I'm still making mistakes, but I don't want to talk about Luke anymore. I don't. I want you to be mine. He let you go—and I've thanked God over and over for letting that happen—because in every way, you're perfect for me, not him." He dropped his hands and folded his arms across his chest.

"I know," I whispered, then cleared my throat. "I *know*, Ben."

"You don't—wait, what?" Ben said, confused.

"I'm not in love with Luke anymore." My voice pleaded with him to understand. "It hurts to be pushed aside and left out—and that's how I feel when I think about him marrying Sara tonight, surrounded by our best friends. But I don't want to go back. I'm different now, in ways that make me feel like I know myself better. I don't need him anymore. But us—but you—"

He absorbed that. "Are you—are you still afraid I could change your mind?"

I threw my hands up. "Yes, I'm afraid. Now you're going to be a rock star. We both know what that lifestyle can be like."

His eyes bulged. "It's—you—" he sputtered. "You're the one who wants me to do this!"

I put my hands on my hips. "Only because I know you have what it takes. Only because you belong onstage, Ben. Your songs—they should be heard because they connect with people, but ..." My voice faltered. "Are you saying you don't want this?"

He was quiet for a minute. "I do. I've wanted it since I was a kid. That doesn't mean it's the right thing for me. I'm not sure. Part of me really wants to try. You're right. It's a once-in-a-lifetime kind of opportunity, and I don't want to look back and think that I was afraid to go for it."

"Four months might just be the beginning," I said.

"Maybe, maybe not."

"Ben, you have so much potential. You could go all the way. I know it."

He shook his head. "I think you overestimate me, Deb. And I don't need a lot of success. I'm fine. It could change me, and I'm happy with who I am. But at this point, we're going. The band deserves this chance. Still—I'm worried about you and me."

I stared at him and I knew. I knew this would most likely be a first step that would change Ben's life.

In Texas, I'd found one of my closest friends to be my stiffest competition for the man I'd loved.

How could I compete with a world full of groupies and whoever else? It might not come to that—but one look at Ben, and I knew it could.

I'd grown used to the way of him. How he smoothed back the top half of his hair and tied it in a knot. How he absentmindedly ran his thumb over the tattoo on his left wrist whenever he was thinking. That flash of smile that so often came my way. And the image of him holding Gilly in her nursery, singing with that voice that melted me—that image seemed to be seared in my mind.

I wanted to tell him about my plans to buy a house, but for some reason, the words wouldn't come. I'd wanted to bring it up several times before but held back every time. I wasn't sure why. Maybe because that was mine alone to hold on to. This moment—the tour—was about him.

"Hey, we're not in any rush," I heard myself saying smoothly. "Just because you're gone for a few months on tour, that doesn't mean suddenly we have to stop being in contact with each other." But even as I said it, I wondered what might happen.

"I don't trust you won't disappear on me," he said with a pointed look in my direction.

"Ben, if you're going to go after this, go after it."

He stepped closer to me. "I was already going after something. She's not very cooperative."

I smiled at that—couldn't help it. "Like I said, we don't have to be in a rush." *And I'm not getting my heart broken a second time.* "I believe in chasing your dreams. I fully support you taking this opportunity, but it makes sense to me that we hold off on getting more serious until we know where this is going for you. I've got to protect my feelings."

"You need to protect your feelings from me?" Ben said in disbelief.

"Yes." I looked him in the eyes. "Ben, please. Let's just keep spending time together as usual. When the tour comes, go all in. After, we'll pick up where we left off."

If there is an after.

Chapter Twenty-One

There really is no place like home.
The Wizard of Oz

Saturday morning, I dragged my guitar out from under my bed. It took a while to tune it, strumming chords and finding my way. When I finally felt ready, I sat cross-legged on the floor of my living room. Through the window, I could see snow coming down with a soft vengeance. Beautiful, swirling, but relentless.

The fire flickered in front of me, warming the space. A notepad rested on the coffee table. I played and hummed, closing my eyes and searching for my rhythm.

I was wounded, you were healed ...

Lyrics sprang through my mind and I scribbled them down. When I'd told Ben before that I wasn't a songwriter, it would have been more accurate to say I wasn't a successful songwriter. I'd tried to write a few songs back in college but never anything I was happy with. For some reason, I'd woken up that morning with music stirring in me. It was time to try again. The wood of my guitar felt right in my hands. The strings spoke to me. Even in a silent room, rhythm surged through my veins.

A few hours later, the floor was littered with paper balls. I lay flat on the floor and groaned my frustration. Then I ate a pint of mint-chocolate-chip ice cream. Then I created a new Spotify playlist. Then I wrote more lyrics and started to sing.

And it might take a thousand years . . .

I stayed up half the night writing lyrics, writing music.

Sunday, I did it all over again.

Christmas was slated to be on Thursday, and I'd volunteered to work, the tradeoff being I'd get Friday off. Andy had Christmas off, so it would be me and an intern. Wednesday evening, I went to an early Christmas Eve service at Ben's church. Paige had left for Kansas. I scanned the auditorium for a good seat and then paused in surprise at Cassidy waving at me from the right side of the church. I went over and slid in next to her and Jake. "Hi! What are you doing here?"

"Ben sent Jake a text, inviting us to come to the candlelight service, so here we are. Gilly is in the nursery. Aren't the decorations so beautiful?"

I followed her gaze around the room. Wooden pallets lined the walls of the room, plain Christmas trees, a few poinsettia plants—the earthy tones felt warm, simple.

Ben climbed up on the stage with just his acoustic guitar, the lights dimmed, and he began to play "Silent Night." In a trim black sweater and dark jeans, he sat on a barstool, flickering candles behind him on wooden pedestals, and began to sing.

Without much fanfare, Ben led the crowd in carols. Then the pastor got up on stage and talked about the birth of Christ. The simple but entirely magical story of a baby in a manger, come to save the world. It seemed almost unbelievable.

When the pastor finished speaking, we bowed our heads to pray. Then the ushers passed out little wax candles, and one by one, the candles were lit across the rows. I shared my flame with Cassidy, and she shared hers with Jake. Then the whole room glowed with glimmering lights, reminding me of the stars over Bethlehem.

Ben climbed back onstage and began to sing "O Holy Night."

My heart ached at the sound.

Maybe my faith had changed, but I believed the story. More than that, I loved the story. I decided then . . . my dance with God might look different now, but I was still willing to dance.

In fact, this dance seemed more real to me.

Parts of me had changed over the past year, but in that moment, I felt like a woman who was growing into herself. Finding her own way. Shadows bounced from hundreds of flickering flames as Ben's baritone brought life to the room. Words of the soul's worth and the night the whole world changed.

My eyes filled with tears as I chose Christmas all over again.

After the service, Ben came over, shook hands with Jake, and hugged Cassidy and me. They left to get Gilly, and Ben draped his arm over my shoulders. I kept silently marveling at how this Christmas Eve was five thousand times better than the tragic one I'd endured last year. I couldn't have known what one year would bring. We walked together out of the sanctuary to my car, and I told Ben how I'd felt during "O Holy Night." The parking lot buzzed with activity as cars left. Snow began to fall in the dark.

"You sang beautifully tonight, Ben."

He pulled me tighter. "Thanks. I'm going to miss this church when we leave for the tour."

"If they don't find a replacement, they'll take you back," I told him.

He shrugged. "When I left the youth camp to come here, I knew it was time for a change. My world is better for it. I feel that way again. God's with me here, on Christmas Eve, with you. He'll be with me there, in the crazy haze of the tour." We stopped in front of my car. "So we're going to my parents' house tomorrow after your shift, right?" Ben asked.

I nodded. "I've got all the presents wrapped and ready to go."

Snow swirled faster around us as Ben kissed the top of my nose. "You and me and a little bit of mistletoe, baby."

I grabbed a fistful of his jacket and directed those lips closer to mine as Ben chuckled.

"More than a little, Ben Price."

When I opened the door for Ben the next afternoon after my shift, he walked in, looked at the luggage situation, and covered his face with his hands.

"It's *one* night, Deb," he groaned.

"It's *Christmas*. All these bags are completely necessary. Start loading."

He obeyed, complaining about how it took two trips and how loaded down my SUV was for one night, blah blah blah. We found one fast-food joint that was open on Christmas, picked up lunch, and got on our way. Ben drove my SUV since it was more comfortable and roomier than the jeep, but I controlled the music. We blasted Christmas music the whole way, singing together, harmonizing. And when we reached his parents' house, Connie and Jonathon came running outside, thrilled to see us. She had hot cocoa and cookies waiting for us and she hugged me so tight. I hugged her back and almost cried because her welcome and acceptance covered my heart and warmed me. She needed me like I needed her.

We opened gifts and ate glazed ham with all the fixings. Late that night, after Connie and Jonathon had retired to their room, Ben and I sat alone by the fireplace, eating more pumpkin pie and watching holiday movies. Then I turned the TV off.

"Can you get your guitar for me?" I asked him, trying not to feel shy. I'd been so relieved he'd brought it.

He jumped up. "Sure." He brought over a worn, loved acoustic guitar, and I ran my fingers over the strings.

"Okay." I settled in, getting situated with the guitar on my lap. "I have one last present for you."

He didn't respond, just waited. I warmed up for a moment, strumming chords, getting familiar with the woody sound of his guitar. Then my fingers began to play. I took a nervous breath and began to sing.

I was wounded, you were healed ...
I was hiding, you were revealed.
I didn't have a heart to steal, you stole it anyway.
I didn't want a song to sing, you sang it anyway.
And it might take a thousand years
To know just what you are to me.
I'm fire and I'm ice and I've tried to warn you . . .
You just say,
Baby, I don't scare easy.
I've danced in rain and I've danced in snow.
And if it means having you, love,
I'll brave the cold.
And when the storm is over,
We're just pieces that fit together.

My voice shook at the last, and I looked up at Ben, whose eyes were wet and glossy. He took the guitar and set it aside.

"So you're an amazing songwriter. Any other surprises?" he asked. I crawled over to kiss him, a smile on my face.

"*You're* the amazing songwriter. But I wrote this for you, humble as it may be."

He took my face in his hands and kissed me. Then we sat curled up together, listening to the fire crackle. I rested my head on Ben's chest, hearing the rhythm of his heartbeat.

"Merry Christmas," I whispered. He kissed the top of my head, and I could almost sense his smile.

"Just say it."

"It's not a good idea. Not before the tour." There was a time when I'd been less cautious, but no longer.

"Say it," he said with a mock growl. "I'll go first. I love you, Debra."

The corners of my mouth tilted up. With the romance of the moment, the beauty of an idyllic Christmas, I couldn't fight my feelings, come what may. "All right, all right. I love you too."

"Was that so hard?" Ben asked in a teasing voice.

I sighed and sat up to face him. "It's not that." I moved over a little, feeling too hot by the fire and by my rising emotion. "I finally feel as though I've moved on from the hurt of losing Luke to Sara. They're married and together—and I'm okay. I don't hate them. I'm settling into this new tempo with God. It's a different relationship from the one I had with him before. Honestly, this one is harder. Maybe it's darker. It feels more real to me. Now ... you. You're my river in the desert, and you're leaving for what could be a whole new career. Of course I want you to jump at this chance—but the future seems uncertain right now. The last year has been filled with uncertainty for me, Ben. I'm over it. I'm sick of uncertainty. Now I'm right back in it, in a huge way, with you. Yes, I love you. I love you and I want the stars for you. I hope you want that for me."

Ben nodded, leaning forward and tucking my hair back out of my eyes. "You know I do."

"I can't help feeling afraid that this will fall apart and I'll be hurt again. So I think some self-preservation is a good thing."

He stared down at the tattoo on his wrist. "I don't think any of this would even be happening if it weren't for you, Deb. I mean that in the best way. I was content, yes, but also just doing the minimum, not pushing for more. I'm nervous and freaked out by the tour—and I like the feeling. I'm working for it again. Those things—nervous and freaked out and working for it—you make me feel them too. And you're more important than a tour. If we get a label and make an album and headline our own tour—but I lose you . . ."

His words faded.

I thought of Luke. I now felt convinced that he'd jumped into a relationship with me because it was so easy and fun for both of us, but it had been out of character for him—to not think through every facet. To not go slow and consider what his heart truly wanted, then make the right decision. I wanted Ben to have that chance, even if he didn't realize he needed it. I never wanted him to wonder what he could have become. If we didn't last, if life took us down different paths, I could go forward with my heart intact, with my rhythm with God, and with love and kindness for Ben.

I had to do things differently. For me.

"We'll just wait and see what happens," I whispered, holding back a wave of emotion. He would go on tour. He'd become the rock star he was always meant to be. I'd buy a new house. I'd have a space that belonged just to me. I'd keep making a name for myself on the radio and travel with Andy to L.A. for the iHeartRadio awards next April. My heart squeezed and I thought of *La La Land.* We'd go in different directions, but we'd be okay.

He stood up and pulled me up with him, sliding his hand around my waist and taking my other hand in his. I pushed every thought out of my head and focused on what I had in this moment. Ben hummed my song as we slow-danced by the Christmas tree.

Chapter Twenty-Two

I can't go back to yesterday . . . I was a different person then.
Alice in Wonderland

I pursed my lips and looked at Karis's social media account. I'd tried my hardest to avoid social media when I'd moved to Denver, but now, with Twenty-Four Tears playing in different cities, I couldn't help but check a hundred times a day to see what pictures were posted of Ben and the band. Karis ran Twenty-Four Tears's many media outlet accounts.

Some of the photos brought an immediate smile to my face. Ben on stage, sweaty and exhilarated, giving his all. Seth on drums now, tearing it up. Bryce, still so cool, a low fedora on his forehead, picking at his base guitar.

Some of the photos made my lips thin out into a straight line and my eyes narrow—after-parties and VIP meet and greets. Ben giving autographs to groups of fans. Selfies with lots of fans—mostly girls. So many comments on social feeds, so many comments about Ben. Usually along the lines of how hot he was—girls drooling over that long hair and his melt-me voice. Comments that I agreed with but that tended to make my blood rise.

It seemed like all the things I loved about him were obvious to everyone else as well. That first month, he'd called and texted me every day. Now, in the thick of the tour, I heard from him less and less. And saw more and more photos and fan sites online.

The fear of losing him didn't feel like a fear—it felt like a reality.

While I'd made valiant attempts at playing it cool with Ben leaving, Andy and Lana seemed to take pity on me, inviting me over for dinner all the time. I'd finally started saying yes. One Friday after work, I went over for pasta and garlic bread. Andy and Timmy played video games while I sat on a high-top chair in Lana's kitchen, sipping a glass of wine.

"I'm following their every move too," Lana admitted, pausing from wiping down countertops. "I watched a YouTube video of their concert in Portland. Ben was amazing."

I couldn't stop feeling glum. "I know."

She sat next to me. My glumness didn't seem surprising to her. "Are you worried? That he won't come back?"

I looked down at my glass. "Kind of. But I don't know if I want him to. How could I not want him to succeed, Lana? It's like he was born for this. I've seen it in him since that first night at Percival's Island. He's got so much capacity and such a kind heart, such a generous spirit. I want him to succeed. I just—I just wish—"

"You weren't in love with him?" Lana asked.

I covered my face for a moment, then looked back up at her. "Ben is where he's supposed to be. I'm where I'm supposed to be. I feel—like I'm finally breathing again. I'm happy. I held on so tight to Luke; I wanted him so much. With Ben, there's something inside me that says 'Let go.' He helped me find myself again. I just—don't want to fall apart if I suddenly see him online with someone else."

"He wouldn't do that to you," Lana said quickly.

Oh, but I knew. I knew no one was perfect.

"Even if things don't work out, I think you'll be okay this time, Deb."

"Yeah," I agreed, but my heart felt sad. "I think so too."

She was correct in that. I knew that this time around, letting go wouldn't break me. That didn't mean it wouldn't hurt.

It also didn't mean it wasn't right.

That night in my apartment, I carried a mug of green tea with me as I turned off lights and made my way to my bedroom. I remembered Addison's question to me so long ago: *The goal is to stay and settle, then? Stay* and *settle* didn't match my restless feelings, but they sounded nice. I'd finally talked to my parents about buying the paired house, and after a million questions and sending my dad all the paperwork and financial information, they'd agreed that it would probably be a good investment. My dad offered to co-sign a loan if I needed him to, but I didn't want that. They both said that if I truly intended to stay in Denver, then buying was preferable to renting long-term.

It occurred to me that I'd missed my mother more this time around. I couldn't remember missing my family much during my time in Texas. Here in Colorado, thoughts of my mother and grandmother and other family members pulled at me more. Despite that, I had no desire to go back to Minnesota for good. That wasn't me anymore, but those people, my people . . . I felt lonely for them.

Buying the house felt a bit like signing my life away. The six-months-before-May deadline I'd set for myself had come and gone, but I'd reached out to Denise and she said there was one house left that would be ready by the end of May. The loan fell through for the couple who was trying to buy it. It was time to decide, in my heart, to stay and settle and let roots grow. To make Denver my permanent home. To sign up for dance lessons.

Let go of Texas. Let go of Ben.

Just breathe.

The last Sunday in March, I went to church. It had been weeks and I felt this inner push to just go. I sat with Paige and enjoyed the new worship pastor at Rock Community. We listened to Eric preach on sacrificial living and then we went to The Egg and I. This time we sat alone in the booth—no Milo and Ben.

"Have you, um, been on Twitter lately?" Paige asked, pouring syrup over her pancakes. I sprinkled salt on my egg and mushroom omelet.

"Yes. I saw the picture," I told her. She nodded.

"Have you talked to Ben?" she asked, her voice overly light. I'd seen the same pictures she had, of Ben and a well-known, young, gorgeous pop singer—looking extremely chummy. Her arms around him and his arm around her waist. Her gaze looking up adoringly at him.

"He left a message on my voicemail last night, but I'd already gone to sleep. All he said was that we needed to talk." I took a small sip of my hot coffee.

"Oh," Paige said. I could hear the dip in her tone.

"It's okay," I told her. "I've sort of been preparing for this. It's only a matter of time before they get a label. I don't think Ben's going to come home. At least, not permanently. If they get a label, they might need to hunker down in a studio and start making more music." I took a bite of my omelet.

"Are you really okay?"

I nodded. "I am. I think I know myself better this time around. And Ben—everything was different with us. In fact, when it comes to Ben, I just really want him to be happy. I'm glad he did the tour. I watched him on YouTube last night. The concert in Seattle," I said, not quite keeping the wistfulness from my words. "He was fire, Paige." I peered at her. "Have you heard from Jason lately?"

I caught the slight flush creeping up her neck. She stabbed a sausage patty with her fork. "Yeah. Ever since he got that sous chef position, he's busier than ever. But it sounds like he loves his work."

I took another bite and savored the taste and then looked at my buzzing phone.

"Is it Ben?" Paige whispered. I nodded.

"Answer it!" she scolded. I clicked on the answer button. I hopped up and moved to the front waiting area.

"Hey, how are you?"

"Good," Ben said. "I didn't want to wait for you to call me back. Because—"

Because lately I hadn't been calling back.

"What's going on?" I asked, trying to skip past the awkwardness.

"I just want to talk to you, Deb. We don't talk much."

I bit my lip. "That's not entirely my fault and you know it."

Ben sighed. "Okay. Fair enough. You knew we'd be busy."

"Yeah, I know. I'm busy too." I wanted to be chill and indifferent, but that never seems to be my forte. "How's Rachel de la Rosa doing?" I said, a snap in my voice.

"What do you mean? She was at the festival we played at in Washington state."

"I'm aware. I mean, all of us in America are aware," I said, regretting the bite in my tone, but there it was.

Ben was quiet for a split second. "Just say what's on your mind."

I gripped the phone tight. Then a few seconds later, closed my eyes.

Let go.

"Ben, maybe we shouldn't talk till after the tour. Until you come back. If you come back."

He paused.

"It's just," I continued, "I really want to be supportive. But I see these pictures of you with girls like Rachel—up close and personal to the extreme—and it's not as easy to brush it off as I thought. I want Twenty-Four Tears to make it. You guys deserve all the success in the world. I mean that. But for my sake, I think we should cool this."

"Deb," he said after a minute, in that oh-so-familiar voice. "I'm still me."

"Maybe," I said, "or maybe you've changed. That's allowed, you know. We change. I've changed. But I don't want to be jealous and worried. That's not who I want to be. Maybe we should just stop this. So you can pursue your dreams."

"And what about you?"

My breath caught. *Oh, believe me. I'm wondering that too.* "I'm buying a house," I told him. "A new paired home actually. It'll be ready at the end of May."

"You're what?" Ben's voice spiked.

I tried to swallow but couldn't, so I ended up coughing. "My job is here,

Ben. My lease is up in May. I need a plan for the future. So I'm buying a house."

"How long have you been planning this?"

Eek. My stomach tightened. "It's been on my mind for a while, but I just recently decided."

"How recent?" he asked, his tone uneven enough to tell me he was angry and trying not to blow.

Um, one and half seconds ago.

"I haven't signed anything yet. But I talked to my parents, talked to the bank—everything looks good to go."

"And you never told me about it."

My heart felt like it was crushed in my chest, weighed down. "I wasn't sure yet, Ben," I said, my voice soft. I tried to keep the pleading tone I felt from seeping into my words. "You've got so much going on for you right now . . ."

"I can't believe you didn't tell me." The hollow sound in his voice hurt worse than the anger.

I blinked back tears. "I think we're going in different directions. It's nobody's fault."

"Deb, please. I know it's been harder than we thought, but—"

"Maybe we can talk sometime when you get back," I said, as gently as I could.

"I keep chasing you, Deb. But you don't seem to want to be chased."

My breath stopped for a moment. Was he right?

"At this moment, I don't know what I want, Ben. You're right . . . this is harder than I thought."

"It's hard, so you're ready to bail?" Ben accused. My lips tightened and I gritted my teeth.

"Bail from what? You're not even here."

"Debra."

I knew what he wanted to say. That I did this. That I started him down this road. Even if he was right, we were here now. "We both know you won't be lonely. I'm the one being left behind here, so spare me the anger." I couldn't believe I'd said those words. I bit my lip hard, my eyes watering. Ben didn't say anything for a moment but the rage came through loud and clear.

"Well, we both know I was never your first choice. I can't compete with that guy forever."

Now I was the one shaking with anger. "Stop trying to fight with me!"

"Baby, you're the one who wants to fight." His tone stayed even but softened a tad. "So let's fight."

I could hardly breathe. Fury came up against all the crazy feelings that came over me when Ben called me baby. I wanted to throttle him. I also wanted to hear him call me that forever. I tried to steady my voice. "I don't want this right now, Ben. Neither do you. You just won't admit it. You need to let it go. Go be a rock star. Fall in love with a new actress or singer every few months. Don't worry about me."

My finger pushed the end-call button—before I could say a bunch of things I knew I'd regret. Then I made my way back to Paige. Her eyes were round, pained, waiting for the verdict. I relayed the conversation to her. She reached across the table and took my hand in hers.

"One thing I'm learning is . . ." Her voice trailed off for a moment and she took a breath. "Sometimes the path leads us back to only ourselves, and that's okay too. We're strong."

I held her hand tight.

That night my phone rang late, waking me up. My hand scrambled in the dark, knocking a water bottle—closed thankfully—to the floor, and I groaned. I found my phone and brought it to my ear. "Hello?"

"Debbie, I don't want you to worry."

I sat straight up at the sound of my mother's voice. "What's happened?"

"As I said," she reiterated in that calming (sometimes grating) way of hers, "everything's going to be fine, so I don't want you to worry. But still, I thought you should know. I've brought Nana to the hospital. I knew she'd been sick but she said it was just a cold—typical!" I heard the frustration in my mom's voice. "She called and seemed scared, so I came over and decided she needed to go to the ER."

"Oh, God." Tears were filling my eyes.

"Honey," she said. "Please listen. She has pneumonia and she's going to be okay. They admitted her and a real nice doctor has talked to us. She's got an IV for fluids and she's taking medicine. They say she'll need to be here a couple of days; then we'll get her home. She's already doing better from that IV. Apparently, she was severely dehydrated. Anyway, I'm here at the hospital. I'd let you talk to Nana but she's worn out and fast asleep."

"No, that's okay. I'll call her tomorrow. I'm going to see if I can come out—maybe next weekend."

"She's going to be fine, Debbie."

"Even so," I said, rubbing my nose. "I need to see her. I should have a few days of vacation time by now. I'll check on flights and let you know."

"That's fine. You don't have to come, but I understand if you want to. And that might boost Mom's spirits."

A huge lump rose in my throat at the thought that I would raise anyone's spirits.

The reminder that I mattered to people.

I hung up with my mom and searched online for discount flights. Every flight looked expensive, but I needed to see Nana. I finally set my phone aside and decided to search again in the morning. I rolled over, part of me breathing relief that it wasn't more serious, another part of me aching to be with my family.

Five a.m. was brutal. I pulled myself together and drove to work, downing an espresso before going on air. During every intermission, I searched flights. After my shift, I booked a flight and worked out my schedule with Andy. I'd leave the next Friday, early afternoon, and come back Monday night. Andy would let one of the interns cohost with him Friday and Monday. I hoped that wouldn't be a disaster, knowing Andy's propensity to get annoyed quickly with interns, but it couldn't be helped.

When I called Nana that afternoon, she sounded weak and tired, and I wanted to be right there with her, turning on *White Christmas* in the hospital room. I promised her I'd be there soon, and she told me not to make a fuss, and I said I'd be there, so get ready.

When I got home later that afternoon, I texted Paige about my grandmother. She was sweet and caring and told me she'd be praying for her, and I knew she would. I wanted to text Addison and Lily but couldn't bring myself to do it. I wasn't sure why.

Of course, they'd say the same—they would pray. And I believed they would because that's who they are . . . but I didn't text them. I felt so far removed from them.

I wanted to text Ben. I knew he'd be hurt that I even had to think about it, but I *did* think about it, and I didn't text him. Because I felt alone and I was alone, and I just needed to hurry up and get to my sick grandmother and see for myself that she was okay. I couldn't bring myself to make the effort to tell people that were nowhere near me, who couldn't really help beyond words and thoughts. And who—when it came to Ben—were off on tour, living an exciting life with girls like Rachel de la Rosa.

Instead, I packed, repacked, shopped for Colorado-ish gifts for everyone in my family, and counted the hours until I was home.

And when I stepped off the plane and into the terminal in Minneapolis, I almost ran to the baggage claim. I grabbed my pink suitcase and rolled it outside, where it was snowing, sadly. My brother's Yukon was sitting in the long line of cars, waiting for pickup. I motioned for him to stay in the car amid the snow. I threw open the backseat door and shoved my suitcase in and then shut the door and hopped into the front seat.

"Brrrr! It's supposed to be spring already!"

"Don't even mention it. Carol planted flowers and she's so upset." My sister-in-law, Carol, who loved flowers and egg quiche and who hadn't changed her hairstyle since my brother met her in the ninth grade. Always long. Always one length.

"Thanks for getting me." I held my hands directly in front of the heater.

"No problem." Brian's eyes darted to me before he changed lanes. "You change your hair or something?"

I figured after living with Carol for so long, a change in hair length was at least noteworthy to my brother.

"Yeah. How're Carol and Jude?" I asked, wondering about my seven-year-old nephew.

"Good. Fine."

I realized that was going to be the extent of his description. "So is Nana still with Mom and Dad?" I asked.

His pointed jaw moved side to side. "She's back home. Mom wasn't sure if you were planning to stay with them or wanted to go out to Nana's."

I bit my lip. As much as I wanted—needed—to see my mom and dad . . .

"I figured you'd want to go to Nana's. So Mom said if that's what you want, she and Dad will plan to bring food tomorrow and I should just drive you out to the lake now."

I exhaled. Something came over me, this sense that I was known. Brian and I had never been best-friend close—he was quiet and liked sports and you couldn't pay him to watch a musical—but we'd always been I've-got-your-back-and-you've-got-mine close. All through our growing up years. And I felt that way about him in this moment.

"That sounds perfect."

We chitchatted on the long drive out to Nana's house, situated about a block from Lake Burston. Old pine trees shaded the houses in the old neighborhood. Brian turned down Beehive Lane, and I saw the faded, worn siding of my grandmother's house. I was out the door before the car was in park. I knocked even as I tugged on the handle. Cold air chilling me to the bone and whipping my curls. The handle turned easily and I pushed open the door. Brian was right behind me, carrying my luggage.

"Nana," I called out softly, in case she was asleep.

"Debbie, girl. Get in here." I heard her voice from the kitchen and I dashed through the house. She was in a blue nightgown, the old-fashioned kind that buttoned down to her knees, and some soft slippers. I had my arms around her in a second, breathing in the smell of her lotion and then crying like someone had died.

"There, there, Debbie," she said softly, but I heard the worry saturating her voice.

"Deb, what's wrong?"

I sniffed loudly and turned at the sound of Brian's voice. I ran my sleeve across my nose and just stood there. "I'm okay," I said. What else could I say?

No one spoke for a moment. I turned to Nana, studying her. She looked pale, and she'd lost weight, but she still seemed all right. Weak and tired, though. "How are *you*?" I asked.

She smiled but the worry lines didn't vanish from her face. "I'm fine. Happy to see you here. I couldn't believe it when your mama told me you were coming. She brought me home yesterday. And she left a big pot of potato soup in the fridge for us to eat this evening. Brian, do you want to stay and eat?"

Brian was already pulling up a chair. "I'll have a quick bite. Then Carol will be expecting me."

I steered Nana to the table and pulled out the soup pot myself, then set it on the stove to warm and retrieved bowls while Brian and Nana asked me a million questions about Colorado and my new job. No one mentioned my emotional spill. Once the soup was hot, I ladled it into bowls. And then Brian had to leave and I dragged my suitcase to the guest room. The one with the pink wedding quilt that had been there for ages. I changed into yoga pants and a large sweatshirt and thicker socks, slid my hair back in a headband, and went looking for Nana.

She was flipping through channels, sitting on the sofa. "There's microwave popcorn, Debbie. Make some, will you? And maybe some decaf coffee."

I smiled. "You bet."

Ten minutes later, we had a bowl of kettle corn between us and two cups of decaf sat on the coffee table. "I brought a couple of movies, Nana," I told her. Her eyes widened with excitement like it was Christmas, so I retrieved them from my bag and let her pick which one we'd watch. I'd ordered a bunch of DVDs online, knowing that Nana didn't have cable, much less streaming digital options. And I'd brought her a new throw blanket I'd found at Homegoods, soft, thick white fur.

She chose *High Society* and I tucked the blanket around her. Nana and I loved every minute. She fell asleep toward the end and I knew her energy had run out. I helped her to bed and then cleaned up. I checked the refrigerator for breakfast options the next morning, then settled into the guest room after turning off lights and checking that the doors were locked.

My phone dinged and I grabbed it.

Ben.

Paige told me about your grandma.

Oh dear. I imagined him working that jaw, trying to figure out how to let me know he was hurt I hadn't told him but still let me know he was worried and cared. I just waited.

Is everything okay? He finally texted.

She's doing better. I'm out here for the weekend. It's good to be home.

I sent the message and stared at that word.

Home.

I could sense the conversation that wasn't happening.

Why didn't you tell me?

Because we broke up.

You mean you broke up with me.

Ben.

Debra.

Okay! I love you. I'm sorry. You haven't kissed Rachel, have you?

Don't be crazy.

Instead, I sighed and punched in another text. Maybe we can talk when I get back.

He didn't have to tell me he'd be praying. I already knew he was. It didn't change anything. I already knew who Ben was.

I sighed and fell back on the pink quilt.

I wanted to know who I was. Where I belonged.

My phone dinged again and I held it up over me to read his text.

If you need me, I'll come.

I set the phone aside and climbed under the quilt.

I heard noises in the kitchen the next morning and jumped out of bed. Nana stood at the stove.

"I wanted to make breakfast!" I argued. "Nana, you're sick! At least let me cook for you." She waved me off and handed me a cup of coffee.

I breathed in the smell of hot coffee before placing my lips to the warm rim of the mug.

"I scrambled up some eggs." She motioned to the skillet on the stove. My stomach rumbled, and I grabbed a plate and scooped up a healthy serving. "There's toast too," she told me.

We sat together at the round table I'd missed so much and ate our breakfast. I told her all about the move and the job and hiking and Paige and even white-water rafting.

"Sounds like you got a boyfriend," she said. I blushed. I couldn't help mentioning Ben in all my retelling of my Colorado adventures.

"We're just friends."

"Hmph." She smiled, then reached over and took my hand in hers. "I sure am glad you came. I've missed you so much."

My heart couldn't take that comment. I started bawling.

"What on earth?"

"It's okay, Nana." I wiped my eyes. "I'm okay."

She sighed. "You keep saying that, Debbie. No one believes you, honey." She stood, walked over to the counter, and grabbed a brown bag. "It's a good thing your mother left us these too." She pulled out a pastry from the bag and set it on my plate and then took one for herself.

"Tell me the whole story. Start with Texas," Nana instructed.

An hour passed easily. We finished the pastries. Nana's brow furrowed more and more as I told her about Luke and Sara getting engaged. About my therapy sessions. About Ben and his tattoos.

And over second cups of coffee and cherry-filled croissants, the tension in my shoulders eased a bit. A few wayward tears surfaced as I neared the end of my story—my conversation with Ben.

"It's been a difficult year for you," Nana said softly. "Maybe it's time to come back home," she suggested.

I didn't respond. Was it? Was that the answer I kept chasing?

"I've changed since I left," I told her.

Nana nodded. "Of course you have. But when it comes to your people, your family—we have to accept each other just as we are. If you want to come back, Debbie, we'd all be thrilled. You don't have to worry about that." She stood up again and I noticed that she supported herself with one hand by clenching the back of the chair.

"How are you feeling really, Nana?" I asked. She inhaled and gave me a smile.

"I'm feeling old, honey. And like I'm recovering from pneumonia. I'm going to go back to my room and take my medication and maybe sleep for another hour or so."

I jumped up, put an arm around her waist, and walked her back to her bathroom, where she waved me off and told me she'd be fine. I showered, dressed, and washed the breakfast dishes.

Then I did what I've always done at Nana's house—wandered around. I looked at all the old collages of family photos she had on the walls. Checked out her record collection that had belonged to my mom. I found a vintage *Purple Rain* record and thought how Ben would have loved it. Every corner of the house felt familiar and comforting. As though, maybe, part of me had been left here, in the cracks in the walls, in the weathered tiles on the floor, in that antique kitchen table that I'd sat at so many times.

I could clearly see me and Brian and our cousins running through the house, like ghosts drifting through the hallways. I could close my eyes and hear yelling and giggling and parents scolding. A wash of emotion flooded me and I had to sit down. Because those days were gone forever. I'd loved them so much, and they were stitched on my heart like rings on one of Nana's quilts—but still, they were my past.

Could a new version of them be my future? What if I married and settled in this area or close by? My children and Brian's could run through the house as we had.

There was a loud knock at the door, and I jumped, startled out of my nostalgia. I rushed to the door, not wanting Nana to wake up.

"Brian! Carol! Jude!" I squealed with glee at the sight of all three of them. Jude held back but managed to mumble "Hello." I didn't mind. Maybe at seven they don't remember well aunts they rarely see. I gave him a side squeeze and Carol a full-on tight hug. Since she and Brian had been together since high school, she was absolutely family to me. Brian carried grocery bags into the kitchen.

"We brought stuff to make sandwiches for lunch this afternoon, in case Nana's running low on groceries," Carol said, walking with me back to the kitchen. I explained that Nana was taking a little nap.

"It's good to see you," Carol said in that calm, restrained way of hers. We put away the groceries while Brian turned on cartoons for Jude. When Brian joined us in the kitchen, I rambled on about how I'd been having a blast-from-the-past moment before they arrived, reminiscing about childhood days.

"It's so nice for you guys that you've never left. You get to keep making more memories here," I said, sadness tingeing my words.

Carol rested her chin on her folded hands and shrugged. "Believe me—there have been days we've wished we'd gone a bit further from home."

Brian nodded. He wiped his hands with a dishtowel, then opened the refrigerator, and pulled out a can of soda. "Yeah. Things haven't changed here much. You moved away and saw new things. I always knew you would."

I absentmindedly ran my fingers over the worn table. "How did you know?"

Brian and Carol laughed. "Deb," Carol said, "whenever I hear the expression that someone needs to 'spread her wings and fly,' I think of you. You were ready for adventure from the time you were in middle school."

I supposed she was right. "Nana says maybe it's time for me to come home."

The two of them exchanged a glance. They reminded me of Andy and Lana.

"Speak," I ordered. "No silent communication."

Brian chuckled. He sucked down half the soda, then sat down. "Dad said you were buying a place in Denver. Did something change out there?"

Only Ben becoming a rock star and me getting left behind again.

"No. He's right. I'm buying this great townhouse. I get to pick out everything—colors, carpet, countertops. I'll be broke, but I'll be living in style."

Carol sighed. "That sounds wonderful. Not the broke part—the choosing part. I'd love a new house. Tell me about Colorado."

I launched into the beauties of Colorado and all the pros of living out there.

"Sounds like the perfect place," Carol said wistfully.

"It's wonderful. You guys should come visit."

"You're always the lucky one, Deb," Carol said, and I couldn't help the almost manic burst of laughter that erupted from me. I coughed and tried to rein back in the crazy.

"No, dear. I'm not." I tapped the table. "Let's not forget what drove me to Colorado. Remember the getting dumped part?"

"He never deserved you," Brian said gruffly, taking off his ball cap and then putting it back on with a vengeance.

I managed a small smile at his loyalty. "Well, it's over now and I've moved on. Literally, come to think of it."

"If you've bought a place, you can't seriously be thinking of moving back here," Brian pushed.

I pushed my hair out of my face. "I don't know what I want, I guess. I'm a little lonely out there."

"You? Lonely?" Carol said in disbelief. She and Brian exchanged more annoying looks. "It's just"—Carol shifted in her seat—"you always make friends so easy. It seems like you find a tribe of people wherever you go."

"That was Texas. And yes, I did find a great tribe of friends. Then it all went up in flames." I took a breath to steady myself. I could feel my heart rate speeding up. "I've made a few friends in Colorado." I looked around the kitchen. "It feels like everything's the same out here."

"But it's not," Carol contradicted softly. "We've changed too. Not so much, maybe. But Nana's getting older, more frail. Your parents are aging. Brian changed jobs last year. We—we—" Her words caught in her throat and she looked at Brian. My eyes darted to him.

He cleared his throat. "We had a miscarriage two months ago."

I covered my mouth. "Oh, Carol." I reached for her hand. "No one told me."

She nodded stiffly. "We didn't tell too many people. We'll try again."

"Sure, you will." I squeezed her hand and she gripped mine in return this time.

"You needed to go, Deb," Carol reminded me. "And there's nothing wrong with that. Just because we stayed doesn't mean we'll never leave. Brian might get transferred somewhere and we'll move. Or maybe we'll stay here forever."

"We'll do what's best for our family," Brian agreed.

"How do you know?" I asked in a small voice. "What's right for your family?"

Brian smiled. "Trial and error, sis. Hey"—he leaned closer across the table—"Nana's right. You always have a home here, and if you want to come back, we're here for you. I know a couple guys I could set you up with."

Carol laughed and I rolled my eyes. "Thanks, but I've met someone."

"The singer?" Carol asked, intrigue lighting up her eyes.

Word gets around.

"Update: we're not really together. But if I found one rock star, I'm sure I can find another."

"Rock star?" Brian echoed. I inhaled and then explained the situation of Ben's band getting to go on tour. Carol's eyes rounded larger as I spoke.

"But that's so exciting!" she said with as much animation as I'd seen from her.

I nodded. "It is. But it also means that things are happening for him. I don't think living in Denver is going to be in his immediate future."

"And you've bought a house," Carol surmised, wincing. She got it.

"If you stay out there, Deb, we'll come visit. I promise," Brian piped up. I felt relief just hearing him say the words.

The sound from the TV in the living room grew louder and Carol jumped up to check on Jude. There was another knock at the door and I rushed to answer it. My parents came in. There were more hugs. My dad held me tight, kissing the top of my head. Then Jude was tugging at his arm, dragging my dad into the living room. Mom had brought a cake and wanted to start making sandwiches in case Nana was hungry when she woke up.

Just like that, I was surrounded by my original tribe. Every breath felt like home.

"Deb, take this tray to Nana. Tell her she does not have to get up—we've got everything under control." Mom handed me a plastic tray that held a roast beef sandwich and chips, along with a glass of water. I disappeared down the hallway to Nana's room and quietly opened the door. Nana motioned for me to come in.

"What's all the noise out there?"

I smiled. "Ninety percent Jude. Ten percent the rest of us."

She chuckled and then yawned. "I like hearing my family in the next room."

I propped pillows up behind her and set the tray on her lap. She popped a chip in her mouth. I sat on the edge of the bed. The four-poster, cherry-wood bed frame was more worn and scratched than I remembered. And the ancient matching vanity in the corner was covered with boxes and clothes, but it was still there. The room smelled the same as it always had. A little musty, a little like old perfume.

"I miss you too, Nana," I told her, needing her to know. "All the time. I watch musicals and remember all the nights I slept over here. I sing showtunes and think of us dancing."

Her blue eyes welled up with tears. "I'm old now, Debbie. I feel it so much right now. And I felt it so much in that hospital. There's nothing that makes you feel old like getting sick does. But you won't ever forget, will you, all those times we've had together?"

I rubbed the blanket that covered her, feeling her bony legs beneath my fingers, and my fragile heart broke in two all over again. "I'll never forget. I promise."

"I'm so proud of who you are. All those people listen to you on the radio. Sometimes your mother comes over and finds the radio station on the internet, so we can hear you too."

I couldn't breathe. I bowed my head and tears fell to the blanket. "Maybe I should come back. I don't know. I don't know where I belong anymore. I love being here so much. But something in me still feels restless."

She touched the curls around my face and lifted my chin. "Honey, this will always be your home. But that doesn't mean it has to be your only. Children grow up and sometimes move away. Oh, it's such a hard part of life, letting them go. I can't even put it into words. But you've had adventure in your heart since you were a little girl. It's okay to chase it. This place, all of us, we'll be part of you wherever you go. And the road home is never too far. You know how to get here, Debra." She pushed aside the tray and I fell into her arms.

I can't put it into words either. But it hurts.

I might not have known where I wanted to end up, but I knew in that moment that I would forever be Debbie Hart, born in Minnesota, musically inclined, adventure seeker, loved by her people.

It was enough to keep me going.

Chapter Twenty-Three

And bring me home at last.
Anastasia, the Musical

The next Tuesday on air, during the Miss Lonely Heart segment, I sat nervously, tapping my pencil on the table. Over the course of the morning, I'd shared all about my trip back to Minnesota, making Andy laugh with stories of how my mother's ceramic cow collection had eerily begun taking over other rooms in my parents' house and my deep concern over that. But now it was time for call-ins and revenge advice.

Andy took a swig of an energy drink right after we took a call from a woman who secretly missed her ex-boyfriend and wanted to reach out to him. I moved close to my microphone.

"Guys, here's the thing. I don't think revenge is the answer. I think, maybe, Miss Lonely Heart has found herself in love again. And while it doesn't seem to be working out, it's reminded me that love is an amazing, beautiful feeling and I need to be open to it."

Andy opened his mouth but I held up a hand to stop him. Then I continued, "I want to hear your stories, and I want to empathize with you. But more than revenge, I want happiness for our listeners. I want happiness for myself."

"So you're in love, Deb, with—"

"Andy!" I squawked. He knew I didn't want to share Ben's name, especially now. Andy grinned. Of course, I hadn't told him about me basically breaking up with Ben.

"Okay, okay." He held up two hands. "But you don't think it will last?"

I sighed with theatric flair. "We're going in different directions, but I only want good things for him. So I'm trying to let him go gracefully."

"Maybe you should fight for him," Andy said, an eyebrow raised. I thought about Ben and I couldn't come up with a witty answer. "All right"—Andy sat back in his chair and tapped the table—"we need you guys to call in. What should Miss Lonely Heart do?"

That night, I couldn't sleep. I ended up reaching for my phone and stalking Ben. I figured *letting go* didn't mean I couldn't follow him online. I mean, hadn't I sort of been the catalyst for helping him take the leap to go on tour? I was invested in Twenty-Four Tears's rise to fame. So I looked at the band photos on their website and read Karis's most recent tweets; then I went to their Instagram account and scrolled through—unable to find the picture of Ben and the pop star. I kept scrolling—up and down—realizing that several pictures had been deleted. They were still on the pop-star girl's feed, but they'd been removed from Twenty-Four Tears's account.

That made me a teeny bit happy.

My relief and happiness ended up being short-lived (big surprise, story of my life) when two days later I just happened upon Rachel de la Rosa's feed to see a new picture of her and Ben and Seth and Karis, taken at that same festival. She was positioned glued to Ben's side, sandwiched between him and the others. Wearing a flimsy little slip of something, she had an arm around Ben's neck, and her lips, spread in an unmistakable smile, pressed into a kiss on his cheek.

I covered her face with my thumb while I studied Ben. The rigidness in his jaw gave me some hope that maybe he felt uncomfortable in that moment. But I was pretty sure that I was the one feeling extremely uncomfortable with the picture, not to mention all the feelings rising up inside me. Jealousy, worry, anger, fear, hurt—emotions that had exhausted me too many times.

Friday, I went to see Dr. Clark. Our sessions had slowed as we'd both felt progress had been made, but I needed to talk, and I felt terrified that holding in such a barrage of feelings would take me back to a place I didn't want to be.

Sitting on that sofa again, I sat with crossed legs and ran my sweaty hands down my jeans. She just listened as I told her everything from telling Ben I loved him at Christmas to the breakup call to the photos of him and Rachel. I told her about going home to Minnesota, missing my family so much but still feeling as though I were searching for something.

"Andy says I should fight for Ben," I said, clearing my throat when the words were difficult to get out.

Dr. Clark's smooth black hair was in a tight bun at the base of her neck. I was having trouble adjusting to her new box-framed deep purple glasses. Maybe recognizing my distraction, she took off the glasses and stuck them in the desk drawer.

"Is that what you think?"

I sighed deeply. "I don't know. I know I don't really want to lose him, but it's not in me to fight right now. I'm too wary of being hurt. I don't think anything's going on with that singer—but what if there was? Or what if he wanted something to happen with her? Or the next girl on the road with him? Or some willing fan who's waiting by the stage? I don't want to be the discarded one again."

"Were you discarded, Debra?" she asked, her voice calm and steady. "Or did Luke learn who he was and what he needed? I think sometimes we have to be brave enough to change directions when we need to. Maybe that's what Luke did. And now you're at a crossroads and have to decide what direction *you* want to go in."

My arms had been crossed tight over my belly, but the tension began to ease. She was right about Luke.

"What if Ben needs to change directions and wants someone else?" I tried to ask the question without my voice trembling, but it didn't work.

"I think—from what you've told me—that perhaps Ben knows who he is at this point in his life."

"But everything has changed for him!"

"Everything has changed for you," Dr. Clark pointed out.

Yes, it had.

"Who are you, Debra? Think for a moment; then tell me what comes to mind."

"I don't know," I cried.

"You do. Tell me."

I clasped my hands for a few seconds and stared out the window behind Dr. Clark's head. A mountain landscape could barely be seen in the far distance.

"I'm just this girl who loved someone once with her whole heart; then he gave it back to her. It's not really a unique story."

Dr. Clark stood up and walked around her desk. She sat on the sofa next to me. "First, every story is unique. Second, that's who you were. Who are you now?"

"I'm—a woman who can take care of herself."

Dr. Clark nodded encouragingly. "Yes, you are."

"I'm comfortable alone. I don't think that was true of me before, but it is now. Sometimes I even crave it. But not all the time. I still love music and theater and dancing and pink lipstick. I like being with Paige. I love my family. I like living in Colorado."

"All good things," Dr. Clark agreed.

"I might not be as spiritual as I was before. Do you think that's okay?"

"I think you're very spiritual, Debra. I just think it looks different for you than it used to, and that's absolutely okay. Your journey is your own." Dr. Clark set one manicured hand on her knee, and I couldn't help noticing how perfect her acrylic nails looked. That made me think of how badly I needed a manicure.

It occurred to me those probably weren't the right thoughts to have during a therapy session.

"How do you feel about Ben?"

"I don't want to lose him, but I don't want to chase him. Does that make any sense? I'm not in a rush this time around. Maybe that means we're not meant to be together."

"Why would it mean that?"

I laid my head back and exhaled. "I don't know. With Luke, I wanted everything fast. I was so convinced that he was my match, and I just wanted to start our lives together as soon as possible. Why wait when you know? That all ended up being one sided, of course."

"Slowing things down this time makes perfect sense. You don't have to chase Ben, Debra, but is some of that fear? Are you afraid of going all in with this relationship?"

I closed my eyes. "Maybe. He could still walk away."

"So could you. In fact, in some ways you have."

I thought of the breakup conversation I'd initiated.

"You know what life on the road is like for a musician," she said gently. "You opened the doors that gave him this opportunity. Would you rather he gave that up and came back home to be with you?"

I shook my head. "No. I did it because I believe in him. I still believe in him."

"What about the house? Have you signed the paperwork?"

I licked my lips and clenched my fists nervously. "Yes. I signed everything a couple of days ago. It'll be all shiny and new." I tried to force my voice to lighten. "And it will be mine. I already bought a new welcome mat for the front porch."

"This is what you want?" Dr. Clark pushed. I didn't answer.

She sighed. "I've wanted to avoid any comparisons, but I think we need to get this out. How are your feelings for Ben … compared to how you felt with Luke?"

I looked at my own unmanicured hands. My empty ring finger.

"So different. I was so different with Luke. It almost makes me sad that Ben doesn't get that side of me. Fun and outgoing and willing and open and passionate. This version of me seems boring in comparison."

"You're definitely not boring." Dr. Clark smiled. "There are lots of facets to who we are. You see me here, in this quiet, calm space—and you'd probably think it was strange to see me screaming on a roller coaster, but that's one of my favorite pastimes."

I bit my lip to keep a chuckle from escaping. "Seriously?"

She laughed and nodded. "You can be more introspective and still love a good party. You can thrive on being around lots of people but then sigh with relief when you have a quiet Friday night at home—just you and Fred Astaire and Ginger Rogers. You can be cautious with your decisions, but once you've made one, you hit the ground running. You can be someone in tune with God but also open to that relationship looking different from what you're used to. Debra, you went from being someone who hated working out to being a woman who likes to run. There's no growth without change."

I thought of Paige. *There's no growth without rain.*

"With or without Ben, you are strong. But being strong doesn't have to mean being alone. You don't have to rush, Debra. You don't have to do anything. Tell me this—how do you feel whenever you're with Ben?"

I didn't answer for a moment, trying to think of the right words. I thought of his tattoos. *Isaiah 43:19.* God making a way through the wilderness and a stream in the desert. *Sadie.*

I pictured him onstage at Percival's, eyes closed, mouth on his microphone, singing "Ruin" from out of his own brokenness. Then at church, both arms outstretched, leading hundreds of people in worship. I saw him flying through the air into the cold water of the river, cooking dinner and breakfast for the campers, handing me a cup of cider, looking at me with longing in his eyes. I remembered how he looked the night we went to the theater—so handsome and so excited to spend the evening with me. I thought of how it was when we danced in the snow. I still felt the fire burning in me as we argued on the phone. And my breath stopped as I thought of the heat rising in both of us every time his lips pressed hard on mine.

Ben.

"I feel like I've found the guy who I want to be the soundtrack to my life."

Sunday morning, I went down to the gym for an hour, then watched Gilly over lunch while Cassidy and Jake went out for a quick coffee date. When they picked her up, I was peppered with questions about how Ben and his band were doing and when he would be back. I was thinking of texting Paige, asking her to come over for dinner, when someone knocked at the door. I picked up Gilly's rattle, figuring Cassidy had come back for it.

I swung open the door and dropped the rattle. Ben Price stood on my welcome mat.

All my frustration over the pictures with all the girls, not to mention me hanging up on him, was temporarily forgotten as I threw myself at him.

"What are you doing here?" I asked when I pulled back from the hug, motioning for him to come inside.

"We need to talk," he said, his eyebrows rising.

"Oh-kay. Pretty sure we could do that over the phone." I closed the door behind him.

He sighed and dropped a duffle bag on the floor. "Not this conversation."

Dread washed over me.

"We need to talk about us. And Rachel de la Rosa," he said with resignation. "Let's sit down."

He sat on the sofa, and I moved to sit by him, still unnerved that he was *here*, in Denver, in my apartment.

"You're making me nervous," I said, trying to chuckle.

Ben scratched his head, then tucked his long hair behind his ears. "Listen, she's cute—"

My chuckle disappeared and was replaced by a firm grimace. "Ben—"

He held up one finger. "Hold on. Just let me talk; then I'll listen to whatever."

I crossed my arms.

"Debra, Rachel is like a teenager."

"Try twenty-five," I corrected.

He rolled his eyes. "I'm *saying*, she's young. She's got a lot of attention and money, and she's out there, doing her thing. We met after the festival at this big get together with the press. People snapped pictures. I talked to her briefly. She was on the way to, unfortunately, being wasted. I hope she's got good people looking out for her. Anyway, that was it. She *has* called me—" My eyes widened. "Carlisle gave her my number. We've since had a discussion about giving out my number. She's called; I've let her know I've got a serious girlfriend. That's it."

"You've got a serious girlfriend?" I echoed in mock surprise, eyes large.

He gave me a stern look. "Yeah. She's a radio show host who tells all of Denver that she's in love with me but keeps trying to break things off."

An unexpected burst of laughter escaped me. I covered my mouth, trying to rein it in. "Have you been listening to the show online?" I asked. He sighed loudly and looked up to the ceiling.

"Of course I listen to the show online." He rested his arm on the back of the sofa and looked over at me, weariness in his eyes. "If you love me and I love you—please stop breaking up with me."

Another short burst of laughter erupted, this one tinged with tears. "You could change your mind. You could do something stupid with some cute pop star and ruin everything," I whispered.

That time, Ben laughed. He rubbed his eyes. "Well, at least we know you'll always keep me grounded." The laughter faded and he touched my curls. "Debra, you're right. I could make a mistake. Or you could. People aren't perfect, least of all me. But if we're working at this—at *us*—I think we'll be okay. No one is perfect. That's not a reason not to be in a relationship when you find somebody you want to be with. And because I love you, I need you to include me when something as important as your grandma getting sick happens."

The rigid strain in my neck and shoulders eased up somewhat.

"I'm sorry." My voice cracked and I started to cry. "I didn't mean—"

"Deb," Ben broke in. He pulled me closer, closing his eyes, holding me, sighing like he'd been in pain before this moment. "It's okay. Just—tell me you want this too."

My arms wrapped around him. "I want this too. What you said about not being my first choice ..." I had to stop and try to breathe.

His eyes filled with worry. "I shouldn't have said that. I'm—"

I shook my head. "No. I want you to say what you're feeling. That's who we are, Ben. But I need you to know that it doesn't matter about being first. You are my only choice because you're the one I want. *You're* the one, Ben." I kissed him softly, then searched his eyes, hoping he believed me.

His gaze met mine, and I could see that my words had met their mark. The worried crinkles at the corners of his eyes relaxed. The tension in his jaw vanished. "I had Karis take down all questionable pictures, and I told her I don't want her posting anything with just me and another girl."

"Thanks for that," I said.

He nodded. "What else can I do? You know there will be more Rachel de la Rosas. You knew that going in. Seriously, I want you to tell me what you need from me."

He looked so tired. Sitting on my sofa, jumping on a last-minute flight just for me—I started thinking he'd already done what I needed. But he was asking for specifics.

"Let me think about that, okay? We might need to be more intentional about talking every day. I'll tell you what ideas I come up with." I massaged his neck and his eyes closed. "Are you hungry?" I asked. "I was thinking about ordering Indian food."

He nodded but didn't open his eyes. "Sounds good."

Later, over chicken curry, rice, and naan bread, Ben talked more about the tour, what Carlisle was doing for them now that he was officially the manager for Twenty-Four Tears.

"We've got a label looking at us. Carlisle is having talks with Just-the-Beats Records."

My fork paused midway to my mouth. "Oh my gosh."

Ben tore a piece of bread in half. "It's not for sure. Bryce is trying not to get his hopes up. But it could happen."

I finished my bite of food, mulling over the thought of Twenty-Four Tears getting signed to a label.

"Does that mean ... will you need to move to L.A.?" I worked hard to keep my voice steady.

He just stared at me for a moment. Then his hand went softly to the back of my neck, his fingers intertwined in my hair. "I know you just bought a house, Deb. I don't want to relocate. I figure I'll just fly out a lot if I need to. We can make it work. If you're here—I'm here. You matter more than the music."

I sucked in a shaky breath and willed my chin not to quiver. "You matter more than the house. I pulled out of the contract."

His brow wrinkled. "What? How?"

"There was a one-week grace period to change my mind. I went to the office at the model home yesterday and backed out."

"You changed your mind?" He held my hand and kept his eyes glued to me.

"I did," I said simply, lifting and dropping my shoulders. "I wanted the house to be"—I paused, thinking of Dr. Clark—"my way of planting roots here. But the money, the timing—I realized that I wasn't sure. And I need to be sure. Yesterday morning I went back to the sales office and met with Mrs. Shumaker. I lost some money—which hurts financially and emotionally—but it was the right thing to do."

With Luke, I'd had no reservations whatsoever. I'd been so ready. But with the house, I'd had just enough uncertainty—maybe that was how Luke had felt. The need to slow down, the sense of being rushed, the fear of making a commitment he wouldn't want to keep. I'd pulled out of the contract, not worried about the money—more worried about signing up for something I didn't really want. Now, thinking of Luke, that terrible night, his eyes glossy with tears, the shame in his voice—I could forgive him for doing what he'd needed to. He let me go and held on to who he was.

On the other side of that was a slightly changed version of myself. And in the mirror of Ben's gaze on me, I could see what he saw. This woman a little wiser, a little more thoughtful. A new current of steadiness that rushed through me like a stream. That thought reminded me of Nana. Maybe I was like her in ways I hadn't realized before.

In that moment, I wanted to dance. Because if I was sure of one thing only, it was that Ben Price had overtaken my heart and I never wanted to be the same again.

I blinked, decidedly keeping all those thoughts to myself. I squeezed his hand. "I've got a couple more months till my lease is up. I can look for another place or sign another agreement for this apartment."

He raised both eyebrows. "So ... this has nothing to do with me?"

A small chuckle escaped me and tears filled my eyes. "It has everything to do with you. As you know—as all of Denver knows— I'm crazy in love with you."

He smiled, relief smoothing the lines on his forehead. "Oh, good. I was afraid I was reading the signs wrong." He kissed my mouth, then the tip of my nose, then my eyes; then he pulled me into a tight embrace. "I'm crazy in love with you too."

I buried my head in his shoulder, overwhelmed by the avalanche of feelings rushing over me. So much love swirled in and over my heart, leaving no more room for anger.

After a moment, Ben tipped my chin upward to face him. "I *really* want you to come out for our last show, end of May. It's in Dallas. I'll fly you there."

"Yes, of course. I'll ask off. I've been storing up vacation time and volunteering for holidays, so it shouldn't be a problem."

Ben wiped a tear from his face with the back of his hand. "We're an *us*, Miss Lonely Heart. And we're not a secret. You can go ahead and tell your radio listeners."

When Ben left that night, I washed the few dishes in the sink, my Pandora show-tunes station playing in the background. I dried my hands and turned on the dishwasher and paused as a new song began. My heart skipped a beat as "Summer Nights" from *Grease* came on. The music filled the small space that was my apartment, and my heart could hardly take it. Heady with feelings and thoughts of Ben and hope for a future I'd given up on—I had to sing. I'd known every word by heart since I was fifteen and they flowed from me now. I twirled through the kitchen, singing about young love and the heat of summer nights (not too loudly. I didn't want to wake up Gilly after all). I clasped my hands together like Olivia Newton John. My hair brushed across my face as I danced from my kitchen to outside on my back porch in my pajamas, performing to glittering lights scattered through Denver's dark sky.

And when the song ended, I fell onto the sofa, sweat glistening on my forehead, my heart aching with something like relief and gratitude and belief and love.

There you are, Debra Hart. I smiled.

A memory flashed in my head. Me and Addison and Lily and Sara. We were at Addison's house and someone had turned the old song "Girls Just Want to Have Fun" on. Addison sang at the top of her lungs. Sara and Lily and I had danced together in the kitchen. I remembered feeling so completely happy in that moment that I wanted to freeze time.

I inhaled deep through my nose and closed my eyes.

Those moments were some of the best of my life.

There was silence for a second and then, softly, the lyrics "Tale as old as time" drifted from the TV sound system over my living room, and I breathed again. Because whose heart doesn't lift at those words? And I knew life goes on.

I would always miss those girls. But in some ways, I would always have them.

Now Ben Price loved me the way girls dream of being loved. And I needed him like an artist needs paint. Like a musician needs harmony. Like a writer needs words. Like people need God.

I was jumping up and down and screaming with thousands of people.

I'd flown to Dallas for the last show on Chasing Summer's tour. They'd tacked on a big musical festival at the end and I couldn't wait to hear the band. Ben had told me to hang out backstage, but I wanted to be with the crowd, cheering on Twenty-Four Tears. Up on stage, in front of a packed stadium, Ben held that microphone, stomping his foot in time, singing to admiring fans, including me. Post-show, I joined the others in the VIP room, drinking champagne, dizzy over the fact that Twenty-Four Tears had just been signed to Just-the-Beats Records. They'd go into the studio in Los Angeles to work on a new album, then headline their own tour—smaller venues at first, across the Midwest.

As I moved around the room, hugging Karis, talking to the guys in the band, and meeting everybody from Chasing Summer, it occurred to me that I felt like myself again, enjoying the excitement, thriving with the loud hum of the crowded room, chatting with everybody. When we weren't together, even from across the room, Ben and I kept sneaking glances at each other. Every time he winked in my direction, flutters rushed through me. As much as I was enjoying the excitement and the crowd and the noise, I couldn't wait to get that guy alone. Once the party finally died down and the room cleared out, Ben and I sat alone on a sofa. He closed his eyes in utter exhaustion.

"So tonight was Karis's last night. She's headed back to Denver." He rubbed his temples.

"And you're headed to L.A.," I said, unable to keep the sadness out of my voice. He opened his eyes.

"Miss me?"

"You know I do."

He reached a tan arm out and pulled me close to him. After the show, he'd pulled back his sweaty hair and tied it back. A homegrown Coloradan, Ben was no match for the Dallas heat and humidity. The guy was wiped. "I need you, Debra."

"I'm here," I assured him, thankful he'd exchanged his sweat-soaked shirt for a clean one. I ran my finger down the side of his face, feeling the scruffiness of his beard. I planted a kiss on his cheek. "All those girls out there—they can cry an ocean of tears. You're my rock star."

Ben smiled. With his arm around my shoulders, his fingers began touching the ends of my hair. "And you're mine." Then Ben sat up, pulling his arm out from around me and facing me. His gaze met mine, searching again. "Don't you get it? I want kids with curly hair like yours. I want to sleep with you and wake up with you. I want to chase dreams with you and make a home with you."

Home.

It wasn't the heat of Texas. Or the mountains in Colorado. Or the lakes of Minnesota.

It wasn't a brand-new house with fresh paint and a welcome mat.

It wasn't Luke.

It was Ben. And my own heart.

"I'm already home. I'm with you," I said the words, knowing they were true. Knowing we were us.

He reached for my arm, his fingers lightly walking their way down to my wrist, distracting me. Playing me as though I were strings on a guitar. "If you really feel that way, Deb, I want you to come to L.A. I want you to come on tour with us. I want you to sing with me. I want you to marry me."

"What?" I shifted on the couch, putting some distance between us.

"That's what I want," he said, patting his chest. "I've thought about it and prayed about it. What do *you* want, Deb?" he asked, studying my response. "This tour has been incredible and fun and opened up so much for Twenty-Four Tears. But I don't want to do it again without you."

What did I want? My dream job? I'd already experienced that twice. Singing with Ben would be a whole new adventure. Maybe we'd write songs together. I could see hotel rooms and cities and going to sleep next to him every night in my future. Tour buses and plane rides. Babies and trips home to see family. Music.

A life beyond anything I'd imagined.

Ben took my hand in his. "At Christmas, you told me I'm your river in the desert."

Tears welled up in my eyes. With my free hand, I touched the verse on his arm. I thought of my nana's words to me: *You'll lose yourself in passion and find yourself in love.* I wanted both with Ben Price.

"When I say I need you, Deb, I mean it." Ben took a shaky breath and tightened his grip on my hand. "Will you marry me? Can we do all this together?" For a moment, Ben, with his tan skin, light eyes, and dark hair, looked as nervous as I'd ever seen him. I smiled at that.

God, I love him so much.

What I felt for him was wild and deep and unpredictable. I wanted to dive in, like I had that day in the freezing water of the river. "I want *you.* And yes, we can do this. We can do whatever we want. You and me and marriage and music."

I kissed him once, then twice. Then paused but he pulled me right back for more. And it was fire and snow and rain and faith and love. Real and lasting.

He settled back next to me, our fingers laced together. Our wrists touching. Two words pressed against each other. His tattoo and my new one.

Healed and *Free.*

A Note from the Author

It broke my heart to break Deb's in *The Last Summer*. But that was Sara's story and the way of it had been settled back when the story first came to me. During the final proofing of *The Last Summer*, one of my editor friends read the novel and sent me an email that said, "Poor Debra!" I told her, "Deb's story is coming!" I'd thought of Debra's story way back during the writing of *The Last Summer*. I had glimpses of scenes. But I wasn't sure I'd ever write the full novel. As the time grew closer for *The Last Summer* to release, I just kept thinking, *I've got to write it. I've got to give Deb a chance too.*

So I did.

During naptimes, and after bedtime, and on Saturday mornings and any time I could find, I typed out Debra's story.

Part of the heartbreak of *The Last Summer*, for me, was the splintered effect in those special friendships. From the time we're very young, friends are so important. And haven't we all lost a friend or gone through a breakup, and felt our heart shatter? Those are deep wounds, and I wanted to dive into what Debra was feeling and show how time—as it so often does—keeps moving on. Eventually we move with it.

It's been my privilege to explore the friendships between Debra and Sara and Addison and Lily and Jason and Sam and Luke. These seven people have been in my head for twenty years and they're special to me. I was so thrilled when Ben showed up—I knew he'd be Deb's best friend and so much more.

My first thought was to dedicate this novel to those friendships in my life that have meant so much, but I soon found that there wasn't room! I think that at every season of life, friendships make all the difference. They have for me. When it comes to my friends—from when I was just a girl in Texas to my college years in Texas and Virginia to life as a young married in Colorado, working on my career and just beginning to grow our family—to now . . . you all know who you are and I'm so grateful for your friendship.

And thank you with all my heart to my sisters, Sara and Laura. Because sisters are gifts you get to keep forever. And you can call them crying at any moment and they'll drop everything. And you can giggle with them over a million inside jokes. And the love never stops.

Thanks to my dad for that first writer's conference you sent me to in Conroe, Texas. You believed in me from the beginning. Your support means everything, and I love you and Mom so much.

Thank you to Marianne for all your invaluable feedback. And to Jessica

Nelson with LPC for your insight and help in shaping and polishing this story.

I want to offer a special thank you to Kollette Decker with Renegade Road for ALL the music advice. Seriously, where would I be? Check out their music at www.facebook.com/coloradocountry1.

As always, thanks to Jeff. I couldn't do any of it without you.

And finally, all my gratitude to the One who creates a way in the wilderness and rivers in the desert.

Made in the USA
Middletown, DE
22 September 2019